Dillinger

S. J. Hawley

Published in 2014 by FeedARead.com Publishing – Arts Council funded

Copyright © S. J. Hawley.

The cover image is a work of the U.S. federal government and is

therefore in the public domain.

First Edition

A CIP catalogue record for this title is available from the British
Library.

WANTED

JOHN DILLINGER

with alias Frank Sullivan

NATIONAL MOTOR VEHICLE THEFT ACT

DESCRIPTION

AGE: 31 years

HEIGHT: 5 feet 7-1/8 inches

WEIGHT:153 pounds

BUILD: medium

HAIR: medium chestnut

EYES: grey

COMPLEXION: medium

OCCUPATION: machinist

MARKS AND SCARS:

1/2 inch scar back left hand;

scar middle upper lip;

brown mole between eyebrows;

moustache

CRIMINAL RECORD

As John Dillinger, #14395, received State Reformatory, Pendleton, Indiana, September 16, 1924: crime, assault and battery with intent to rob and conspiracy to commit a felony: sentences, 2 to 14 years and 10 to 20 years respectively:

As John Dillinger, #13225, received State Prison, Michigan City, Indiana, July 16, 1929: transferred from Indiana State Reformatory: paroled under Reformatory jurisdiction, May 10, 1933: parole revoked by Governor-considered as delinquent parolee:

As John Dillinger, #10587, arrested Police Department, Dayton, Ohio, September 22, 1933: charge, fugitive: turned over to Allen County, Ohio authorities:

As John Dillinger, received County Jail, Lima, Ohio, September 28, 1933: charge, bank robbery: escaped October 12, 1933:

As Frank Sullivan, arrested Police Department, Tuscon, Arizona, January 25, 1934: charge, fugitive: turned over to Lake County, Indiana, authorities:

As John Dillinger, #14487, arrested Sheriff's Office, Crown Point, Indiana, January 1934: charge, murder-bank robbery:

The United States Marshall, Chicago, Illinois, holds warrant of arrest charging John Dillinger with feloniously and knowingly transporting Ford V-8 four door sedan, motor number 256647, from Crown Point, Indiana, to Chicago, Illinois.

Law enforcement agencies kindly transmit any additional information or criminal record to the nearest office of the Division of Investigation, U.S Department of Justice.

If apprehended, please notify the Director, Division of Investigation, U.S Department of Justice, Washington D.C., or the Special Agent in charge of the Division of Investigation listed on the back hereof which is nearest your city

Issued by J. Edgar Hoover, Director

You get to recognize a killer in prison. There's a lot come in that way or they turn when they're inside. First we thought he was just a hard-headed hick who got a lousy break. Then you'd see him in a fight, and it was like he didn't care whether he got killed or the other guy, just so someone got it. We learned to keep out of his way.

Even inside, cons joke and are friendly. But year by year, Dillinger just got quieter and madder. I used to sweat every time he looked at me. He always had this expression on his face, his mouth twisted on the left side, like he was under pressure every minute. Some guys try to look tough, then they forget and it's gone. But he had that look all the time. I tell you, I knew as soon as they let this guy out, someone was gonna walk away from his hat.

ONE

CROWN POINT

A jail is just like a nut with a worm in it. The worm can always get out

– John Dillinger

One

Midway Airport, Chicago

Tuesday, January 30, 1934

Johnny blinked at the flash of sodium powder as he emerged from the American Airways Tri–motor. Glanced at the snappers swarming the runway as he descended the steps. This was what it must be like for Tracy or Fairbanks. Edward G.

No steel bracelets for *Little Caesar*, though. Harness bulls packing the tarmac. Khaki-clad State Troopers. Dicks in squashed fedoras and off-the-rack suits. He might be getting the same attention as Tracy or Fairbanks, but it was the steel bar hotel for him rather than the Ritz or Hilton at the end of the day.

No Mary Pickford either for a guy the Indiana authorities had shanghaied out of Tucson for killing a cop. And nobody left to bust him free of the joint the way the boys had at Lima. Not with three of them facing the chair in Ohio for the sheriff they'd gunned during the breakout. Red shot full of holes outside a bank in East Chicago. He wanted to make it over the wall at Crown Point, he was going to have to do it alone.

A couple of dicks broke loose from the mob as he exited the plane and strong-armed him into the back of a paddy wagon. They sat opposite him as the van joined a convoy of police flivvers, sirens yowling, outriders clearing the way. A Mutt and Jeff team in matching hats and overcoats.

The small one leaned forward, a white-haired bruiser with a stogie pegged in the corner of his mouth. Black-rimmed cheaters. He opened his coat to reveal the worn wooden grips of his service .38 in a shoulder holster. Removed the stogie from his mouth as he spoke. "The name's Stege. Captain Stege. Number one man on the Dillinger Squad. I got fifteen notches on my piece already. Last three was racket boys we thought was you and your crew. No loss to anyone. I'd give my left nut to drop the right punk this time out, though. Make it sixteen, you get me?"

Johnny raised his hands in front of him. "Take the cuffs off me. I'll see you get the chance."

Stege knocked ash from his cigar. "You think I wouldn't?"

"Tough guy. I wasn't wearing these things, I'd hammer that piece up your ass."

Stege blew cigar smoke in his face. "You'd do *what*, you bastard?"

Stege's companion squirmed in his seat. "Christ sake, Jack. Keep your mind on the job. Hamilton tries to spring him while you two's in a pissing match and we won't stand a chance."

Stege replaced the stogie in his mouth. He stared at Johnny as the police convoy wound its way beyond the city limits. Crossed the county line. "I hope to Christ your sidekick does try something, you murdering son-of-a-bitch. Anyone tries to stop us and you're the first man dead." He waited for a response. Got nothing. "Just try something," he said hopefully, and settled back into his seat.

They rolled into Crown Point around eight a.m. A trim matron in a tweed suit, lace at the neck, descended the jailhouse steps as they pried him out the back of the wagon. She caressed the .45 on her hip. "I'm Sheriff Holley. I'll take over from here, gentlemen."

Stege did a double-take at the sight of a female sheriff. Recovered manfully. "Okay, Sheriff. He's all yours." He placed a hand between Johnny's shoulder blades. Propelled him forward. "I'll see you at the execution, asshole. Book me a front row seat."

"Get in closer, Stege. Sit on my goddamn knee when they throw the switch."

The reporters clustered beneath the portico of the red-brick jailhouse perked their ears. Scribbled that down. They trailed him through the stone-faced entrance of the building. One threw him a question as an adolescent-looking deputy with a Thompson escorted him towards the desk for processing.

"No hat, Johnny. Going for the college look?"

He gave that lopsided grin. The one the Janes went for. "One of those cops out in Tucson. Somebody grabbed themselves a souvenir before I got on the plane."

The pressmen traded looks as they bent over their notebooks. He knew what they were thinking. This guy was different from the tight-lipped Syndicate guns they were used to dealing with. The mute wops in parrot-coloured shirts. Tiger-striped neckties. He had that elusive something. Charisma. Star-quality. Call it what you will. Whatever it was, it was going to play well beneath the headlines. A stir of excitement rippled through the pack as a second scribe fired a question.

"Glad to see Indiana again, John?"

"About as glad as it is to see me." He picked up on the mood of the crowd. Nodded towards another reporter. "Got a question, buddy?"

"You're credited with smuggling the guns into the state pen for the September 26th break. Any truth in that, John?"

"I'm not denying it. Leave it at that shall, we?"

"How'd you get them in?"

He shook a finger at the hack. "You're too inquisitive." Let that smile spread over his face again. "I met a lotta good fellas in the joint. I wanted to help them out. There's no denying I fixed that break last September when those ten guys got away. Why not? I stick to my friends and they stick to me."

The press had fanned out around him now in a semi-circle. The cops stood back. Gave him the floor. He held up his manacled hands to the Sheriff. "Any chance I can lose these, Mrs Holley?"

The Sheriff raised a pencilled eyebrow at a bespectacled figure in crumpled pin stripes. A shaving cut on his chin. The guy looked like a farmer in his Sunday go–to-meeting clothes. A broken-down schoolteacher: Lake County prosecutor Bob Estill. He gave the nod.

Johnny circled his hands as the deputy removed the cuffs. "Okay, thanks." He shook the circulation back into his fingers. Despite the machineguns, the iron bars, he was the guy in control of the situation and he knew it. He was beginning to enjoy himself. "Any more questions?" he asked, shucking his jacket.

"Think you can beat this rap, John?"

He dipped in his vest pocket. Smirked as the bulls tensed. Unwrapped a piece of gum. "I never killed that cop O'Malley," he said, feeding the gum into his mouth. "I never had anything to do with that stick-up. I was in Florida when the East Chicago job was pulled and I can prove it." He indicated his face. "Think I got a tan like this on Lake Michigan in winter?"

Scattered chuckles. Another voice from the floor.

"Pretty hot in Tuscon as well, Johnny?"

Flashbulbs popped.

Goddamn Tuscon.

They'd been a long way from their Mid–West stamping ground. On vacation. The cacti and hitching rails had been a different world from the hard grey skies of Indiana and Ohio. They'd been off their guard. Sloppy. And they'd paid the price when the local cops picked them up at the tourist court without firing a shot. "Those cowboy cops pulled too fast for us. I'll give them that. We thought they were rubes and flashed our rolls. Drank too much. They picked our mug-shots out of *True Detective* and scooped us one-by-one without alerting the others. Pie on the sill for them."

"So that only leaves Three-Fingered Jack Hamilton still on the outside," the reporter continued. "Isn't that right, John?"

He saw Red stumble and fall as the bullet struck beneath his partner's steel vest as they exited the First National in East Chicago. The red slick engulfing his hands, his suit, as he hauled the guy into the back of the Terraplane. Laid rubber down Chicago Avenue as they pulled for the sticks. "Red took a gutful of bullets in East Chicago. So I heard. He never made it beyond the county line. The guys wired him to a manhole cover and slipped him in the Calumet River. I had a whole sack of money to pass onto his family, but the cops took it off me in Tucson." His face was grim as he chewed the stick of gum. Went for pathos. "I tell you boys, things had gone different with me as a kid and none of this would have come to pass. Nine years in the state pen for a first offence was too much. I was just a farm boy fell in with bad company and took to drink. I threw myself on the mercy of the court and pulled ten-to-twenty for jack-rolling some guy. If things had been different…"

There was an intake of breath from the deputy holding the Thompson on him. "Jesus Christ."

Johnny resisted the urge to wink at the kid. He'd pushed it as far as he could. "Time we wrapped this up, guys. Any more questions before we call it a day?"

"What do you think of Roosevelt, Johnny?"

Of course. The President's birthday. "You can say that I'm for him and the National Recovery Act. Especially the way he's kept the banks open."

Laughter. They liked that one.

"And how long does it take you to go through a bank, John?"

"One minute and forty seconds flat." He snapped his gum. "One last question before I go upstairs."

"What do you think of being held by a female Sheriff?"

He gave Mrs Holley a quick appraisal. She was older than he went for, but a nice-looking gal. You spent your salad days locked in a steel box with nothing but a contraband copy of *Artists and Models* and a vivid imagination for company and you got to appreciate a good-looking dame. The fact she might be the last attractive woman he ever clapped eyes on was something he didn't want to consider right now. "I think Mrs Holley seems a fine lady." He realized he'd drifted within touching distance of the prosecutor, the latter seeming uncomfortable with the scrum of reporters. "I like Mr Estill fine too."

A cameraman shouldered to the front of the crowd. Turned up the brim of his hat. "A shot with the prosecutor, John," he said, dropping to one knee with his camera.

Johnny leaned on the prosecutor's shoulder. The prosecutor's arm came up automatically. Draped across Johnny's back. He matched smiles with Johnny as the shutter closed, catching the county prosecutor and the man he'd vowed to burn for the murder of an East Chicago cop arm-in-arm. Buddies for the camera.

It was an image that Lake County voters would be reminded of six months later when copies dropped into their mailboxes as Democrat Estill ran unsuccessfully for re-election. The rest of the country would wake to the shot the next morning as the wire services splashed the image of the regionally-notorious bank robber coast-to-coast.

The mocking eyes and sardonic smile would set female hearts beating faster from New York to San Francisco. The off-the-cuff wisecracks and cool bravado give heart to Depression-weary clerks and factory hands. Inspire a generation of pool hall cowboys. John Dillinger had walked into the Crown Point Sheriff's office just another yeggman. He woke in his cell the next morning a star.

<u>Two</u>

Stardom was the last thing on his mind the following day, however, as he greeted the elegant figure entering the cellblock, a tall, soulful-eyed sheikh in immaculate blue serge and a pearl grey fedora, a slim black cigarette holder clamped in his mouth. Correspondent shoes.

"Zark."

"Johnny Boy." A square-cut emerald glinted on the newcomer's pinkie as he threaded a manicured paw between the bars. "How's it going, pal? They treating you well?"

"Well as can be expected." He caught a whiff of Bay Rum as he shook. Retracted his hand. "I bring you out your way, buddy?"

Zark inserted an Abdullah in the cigarette holder. Shrugged. "I got a legitimate interest in the case. The cop you killed was East Chicago. I'm here representing the department." He offered Johnny a cigarette. Lit them both up with a thin gold lighter. "That First National thing. It should never have happened. Why didn't you come to me, you was gonna knock over the bank? I coulda pulled the cops off the streets. Tipped you when the vault was full. Nobody had to get jugged. Nobody get hurt. It's the kind of play

18

I'd a figured from someone like Nelson. I thought you had more sense."

"Yeah, well. It's done now. No use crying over spilled milk. Is there?"

Zark looked at him coolly. "No. I guess not." He exhaled a plume of smoke at the ceiling. "How you doing, anyway, John? Anything I can get you? Commissary? Smokes?"

"How about a woman?"

Zark showed his teeth around the cigarette holder. "Missing Billie?"

"And how."

"Try sweet talking Mrs Holley. She's a doozy, ain't she?"

Johnny picked a strand of tobacco from his lip. "I seen worse." If there was one thing made jail unbearable to him, more painful than the armed guards, confinement, lack of freedom, it was doing without a broad. Especially the dark-haired former hatcheck girl from the College Gardens back in Chi. "A female sheriff, though. What the hell's that about?"

"Her old man was killed in office. She stepped in till the next election. Keeping the seat warm for her nephew, they say. The deputy walked you in here with the Thompson." He tipped ash from his Abdullah. "Sure there's nothing I can get you while I'm here?"

"What about a mouthpiece?"

"Don't know that it's a lawyer you need this time, Johnny. More a miracle worker, I'd say."

"You're connected, though. You can find me a lip. A Syndicate lawyer."

Zark replaced the cigarette in the holder. Set it between his lips again. "Sure I can. If that's what you want." Smiled. "Yeah, I can find you a lip, Johnny. You can pay the price, I know just the guy."

Johnny watched the fixer out the cellblock. Pulled on his cigarette. So he'd got himself a shyster. That was something, anyhow. A guy with Zark's connections promised to find him a lip, it was good as done.

Even a mob lawyer might not be enough to spring him, though. Not with the rap he was facing. Too many people had seen him drop that bull outside the First National a few weeks previously. They had Wilgus, the dead guy's partner, as chief witness. Even with a decent mouthpiece, his chances were slim.

There was an alternative, though. Busting out. He was an old hand at that.

The papers had boasted that Crown Point was escape-proof. There were half a dozen barred doors and some fifty guards between his second floor cell and the street. Floodlights. Vigilantes from the Farmers' Protective Association. A squad of National Guardsmen to beef up the hacks.

It would be a difficult can to crack. Difficult, but not impossible. You could walk out of any place if the fix was in. He'd proved that when he broke his old partners out the state pen in September.

Harry 'Pete' Pierpont. Charles Makley. Red Hamilton. Russell 'Booby' Clark. He'd been nothing but a two-bit jack-roller until the guys had turned him out as a yeggman, an armed robber. They'd taught him the intricacies of making a jug. Running a git. Given him the training. The contacts. Promised him a place on their string once he was paroled.

All he had to do was help them crash out the place. Pull a couple of jobs with guys they knew on the outside and raise the money to fund their escape.

The guys they put him in contact with were a couple of punks named Shaw and Parker: the White Cap gang, named for the headgear they wore to knock over a target. "All they see is the hat and shades," Shaw said, donning the latter as they parked outside their first target, a Haag's drugstore in Indianapolis. "They give a description and it could be anybody. President fucking Roosevelt. Better than a mask, for Christ sake."

They'd swaggered into the drugstore. Displayed their rods. Shaw took the main cash register, Johnny the smaller one by the soda fountain. "Look the other way," he said, as the three kids behind the counter gaped at his map.

They faced towards the other counter, where Shaw was ransacking the till.

"Don't look at me," Shaw said, brandishing his pistol at them.

They switched their gazes back to Johnny. "I said look the other way," he repeated. He snatched the cash from the drawer.

Glowered at Shaw. "You finished?" he said, retreating towards the door.

Shaw waved a handful of notes at him. "Ready to go." He followed him out to the car. Found the latter boxed in at the curb between a beer wagon and a farm truck. "What the hell?"

Johnny thrust his head in the driver's window. "Get this thing on the road. Do it. Now." He simmered as Parker bumped between the two trucks. Worked the getaway car loose from the parking slot. "Next time…"

"What?"

He took a deep breath. "Never mind." Compared his take with Shaw's as they peeled off from the drugstore: a couple hundred dollars. Not enough. Not nearly enough for the prison break. "Know anywhere else we can hit, kid?"

Twenty minutes later, they stopped outside a City Foods supermarket. "This time, Parker," Johnny said as he exited the car. "This time make sure you can actually get the thing away from the curb when we're finished okay?"

Parker gave him a wounded look. "What do you think I am, stupid or something?"

23

Johnny bit back his retort as he accompanied Shaw through the door of the supermarket. Pulled up short as the manager shook his head. "You guys again? What is it, twice in the last two months?"

Shaw avoided Johnny's eye as the latter skewered him with a look. Flaunted his piece at the manager. "Forget the wisecracks. Empty the till, okay?"

The manager hit the 'no sale' key. Showed them the empty drawer. "The management started to collect after the last time you hit the place. You missed their guy by a good half hour."

Johnny lowered his pistol. Glared over his shades at Shaw. "Come on, you. You got some explaining to do."

Shaw tarried a moment. Began to loot the cigar counter. "I'm not leaving empty handed."

Johnny lodged his pistol in his belt. Stalked outside. "Fine. Have it your own way." He climbed into the car. Rocked back in his seat as Parker took off, leaving Shaw on the sidewalk with an armful of guinea stinkers. "Stop, for Christ sake. Stop the car."

Parker stood on the brakes. He reversed the car up the street as Shaw panted up to them. Took off again as his cohort collapsed into the back. Ran a red light. Johnny elbowed him aside as he hit the brakes again in the face of an oncoming bus.

"If you can't drive, give me the wheel."

He steered them towards his father's farmhouse and safety. Slept in his old bedroom while the other two put up in the barn. He listened to the old man snore other side the wall as he considered his options. Cutting hay and hoeing turnips seemed like the smart choice compared to pulling another stick up with Shaw and Parker. How two half-wits like that stayed on the outside while good men like Pete and Red were locked down in the pen was beyond him. Dumb bastards couldn't find their own assholes with a map and a flashlight.

Nevertheless, he pulled another job with the duo a few days later, hitting the Bide-a-Wee tavern in Muncie, Indiana, just before closing. The take this time: seventy dollars and change. Johnny distinguished himself by pinching some woman's ass on the way out. Slugging her beau when he objected.

The cops I.D.' their getaway car, though, a green sedan with yellow wire wheels, and picked up Shaw and Parker the next day. The two of them drew ten to twenty apiece in Johnny's old alma mater, Indiana State. The career of the White Cap gang was over almost before it had begun.

Johnny escaped the pinch, however, backing his ride unseen out the driveway of Parker and Shaw's hideout when he made the patrol wagon in front. His next target, the first on his own, was a bank in nearby Dalesville rather than a drug store or supermarket. The take, $3500 and a handful of diamond rings from the vault. Two weeks later, he lifted ten grand from the First National Bank in Montpelier. On September 6, the State Bank of Massachusetts in Indianapolis yielded $24,000, the second costliest bank raid in Indiana history.

In between jobs, he took time out to visit the World's Fair in Chicago with Mary Longnaker, sister of the fairy cleaned his cell for him in the pen. She was a sweet kid, the first woman he'd had since he raised and he was crazy about her. Couldn't keep away. Which is how the cops got onto him later that month, tipped by a jealous landlady.

They caught him in his BVDs as he leafed through a handful of photographs showing him and Mary at the fairground, sharing ice cream cones, ogling the World of Tomorrow pavilion. The Old

26

Heidelberg Inn. Posing with an obliging bull as a passer-by worked the camera.

He'd almost pulled on them as they came through the door. A guy in plain clothes comes at you with a scattergun and you tend to fire first and ask questions later. They'd identified themselves in time, though, and thrown the cuffs on him. Hauled his ass into the lockup at Lima and grilled him about the banks he'd knocked over in the last couple of weeks.

The escape had already gone down by then, however, the pistols he'd bought smuggled into the prison shirt factory in a bale of thread by a bribed contractor. The guys had used the artillery to take a couple of guards hostage, walking them through the main gate under the eyes of their rifle-toting colleagues on the walls, the gun bulls taking them for transfers under escort.

They'd holed-up with Mary Kinder, an old girlfriend of Pierpont's, in Indianapolis and knocked over the First National in Makley's hometown of St Mary's, Ohio for funding, before turning their eyes to Lima just a few miles to the north. Johnny had played it cool as he'd sat in the Sheriff's lockup and waited for them to come for him. It was just a matter of time.

They sprang him after supper on Columbus Day. Thursday, October 12. They'd had pork chops and mash potatoes that night. Corn bread. Coffee. Apple cobbler to follow. A good meal. He'd eaten worse in restaurants on the outside. Sheriff Sarber's old lady was a hell of a cook.

The Sheriff himself wasn't a bad old guy, a former Chevy salesman in his forties who'd stood for office when his dealership folded in the Crash. The light caught his bald spot as he laboured over paperwork at his desk, his gun belt slung from the back of the chair. His wife sat nearby, working a crossword puzzle, while a deputy played with the Sarber's Labrador, Brownie, on the davenport by the stove. It was a cosy, almost domestic scene mirrored by the guys in the cellblock as they played pinochle, belts loosened, shoes kicked off as they dealt a greasy deck of cards on the recently-cleared dining table.

The guy holding the deck shuffled and split with the practiced moves of a professional dealer: Art Miller, a rackets guy from Toledo being held for second-degree murder. "Deal you in, Johnny?"

Johnny signed off on the letter he'd been writing his old man.

Dear Dad,

Hope this letter finds you well and not worrying too much over me. Maybe I'll learn someday that Dad that you can't win in this game. I know I have been a big disapointment to you but I guess I did to much time, for where I went in a carefree boy I came out bitter towards everything in general. Of course Dad most of the blame lies with me for my enviroment was of the best, but if I had gotten off more leniently when I made my first mistake this would never have happened. How is Doris and Frances? I preferred to stand trial here in Lima because there isn't as much predujice against me here and I am sure I will get a square deal here. Dad don't believe all that the newspapers say about me for I am not guilty of half the things I am charged with and I've never hurt anyone. Well Dad I guess this is all for this time, just wanted you to know I am well and treated fine.

From Johnnie

He sealed it into an envelope. The hell he'd put the old man through since he was a kid. If there was one thing he felt guilty about, it was that. The least he could do was reassure him things were okay at the moment. He'd have the Sheriff pass it on through his lawyer in the morning. Assuming he'd still be there, that is.

He joined the rest of the guys at the table. "Sure. Deal me in." Played mechanically, stealing regular glances towards the door. He'd been there since the 21st. Almost three weeks now. The boys had busted out on the 26th. They'd be here soon. That was a given. All he had to do was wait.

It happened as he took a stint as dealer. Three guys, well-dressed, hats low over their eyes. The light grey orbs of the leader, a tall, collegiate-looking athlete, were still visible, however, as he approached the Sheriff's desk.

"Prison officers. We've come for John Dillinger."

The Sheriff raised his eyes from his papers. Set down his pen. "I don't know anything about this. I haven't received a phone call from the pen. Any mail." He began to rise from his desk. "Can I see your credentials, please?"

The leader reached inside his coat. "Sure." He shot the Sheriff twice in the chest as his companions drew on the deputy. "Here's my credentials, you son-of-a-bitch."

The Sheriff tipped backwards out the chair. Stretched a hand towards his gun.

The grey-eyed man beat him to it. Jerked the Sheriff forward by the collar. "Where's the keys, you bastard?" He brought his pistol down on the Sheriff's head. Once. Twice. "The keys to the cell block. Quick."

Mrs Sarber started forward. "Don't hit him. Please don't hit him again, boys."

The second raider, a well-built, affable-looking sort with a moustache, restrained her. "Give us the keys, honey, and he won't get hurt."

The deputy cringed beneath the gun of the third intruder, a portly, distinguished figure in his forties, a businessman by appearance rather than a killer. "In the hallway cupboard. The cupboard by the cell block."

The grey-eyed man signalled the man with the moustache. "Booby."

"Got it, Pete." He unhooked the key from inside the cupboard and worked the lock. Smirked as Johnny threw in his cards. "Not staying for a last hand, Johnny?"

"Think I'll sit this one out, Russ." He snared his coat. "Coming with us, Art?"

"My lawyers will straighten it out for me. Racket guys don't do time in this neck of the woods." He clasped his hand. "Luck, Johnny."

"You too, Art."

He stood aside as Pete forced Mrs Sarber and the deputy into the cellblock. Put a bullet over the heads of the other prisoners as they surged towards freedom. "The rest of you bastards get back. We only got room for Johnny."

Mrs Sarber clung to the bars as the door closed behind her. Faltered at the sight of her husband. "He's hurt, men. Can't I stay with him a little longer?"

The distinguished-looking man grimaced as he turned the key on her. "Sorry, lady. Someone will be along soon, though. They'll have heard the shots." He darted a tight grin at Johnny. "Speaking of which - "

"Sure, Charley." He strode briskly towards the outside door. Spared a glance at the Sheriff lying tangled amongst the furniture on the office floor. "Did you have to do that?" he said, as Pete fell into step beside him.

Pete made an angry gesture as he accompanied him into the street. "You wanted to get out of there, didn't you?"

"Yeah, but - " He let it go as he dropped into the back seat between Russ and Charley. Acknowledged Red at the wheel. Pete was the wild man of the bunch. The guy had been in the nut-house as a kid. You couldn't argue with him once his blood was up. Not if you wanted to keep your head on your shoulders, anyway

Besides, what was done was done. He couldn't help Sarber now. And he was out. That was the important thing. Out and free and the law couldn't touch him. For now at least. The fact that the others would be looking at the electric chair for that night's work wouldn't become apparent for another three months.

He compared the Crown Point lockup to the cell in Lima as he finished his cigarette. Scored it out on the sole of his shoe. Yeah, he could beat this joint without standing trial. Indiana State was a different proposition, though. Which was where a good lawyer came in. A lawyer could keep him here in the county jail rather than see him transferred to the pen. Buy him time to make a break.

Yeah, all he needed was a good lawyer. Or at least, a crooked one. A lawyer like the one Zark promised to set him up with. Syndicate mouthpiece Louis Piquet.

Three

Crown Point, Indiana

Friday, February 9

Johnny was dressed in an open-necked, collar-attached blue shirt and vest. No jacket. The same outfit he'd worn when he arrived back East. The one the public knew from the newspapers.

He worked his smile as he passed through the news photographers thronging the courtroom. Put on a good show for the press as he approached the bench. If it kept the public happy, brought him some support, so be it.

Besides, he enjoyed the attention. A guy could get sick of it after a while, but that wouldn't be a problem here. He wouldn't be around long enough for it to become a pain in the ass. You could bet your bottom dollar on that.

He stopped before the judge, hands shackled, a Thompson notched in his ribs. "Louis?"

Louis Piquet came up from behind the defence table as if at the sound of a timekeeper's bell. A plump, putty-nosed cherub, he stood barely five feet four in his hand-lasted Oxfords, a diminutive

35

figure amongst the surrounding figures in derbies and fedoras.
Stetson hats. His hair added another three inches to his height,
however, a tightly-curled, salt-and-pepper mass swept up in a *Bride
of Frankenstein* pompadour, a dramatic coiffure that reflected his
style in the courtroom and his no less colourful personal history.
For those inclined to believe it, that is.

By his own account, Piquet had been a rod-riding hobo who
went on to tour Australia as part of the Sanford track team and
fought as a welterweight on the West Coast, returning to Chicago
only after being wiped out by the San Francisco earthquake. He'd
taught himself law while working as a barkeep, passing his bar
exams on the twelfth attempt, before using his talents as a
Democratic ward-heeler to land himself the post of city prosecutor.
After sending up a Syndicate patsy for the murder of crime reporter
Jake Lingle, he'd gone into private practice and been rewarded by a
string of underworld clients whom he'd sprung via a combination
of courtroom melodramatics and under the table payoffs.

Which was the reason he'd been parked opposite Johnny in
his Crown Point jail cell four days earlier, tapping a coin against the

bars in case the place was bugged. "Dick Tracy stuff," he'd said, rolling his shoulders. "You never know."

Johnny held his mud. It seemed over the top to him, but he figured it was the lawyer's style. "I want you to represent me," he said. "I didn't have anything to do with the East Chicago job."

"I don't believe you did."

"I can prove I didn't." He bent his head to the mouthpiece's ear. "Here's what happened, see?"

Piquet raised his hand. "Before we take up too much of each other's time. Innocent or guilty, you're in a pretty hot spot here. I suppose you know it's going to cost money to put on a strong defence. How much have you got?"

"My old man back in Mooresville has about three thousand dollars."

"That all you have?"

"That's all."

"Hell, you don't need a lawyer. You need a doctor."

Johnny pondered. "That's all I have in cash. But -" he dropped his voice. "I have a third interest in a quarter of a million dollars hidden up in Wisconsin. I'll arrange with the boys to have your fee cut out of that."

Piquet tapped louder. "Cash?"

"Bonds. You can move those, can't you?" He shook his head impatiently as the lawyer hesitated. "Read the newspapers. I'm not some punk stuck up a liquor store. Robbed a gas station. The man who walks Johnny Dillinger out a courtroom can write his own ticket when this is all over. You ought to be paying to represent me. Not the other way around."

Piquet walked the coin over his knuckles. Guffawed. "You might think of a career on the other side of the courtroom once you're out of here, Mr Dillinger. I'll tell you that for nothing."

Well. That was as maybe. For the moment, however, the ball was in Piquet's court. Johnny just hoped the lip's performance matched his appearance as he stood before Judge Murray in exquisitely-cut grey flannel and a white-on-white shirt, blue handkerchief, speckled tie, hand adjusting the latter as he inclined his head towards the bench.

"Your Honour." He swept his paw towards the accused. "Are we to have a hearing in accord with the laws of this state and of this nation, or are we to witness merely a mockery of the name of justice? Is the state to be permitted to continue inciting an atmosphere of prejudice and hatred? The very air reeks with the bloody rancour of intolerant malice. The clanging of shackles brings to our minds the dungeons of the czars, not the flag bedecked liberty of an American courtroom" – a reverent glance at the Stars and Stripes above the judge's head - " I request the court to direct that those shackles be removed."

Estill was up on his feet. Finger stabbing at Johnny. "That is a very dangerous man, your honour."

Judge Murray noted the shotgun-wielding vigilantes. Deputies. National guardsmen in tin hats and webbing. "Remove the handcuffs from the prisoner," he said.

Piquet bowed graciously. "Thank you your honour." Smirked at Estill. "May I also point out that this is a civil court and not a military court-martial. Could anything be more prejudiced than machineguns pressed into the defendant's back, and an army of guards cluttering up the room? May the court direct that all guns be removed from the courtroom?"

The deputy at his back stirred. "I'm responsible for the safe-guarding of this prisoner," he said, tightening his grip on the Thompson.

Piquet regarded him with astonishment. "Who are you?" he demanded, eyes popping like Eddie Cantor's. "Are you a lawyer? What right have you to address this court?"

The Deputy opened his mouth to speak. The judge, a corpulent, frog-faced figure in black, pince-nez perched on a glowing plum of a nose, made a levelling motion with his hand. "Remove the guns," he said.

Piquet grinned furtively at his client as the guards trooped from the wood-panelled courtroom. Johnny grinned back. Naughty schoolboys in front of the principal. The lawyer wiped his face clear as the room settled down again. Came back for the second round.

"Thank you, your honour. Now that the court resembles a palace of justice rather than an armed camp, I feel we may now be able to proceed to the reason we are here. To whit, the establishment of my client John F. Dillinger's innocence of the crime of murdering the unfortunate Officer O'Malley in East Chicago last month. In order to prove my client's innocence of the said charge, I respectfully ask that I be granted a delay of thirty days and a date in March in order to locate and transport witnesses from Florida in order to prepare my defence."

Estill was on his feet again. "Ten days should be plenty," he said, addressing the Judge.

Piquet bristled. "That would be legal murder. There is a law against lynching in this state."

"There's a law against murder too."

"Then why don't you observe it? Why don't you call back your men with their machineguns? Why don't you stand Dillinger against a wall and shoot him down? There's no need to throw away the state's money on this kind of mockery. Why isn't John Dillinger entitled to the consideration of a hearing? Your honour, even Christ had a fairer trial than this."

Murray worked his gavel. "May I remind you gentlemen that this is a court of law rather than a school yard. If you cannot restrain your tempers, I'll hold you both in contempt."

Piquet bent from the waist. "My apologies, your Honour. For the record, myself and Estill have nothing but the greatest regard for each other."

Murray hid a smile. "He'll be putting his arm around you next." Waited for the mirth to subside. "As to your request. The defence is granted a delay until March 12th to prepare its case."

Estill exploded. Threw his arms wide. "Your Honour, why don't you let Mr Piquet take Dillinger home with him, and bring him back on the day of the trial? You've given him everything else he asked for."

"That will be enough from you, counsel."

Piquet repeated the bow. "Thank you, your Honour." Winked at Johnny.

Johnny returned the wink as he was led from the courtroom. "Attaboy, counsel." He helped himself to a stick of gum as the deputy returned him to his cell. Reclined on his bunk and clasped his hands behind his head. He sat upright as Piquet joined him in the cell a few minutes later. Popped the gum between his teeth. "Nice going, Louis."

"Wasn't it, though? Did I show Estill a few tricks there or what?"

"Some performance, counselor. You made old Bob look a sucker. I'll give you that." He tightened his jaw on the wad of gum. "It won't come to anything if they ship me to the pen, though. They get me back to that place and I'm cooked."

"Quit worrying. You're not going back to the pen. I threatened to file for a change of venue if they shipped you off to the hoosegow. Told them it was too far to travel from Chicago if I was going to conduct a proper defence."

"And they went for it?"

"Murray and Estill are ambitious. You're big news, Johnny. No way those two are going to risk losing you to another court."

"And the Sheriff. What about her?"

"She's made too many claims about this place being escape-proof to let you go to the pen. I made a few cracks about this being too big a job for a woman and she dug her heels in. She might have a badge pinned to her chest, but she's still a dame. And if there's one thing I know, it's how to handle a dame." He dug a coin from his pocket. Began to tap on the bars. "This problem you have with going back to the pen, though. Are you planning what I think you're planning, Johnny?"

"You should know better than to ask me that, counselor." He edged closer, their heads almost touching. "You're connected, Louis. Know the pols. Can we put the fix in here?"

"You're too hot, Johnny. Too famous. And Murray and Estill know there's an election coming. The political rewards for putting you away are worth more to them than a bribe. Likewise, if they let you walk in the face of the evidence against you -" He grimaced. "Not something a defence lawyer likes to admit, but if you are planning to do what I think you're planning to do…"

"A gun, then. You can get me a gun, Louis?"

"And what the hell do you think would happen if they caught me? You don't seem to understand, John. Ever since that picture with Estill, you're headline news. Above the fold on the *New York*

Times. You're red-hot, man. Anyone who touches you is likely to go up in flames."

"I'd pay you, Louis. Pay you well. That stack of bonds up in Wisconsin."

"The more I hear about those bonds, the less I like the sound of them." He tapped away with the coin. "It just so happens that someone has been in touch with me on the other side of the wall, though. Someone who's willing to front the money for your defence. Provide a safe-house on the outside. Plastic surgery if you want it."

"Who?"

"I'll tell you that if you make it out the place. Here - " he produced a fountain pen. Scrawled a number on the back of a business card. "Call me once you're back on the street. I'll put you together with your mystery benefactor when you phone me. Use my connections to put you on ice. Assuming I'm going to see payment for my services at some point, of course."

"Keep your hair on, counselor. You'll get paid." He switched his attention to the Tommy gun-toting guards patrolling the corridors. The barred windows. Steel doors. "Assuming I get out of this joint in the first place, that is."

Piquet flipped the coin. "I got faith in you, Johnny." Quit the cell. "See you around, pal."

Johnny removed his gum. "You too, Louis." Stuck it to the underside of the bunk. He had time to prepare now. Plan his move. With the threat of being shanghaied to the state pen removed, the biggest obstacle to his escape was gone. Things were beginning to go his way. Play his hand right at this point and he was already halfway over the wall.

Four

Saturday, March 3 – 9.15 A.M.

He has none of the looks of the conventional killer – none of the advertised earmarks of the crook. Given a little more time and a wider circle of acquaintances, one can see that he might presently become the central figure of a nationwide campaign, largely female, to prevent his frying in the electric chair for the murder of Policeman Patrick O'Malley.

Johnny razored the article from the read-to-pieces copy of the Chicago *Daily News* and buttoned it into his shirt pocket, tossing the blade onto the whittled section of bed board beneath his bunk as he unscrewed the razor's handle. He wired the black metal tube to the carved wooden pistol grip cached beneath his mattress. Smiled as the stewbum janitor approached the cellblock with his bucket and mop, a pair of trustees tailing him with soap and toilet paper. A last daub of boot blacking and he was ready to go.

It was good to know the female newspaper readers of America were behind him, but that didn't unlock his cell for him or remove the steel doors in his path. With a lot of nerve and a little luck, though, the wooden gun in his hand would provide all the

47

support he needed to get him out of Sheriff Holley's lockup and back on the streets where he belonged.

He waited for the guard to spring the door before making his move. Sank the gun in the janitor's gut. "Come on, Sam. We're going places." He faced him towards the guard. "You're going to be good, aren't you, Sam?"

The janitor blinked bloodshot eyes, last night's beer on his breath. "I'm always good," he said, baffled.

"Atta boy, Sammy." He threw a glance over his shoulder as he covered the guard. "Want to take care of the janitor, Youngblood?"

A hulking black shape appeared at his elbow, a toilet plunger held like a billy club. Herbert Youngblood, murder one. The only guy desperate enough to come in on the break with him. "I got him, Johnny."

"Swell." He stashed the two captives in a nearby cell. Shoved the trustees in after them. "No gun, Bryant?" he asked, patting down the guard.

"No guns in the cell block. Official policy."

"What the hell. We'll just have to improvise." He beckoned the janitor forward as Youngblood made to lock the cell door. "Come on, you. You're gonna get me out of here."

He padded out the cellblock. Took a slant down the corridor. Seventy feet away stood the warden's office. Voices sounded inside. The chink of crockery: guards at their morning coffee. "How many?" he asked the janitor.

The janitor humped his shoulders. "There's four doors between you and the outside, though. You'll never get away with it."

Johnny thought a moment. "Got a pencil?"

"Sure."

"Draw me a map."

The janitor sketched a diagram on the back of a cigarette packet. It was pretty much how he'd figured it. Four doors between him and the outside. The corridor as the only way out. There was a flight of four steps bisecting the corridor, though. It put him just above the guards' line of sight. "Who's that?" he asked, as a figure emerged from the office.

49

"Ernie Blunk."

"Call him over." He sank back into the shadows as the guard approached. Pounced as he reached the steps. "Get up here, you son-of-a-bitch or I'll kill you." He walked Blunk back to the cellblock. Left him with Youngblood. "Now the jailer, Sam. Call him up to the steps."

The janitor squared his shoulders. "I'll be goddamned if I'll help you get out of here. I'm not going any further. Shoot and be goddamned."

Youngblood raised the plunger. "Rummy bastard."

Johnny stepped between them. "None of that. I'll handle this." He shunted the janitor back into the cell: the old lush had sand, he'd give him that. "Contrary to what people say, I'm no killer. But I'm gonna get past those hacks today, come what may."

"They'll plug you before you get halfway down the corridor."

"You think so?" He cut Blunk loose from the pack. Frogmarched him towards the steps. "I'm gonna make it outta here and you're gonna help me."

"You can't. They'll kill you."

"I got everything to gain and nothing to lose. You can either be a dead hero or a live coward, but I am going to get out of here, whatever it takes."

"Not with my help, you won't."

Time to bluff. "That a wedding ring on your finger, Ernie? Got a wife at home? A baby?"

"You son-of-a-bitch."

"I'll take that as a yes. Now down to the steps and call the warden."

He stood behind Blunk as the guard hollered to the warden: Lew Baker, a former jeweller. Motto, 'I used to sell watches, now I watch cells.' Bunched his fist in the turnkey's shirtfront as he mounted the steps. "How many in the office, asshole?"

"Four." The warden's face fell as he realized what he'd done. "Christ, Ernie…"

"Never mind, Baker. At least you'll have something to tell your grandkids when you get older. As long as you behave yourself, that is." He steered him towards Youngblood. "Now get in the cell."

He made Blunk summon the other guards one-by-one. The last guy made a grab for the gun. Johnny slugged him and turned him over to his accomplice. "Sure that's the last one, Ernie?"

"Find out for yourself."

He dumped Blunk in the cell. "Well. Let's see what we can see." He sidled down the corridor. Hung an eye around the office door.

Coffee cups. Paperwork. No guards. A brace of Thompsons leaning against the wall. He hefted the machineguns in his hands.

A Thompson held a hundred rounds per magazine. It could lay down a thousand rounds a minute. Stop and demolish a moving automobile. Blow a prison door off its hinges. Twenty pounds a piece of life insurance for the man that carried them. He transferred one to Youngblood as he returned to the cellblock. "Where are the cars kept, Baker?"

"In the garage. In back."

"And where are the keys?"

"In the cars."

He collared Blunk again. "Come on, Ernie. You're walking us out of here." Waved the others back with the Thompson. "The rest of you against the wall of the cell, if you know what's good for you."

Baker looked grave. "You'll never make it to the garage, John. The guards outside will cut you down in the street."

He produced the wooden pistol. "I keep forgetting." Rapped on the bars of the cell with it. "This place is escape-proof, right?"

The warden's face sagged. "I'll be a son-of-a-bitch."

Johnny replaced the pistol at his waist. "I wouldn't doubt it for a moment, warden." He signed to Youngblood. "Come on, Herb. We're going for a drive."

He studied the map as they walked back down the corridor. Opened the rear door of the warden's office. A white-aproned figure looked up from a steaming cauldron of stew, drawing back his ladle like a cudgel at the sight of the machineguns. Blunk shook his head.

"I wouldn't, Bill. These guys mean business."

The cook dropped the ladle. Joined the brace of guards Youngblood had collected as they warmed their hands at the ovens. They stood with their hands brushing the ceiling as Johnny unhooked a hat and raincoat from the back of the door. Squinted outside. "Okay, we're clear." He moved them into the street.

They made a strange procession as they trailed along the front of the jail: Johnny, the chef, Blunk and the guards, Youngblood at the rear. The street was empty, though, and the passing motorists ignored them as they turned the corner and entered the garage at the back of the building. Just a couple of hacks escorting prisoners to the cells.

Their luck ran out as they hit the garage, however. "No keys," the trustee said, as he left off polishing the Sheriff's Nash and gawped down the muzzle of the Thompson. "They're in the warden's office, I think."

Johnny tightened his grip on the machinegun. "You know what I'll do if you're lying," he said.

The trustee blanched. Edged away from the car. "See for yourself," he said.

Johnny searched the glove compartment. No keys. He gnawed his lip as he straightened. "That son-of-a-bitch, Baker. I ought to kill him." He nodded to Youngblood. "Keep these bastards covered. I'll go back and check."

He marched Blunk and the trustee back to the kitchen door. Surprised a National Guardsman and a trio of vigilantes in check shirts and hunting caps. He took their guns and secured them in the larder while the trustee ransacked the warden's office for the keys. No dice. "You know where the nearest garage is, son?"

"Joliet Street. Down by the Criminal Courts Building."

He returned Blunk and the trustee to the jailhouse garage. Twitched the machinegun towards the entrance as a woman appeared in front of him. "Mrs Baker. Why don't you join us?" He added her to his haul. Panned the gun barrel towards the captives. "These guys giving you any trouble, Herb?"

"No trouble at all, Johnny."

"All right, then. Lock them in the office and follow me. We're going for a ride."

They sandwiched Blunk between them and set off down the side of the Criminal Courts Building. Their luck held. There were no deputies or Guardsmen in front of the court. No one to challenge them as they crossed the street to the garage and buttonholed a couple of mechanics bowed over an engine. "Which is the fastest car in the place?"

One of the mechanics lifted his head. "The V-8 Ford." He dipped beneath the hood again.

"You better get over here. Show me which you mean."

The mechanic concentrated on the engine. Didn't seem to hear him.

"Get over here, asshole. Do it now."

The mechanic's face dropped. "What the hell?"

Blunk licked his lips. "You better do as he tells you. This guy means business."

The mechanic wiped his hands on his overalls. Led them across to a black police Ford with a red light and siren. "I thought you was deputies," he said, eyeballing the Thompsons.

"Ever see a black deputy, kid?"

"I never seen a woman sheriff till I moved to Lake County." He opened the car door. "Want me to drive?"

"Blunk can do the driving. You get in back with Youngblood." He took the shotgun seat. Pointed the Thompson at the second mechanic. "Open the doors."

The mechanic thumbed the air-compressor button. The garage door swung up. They hit the street, coming close to sideswiping a taxi-cab as they swerved onto Joliet and crossed the town square. Johnny punched the Thompson into the jailer's side as they narrowly missed a utility pole. "Pile this baby up and you're the first to die."

Blunk shied like a startled horse. Ran a light. "Jesus. Jesus Christ."

Johnny withdrew the barrel. "Ah, hell." So much for the *Public Enemy* routine. "You know I'm not going to hurt you, Ernie, long as you do what I say. But calm down, for Christ sake. Keep your foot off the accelerator and your eye on the road."

"Sure, Johnny. Whatever you say."

"Just take your time, Ernie. Thirty miles an hour is fast enough, okay?" His attention piqued as they passed the First National. The Commercial. A couple juicy banks there. Perhaps he should have hit them on the way out. He rummaged in the glove compartment. No Rand McNally. "You know where the turning is for Route 8?"

"We passed it a couple blocks back, Johnny."

"The next main road, then." He concentrated as they proceeded up Pennsylvania Avenue, parallel with the railroad tracks. Spotted a junction. "And left here. Stick to the cat roads till we hit the highway. Away from the bulls."

They passed through the suburbs. Drove into farm country. Johnny put up the Thompson as they headed into the sticks. Chin-nodded towards a side road as they approached St John, next town down the pike. "Up there, Ernie. I want the light and sirens gone before we get any further. And fit the chains. Those gravel roads are hell in the rain. Be damned if I'm going to get stuck after what I pulled at the jail just now."

"Okay, Johnny. You're the boss."

The deputy slewed the car to a halt at the side of the road. He joined the mechanic in stripping the incriminating fixtures from the Ford and fixing the chains. "This' going to take time, Johnny. Half an hour, say."

Johnny rested his foot on the fender, humming beneath his breath as they worked. "That's no problem. What's time to me?" He drooped an eyelid at Youngblood sitting silently in the rear of the car. "They've been pretty swell guys so far, ain't they, Herb? What say we take them down to Ohio with us? Bust out the rest of the boys?"

Youngblood grunted. "What say we put a bullet in the motherfuckers instead? Stop them squealing to the law?"

"No telephone lines out here, Herb. By the time they raise the alarm, we'll be long gone." He hopped back in the Ford as they finished fixing the chains. Tossed the light and siren in a ditch. "Here -" he pressed a couple dollars on them as they stood by the car. "For cab fare. Herb had a collection from the hacks in the cell. I'd give you more, but it's all I can spare. What the hell. I'll remember you at Xmas, okay?"

The mechanic folded the bills into his overall pocket. "Think I'll hang onto this, Johnny. Might be worth more than a few bucks in years to come. A souvenir of Dillinger."

Johnny chuckled as he put the Ford into gear. "You ought to come with us, son. You're wasted as a grease monkey." He sprayed gravel as he took off down the road, leaving the two hostages standing forlornly by the roadside. Pity to put a couple of regular guys like that through the mill, but it couldn't be helped. The money they'd earn from the newspapers should more than make up for it. He broke into song as he turned back onto the main road.

'I'm headin' for the last round up

gonna saddle old Paint for the last time and ride

So long old pal

it's time your tears were dried

I'm headin' for the last round up

Git along

little dogie

git along.'

They made for Chicago. Crossed the state line. Those two guys by the road there. If nothing else, the last couple of hours should keep them in free drinks for the rest of their lives. Damned if he hadn't done them a favour.

'I'm headin' for the last round up

To the far away ranch of the boss in the sky.

Where the stray are counted and branded

there go I

I'm headin' for the last round up

Git along little doggie

git along.'

TWO

PUBLIC ENEMIES

under-filth… rats crawling from their hide-outs to gnaw at

the vitals of our civilization – J. Edgar Hoover

One

North Side, Chicago

Saturday, March 3 – 12.30 p.m.

I am for John Dillinger. Not that I am upholding him in his crimes: that is if he did any.

Why should the law have wanted John Dillinger for bank robbery? He wasn't any worse than bankers or politicians who took poor people's money.

Dillinger did not rob poor people. He robbed those who became rich by robbing the poor. I am for Johnny - Letter to the editor, Indianapolis News, May, 1934

Johnny checked the street sign: Wellington Avenue. Craned his neck out the window as the Ford crawled down the gutter. There it was. 434. And loitering in the doorway, hat brim down, hands in pockets, was Piquet. Just like he'd said in the phone call.

"Hi, counselor." He indicated the building. "This where I'm staying?"

"Just while we talk. We'll be moving you somewhere safer after tonight."

"Got any dough?"

"Sure." Piquet separated a couple hundred from his roll. "First time I ever paid a client rather than the other way around."

"Don't worry. You'll get your money." He reached a hundred to Youngblood, hunkered down in the back seat beneath a raincoat with a Thompson. "Sorry, Herb, but they'll be looking for a black and tan team. Best we split now."

Youngblood took the money. Relinquished the Thompson. "Can't carry that with me on a streetcar. Let me have a pistol instead, John?"

"Sure." He gifted him a Smith and Wesson. Offered his hand. "Hate to see you go, Herb."

Youngblood shook. "You too, John. Take it easy, you hear?"

Johnny watched him lope through the traffic and vanish down a side street. "One of the good guys. Wish I could keep him aboard a little longer."

Piquet nodded. "You can't beat a good shine. Treat 'em right and they're faithful as dogs." He moved towards the stairwell of the building. "Anyway, come on up. There's someone waiting to see you."

They ascended the staircase, Johnny packing a Thompson beneath the raincoat. He followed Piquet into a railroad flat. Set the safety on the Thompson at the sight of the figure hunched on the brown horsehair couch. "Red."

The dark-haired man finger-brushed his temple. "So much for the dye job."

"I never seen a brunette with freckles like that. And you can't do much about the fingers."

Hamilton curled his mutilated hand. "Guess not." A former lumberjack and deckhand on lake steamers turned bootlegger, Hamilton had been doing a twenty-five year stretch for bank robbery when he fell in with Johnny. Embittered by the authorities refusal of a furlough to attend his mother's funeral, he had been one of the ringleaders of the September prison break. "You're looking good, anyway, Johnny."

"You too," Johnny lied. Truth be told, Hamilton had aged since he'd last seen him. The worried pleat bisecting his partner's eyes, the lines grooving his forehead. And the guy was pale. Ill. He'd lost weight. "That thing in East Chicago," he said.

"It hadn't been for that, I'd a been lifted with the rest of you guys in Tuscon. Heading for the chair with Pete and Booby. Fat Charley."

"Still." East Chicago. It should never have happened. There was a right and a wrong way to knock over a jug and they'd gone about hitting the bank in the lakeside port like a pair of schoolboys raiding a melon patch.

A professional spent time casing the place beforehand, noting the location of the vaults and the tellers, the delivery times, the entrances and exits. He counted the guards. Charted the local beat and traffic cops. Recorded the times they came on and off shift.

Most importantly, he planned a git. He timed it out as he practiced the run. Stashed gas along the route. Carried a medical kit. Packed corks to plug bullet holes in the gas tank. Roofing nails to puncture the tires of pursuing police flivvers. He had any sense at all, he knocked out the rear window of the getaway car to give a clear field of fire.

Instead of which, they'd hit the place almost on a whim. They'd blown most of their spending cash on a jaunt to Miami and were impatient to join the rest of the guys out West. There was money coming from the stolen bonds he'd later promised Piquet, but the fence was stalling and he couldn't be bothered to wait. Not when there was a full bank hanging like an apple on a tree. Waiting to be picked.

Besides, he was bored. It was almost two months since he'd cracked a jug and he missed the thrill. Missed his name in the headlines. And he was getting cocky. The elaborate planning was beginning to seem unnecessary. He'd pulled a couple dozen jobs without a hitch. Why should this place prove any different from the rest?

Things had gone as they always had at first. He'd broken the Thompson from the trombone case he used as a carrier and vaulted the barrier like Fairbanks. Brimmed an army barracks bag as Hamilton threw down on the staff. The alarm was ringing, but no sweat. The alarm always sounded at some point. Small town cops were no match for a couple of practiced yeggs with machineguns. They were cutting it fine, though. Time to wind it up. Hit the street.

"Oh Jesus."

Cops. Half a dozen of them lined up behind cars and lampposts with BARs and pump guns. A couple on the sidewalk. He only had a second to register before they opened fire.

Bullets impacted the steel vest he wore beneath his jacket. Plucked at his coat tails.

Ruined his suit.

He spun and crouched. Tucked the stock of the Thompson into his shoulder. The burst hit O'Malley full in the chest as he emerged from behind a Buick, flattening him to the sidewalk. The dumb flatfoot never had a chance.

Killing the cop. The way it would play in the newspapers. So much for the counter-leaping Robin Hood that hurt only the rich guys. The gentleman bandit that wisecracked with bank staff as he took down the vaults. The bull had a wife and kids, for Christ sake. A family man. What the hell would the public think of him if he was convicted of killing a good egg like Officer O'Malley?

It wasn't just O'Malley that had gone down, though. Hamilton. The poor schmuck had always been a lead magnet. The extra digit he'd lost on that Illinois job, for instance. The papers should be calling him Two-Fingered Jack by now.

The bullet he took beneath the vest, though. That was no missing finger. Two months later and the guy still didn't look right. The way he bent forward as he stood, stroking his stomach with his fingertips. "Still giving you pain, Red?"

"It'll pass. Better a pain in the stomach than a date with Old Sparky."

"We still got to do something for those guys in Ohio. See if we can crash them out of there."

Piquet leaned against the doorframe, arms folded. "I've been down to visit the boys for your colleague here. They've called in the regular army to defend the place. Sandbagged the outside of the building. Set up heavy machineguns. They're searching people as they enter and leave the courthouse. There's no way anybody's going in or out of the place without the doughboys' say so. The only way they're getting out of that place is with a good lawyer."

"Like you, you mean?"

"They know my reputation down there. The bastards threw me in the slammer when I showed my face. The brass hat in charge threatened to horsewhip me when they found I'd got hold of the jury list." He studied the two yeggmen from beneath his pompadour. Worked his tongue behind his lip. "Besides, I'm still waiting for the balance for representing you before I take on any more clients. In case you'd forgotten, Johnny."

Hamilton stirred. "You'll get what's coming to you. We're going to be in funds by the end of the week. Enough to buy those guys down in Ohio a good lip while we're at it."

Johnny shot him a look. "We can contact you at your office, counselor?"

Piquet uncrossed his arms. "You've got my number, Johnny. Call me when you've got the scratch, okay?"

Johnny clicked his tongue as the mouthpiece left. "I thought you were going to spill in front of the lip for a minute, Red."

"The bullet hit me in the gut, Johnny. Not the head. I ain't stupid, you know." He parted the blue velvet drapes as Piquet reached the street. Watched him manoeuvre a black Studebaker into the traffic. "You trust that guy, John?"

"As much as I trust any lawyer."

Hamilton let the drapes fall. "It don't really matter none. Tommy Carroll's picking us up before morning, anyway."

"The pug?"

"You know the guy?"

"I heard good things about him."

"He learned to use a machinegun in the AEF. Hell of a tiger. One of the bunch I been running with since the rest of you were lifted out West."

"These the guys fronting the money for Piquet?"

Hamilton nodded. "They put up some for the guys in Ohio as well. Kept me on ice while I got over the East Chicago job." He propped himself against the windowsill. "The guy running the string. He's real eager to have us on board, Johnny. Especially, you."

"Anyone I know?"

Hamilton hesitated. He concentrated on the rose-patterned wallpaper behind Johnny's head. *Washington crossing the Delaware* above the fireplace. "The kid Jimmy," he said, fiddling with the window sash. "You know, the guy from Back of the Yards."

"Nelson. That's who you're talking about, right?" Jesus. That was all he needed. Babyface Nelson. He'd heard plenty about the diminutive killer when he was in the joint. All of it bad.

The runt had started as a beer runner for the Touhy mob up in Des Plaines, according to the grapevine, before making his name leading armed burglaries into Chicago's Gold Coast: at one point, he'd personally ripped twenty grand's worth of ice from the neck of one Mary Thompson, wife of Hizzoner the mayor, Big Bill.

From there, he'd graduated to knocking over banks and nightclubs, roadhouses, a series of heists distinguished by the mayhem he'd left in his path. Rumour was he'd once shot a guy in a stick-up for smiling at him, a rumour that was all too easy to believe. From what they said of Nelson, anything was possible.

A sentence of one year to life for armed robbery had temporarily put a crimp in the kid's style, but a smuggled gun on the train taking him to Joliet had enabled him to escape west to Reno. He'd paid for his keep in Nevada by bumping a couple of witnesses against Bill Graham and Jim McKay, the town's gambling boss', before heading out to the West Coast, where he'd resumed his old trade of riding shotgun on booze shipments.

Now, though, it looked like Repeal had put him out of a job and he was back in his hometown and ready to go to work. All he needed was a couple of recruits crazy enough to work with him. Recruits like himself and Hamilton. "Christ, Red. Goddamn Nelson. What were you thinking? You know the rep he's got. Throw in with Babyface and we're on a one -way trip to the morgue."

"We owe him, Johnny. Money he put up for lawyers. Doctors. Money for safe-houses while I got on my feet." He turned down his mouth. "Besides, no one else will touch you, John. That thing in the papers. Every reader in the country knows your face since that photo with the prosecutor. Nelson's the only one screwy enough to give you a chance."

Perhaps Red had a point. And this didn't have to be no long-term arrangement. One job, two at the most with the squirt and he'd

74

be able to square his debt and pick up some travelling money. Fund a lawyer for the rest of the boys.

After that, he could cut out with Red and begin to make plans. Start looking at finding a hiding place abroad. Altering that mug he'd managed to splash all over the front pages. "You worked with the guy as yet, Red?"

Hamilton shook his head. "He's the best wheelman in the business, though. Used to race stock cars. Good with a gun - " he flinched at the expression on Johnny's face. "And he's a city kid. Grew up with the rackets boys. Got the connections us Hoosiers can use if things get tight with the law."

Johnny wasn't so sure of that. The way things were going with the Touhy mob, Nelson's connections were more likely to get him hit than save his neck from the bulls. Still. "What about the rest of the string? Anyone I know?"

"Eddie Green. You'll a heard of him. Best damn jug maker in the business."

Fast Eddie Green. A navy vet and sometime machinegunner for the Barker mob, Green had served eight years for armed robbery in Minnesota and had good connections in the St Paul underworld. The kind of guy could line them up with plenty of well-stuffed banks, once they started to roll. The kind of guy you wanted on your team if you wanted to make money. "Okay," he said. "That's jake. They say good things about Eddie." He peeled a stick of gum. Folded it into his mouth. "Anybody else I know?"

"An old buddy from Indiana State. Guy as raised a couple months before you did."

"We talking about Homer here?"

"Van Meter's the guy hooked me up with Nelson and his crew. Gonna be like old home week once we get back together again." Red spread his hands. "This' one of the best goddamn outfits I ever worked with, John. We manage to keep a lid on the little guy and I figure we can make some real money once we get to work."

Johnny nodded. "From what you were saying earlier, I figure you already got something in mind, Red."

Hamilton nodded in turn. "We're ready to roll the day after tomorrow. If you think you're up to it, John."

Two

The uniformed Negro chauffeur glided the black and grey Pierce Arrow to the curb outside the Banker's Building on the corner of Clark and Adams. "Anything else, Mr Purvis, suh?"

The doll-faced little man in the rear seat shook his head. There was a hint of magnolia in his voice when he spoke. "Thank you, President. That will be all." He entered the office block and summoned the elevator: the Nineteenth floor. Whistled off-key as he stepped into the cage. Melvin Purvis, Special Agent in Charge of the Chicago FBI office, was feeling pleased with himself. Eighteen days earlier, he'd nailed suburban mobster Roger Touhy for the kidnap of international swindler Jake 'the Barber' Factor, after first failing to convict the Irish hoodlum for snatching St Paul brewer William Hamm. He'd sent the harp down for a ninety-nine year stretch.

There were dissenting voices that contested the verdict. Doubters that said Factor's kidnapping had been faked in order to avoid extradition to Great Britain. That the whole thing had been a put up job by Factor and Capone successor Frank 'the Barber' Nitti – the two clippers having supposedly worked together in the same

Halsted Street tonsorial parlour at one point – aimed at removing the last holdout to Syndicate rule in Chicago.

There was also the fact that a second St Paul brewer, Edward Bremer, had been kidnapped under almost identical circumstances to Hamm while Touhy was being held over the Factor case, something critics failed to believe was a copycat crime.

There were always people ready to carp at a fellow on the rise, though. Jealousy was an unavoidable consequence of success. You had to expect a certain amount of sniping when you generated the kind of press that had come his way for putting the mick in the can.

It wasn't just the press that had been forthcoming with their praise, either. He could quote the memo from Mr Hoover from memory. "This is a splendid piece of work, which was consummated only by the untiring and resourceful efforts of the entire Chicago staff." Or rather, he could quote the memo from *John,* from memory. Hadn't the Director admonished him to, "stop using *mister*"?

In fact, the whole tone of their correspondence had taken on a – well, intimate, tone. The Director liked to rib him about his good looks, especially after the newspapers had picked up on them. What was it? "I don't see how the movies could miss a 'slender, blonde-haired, blue-eyed gentleman.' All power to the Clark Gable of the service."

It made him a little uncomfortable, he couldn't deny that. Especially after the rumours he'd heard floating about the cocktail circuit in Washington. But there was no denying it felt good to be the man upstairs' blue-eyed boy. And he had to admit, catching his reflection in the polished surface of the elevator doors as he emerged on the nineteenth floor, the sharp-suited gent with the puff handkerchief and rakishly-tilted fedora, a comma of hair breaking boyishly over his forehead, cut a damned attractive figure. Whatever else you might think about Mr Hoover – John – the director had taste.

He sauntered down the hallway from the elevator. Traded quips with the local reporters and wire service men smoking and cracking knuckles on the chairs outside his office. He greeted his secretary, Doris, as he pushed through the swinging gate beside her desk. Dropped her a wink. Tried not to think about what the slender blonde wore beneath the high-necked blouse and skirt as he entered the bullpen and threaded his way between the one hundred identical desks where the agents attached to the Chicago office worked their ongoing cases.

The desks he passed were functional. Uncluttered. Each came equipped with a single black telephone and blotter. Personal photographs or other memorabilia were forbidden. Work was either completed by the end of the day or returned to the file room, the office's inner sanctum: only the clerk or her assistant were allowed to retrieve one of the three carbon copies of every memo, teletype or telegram filed in the grey metal cabinets inside.

The agents manning the desks followed a similar uniform pattern, young college graduates of North European stock – the only Jew in the Bureau, second in command Pop Nathan, had been inherited from the Director's predecessor – accountants or lawyers who preferred government service to starving in the Depression.

Many, like Purvis, were Southern. Often they were graduates of George Washington University, Hoover's alma mater, especially his old pledge, Kappa Alpha. For many years, the Kappa house would serve as an unofficial hostel for visiting agents.

The men's personal appearance was as standardized as their background, dark suits and sombre ties with black shoes and black socks, trimmed hair, neatly parted, being compulsory. 'Personal appearance' was one of the categories the agents were rated under, the ranking running from 'neat' to 'flashy', 'poor' or 'untidy.' Careless grooming or deviation from the dress code could lead to disciplinary action against an agent, part of the draconian code of conduct enforced by Washington.

Other infractions that could see an agent carpeted included eating at the desks or making a single typographical error when typing up a report. Bad timekeeping was particularly frowned upon, a misdeed traceable due to agents signing on entry and exit. A minute's lateness meant the SAC had to explain why to the Director. Two 'tardies' meant suspension.

"I want the public to look upon the Bureau of Investigation and the Department of Justice as a group of gentleman," the Director had once told an audience. "And if the men here engaged can't conduct themselves as such, I will dismiss them."

He was as good as his word. When the Special Agent in Charge of the Denver office offered an inspection team a drink, he was summarily dismissed from his post.

It was all part of Hoover's attempt to build a streamlined, professional operation out of the 'Department of Easy Virtue' he'd inherited ten years earlier, a replacement for the patchwork of inefficient, often corrupt sheriff's offices and municipal police departments that operated at local level. With its groundbreaking fingerprint department and ballistics laboratory, it stood as a model for what a national, federally directed law enforcement agency should be. All it had needed was a target to operate against.

Created in 1908 to investigate antitrust cases, the FBI's remit had expanded to cover an odd assortment of offences, sedition, federal prison breaks and crimes on Indian reservations amongst them. Under Hoover, it had found itself investigating corruption in the Atlanta penitentiary and murder and theft of oil-rights on Oklahoma Indian lands. It was hardly enough to justify the Director's plans for expansion and modernization, or indeed, his own career. There were plenty of people in Washington who would have been happy to see the obsessive little bulldog behind the Bureau get what they believed was coming to him.

The interstate crime wave that accompanied Repeal and the Depression had been a godsend, then, giving Hoover's largely functionless organization the target needed to justify its existence. More, it catapulted the Bureau into the centre of current political debate, success in the War against Crime being seen as a test case for federal intervention at state level, a success the Roosevelt administration badly needed as it struggled to get Depression-busting NRA legislation through Congress.

If the Bureau could prove itself against the gangs of Mid-Western yeggs and kidnappers crowding the headlines, helping usher in the President's New Deal, the Director would gain the support he needed to transform the FBI into a national police agency, outmanoeuvring his competitors in the Treasury's Secret Intelligence Unit, negating the exposure the T-men had received for nailing Capone. In such a political climate, the press coverage generated by Touhy's apprehension could prove the decisive factor in locating Hoover at the apex of the United States' law enforcement hierarchy.

And the thing of it was, it was all down to the good-looking little fellow easing behind his desk to start another day fighting crime with typewriter and forms in triplicate.

Purvis inspected the image reflected in the window. Redefined the parting in his hair. When you came down to it, you couldn't really blame some guys for being jealous.

There was a knock at the door. He hastily faced front. Snatched a memo from the top of the IN tray. "Come."

Doris. The flush in her cheeks. Like someone had slapped her face. "Big news, Mr Purvis." She fluttered a telegram at him. "It just came through the wire."

He read the message through. Paused. Read it again. 'Dillinger escaped.' Holy Christ. He couldn't believe it. Crown Point jail. Hadn't they claimed it was escape-proof?

That was your local law for you. Inefficient. Corrupt. He wouldn't be surprised if the bank robbing son-of-a-bitch hadn't bought his way out of there, although leaving a woman in charge couldn't have helped. He wasn't the first man to question the wisdom of having a woman as sheriff, and he was sure he wouldn't be the last.

It was the final line of the message that had him riveted, though. 'Fugitives crossed the state line into Illinois in a stolen car.' Interstate transportation of a stolen motor vehicle. Violation of the Dyer Act. A federal offence.

This was it. The chance the Bureau had been waiting for. That he'd been waiting for. The chance to go after the most notorious mobster in the country.

He looked masterful for Doris as he speared the phone. Tried to keep his voice steady as he connected to the Washington switchboard. "Purvis, Chicago. Get me Mr Hoover." Or John, he thought, as Doris gazed worshipfully on. Forget the *mister.*

Three

Sioux Falls, South Dakota

Tuesday, March 6

The green Packard slowed outside the Security National Bank and Trust Company. Came to a halt.

"Looks like a fat one," Johnny said, clearing frost from the windows.

Eddie Green nodded as he unfurled the git, a slim, blade-faced yegg with piercing brown eyes, the hair shaved in question marks over his ears. "We should have a good payout today. Trust me on this one."

The husky black-Irishman in the shotgun seat prepped his machinegun. Crossed himself: Tommy Carroll, car thief, burglar and latterly armed robber, a fashion plate and relentless womaniser, despite the scars on his neck and jaw and a mouth that twisted distinctly to the right. In and out of jail since the army, he'd attempted to go straight the previous year, marrying and opening a restaurant in Mankato. A few months working a hotplate had been enough for him, however, and, after dumping his wife for a nightclub singer, he'd traded his spatula for a Thompson and thrown in with Nelson on a string of bank raids. "Better pay than I ever got hiring out my head for a punch bag, anyway," he said, massaging the flattened bridge of his nose. "Right, Jimmy?"

Nelson scowled. He tugged the peak of his newsboy cap down over his brow. Turned up the collar of his suede windcheater like a soda jerk playing Cagney. When the runt tried to act tough, he looked like a sixteen-year old. "Long as you throw lead quicker than you did your fists, Tommy, that's all that matters."

Johnny admired himself in the wing mirror. Tilted his hat. "Things go to plan and there's no need to use the heaters at all. Hear me, Jimmy?"

The kid's scowl deepened. "Where the fuck you get off giving me orders, Dillinger? I'm the guy invited you into this crew and you better not forget it, see?"

Van Meter snickered, a rubber-lipped string-bean with the perpetual 'who me?' expression of the class cutup. A former busboy and waiter, he'd received a twenty-year sentence for armed robbery and ended up in the prison shirt factory with Johnny, entertaining his fellow inmates by lassoing horseflies with lengths

87

of thread and throwing his body out of joint to imitate a cripple. He'd lost several teeth to prison guards who found his antics less amusing, especially after he felled one of them with a lead pipe during an escape attempt. "Listen to the punk. The guy had a box to stand on and he'd smack you in the mouth."

Nelson positioned the Colt machine-pistol on his lap. The Colt automatics Nelson had converted to fire on full auto were like carrying a pocket machinegun. With a suppressor and pistol grip fitted in front of the trigger guard and a twenty round clip, they gave you plenty of punch for half the size and weight of a Thompson. Johnny suspected the runt found them easier to handle than a full-size sprayer, although he had too much sense to call Nelson on that one. "I don't need to stand on no box to deal with an asshole like you, Van Meter," the kid said, slipping the safety. "I can cut you down to my size any time I want."

Green clamped down on Nelson's wrist. "Easy, Jimmy. We're all pals here, ain't we?"

Johnny shot a warning look at Van Meter. "That's right. All in this together, yeah?" He'd always found Van funny, the reason he'd walked the yard with him in the pen, but he knew a lot of guys

88

took him the wrong way. That was the reason he'd never teamed him with Pierpont and the others first time around. Put Van together in a room with Pete and there'd be hair on the walls by the end of the day. The effect he had on some guys. "But I mean what I said before. Things go okay and you got yourself a couple new guys on board, Jimmy. But you start spraying lead like it's the start of the hunting season..."

"Yeah, yeah, all right. Quit griping, for Christ sake. I get what you saying, all right, Dillinger?"

Hamilton tilted his chin towards the stone exterior of the bank from his position in the driver's seat. "We're drawing attention sitting here arguing. A couple of bank clerks been watching us through the window. We don't start moving and they'll sound the alarm."

Johnny primed his Thompson, a memento of Crown Point. "You're right, Red." He opened the door. "Best stow the bullshit. Cut to the chase."

They filed out the Packard and crossed the sidewalk. Green stood guard by the car while Carroll took position by the door of the bank, the skirts of their overcoats flapping open in the breeze to reveal the Thompsons underneath. Hamilton remained at the wheel. The other three entered the bank, their heels sounding hollowly on the polished marble floor. Van Meter strode to the exit and pulled a sawn-off from beneath his trench coat. Nelson, meanwhile, took centre stage, flourishing his machine-pistol. "This is a hold up. Everybody on the ground." He started as the alarm rang. "Who set that alarm off? Who?"

Johnny mugged at Van Meter as he went over the barrier. Goddamn punk. He moved from cage to cage, shovelling money from the counter into an empty sugar sack, menacing the teller beside him. "Is that all of it?" He followed his involuntary glance toward the vault. "You know the combination?"

He covered the other members of staff as the teller shook his head. "Which one has the combination?" Made a show of arming the Thompson as they remained mute. "I'm not monkeying around here. You either speak up and open that vault or I turn loose with the chopper and wipe out the whole damn bunch of you."

The bank staff swivelled their eyes towards a mousy, middle-aged individual attempting to merge with the wallpaper. Johnny yanked him forward by the tie, his collar button pinging on the floor. "Smart guy." He planted his boot in the guy's ass. "Well, what the hell are you waiting for? Get busy and open the safe."

The teller struggled with the lock. "Shit." Started again.

He yelped as Van Meter appeared beside him. Goosed him with the scattergun. "Crack that lock, you son-of-a-bitch or I'll cut you in two."

Open sesame. The two bandits exchanged smirks as they helped themselves to the cash inside. Johnny risked a peek over his shoulder as he filled his sack. There was a growing crowd outside. Buncha hicks. Treating it like a day at the circus. A couple of guys stood with their hands in the air, one in a cop suit. No sound of gunfire, though. Green steady by the car. It looked like things were going to be jake.

Nelson, though. The alarm seemed to be working him into a frenzy. He hopped around the lobby like a bantam, jabbing the Colt into the terrified hostages' faces as he accused them of setting the damn thing off.

"Take it easy," Johnny called to him as they finished up at the vault. "Let's concentrate on the money, all right, kid?"

Nelson gave him the finger. "Fuck you, asshole." Caught a movement in the street. "Son-of-a-bitch." He bounded onto the counter. Loosed a volley through the window. Women screamed as a Highway Patrol motorcycle skidded across the hardtop and collided with a telegraph pole, the rider kicking in the gutter. "I got the bastard. I got him."

Van Meter sucked in his breath. "Jesus." He looked towards Johnny. "We finished here, John?"

"We need some hostages, though. The bank staff."

They crowded the tellers through the doors, collecting the other guys on the way to the car. They had to muscle their way through the rubberneckers gathered on the sidewalk. The schmucks didn't seem to understand the danger they were in. They acted as if this was a gangster movie rather than the real thing. No one moved as Nelson shot out the bank's windows. At least the cops that were arriving on the scene couldn't open up on them without hitting Joe Public. That was something, he supposed.

They piled into the car. Bunched the hostages on the running boards, four girls and the guy from the vault. "Hold tight now."

One of the girls winced. Held out her arm. "I can't. I sprained my wrist."

Nelson made to say something. Johnny cut him off. The broad was cute. A blonde. Like Harlow, for Christ sake. "Okay, sugar. You don't have to come."

A clang came from the front of the Packard. Steam rose from the hood. A bull disappeared into a doorway, smoke twisting from the barrel of a hunting rifle. The radiator. Johnny clapped Hamilton on the shoulder. "How we doing, Red?"

Hamilton squinted through the moisture clouding the windscreen. "We can still make it, John. Grab another car at the edge of town."

He rubbed at the glass with his sleeve. Drove slowly towards the city limits, thirty miles an hour tops. A road sign loomed ahead: Route 77. The highway south.

"Pull her over, Johnny?"

"Sure, Red. When you're ready." He jumped down into the road as Hamilton braked. Scanned the highway for pursuing cops. "Got the nails, Eddie?"

Nelson elbowed Green aside. "I'll do it." He broke the sack open on the road behind the Packard.

Johnny whistled tunelessly as he watched the runt at work. "You're getting nails under the car, Jimmy."

"I know, I know. Think I'm blind for Christ sake?" He swept the nails from beneath the wheels. Pointed his Colt at the hostages as they stood shivering at the roadside. "Okay, assholes. Back on the running boards."

The guy from the vault spread his arms. "The girls are freezing. They can't hold on much longer."

Johnny gestured with his piece. "Okay, then. Get in the car."

The girls squeezed in the back seat. Snuggled on the laps of the bandits. The male teller stood awkwardly, hands hanging loosely by his sides.

"What about me?"

Nelson deadpanned. "You're through." He laughed as the teller cringed in anticipation of a bullet. "Easy, fella, we don't need you anymore. Come on boys, let's hit the road."

Four

Purvis studied the files on Dillinger. The sheaves of press cuttings assiduously collated by his agents, filed and sorted by date order and location. The yeggman had had a good run in the months since his colleagues had sprung him from the Sheriff's office in Lima. Police stations robbed for firearms. Banks looted. Law officers killed.

And the way he'd waltzed out of the lockup in Crown Point. The way he'd showboated. Played to the crowd. It was as if the son-of-a-bitch had anticipated the headlines, deliberately rubbing the law enforcement community's nose in the dirt. What was it Estill had said afterwards? "From what I hear, I'm surprised Dillinger didn't serve tea to the guards before he left."

Estill was bitter. You couldn't blame him for that. The photograph and the subsequent escape had destroyed his political career as surely as if he'd let the bandit out the cellblock himself.

The other quotes in the press, though. They acted as if it was some kind of game. The idiots seemed to be rooting for the bastard. It was as if they'd forgotten what he was. What he'd done. None of them gave a damn about the widow and orphans in East Chicago, mourning a man who'd worked hard for his family. Protected the community. Tried to do his job.

The clipping in his hand, for instance, talked of the, "half-comic exploit of Dillinger in taking complete possession of the fortress-like prison." Described it as, "typically Dillinger-like. It was marked by desperate courage, unhurried precision, and an occasional laugh for punctuation."

He found that kind of attitude hard to believe. Referring to the fact of a cop killer menacing officers with a machinegun as, "half-comic." The mention of, "an occasional laugh for punctuation". He'd like to see some of the vultures worked for the press looking down the barrel of an automatic weapon. See them crack a laugh with a loaded Thompson tucked beneath their noses, the pricks.

It wasn't just the newspapers that were using Dillinger as a springboard for comedy, though. The public was trying to get in on the act as well. There'd been suggestions that Crown Point be renamed 'Clown Point' or 'Dillinger'. A letter had actually been delivered to the town bearing the address 'Wooden Gun, Indiana.' Similarly, wooden pistols had been handed out as party favours at a

96

Republican dinner in Indianapolis. Back in Dillinger's hometown of Mooresville, a notice had gone up on the city hall bulletin board:

JOHNNY ISN'T WITH THEM ANYMORE

It was beyond him. The press and public didn't make these two-bit thieves out to be latter day Robin Hoods, they wouldn't be the problem they were. Or at least, there wouldn't be the pressure put on guys like himself to bring them in. Not that that itself would be a problem if the Bureau were more effective in tracking the bastards down.

Aside from his own success in nabbing Touhy, the only underworld casualty so far had been half-assed bank robber and kidnapper George Barnes, arrested by the Bureau's Bill Rorer back in September. The Director's publicity machine had inflated Barnes into criminal mastermind 'Machinegun Kelly' and gained the Hoover's agents a snappy new nickname from Barnes' blurted, "Don't shoot, G-Men," as he surrendered. Otherwise, the yeggs had left the federal men looking like a bunch of incompetents.

The Hamm and Bremer kidnappings were still unsolved, although, in his heart, he was convinced Touhy had pulled the former. Pretty Boy Floyd had seemingly vanished off the face of the Earth for the last six months, despite a thousand-strong trawl of his Cookson Hills stronghold by law officers and National Guardsmen. The Barkers had left no trace behind them aside from a blood spoor of dead law officers and despoiled banks. Ditto Kansas City Massacre gunman Verne Miller, the few leads agents had managed to unearth evaporating into thin air before the suspect turned up naked in a Detroit ditch, skull fractured, garrotte around his neck. And Dillinger…

He surveyed the office buildings and department stores of the Loop standing below his nineteenth floor window. The stockyards. Rail depots. Tenements. Taverns. Gambling joints.

Somewhere out there, amongst the teeming mongrel hordes of the city, the hebes and polacks, guineas and micks, was an All-American farm boy with an easy grin and a nice line in wisecracks, a Thompson under his arm and a roll on his hip. Some whore warming his bed, he shouldn't wonder, while he lived the good life at the banks' expense, thumbing his nose at the cops.

It was tantalizing. Frustrating. He knew the guy was out there. Probably within a mile or so of where he now stood. If he could only reach down into the streets from his eyrie, put his finger

98

on the fuck like some kind of federal Kong. Crack the bastard beneath his thumb like a tick.

The rewards for the agent that could pull that off, both within the Bureau as it stole the spotlight in Washington and on the national stage as a whole. That was something to think about. Yeggmen weren't the only individuals that could be made or broken by the press. For a good-looking guy with a law degree and a couple of scalps on his belt, the sky was the limit.

Local office should be no problem if he could make the right connections with the party machines. When you saw the snuff-dipping crackers and Klan apologists that represented his own neck of the woods in the Senate, he could see that the chamber was crying out for modern, educated fellows like himself. And if they could elevate a simpleton like Harding or a cripple like Roosevelt to the Presidential office. A guy as married his own cousin like some hillbilly, for Christ sake...

That was if he nailed Dillinger. Put a bullet in him or sent him to the chair. As it was, all he had to go on was a filing cabinet full of press clippings and neatly-typed reports, three carbons apiece. His agents were experts at collecting information and condensing it into files. What they weren't so hot at was actually tracking down suspects. Making arrests. A Bureau staffed by lawyers and accountants might look good to Mr Hoover – John – back in Washington, his own personal set of shiny tin soldiers in the War against Crime, but they made even the average rural sheriff's department look good when it came to taking down the opposition.

Still, he figured he had a few days grace to get his investigation under way. Dillinger would be lying low like a hunted animal as he attempted to establish himself on the outside. He would be vulnerable. Off-balance. A state that would work to the benefit of a dedicated team of investigators operating on scientific principles and backed by the laboratories in Washington.

That was what Purvis hoped, anyway. At the very least, Dillinger would take time to put together a new gang. It would be a while before he became active again as an armed robber. Wouldn't it?

He turned away from the window as Doris cleared her throat at his back.

"Yes, sweetheart?"

"Something's just come over the wire, Mr Purvis. I thought you ought to see it immediately."

"Okay, Doris. Thanks." He gave his attention to the sheet in his hand as she returned to her desk. Let the memo drift to the floor as he registered the dateline: *Sioux Falls, South Dakota. Tuesday, March 6.*

He couldn't believe it. Three days out of jail and the Dillinger mob was already back in business.

Five

St Paul, Minnesota, March 7

They made Minneapolis-St Paul sometime after midnight, relaxing as they crossed the Mississippi into the latter. The cops had closed on them when the Packard finally gave out a few miles back, a police flivver appearing as they hijacked a passing Dodge and transferred gasoline cans from the now defunct getaway vehicle. Nelson had put a volley over their heads, however, and the cop car had reversed smartly up the highway and vanished, leaving them free to cut loose the hostages and head for the Twin Cities and safety.

St Paul was the northern equivalent of Hot Springs, Arkansas or Joplin, Missouri, a place where a hard-working yegg could relax and enjoy himself without police harassment. The system had been set up by the O'Connor brothers, police chief and Democratic party head cum saloon owner respectively, at the turn of the century. A guy kicked back part of his take as he arrived in town and, as long as he kept his nose clean, he would be guaranteed freedom from arrest or extradition.

The O'Connors grew fat on graft from their gangland clients while the public enjoyed a crime-free environment and showed their appreciation by keeping the brothers in office. The system proved durable enough to survive the pair's retirement, the mantle of underworld fixer passing first to Dapper Danny Hogan and then, following the Irishman's explosive demise in 1928, to his probable assassin, Dutch Sawyer, proprietor of the Green Lantern Tavern at 545 Wabasha Avenue, the establishment the mud-flecked Dodge rolled to a halt outside of in the early hours of Wednesday morning.

Johnny worked the kinks from his back as he stepped out the car. "The fix is in?" he asked, as they gathered on the sidewalk outside the bar.

Nelson punched his hands into his pockets. "You think I'd drag you all the way out here without making arrangements?" He tipped his head at Hamilton as the latter stayed behind the wheel. "Park in the alley down the side. We can schlep the money up the outside staircase to the office without attracting attention. Get Dutch to take care of the car for us before it's traced."

They mooched into the bar, a long, narrow room bright with lights and music. The place featured blackjack, poker and roulette wheels and was populated by hard-looking guys in expensive suits, peroxide blondes draped decoratively over their arms. Fanny Brice was walking her baby back home on the jukebox as they lined-up along the mahogany counter, elbows on the woodwork as they took in the scene.

The skinny guy behind the jump smiled gold at them, a towel slung over one shoulder. He wore a clean white apron over a candy-striped shirt with green silk sleeve garters and a polka dot bowtie. "Jimmy."

"Pat." Nelson boosted himself up by the brass foot rail to lean on the counter. "The Dutchman in?"

"Sure, he's upstairs. Been expecting you all night."

Nelson treated the others to a self-satisfied grin, showing them he knew how to run a string. "Okay if I go on up?"

"Sure, Jimmy. You know the way." The barman drew a fistful of steins from beneath the counter as Nelson strutted towards the stairs. "Something to cut the dust, gents?"

A chorus of affirmatives. They propped their elbows on the bar as the beers arrived. Van Meter lifted his mug.

"Here's how." He clinked glasses with Johnny. "That kick you gave that jugger. I thought you was like to put your boot through his ass."

Johnny blew the froth off his Hamm's. "Opened the vault, didn't he?" He took a swig. It was a good brew. Thank Christ for Repeal. He lowered the stein. Wiped the foam moustache from his lip. "The kid Jimmy. Way he acted out there today. Be honest with me, Homer. What do you think?"

"The jug was a fat one. And he's put together a good string. Looks like he's planned things with the Dutchman as well."

"The bull on the motorcycle, though. Tommy could have handled that. There was no need to take him out the way he did." He set down his beer. "You reckon he was a goner?"

Van Meter shrugged. "Check the newspapers tomorrow. We'll soon find out." He parked his beer beside Johnny's. "I know what you mean, though. The runt's looking for an excuse to use a gun on someone. Handle him the wrong way and it might be one of us."

Johnny kicked his ankle as Nelson reappeared at the foot of the staircase. "Everything copacetic, Jim?"

Nelson inclined his head. "Get Hamilton and bring him up here with the cash. I'll introduce you to Dutch and we can do business."

Sawyer turned out to be a pear-shaped Jew in a black silk suit and checkerboard-patterned tie over a white on white silk shirt and highly-polished black wingtips. Argyll socks. "Good to meet you, boys," he said, shuffling from behind a walnut desk as they entered the office. Shaking hands. He conjured a bottle of Johnny Walker Red from the dark wood cabinet in the corner. Glasses. Broke the seal. "A celebration," he said. "Jimmy says you had some kind of score today."

Nelson hooked his thumbs beneath his armpits as Hamilton dumped the sacks on the oxblood carpet. Displayed his teeth. "My boys did pretty good the first time out, Dutchman. I think they gonna have a future with me, if they play their cards right." He shook his head as Sawyer made to pour him a drink. "My old man put me off that kick for life, the rummy fuck."

"Me neither," Johnny said. "That's how I come to be locked up in the first place." He chin-nodded towards the humidor on the desk. "I'll take one of those cigars if you're offering, though. Nothing wrong with a good smoke, far as I can see."

Dutch snipped the end off one of the Cubans. "They do say it's good for you." He ignited the cigar with a heavy silver desk lighter. Offered them around the rest of the group. "Though you probably got a point with the hard stuff. This' good liquor, but the panther piss they was knocking out during Prohibition was enough to put anybody on the wagon."

Nelson eyed the others disapprovingly as they savoured their drinks. He bit the inside of his cheek. "It hadn't been for Repeal, I'd still be running wet goods for Roger Touhy rather than knocking over jugs."

Sawyer contemplated the depths of his glass. "Hard for an honest man to make a living with the Depression. Even harder for a dishonest one now they legalized booze." He prodded the sacks with his toe. Killed his drink. "You guys seem to be doing all right, though, from what I can see. You want to cut it up now? See what you got?"

Eddie swung up one of the sacks. Emptied it onto the desk. "Mighty nice," he said, reaching for the second sack.

Nelson beat him to it. "Who the hell elected you bookkeeper? I'm the leader of this string and you better not forget it." He added the contents of the second sack to the pile already on the desk. Sorted and stacked the cash into bricks. "$46000 and change," he said, a smile breaking over his face as he finished. "Not bad pay for a morning's work, eh, guys?"

Sawyer nodded. "Not bad at all." He topped up their drinks. "I ought to lay off this stuff. Ulcers. I got a hole-in my stomach you could drive a Mack truck through. The sawbones would go crazy, he saw me with a glass in my hand."

Van Meter gave a loose-lipped grin. "No doctor here now, Dutch."

Sawyer upended the bottle. "What the hell. You only live once, right?" He hit his drink. Shuddered. "Jesus. This' good stuff." He slanted his head towards the cash on the desk. "Me and Jimmy agreed I get ten percent of the haul as my end. That covers safe-houses and police protection as long as you stay in St Paul. Also I move any bonds you got through my connections. Again I take ten percent off the top as my commission. You need a clean car, untraceable hardware, I can fix that for you too. If that's okay with you guys?"

Johnny looked to the others. "Sounds jake to me. We got a whole buncha bonds upstate we been trying to unload the last few months now. What do you say, Homer? Red?"

Nelson broke in. "That's fine with me, Dutch. And what I say goes around here, all right boys? Tommy? Ed?" He clucked his tongue as the two reluctantly nodded. "All right then. The rest gets cut up six ways. I'm keeping back a couple a grand off both youse and Red, though, Johnny, to cover what I fronted the mouthpiece and the doctors for Hamilton." He gave them a challenging stare. "That okay with you guys?"

Johnny kept his voice neutral. Expression blank. "Guess I can live with that, Jimmy. You're the boss after all. Right, Red?"

"No arguing with the guy as gives the orders, John."

Nelson looked at them appraisingly for a moment. Puffed his chest. "All right, then. We'll get the cash carved up and let the Dutchman have his office back. After that you can hole-up in the apartments Dutch found for us and get some rest. You're going to

need it. We go again in a week's time."

Six

Lima, Ohio

Sunday, March 11

Purvis sat in the upper gallery of the courtroom and evaluated the spectators. Farmers. Housewives. Grocery clerks. No sharp-suited, dead-eyed individuals with pistols bulging their jackets. Painted molls. The security in court was enough to deter even the boldest mobster from staging a prison break, but he was taking no chances. Not with the Dillinger mob's track record when it came to escape attempts. The bastards seemed to walk through steel bars as if they didn't exist. If Dillinger himself was finally going to surface after his own escape from the joint, Lima would be the place.

Staking out the trial was a gamble, but one the Chicago SAC felt compelled to take. It was either that or explain his failure to trace the escaped mobster to Washington. The memo he'd received from the Director shortly before departing the Office had left him feeling distinctly queasy.

"In talking with you last evening, I gathered that you had practically no underworld informants or connections with which your office could contact in the event of an emergency arising… I am somewhat concerned."

Compared to some of the rockets Mr Hoover – 'John' seemed out of the question at the moment – was known to launch at his SACs, the tone was mild. It was the first sign of a frost between them, though. A frost that could turn into a full scale Ice Age if he didn't come up with something on Dillinger and come up with it fast.

Not that he could blame Mr Hoover, mind. The Director had hit on an uncomfortable truth. The Chicago office had turned up zip on the suspect so far and was rapidly running out of leads. Agents had swarmed over Crown Point, making notes, questioning jailers and prisoners. They'd interviewed everybody but the jailhouse cat in the quest for information. Produced zero evidence as to the bandit's whereabouts.

Others had staked out family and known associates of Dillinger and again came up with nothing. Purvis had looked into the possibility of mounting wiretaps on suspects' phones, but found that was illegal under Illinois law. He'd also forked out five dollars a day from the Office budget to a supposed informer who'd

112

launched the federal men on a raid that netted a forty year old female beautician and a possible lawsuit from the irate householder. How he was going to justify that at the next accounts audit had him stymied.

The Bureau's lack of local roots was beginning to tell. They weren't plugged into the underworld circuit of snitches and rumour-mongers and the city police, incensed by a bunch of college boys from Washington muscling onto their turf, refused to share their leads with them. It wasn't as if he could blame police corruption for once. Even the notoriously honest Captain Stege, head of the Dillinger Squad, refused to divulge to him.

Which was why he found himself sitting in an oak-panelled courtroom in Ohio waiting for the nation's most notorious prison escapee to show his grinning face again in public. If he couldn't track the asshole by normal police methods, he'd play it cagey. Let the son-of-a-bitch come to him. That was the plan, anyway.

Things seemed quiet enough at the moment, though. If the attempt came, it would probably be somewhere less public. When the prisoners were being transferred, for instance, or escorted from the cellblock, both eventualities he'd covered using the half-dozen agents that had accompanied him from Chicago. He felt he could relax his vigilance for the time being. Concentrate on the guy in the dock.

Despite the publicity generated by Dillinger, Pierpont was the real power behind the mob. The danger man of the bunch. The bastard had over a dozen bank robberies to his credit by the time he was incarcerated in the state penitentiary and had pistol-whipped bank staff or customers on at least two occasions. He'd also served two previous prison terms and a spell in an insane asylum.

Prison reports indicated Pierpont suffered from bouts of sleeplessness and mania. He'd refused to speak to prison officials or co-operate in having his photograph taken. More to the point of Purvis' presence, he had attempted at least two prison breaks previous to his successful escape in September. Puzzlingly, as far as the federal man was concerned, he neither smoked nor drank.

The statements the prisoner had made on the journey back east had seemed to support his status as mad-dog killer. Reporters who gained access to him on the train picked up a couple of gems as Pierpont provided counterpoint to his buddy's Robin Hood image.

"Those who died deserved to die," he'd told one eager scribe. "And there are plenty more who deserve it and are still alive." He'd stared out the window at the flat brown plains. Grain silos. Mortgaged farms. "In the last few years of my life there's never been a day that some incident hasn't occurred to make me hate the law. I suppose I'm what you'd call an abnormal mental case. A case for a psychiatrist. Maybe I am. But once I was normal. Place your own construction on what I've said."

"Your conscience doesn't trouble you at all?"

"My conscience doesn't trouble me one iota. I stole from the bankers. They stole from the people. All we did was raise the insurance rates."

He picked up on the same theme again as he sat shackled hand and foot under Purvis' scrutiny, the manacles in curious contrast to the tailored suit and collegiate aura the grey-eyed killer projected from the dock. "I engineered robberies worth $300,000?" he replied, in answer to a question – or rather, taunt – from Prosecutor Botkin. "Gee, I wish I had." He mused for a moment.

"Well, at least if I did, I'm not like some bank robbers – I didn't get myself elected president of the bank first."

The judge frowned as the spectators broke up. "Strike that from the record," he said.

Botkin, meanwhile, continued to prod. "That's the kind of man you are, though, isn't it, Pierpont? A thief? A bank robber?"

The prisoner rose as far as his shackles allowed him. "That's right," he said, voice breaking, as the bailiffs moved to restrain him. "And damn proud of it, too. I'm not the kind of man you are. Robbing widows and orphans. You'd probably be like me if you had the nerve."

Pierpont subsided as the bailiffs wrestled him down, the rest of the trial proving anti-climatic as he refused to rise to any further barbs from Botkin. Purvis returned his attention to the spectators, only focusing on Pierpont again as his lawyer, Jesse Levy came to make her closing argument, an emotional plea delivered as the prisoner's mother sobbed at the defence table. "I now leave the fate of Harry Pierpont in your hands and, 'Even though I walk in the valley of the shadow of death, I fear no evil.' I know God is with me, with the defendant, in the hearts of every one of you." She paused as the defendant and his mother reverently lowered their heads. "So I hand him over to you, and I pray God in his goodness will show you the way to do the right thing."

Botner's rejoinder was blunt and to the point. "If this evidence doesn't require the death penalty, I don't know what I'm talking about. It is our duty to uphold the law and impose the proper sentence. Members of the jury, if you'll do this, you will have nothing to fear or regret. The only thing you need to fear is violation of that thing that your conscience tells you to do."

No contest.

"Have you anything to say?" the judge asked as, fifty-five minutes later, the jury delivered their verdict.

Pierpont sat with a half-smile on his face. "No. Not a word." He kissed his mother as he was unchained and led through lines of National Guardsmen beneath Purvis' gaze.

Makley called to him as he was escorted back to the cellblock. "Well, Pete, what was it?"

Pierpont shrugged as the guards secured him in his cell. "Well, what would it be?"

Seven

Mason City, Iowa

Tuesday, March 13

The navy Buick stopped outside the First National Bank's seven-storey façade shortly after two that afternoon. The bank was heavy with the profits of the local cement plants, still thriving despite the Depression, a quarter of a million dollars, according to Green. Forty thousand dollars per man. Enough to buy long-term protection from the Dutchman. Or even better, a fresh face for a yegg who'd found himself featured alongside Carnera and Lindbergh on the nation's news stands.

Johnny twisted the sling of his Thompson around his right forearm, relocating the .38 Colt to his pants with the left. Billie would be meeting him in St Paul after the job. Everything went to plan today and it might be the beginning of that fresh start he'd promised himself with his slice of the take. A new life abroad with the woman he loved.

That was if the job went as planned. They weren't the only ones who knew the worth of the prize secreted behind the redbrick walls of the bank. A guard sat in a steel cage attached to the inner front wall of the establishment, a gun port in a bullet-proof glass panel enabling him to dominate the lobby with the gas gun and rifle that shared the enclosure with him.

Which was why they'd waited until mid-afternoon to storm the building, the time of day when business was at its height. The hostages they'd piled onto their getaway car in previous robberies had taught them the value of operating in a crowd. There weren't many lawmen that would open fire indiscriminately on a mob of civilians. That was what they were betting on, anyway, as they disembarked from the car.

Carroll remained at the wheel this time, while Green, Hamilton and Van Meter entered the bank, leaving Johnny to play the tiger, standing in the cold while the others took over the building. That was the plan, at any rate. What they'd agreed in St Paul.

The coast was clear, though. No bulls.

Screw it. Johnny abandoned his post and hoofed open the door. Why should he stay on the sidewalk while the others had all the fun?

119

It was bedlam inside the bank. Green dominated the centre of the floor with his Thompson, forcing customers to the ground, while Van Meter dealt with the bank staff, triggering a fusillade at a fleeing bank official as he slammed an office door in his face. Hamilton, meanwhile, was behind the counter, bundling cash from the drawers into an empty laundry bag, before nabbing a teller and propelling him towards the vault.

"You. Open that door."

The teller unfastened the barred gate leading to the vault and propped a bag of pennies as a doorstop. He smiled as Hamilton seized the bag, letting the gate swing shut between them.

Hamilton mottled. "You asshole. You did that deliberately."

"You grabbed the bag, buddy, not me."

Hamilton wedged his pistol between the bars. "I can still plug you from here, you fuck." He gestured towards the door of the vault. "Get that door open. Do it now."

The teller took his own sweet time rotating the dial. He plodded slowly into the vault. Returned with a single bag of notes.

"The gate's locked. How'm I supposed to get the money out through a locked gate?"

Hamilton tucked his pistol beneath his arm. "Jesus Christ." He reached through the bars. "Here." Took the bag of notes from the teller. "Singles?"

"I didn't look. Just the first thing I put my hand to."

Hamilton transferred his pistol back to his hand. "You better give me the big notes and do it damn quick, or I'll drop you where you stand, you sorry son-of-a-bitch. Now get back in that vault and start passing out the cash."

In the chaos overtaking the lobby, they'd forgotten about the guard in the cage. Now he made his move. As Green stood with his back to the gun port, the guard opened fire, staggering the yeggman with a gas cartridge between the shoulder blades.

Green went down hard. Came up firing. The guard grinned as bullets starred the glass but failed to penetrate. He aimed the gas gun again. Squeezed the trigger. Nothing. He swore beneath his breath. The two antagonists glared impotently at each other, the guard attempting to prise open his gun with a jack knife, Green struggling to regain his wind after the blow from the gas canister.

Then Van Meter joined the fray. He unleashed a long burst at the cage. The guard dropped the gas gun as a single round ricocheted through the gun port, slicing his cheek. His hand went to his face, coming away bloody.

The guard shrugged the wound. He traded the gas gun for the rifle and worked the bolt. The lobby was too crowded to fire safely, though. He paced the cage like a trapped animal, weapon at port arms as the raiders gave him their backs, cannoning into Johnny as he took in the show.

"What the hell're you doing inside?" Van Meter said, changing magazines on his BAR. "You supposed to be watching the door."

Johnny retreated towards the entrance. "Just making sure you boys was okay in here. I didn't want to miss the fun." He leered as he stepped over a female bank clerk lying on her back rather than her stomach. "You ought to turn over, sugar. This' bank raid, not a directors' meeting."

Van Meter rolled his eyes as he followed him out the door. "Christ Almighty, John. Ask her for a date, why don't you?" He canted his head towards the shoe store across the way. "I'm going to cover the street from that side. Round up a couple hostages in the process."

Johnny eyeballed the passers-by gathering around the front of the bank. "I'll do the same this side. Cover the guys as they come out the lobby." He moved on the crowd. Something he could never get over was the way the rubes treated an armed raid like some kind of sideshow. There was even a guy with a newsreel camera, for Christ sake. Where the hell had he sprung from?

He reluctantly shoved the guy to one side and kicked over the tripod, lining the cameraman up with another half-dozen citizens between him and the street, hands raised. "What the hell happened to Nelson?"

"Eddie got him to cover the back. Told him he expected the cops to come that way. Keeps him out our hair till we finish the job."

Finishing the job. Easier said than done the way things were going in the bank. The place was filling with white vapour, like something out a Lugosi movie, hostages booting the gas canister between them as they tried to escape the worst of it, like kids playing kick the can. The fog worsened as a bank official appeared on the mezzanine and pitched a second canister into the lobby, thickening the atmosphere to Transylvanian proportions.

Johnny's eyes watered. He drew his pistol with his free hand as he backed away from the door. The guys wouldn't be able to stand it much longer. Better make sure things stayed copacetic on the street. He jabbed the Thompson at the row of hostages as their hands began to descend. "Come on now," he chided, like a scolding schoolmaster. "Can't you do better than that?"

He propped the Thompson against his hip as their hands shot skywards again. Put a pistol bullet through the radiator of a car trying to pass in front of the bank. His eyes burned from the fumes curling out the doorway. He wiped the tears with the plaid muffler around his neck as Van Meter stood another rank of hostages along the curb. Where the hell were the others?

A blast of machinegun fire from an alleyway to his left: Nelson announcing his presence as he emerged from the rear of the bank. He opened up on a truck heading into the war zone and

124

ventilated the hood. Giggled like a kid as he shot up the cars parked opposite and the neighbouring storefronts. He swerved his gun towards an elderly guy with a portfolio as he cornered from the next street. "Stop right there, asshole." Blew the guy off his feet as he kept on coming. He kicked the portfolio out of the old guy's hands. Searched it: a teacher at the local deaf school. "Dummy bastard. I thought you were a cop."

The dummy proved he could lip read. "Don't shoot me again," he moaned, nursing a leg wound. "I'm not a cop, Mr. Swear to God."

Johnny looked away in disgust. Called into the bank. "You guys nearly done in there?"

A strangled shout from Hamilton. "Just give me three more minutes, for Christ sake."

Three minutes were more than they could spare, though. Things were hotting up on the street. There was a loud crack from above. Something like a red-hot poker seared Johnny's arm. He turned in time to see a figure whip back from an upper floor of the bank. Emptied his pistol at the sniper. His arm went numb as he thrust his head back in the lobby, the Thompson dangling uselessly as he hollered. "That's it, you guys. It's time."

Hamilton appeared from the fogbank clutching the laundry bag, eyes tearing less from gas than frustration. "All that dough and I couldn't touch it." He joined Johnny and Van Meter as they herded the hostages before them. "That son-of-a-bitching teller. I should have dropped him when I had the chance."

Eddie Green was last out the bank. He knuckled his eyes. "We'll have to swallow it. Get out of here with what we can." He snapped off a single shot as a bystander ogled him from behind a parked car. "Pull that turtleneck in or I'll cut it off for you."

Another shot. The guy in the upstairs window again. Hamilton stumbled as the round slapped him in the shoulder. Johnny caught him with his good hand. Heaved him into the Buick. Goddamn Red. The guy couldn't go for a leak without someone putting a slug in him. He should have guessed it'd happen again.

He nudged Green as the latter spattered the upper story of the bank with pistol shots. "Grab those assholes from the bank. Load up the car. The only way we'll get out of here without that bastard puts a hole-in all of us."

They mounted a string of hostages on the running boards, two on the front fender, a couple more on the back, then crowded a half-dozen broads inside as they moved off. One of them hollered as they passed an apartment house, a bottle blonde with Betty Boop eyes.

"This is where I live. Let me off."

Carroll braked. Opened the door for her. The broad wiggled out the passenger seat. Trotted inside. One of the guys on the running board tried to follow her. Nelson snagged him. Yanked him into the car. "Get back here, you." He glared at Carroll. "What the fuck do you think you're doing, you dumb harp?"

Carroll smiled sheepishly. "I always had a thing for blondes," he said.

Johnny watched her ass into the hallway. "She was kind of cute at that."

"Jesus Christ. Only you bastards could think of cooze at a time like this." He punched Carroll in the arm. "Put the car into gear and drive."

They puttered towards the edge of town, picking up speed as they hit Highway 18. Nelson glanced behind them. "Cops." He ran a Springfield out the back window as the patrol wagon closed and squeezed off a couple of shots. "I can't hit nothing while we moving. Pull over, for Christ sake."

Green consulted the git. "No need for that, Jimmy. We can make the sand pit before them. Switch cars."

"I said pull the damn car over, didn't I?" He sprang from the Buick as it slowed, replacing the Springfield with his machine-pistol. "Okay, you cocksuckers. You asked for it and now you gonna get it."

The burst from the Colt went high. Missed the patrol wagon completely.

Van Meter gave a slow handclap. "Nice shooting, Jimmy."

Nelson reloaded. "Shut the fuck up, Homer." He threw a chest as the Mason City cops aped their Sioux Fall counterparts and reversed over the horizon. "Still telling me I can't shoot, you skinny fuck?" He pitched the gun into the Buick. Broke out the roofing nails from the trunk.

"Careful with the tyres," Green said.

"Fuck you too, Eddie." He hard-eyed one of the hostages on the fender. "Who you looking at, asshole?"

Johnny wadded a handkerchief against his wound. The numbness was beginning to fade from his arm. It felt like someone was turning a hot iron in his shoulder. "Time we cut these people loose, Jimmy. Before they make the other car."

Nelson discarded the nail sack. "What am I, stupid or something? You think I don't know that?" He began to prise the bank staff off the bodywork, dispatching one of the male tellers with a kick in the tailbone. "Get up there and tell those fucks in the flivver to back off or we gonna kill everyone in the car."

Johnny looked at Hamilton. The guy was kind of grey. "How you making it, Red?"

"Getting used to it, to tell the truth, John. Wouldn't be a bank job if I didn't take a bullet someplace."

Green cut away Hamilton's shirt, cleaning the wound with grain alcohol. "It ain't nothing. A through and through. You'll live." He broke a morphine vial from the medical kit. "Need a shot for that, Red?"

Hamilton 'uh –uh' 'd. "I'll take a shot from the booze, you can spare it, though."

"See what I've left when I've patched up, Johnny."

Johnny worked his head. "I'm jake. The slug only creased me." He removed the wadded handkerchief from the wound. The bleeding had almost stopped. "Let Red have a drink if he needs it, Ed."

Homer rubbed his mouth. "I've not had a shot of M since before Indiana State," he said.

Nelson glowered at him as he re-seated himself in the car. "Goddamn hophead. You start using that shit when I'm around and you're off the crew." He locked eyes with Johnny. Red. "No matter how tight you might be with some guys."

Johnny averted his eyes. This wasn't the time or he place. All he wanted was to get back to St Paul and get some professional medical attention. See Billie. "Your string, Jimmy. What you say goes. Now how about you get us out of here and back to the

Dutchman's. Soon as we get back to the Lantern, we can see what the hell the take is."

Eight

Makley's trial proved dull after Pierpont's theatrics. The genial-looking defendant donned silver glasses to consult the legal papers spread before him on the defence table and apologized for being unable to provide the correct spelling of his surname.

"It's been so long since I've used my right name that I wouldn't know. You better look it up on the record."

Similarly, when a retired college professor was excused from the jury after stating, "no man who attacks a sheriff deserves mercy," Makley agreed, saying, "those are my sentiments exactly. I am for the old guy."

Not that the act fooled Purvis. The fat man had been a con artist before he'd turned first to bootlegging and then to bank robbery during the course of the twenties. At one point he'd stolen a furnace salesman's car, traded it in for a new Terraplane and sold the car salesman a furnace in the process, using a brochure he'd found in the glove compartment.

It was best to remember that Makley had heisted approximately half a million dollars from banks in Indiana, Ohio and Missouri before his incarceration in the state pen, killing at least one police officer in the process. He might come over as a mild-mannered Rotarian, but there was no real difference between him and Pierpont when you came right down to it. Both of them were as much the predator as a timber wolf, enemies of society, and needed to be treated as such. Purvis only hoped the jury would do the right thing when the time came.

As it was, the SAC had nothing to worry about. Fat Charlie's display of geniality did him no more good than Pierpont's grandstanding.

"What did they give you?" Pierpont asked, as his co-defendant returned to the cellblock.

Makley rolled his shoulders. "I got everything," he said. Left it at that.

Nine

They sat around the Dutchman's office. Drank his whiskey. Smoked his cigars. Johnny and Hamilton sported fresh bandages on their upper torsos, courtesy of a sawbones arranged by their host. The quack had confirmed what they'd thought in the Buick: the wounds were nothing. Flesh wounds. Which didn't stop the bastards smarting. The whisky helped, but not so you'd notice. Johnny's shoulder hurt like a son-of-a-bitch.

"You going to make the split, Jimmy?"

Nelson sifted through the greenbacks on top of the desk. "That's why we here, ain't we?" He counted the cash, grimacing as he handed a wad to Sawyer. "Sorry, Dutch. Not as much as we were expecting. Things didn't go to plan at the bank."

Hamilton poured himself a refill from the rapidly-emptying bottle. "The money was there. On the other side of the bars. I could almost touch the bastard." He looked like he was about to weep. "That frigging bank clerk. It wasn't his money. Why risk a bullet for twenty bucks a week?"

"You shoulda plugged the fuck," Nelson said, sliding his cut towards him. "That's what I woulda done. Cut him off at the neck and have done with it. No messing."

Van Meter snorted. "And how much dough would we a pulled outta the place then, smart guy?"

Nelson rippled the banknotes between his fingers. "Keep riding me, Homer, and see where it gets you."

Johnny exchanged glances with Hamilton. They'd purposely given the little the guy the centre of the room while they made the split, putting their backs to the wall. The way the runt had acted at the bank, they'd half-expected the screwy bastard to turn on them, especially after they'd come up short. Grab the whole roll for himself. "Easy, Jimmy. We're all friends here, ain't we?"

"Sure," the Dutchman said. "A real friendly bunch, right, Jim?" He let his tone harden as Nelson kept his lip buttoned. "I said right, Jimmy?"

Nelson uncoiled. Sawyer was too powerful for him to buck. He got wrong side the Dutchman and he'd be leaving the Lantern in a beer barrel. "Sure, Dutch. Whatever you say. We're a real buncha pals, us guys. All for one and one for all. Right, Homer?"

"I was just kidding. Having fun with you. Don't you know when you being kidded, Jimmy?"

Sawyer nodded. "Guy was just making a joke," he said.

Nelson's eyes narrowed. "I think someone's needling me, I take it kind of personal. You know what I'm saying?" He made a magnanimous gesture. "But a guy wants to make a joke, that's fine. I like a joke as much as the next guy, okay?"

Okay. The atmosphere lightened as Nelson reached for a smile. Sawyer clapped his hands together.

"Okay, then. You didn't get as much as you was after and you're sore, but what the hell. You'll get lucky next time. Anybody wants to hang around downstairs, the drinks are on the house tonight. And I know a good cathouse up town, you want to get your ashes hauled." He pointed his chin towards Johnny. Hamilton. "Although the look of you guys, you probably want to rest up after what you been through today. Am I right?"

Johnny set aside his half-finished drink. Medicinal or not, it was something he could do without. "You never spoke a truer word, Dutch. Someone wants to drop me at the apartment, I could sleep for a week."

Nelson slapped him on the back. "You guys get fit and rested. I need you for another job I got in mind. Soon as Eddie's cased the place, I'll let you know."

Another job with the maniac in the newsboy's cap and windcheater would be more than Johnny's nerves could stand. The guy had a knack for picking jugs, though, and with the shortfall from Mason City, it would need at least one more big job before he could pull out of the heist game the way he'd planned. One more job before he could start that new life with Billie he'd promised himself. "Okay, Jimmy. That's swell. Pick us another good one and I'll be ready to roll as soon as I'm mended."

Ten

Next up in the Lima courtroom, Booby Clark. This time, Levy tried a novel strategy in defence. A directed verdict of not guilty as Clark, "doesn't believe in capital punishment."

It was a tack that, if nothing else, rendered the judge speechless for several seconds as he attempted to come to terms with her plea. "That is utterly silly for you to say," he managed eventually, "because he is on trial for murder that he doesn't believe in capital punishment."

"Well, it may be utterly silly, but nevertheless there are certain guarantees under the constitution that this defendant is entitled to, and he does not believe in it, and he makes this motion and he deserves the court rule on it."

The ruling was adverse.

Clark, meanwhile, seemed to take being on trial for his life in his stride, twice dozing off during the procedures. A beer runner turned bank robber and a persistent prison escaper, he was hardboiled enough to take whatever the system handed him. Or perhaps he had a premonition of what was to come. After only a short deliberation by the jury, he received a verdict of guilty, but with a recommendation of clemency. Clark just blinked until Jesse Levy put a hand on his shoulder.

"Well. That saves you, kid."

Makley and Pierpont, meanwhile, were sentenced while the jury was out on Clark. They were to die in the electric chair on July 13, the first death sentences to be passed in Allen County for fifty years.

Back in the cells, Pierpont lost his composure. "This' the first time I've felt nervous in a long time," he said, as his hands quivered. "I guess it's that unlucky thirteen."

"What do you mean?" a guard asked.

"Thirteen letters in my name. Born on the thirteenth of the month. Burned on the thirteenth of the month. Shit, even the Judge, Emmett Everett. Thirteen letters again. I should have known as soon as I walked I the courtroom."

Makley chewed gum stoically. "We all have to die once."

"Yeah, well. Perhaps that's so. I wasn't planning on it happening anytime soon if I had a choice in the matter, though."

THREE

G-MEN

Well, wasn't he a rat? Wasn't he everything that was low and vile? Didn't he hide behind a woman? Didn't he shoot from ambush? Wasn't his whole career as filthy as that of any rat who ever lived? – J. Edgar Hoover

One

The Lincoln Apartments, St Paul

Saturday, March 31

I think I was happier with John Dillinger while we were living in the Twin Cities than I ever was before or since – Billie Frechette

Johnny lounged in his union suit reading the newspapers. He'd had a pleasant few weeks recuperating from the bullet wound in his shoulder, treating himself to a couple of blue suits and a brown double breasted. He'd spent another part of the take on getting his teeth fixed – a country upbringing and a prison diet didn't do much for that Hollywood smile – and at night, when it was safe, took in a movie.

Occasionally, he'd visited a nightclub with the others. Joints like the Mystic Caverns and the Castle Royal, pleasure palaces sunk into mushroom caves in the sandstone bluffs overlooking the Mississippi, or the mammoth Boulevards of Paris and the adjoining Coliseum on the corner of Lexington and University Avenue, the latter boasting the world's largest dance floor. Sometimes underworld banker and gambling czar Jack Peifer's Hollyhocks, out on the edge of town.

Other times, he'd stopped by the Green Lantern to plug into the underworld grapevine. It was a chance to make connections for future jobs, fence loot or catch up on his contemporaries. The place was an employment exchange and post office for the guys working the circuit as much as it was a drinking den. Anyone who was anyone in the bank game would pass through the joint eventually. All you had to do was wait.

Walk in the Lantern any day of the week and you could find Barker gang leader and Karloff lookalike Ray 'Old Creepy' Karpis in the back room, drinking milk for his nervous stomach. Federal prison escapees Tommy Holden and Jimmy Keating would be discussing their golfing handicaps between stick-ups, while Harvey Bailey held court from a corner booth following his quarter of a million dollar robbery of the Denver mint: a rogue's gallery of American bandits, all openly going about their business, all untouched by the law. It was that kind of a place.

His nights on the town were rare, though, business as much as pleasure. Mostly he'd stuck close to home as his arm healed.

He'd spent the time playing poker with Hamilton and Van Meter, ordering takeouts from the deli down the block while he listened to the radio, cleaning his guns or pressing his pants. Making love to Billie.

Billie Frechette. The main reason he broke out the can. The former hatcheck girl had been waiting for him in the apartment when he returned from the Mason City job. She'd squealed and bounced into his embrace as he walked through the door. "Johnny."

He'd caught her in his one good arm. Locked into a kiss. "Piquet?" he said, as he came up for air.

"He got word to Mr Sawyer. Had him send me up here when I got off the train."

"No one else knows I'm here, though?"

"I haven't told anyone. And Mr Piquet only knew enough to pass me on to Mr Sawyer." Her brow creased. "Did I do wrong, Johnny?"

He drew her to his chest. "Jesus, kid. What a thing to ask."

She was fixing dinner at the stove as he reclined on the bed, baking powder biscuits and fried chicken with all the trimmings. A sweet kid. She'd been looking for somebody after her boyfriend had been sent down for mail robbery and he'd been fresh out the joint and hurting. No wonder they'd fallen for each other the way they had.

It had been the night after the Greencastle job and he was horny as hell. Hanging out in the College Gardens with Red and Pete and eying the broads. The guys had suggested a whorehouse for later, perhaps Anna Sage's new crib on the North Side, but then he'd spotted the hatcheck girl on the way out and all thoughts of blowing his wad on a hooker vanished.

He'd made small talk with her. Asked her when she got off. They'd hooked up later at an after hours place. Danced to the jukebox on the pocket-size dance floor. The Carioca. Afterwards, they'd went back to the railroad flat she shared with a waitress from the club and screwed like jackrabbits. Ever afterwards, he'd ask for the Carioca when they were out in a cabaret. Called it their tune.

He hummed a few bars of the chorus as he lay on his back. Their tune. She liked that. Thought it was romantic. Well. That was one word for it. Ever since that night, he could never hear the opening bars of the number without getting a hard-on.

Her trim brown body in halter top and shorts. Bobbed hair. Eyes you could drown in. Cheekbones. The French in her. She'd grown up on the Menominee Reservation in Wisconsin, but she looked more like Claudette Colbert than Minnehahah. Parisian as hell. Jesus, she was some piece of ass. Then again, Margaret Dumont would have seemed like Carole Lombard after nine years with nothing more than his right hand or some jailhouse wife for company.

Going without. It could really screw a guy up. A fella could go in the big house straight as the proverbial die. Come out queer as a fucking geranium after a few years celling with some pansy. It was something he'd never got a taste for, though. The old yardbirds might swear there was nothing tighter than a young boy's ass, but cornholing some fairy while you pictured Clara Bow was nothing like the real thing. It never could be.

He caught her around the waist as she moved past the bed. Nuzzled the back of her neck. "Hey, sweetheart. Wanna keep Daddy company a while?"

She giggled. "Jesus, Johnny." Dodged out of reach. "You want the dinner to burn while we make out?"

146

He mock-growled. Reached for her again. He'd always been a horny bastard, even before he went to jail. More than twenty-four hours without tearing off a piece and he went to bed with a headache. "Screw the dinner. Let it burn."

She skipped backwards. "Uh-uh. I'm not spending all day slaving over a hot stove for you just to let it go up in flames." She canted her head at the newspapers spread open on the bed covers. "What about the *Daily News* there? You get a mention today?"

He let her dance out of reach as he riffled the pages. There was only one thing excited him more than a roll in the hay with Billie. "That Texican punk. Barrow. He knocks over a bank in Dallas and gives some old farmer at the counter his money back. 'We don't want your money. We just want the bank's'." He slapped the sheet with the knuckle side of his hand. "Hell, I was using that line last fall. Six months later and this no-account asshole starts using it for hisself. He'll be wearing a skimmer next. Vaulting the counter. Doing that thing I got from Fairbanks."

"This guy's on, what was it? – page five, though. You was front page above the fold for Sioux Falls. Mason City. And everybody knows the picture from Crown Point."

"Yeah, they do, don't they?" His expression flattened. "That's the problem. The Big Fella liked to see his picture on the front page, too. That's why he's doing eleven years on the Rock right now. And they're looking to nail me for a damn sight more than tax evasion."

Still. The press had its uses. The newspapers and radio had him placed all over the country while he was holed-up safe in the Twin Cities. So far he'd been identified perusing the new spring goods at a State Street store in Chicago; negotiating for a twelve cylinder Ford in Springfield, Missouri; buying a half-dozen cravats in Omaha; bargaining for a suburban bungalow in his old hometown of Mooresville; drinking a soda in a drug store in Charleston and strolling down Broadway swinging a Malacca cane. He'd also been reported as buying a fishing rod in Montreal and holding a dinner party at a hotel in Yucatan. Ships had even been searched as they docked in Glasgow and Londonderry after Piquet had joshed with reporters as to his client's whereabouts. The one place he hadn't been sighted, thanks to the Dutchman, was the red brick apartment block in St Paul.

It was more than just the way the papers sent the law running up it's own ass, though. It was hard to resist the press coverage he'd been getting. He'd been pretty much ignored as a kid, what with his old lady dead and the old man running the farm and the grocery store. The most attention his father gave him was to paddle him with a barrel stave when he was caught playing hooky or stealing coal. Chain him to the delivery cart when he was making his rounds. To find half the country following your exploits like it was some kind of movie serial, cheering your face in the newsreels like you were the blessed Doug. Damn, that was something else again.

The letters in today's *News*, for instance, in reply to an editorial knocking him for hitting the banks:

"This person calls Dillinger cheap. He isn't half as cheap as a crooked banker or a crooked politician because he did give the bankers a chance to fight, and they never gave the people a chance"

He borrowed the nail scissors from the vanity set beside the bed. Ran them around the letter. Pretty good. Almost as good as the one he'd saved from *Time* after they published the *Dillinger Land* board game: starting block Crown Point.

"Great desperadoes from little urchins grow. When John Dillinger was ten he, like Tom Sawyer, was a poor country boy. Sometimes he may have dreamed of being another Abe Lincoln or Jesse James… but not that he would achieve a great unwritten odyssey: Through the Mid West with a machinegun."

Headlines weren't everything, though. They'd gone as far as writing a song about Pretty Boy down in the Cookson Hills, which was more than they'd done for him. The Tulsa-born yegg had one over on him there, he had to admit. He wanted to compete with Floyd, he better start burning tax records same as the big Okie next time he knocked-over a jug.

A car drew up outside the apartment. He retrieved the Thompson from beneath the bed. Buckled the belt containing his git money. "Want to see who that is, honey?"

She folded back a corner of the wired-down blinds. "Homer. Probably come to play cards again." She returned to the stove as he relaxed. Chased the chicken round the skillet with a spatula. "I got your favourite for dessert. Coconut cream pie. And there's a couple bottles Schlitz Special Repeal in the icebox you want it."

He slanted the Thompson across the dresser. Padded up behind her. Moulded himself to the contours of her body. "Know how to treat a man, don't you, sugar?"

She wriggled like a puppy. "I sure wish Homer would have put off his visit till later," she said, snuggling herself against him.

He groaned. "He'll be up in a couple a minutes, though. More's the pity." Peeled himself away from her. "I better put some pants on," he said, rearranging his skivvies. "There's being pleased to see a guy and there's going over the top."

Billie put her hand to her mouth. "If those nuns in the Indian School could see me now." She uncapped a couple of beers. Handed one to Johnny as he dressed. "Here he is," she said, as footsteps sounded on the landing outside. "I'll put out an extra plate for him. There should be enough for three if I make extra biscuits."

Johnny hefted the Thompson. Slammed home a magazine. "Turn off the stove, sweetheart."

"Johnny?"

"There's more than one guy out there, Billie. More than one set of footsteps."

"Perhaps he - "

"Quiet."

A hammering at the door. Shave-and-a-haircut. Not the usual slow- fast-slow they used as code. "That ain't Homer." He tucked the machinegun against his waist. "Keep it on the chain, sugar. Ask them what they want."

She tiptoed over to the door. "Yes?"

Two beefy figures in rumpled overcoats and heavy shoes. They had to be cops. What happened to the fix? "St Paul's police. Is Carl there, ma'am?"

"Carl? Carl who?"

They used the pseudonym Dutch had put on the lease. "Carl Hellman."

"He's just left. Won't be back till this afternoon. Call back then, all right?"

One of the dicks stuck his foot in the door. "Are you Mrs Hellman?"

"Yes."

"We'll talk to you instead."

Billy swallowed. "Okay, then." She closed the door as he withdrew his foot. "I'm not dressed, though. You'll have to wait until I'm dressed." She shot the bolt. "Bulls, Johnny. What are we going to do?"

"Throw some things in the large bag. The guns. Money. Anything that could incriminate us." He zeroed the Thompson in on the door as the cops banged again on the woodwork. "Don't worry, sugar. I'll take care of this."

"Christ, Johnny. Don't. Not after that thing in East Chicago."

"No such thing as half a virgin, doll. They can only fry me once." He drew a bead on the door. Put up the Thompson as shots sounded outside the building. "What the hell is that?"

Christ, he'd forgotten about Homer. He turned back the blinds as one of the dicks from the door bolted out the building, Van on his tail. The dick skidded on the sidewalk. Came up shooting. He chased Van Meter back into the hallway, the outlaw throwing a shot over his shoulder as he ran. Tough on Van, but this was his chance. "If there's anyone outside that door, they better stand back."

He raised the Thompson again. Billie screamed as he tattooed a row of bullet holes diagonally across the woodwork, shafts of sunlight stabbing into the room.

"Shut up, you dumb bitch." He rammed the gun barrel between the chain and door jamb. "Get the bag and follow me." Tore up the walls of the landing with another spray from the Thompson, emerging into a cloud of plaster dust.

"Johnny?"

"Come on. It's clear." Johnny reloaded as he moved down the hallway, Billie dragging the suitcase two-handed at his heels. He went through the back door in a crouch. Straightened as he entered the alleyway. Found it clear. "Gimme the case."

"Here."

He exchanged the case for the car keys. "Run ahead and open the garage." Chucked her beneath the chin. "You're doing swell, little sister. Keep your nerve just a few minutes longer and we'll be out of here free and clear."

She hurried ahead to the garage as he strolled inconspicuously away from the apartment block, the Thompson held close to his leg. Backed their black Hudson into the street.

"Easy," he said, as he joined her. Dumped the luggage and machinegun in the back. "We don't want to attract attention. Take it slow now, you hear? No more than thirty."

She gaped at him. "Jesus. Oh, Jesus Christ."

"What?"

"Your leg."

He stared down at the spreading bloodstain on his pants. Son-of-a-bitch. A ricochet. He'd shot himself in the thigh.

Two

Purvis stepped off the train at St Paul station. He regretted again the time he'd wasted covering the Dillinger mob's trial while their erstwhile leader ran riot across the Mid-West. In the month since the elusive yeggman had sprung himself from Crown Point, he'd conducted two major robberies, escaping with an estimated $100,000. The bastard hadn't left a trace behind him. He'd made the Chicago FBI men look like the bunch of ineffectual pen-pushers their critics accused them of being.

Dillinger and co. Goddamn outlaws. They should have become extinct with the passing of the Frontier. The railroad and telegraph had made it almost impossible for armed robbers to operate. For the first two decades of the twentieth century, most bank raids were by stealth, the burglar and safecracker taking over from the horse-borne bandit when it came to cracking a jug.

By the twenties, however, the wheel had taken another turn. Technology had made safes and bank vaults increasingly difficult to open and had, at the same time, gifted yeggs with the ideal means of escape in the form of the automobile. A gang could hit a bank and make it safely over the state line in only a few hours, compared to the several days it might take on horseback.

With the Thompson gun acting as backup and a network of corrupt city governments providing havens across the Mid-West, the only thing preventing an explosion of bank robbery was Prohibition. Illegal hooch was an easier and more profitable way of making a living than knocking over banks. There had been armed robbers during that decade, notably Eddie Bentz and Harvey Bailey and, until his death in a shootout with police, cashiered Prussian officer 'Baron' Lamm, father of the planned and timed modern bank job.

They had been anomalies, though. It wasn't until Repeal that the current crop of bandits had sprouted like weeds across the flat prairies of the American heartland, becoming a curse to hardworking government operatives like himself.

Still. It wasn't his job to ponder the whys and wherefores of the current situation. His job was to apprehend the sons of bitches and clap them in jail. Particularly Dillinger.

Which was why he was here in the Minnesota state capital being greeted by his fellow rising star as a federal crime-buster,

Inspector Bill Rorer, the man who had arrested Machinegun Kelly a few months previously and had, the evening before, ordered the raid on the Lincoln Apartments that came close to nailing Dillinger. A lean, intense-looking individual in the customary dark suit and tie, he had the air of a military man about him, the upright stance and aggressive manner of the marine lieutenant that had once gone over the top with Pershing's boys in France.

"Purvis?"

"Call me Mel."

They shook. Rorer took his overnight bag and led him through the station crowd to a waiting sedan. He saw his guest into the rear of the car before joining the driver in the front, angling his head over the seat to talk as the car cut into the city traffic. "We've a hotel room booked for you, but I thought we could stop off beforehand. Check out the crime scene. I know the old man's pressuring you for results on this one or you wouldn't be here in the first place."

"I need something to show Washington. We've come up with squat at the Chicago end. It probably makes sense to pool resources. Though I doubt my ass is in a sling to the same extent as yours after last night's raid."

"If I'd actually thought it was Dillinger, I'd have launched a full-scale operation. The number of cranks we get everyday claiming to have seen the bastard, though. Every old lady with a single guy living downstairs thinks the poor schmuck's planning to knock over the local First National."

"At least you winged the guy. That was something, anyway."

Rorer tipped back his fedora, revealing a prematurely-balding head. "Yeah, there's that. Try telling the guy in Washington, though."

The blood spoor leading away from the apartment had been small consolation as far as Mr Hoover was concerned. The fact of the matter was that the raid had been bungled. Dillinger, his girl, and a third individual, tentatively identified as Homer Van Meter, had all walked from what should have been an airtight trap. There'd been no backup. No one guarding the rear of the apartment block. And last but not least, a member of the notoriously corrupt St Paul's police department had accompanied the agent who visited the apartment.

It was hard to gauge whether the Director was exercised about the local law acting in with collusion with the bandits, or whether his concern was with sharing any future credit with the city police department, but a series of scalding missives had heated up the wires between Washington and the various field offices in the past twenty-four hours, prohibiting co-operation with their local counterparts. Agents were forbidden to participate in joint operations with police unless, 'short of equipment, like machineguns or gas guns.'

Rorer massaged his chin as they passed the Federal Courts Building. "Christ, I thought we still had to have local law along when we made a pinch. Besides, we need someone who can handle a piece. Most of our boys have never fired a gun outside of a shooting gallery."

Purvis held his tongue. He was enough of a politician to know when to speak and when to keep his mouth shut. Rorer was right about the agents' role, though. They'd simply been investigators until several agents had been killed in the Kansas City Massacre barely a year before, forbidden to make arrests or carry a gun.

Even when the restrictions were lifted on the back of the KC shootout, the results were pitiful. Pistol training often consisted of potting at bottles on fence posts. Agents trained on local police ranges, if they where lucky, or in at least one instance, on an agent's upstate farm. Lawyers or accountants who could handle a gun, like AEF veteran Rorer, were few and far between.

Hoover – Mr Hoover – had always tacitly admitted that his clean-cut young graduates were unable to go head-to-head with chopper-wielding hoodlums. A small coterie of 'cowboys', veteran South-Western lawmen hired from sheriff's departments or the Texas Rangers, went habitually armed. Hard-drinking, tobacco-spitting throwbacks to the Old West, Bowie knives in their boots, their misdemeanours were wincingly overlooked by the Bureau due to their effectiveness in neutralizing the opposition.

Most of the college boys had expected the old-timers to be quietly put out to grass as the Bureau shaped-up as a crime-fighting organization. Now, however, the word had gone out for more legal gunfighters. A new influx of hardnosed city cops and Western pistoleers had begun to infuse the deejays with an added aggressiveness. An aggressiveness Rorer was to exploit to the full, as the events of the next few day's would show.

They parked up outside the U-shaped apartment block and stepped from the car. Their way was barred by a tall, bespectacled figure in a freshly-blocked homburg and banker's pin stripes: Big Tom Brown, six feet three inches and 280 pounds of civic corruption hiding behind a detective' shield. The former city police chief had been demoted to detective following one scandal too many, but still wielded considerable clout as the police force's bagman and fixer par excellence. "Bill," he greeted, firing a cigar. "Always nice to see the government keeping us local boys on our toes." He blew a fragrant smelling cloud in Purvis' direction, chuckling as the little man strangled a cough. "Who's your boyfriend? Edgar Bergan know you sneezed his dummy?"

Purvis kept his face immobile. He'd heard the Charlie McCarthy cracks before. "Melvin Purvis. Special Agent in Charge, Chicago FBI office. And what the hell does a local flatfoot like you think you're doing messing with a federal investigation?"

"One of my officers got shot at too. You college fruits aren't the only ones these pricks like to use for target practice." He took

162

another pull at his cigar. "Not to worry, though, Rorer. Your boys got this place sewn up tight. I tried to take a look see at the crime scene and some asshole with an Ivy league accent threatened to arrest me."

Rorer grinned tightly. "Nice to see my boys on the ball," he said, making to walk past the city detective's bulk.

Brown stepped reluctantly aside. "Pity they weren't as alert last night, ain't it, Billy boy?" He chewed on the cigar as they entered the apartment block. "Good luck, anyway, fellas. You Sherlock Holmes types got a whole empty apartment to play with now. Hope it keeps you occupied while some real lawmen get down to busting the bad guys."

Rorer cast a look over his shoulder as Brown ambled down the sidewalk. "I hate to admit it, but the bastard's probably got us beat. Him and his cronies will have already tipped Dillinger and his crew as to what's happening with the investigation. Unless we get lucky, the assholes are going to skate again."

"At least your men kept him from the crime scene," Purvis said, as they ascended the staircase.

"That's true, I suppose. There might be something we can use if the place hasn't been dry-cleaned by Brown. I just hope the fellas inside had the sense to keep their mouths shut around him. Didn't let anything slip the big lug could pick up on."

The apartment was a mess, the floor strewn with clothing and upturned suitcases, as if someone had packed in a hurry. There were newspapers splayed on the bed. A pan of fried chicken dried-up on the stove.

A half-dozen Federal agents sifted the evidence, dusting for fingerprints. Not that there was any lack of forensics for them to work on. One of the agents threw open a closet door for their inspection: a Thompson sub-machinegun with a fully loaded drum, two Browning Automatic Rifles and what looked to be a .38 Colt. There was also a   bullet-proof vest, a spare Thompson pistol grip and a couple of twenty round clips for the Colt.

Rorer puffed his cheeks. "Looks like we hit the jackpot this time, Mel. If this wasn't Dillinger, I'll eat my hat."

"There was another Thompson in the car downstairs," the agent added. "That and a .351 Winchester. Ammunition."

Rorer stared at him. " 'Sir'," he said.

The agent swallowed. "Sir."

A second agent cleared his throat. "We found this as well, Mr Rorer. I think you might like to see it. Sir." He presented a dime store notebook to his superior.

Rorer thumbed through the closely written pages. "Here, Mel. What do you think of this?"

Purvis read over his shoulder. *000-Rt. On N. 3d-X St. X St. - .02 X Stop St. symbol. Spanish Moon Café.* "What the hell is it?"

"A getaway map. What they call a 'git'. Run that route in a car and I guarantee you'd beat the traffic out of town by a country mile." He flipped the page. His expression grew animated. "Now then. This is more like it. Take a look at this."

Three

They left Minnesota. Drove across Iowa, Illinois. Indiana. Slept in the car. Washed up in Mooresville the following weekend, shortly before twelve. Johnny hid the Ford behind a haystack two fields back from the old man's farm. Limped across the meadows leaning on Billie. Tried the back door.

"Who's there?"

He felt nervous at the sound of John Dillinger Senior's voice. More than when he was taking a jug. "It's me, sir. Johnny."

The old man wrestled with the bolt. Blinked out into the yard. "John? Is it really you?"

"Kind of cold out here. Can we come in, dad?"

The old man did a double take. "Good God, yes. Come on in. Make yourself at home." He put down the lamp he was carrying. Hurriedly pulled the drapes. "They've been asking questions. Watching the farm. You shouldn't have come, John. It's too dangerous. If they saw you come in here…"

"The feds can't find their – their derrieres with a map and a flashlight. I'm not worried about the feds." He saw the way his father was dressed, bib overalls unfastened over long handled underwear. Thick woollen socks. No shoes. "We get you out of bed, dad?"

"I was still awake. Reason I heard you coming through the yard." He glanced at the squirrel gun leaning behind the door. "I thought it was – I don't know what I thought it was. Way things have been since you – you know…"

Johnny took his hat off. "I never meant to bring trouble to your door, sir. To shame you like this."

"You're still my son. No matter what you've done." He shuffled towards the larder. "Have you eaten? You and -?"

"Billie Frechette. My wife."

"Your 'wife'?"

"Well. We haven't had a chance to ah, formalize things yet. But as soon as we're clear of trouble…"

The old man frowned. "I see." Inclined his head towards the young woman. "Pleased to make your acquaintance, anyway, Miss Frechette."

"You too, sir. Mr Dillinger."

167

The old man produced pie. Bread. Smoked ham. "Unless you'd rather I cook you something. The stove's out, though. If you want to help me fetch kindling…"

"Cold's fine, sir." He pulled out a chair for Billie. Seated himself beside her. "You joining us, dad?"

"Eat at this time and I'd never sleep." He fetched a jug of buttermilk from the larder. Poured two glasses. "You eat hearty, though. Good home cooking. Something you'll have missed in the city."

Johnny nodded as he made sandwiches. Sliced the pie. Peach. Like he'd had as a kid. "Audrey bake this?"

"Your sister's a fine girl. Takes good care of an old man."

"Unlike me, you mean."

"I never said that." He watched his son eat. Adjusted the strap of his overalls. "You were wild as a youngster, but you were never mean. You always had a good heart. I've never blamed you for what you've done. What they say you've done in the newspapers."

"Thanks, dad. That means a lot to me."

168

"Perhaps if I'd been less strict with you as a boy. Spared the rod."

Johnny rested his fork on his plate. "Dad. Please."

"You were a young colt. Untamed. I thought you needed to be disciplined." He passed his hand across his eyes. "You were a child, though. Not an animal. If I'd treated you as my son rather than as a mustang to be broken …"

Johnny wanted to put his arm around his father. Tell him everything was all right. That he respected him. Loved him. That all he wanted was the old man's approval. "It's okay," he said, coming around the table. Pummelling him on the back. "I don't blame you none. It must have been hard when my mother passed on. Raising a son on your own. I know I was a rowdy kid. Trouble I brought to your door. "

The old man trawled a handkerchief from his overalls. Honked. Dried his eyes. "Seeing me like this. And in front of your young woman as well."

Billie fluttered a hand at him. "No problem. Mr Dillinger. No problem at all." She abandoned a half-eaten sandwich. "Johnny talks about you often. If you knew the respect he feels for you. Love."

Johnny coloured. "Christ, Billie." Saw his father flinch at the blasphemy. "Sorry, dad."

His old man sighed. "The city for you. Why I sold the grocery store. Moved you out of Indianapolis as soon as I could." He bunched his handkerchief. "Too late, though. I know what it's like when the city gets a grip on a boy. You can't hold a young fellow down on the farm once he's got a taste for the bright lights. The noise and the bustle."

"I'm still a farm boy at heart, dad."

"Difficult to believe to look at you, son. The Sunday go-to-meeting clothes. Cologne. You look like a businessman. Lawyer. Something like that."

Johnny laughed. "You trying to insult me, dad?"

The old man smiled. Looked vaguely confused. "Just – you've grown up to be a fine looking young man, John."

Johnny's ears burned. "Cripes, dad."

"If only I'd been a better father to you. Perhaps you could have been that businessman. That lawyer."

"Instead of a yeggman, you mean?"

"I made mistakes. I know that now."

"If they'd treated me right in court. Given me a decent sentence. I could have straightened out after that thing with Mr Morgan. Been a good citizen. Made you proud of me. Instead they buried me alive. Threw away the key. There was nothing else I could do when I raised. I had no skills. No one would employ me." He shrugged. Invisible stripes. "Knocking over jugs. That was the only thing the reformatory taught me. Nothing to do with you, pops. They hadn't locked me away for nine years just for snatching some guy's roll and I coulda been someone decent. A son you coulda been proud of."

"It's still not too late," Billie said. "We ever get out from under all this, Mr Dillinger, we intend to settle down. Raise kids. The same as regular folk."

"That's a nice thought, dear. But the way things are between Johnny and the law..."

171

Johnny finished his pie. "I'm looking for that one big score. That one hit that gives me enough to get out of the game. Get myself abroad. Look out for my old man like the son he always wanted." He wrinkled his eyes at his father. "A new start in the sun, dad. What do you say? Spend the rest of your days on a beach while some senorita fans you with a palm leaf? Feeds you grapefruit? Oranges?"

The corner of the old man's mouth lifted. "It's a nice idea, John, but I'm too old to move. This is my home now. The place I've sunk my roots. This is where I intend to live out my days. Where I intend them to bury me." His smile faded. "As long as things work out with the bank, that is."

"They're looking to repossess the place?"

"No. Not yet, anyway. Foreclosure, though. It's always a threat these days. Things aren't as bad for us here as they are in the Dust Bowl, but they took over the Hansen place down the road there, just a few days ago. The crop fails and I don't know what I'll do. I swear to the Lord."

Johnny delved in his pocket. "Here." Produced a roll of bills. "I can only spare a few grand now, but I'll send more later when I can."

The old man pushed his hand away. "No, John. Thank you, but I can't."

"My money not good enough for you? That what you saying?" He folded his father's fingers around the roll. "For all the heartache I caused you. For the support I shoulda been giving you when I was locked up in the can."

"No, John."

"Take it. It's the bank's money, anyway. You'll just be giving them back what I borrowed. But without paying the interest." He backed away before the old man could return the roll. Supported himself on the back of Billie' seat. "We ought to let you get back to bed. Early start for a farmer, I know."

The old man hesitated. Trousered the money. "I never could get you up for your chores of a morning, John."

"One reason I prefer the city."

"You staying the night, son? You and your young lady?"

"We ought to be gone before sunup. Before the feds spot we're here."

"There's no need to stray outside. And you can leave after dark. Or I can hide you in the back of the truck when I go into town."

Staying the night. Making an exit in his father's truck. It might not be such a bad idea at that. "We need to phone around. Find somewhere safe in Chicago. Drive me down to the drugstore in Mooresville and you'd be doing me a favour, dad." And there was his leg. They'd had the thing patched up by Doc May, an underworld sawbones, as they fled St Paul, but the wound was throbbing like a pump. It would probably do him good to rest some while it healed. "Whaddya say, Billie? A couple of nights on the farm before we head back to the city?"

"If Mr Dillinger can find us a place to sleep."

"No problem, dear. I'll take the spare room. You can have my bed. It's the only double I have."

"You're okay with that, dad?"

"Giving up my bed to my son and his wife? Why should that be a problem for me?" He extended his hand across the table. Patted Billie on the wrist. "You and Johnny settled down together. Something for us all to dream about. Even if it's only for one night. Welcome to the family, Miss Frechette. Or can I call you Billie?"

Four

2214 Marshall Avenue. The address in the notebook. The place looked deserted. Whoever lived there would have lammed by now. Tipped off by the cops. Nevertheless, Purvis was glad of the .38 Special in his shoulder holster as the manager unlocked the door for them. Shooting it out with the Mid-West's premier bank robbing team hadn't been high on his list of priorities when he first entered law school.

The apartment was empty, though. Or rather, empty of people. The cupboards yielded road maps and airline schedules, suits and hats with the labels cut out. A Thompson under the bed. And ammunition. Lots of ammunition.

"A regular bandit's cave," Rorer said, as his subordinates bagged receipts and laundry tags. Checked for fingerprints. "All we need to do now is track down the son-of-a-bitch who was living here."

Purvis hooked a two-foot length of cord from a wardrobe on the end of his pistol. "What's this?"

"Dynamite fuse. Looks like the bastard was ready to start a war, doesn't it?" He wheeled as the door opened. Pulled his gun. "Behind you, Mel."

Purvis scrabbled at his holster. Realized he hadn't unbuttoned his coat. A shamefaced grin spread across his face at the sight of the figure standing in the doorway. If this was Dillinger, the wanted posters certainly didn't do him justice. "Come on in, honey. No one's going to hurt you here."

The willowy high yellow shuffled inside. Bulged her eyes as she relinquished her suitcases. Tomming it for Mr Charley. The way they did back in Carolina when you caught them on the hop. Purvis knew how to talk to a shine, though. Firm but fair, unless they were one of the bad ones. A good nigger would usually co-operate, if you handled them right. "What's your name, sugar? What are you doing in this place, huh?"

The Negress trembled as he laid a hand on her wrist. The fear was more than just an act. "Lucy, suh. Lucy Jackson. I'm the maid here. And that's my sister outside, Leona Goodman." She peered timidly at the agents as Rorer dispatched one of his men to round up her sibling. "And might I ask what you gentlemen is doing in Mr Stevens' room?"

Rorer fanned his badge at her. "We ask the questions, nigger. Not you. Who the hell is 'Mr Stevens'?"

Purvis made a lowering motion with his hand. "Easy, Bill. I'll handle this." Panic the spook and she'd be no use to anyone. "The suitcases, Lucy. You want to tell us what's inside?"

"Nothing, suh."

Purvis looked at her chidingly. "Lucy. Come on now."

"Swear to God, suh." She opened one of the suitcases. Nothing but air. "Mr Stevens sent us to clear out his apartment for him. Said he'd pick up the cases from my place tomorrow night."

Rorer's mouth twisted. "And you never thought to ask why he couldn't clear out the place himself?"

Purvis waved him down. That wasn't important. They were onto something here. He could feel it. "Don't worry, Lucy. You didn't know what you were getting into it. You're not in trouble. Not if you do what we say." He took a notebook from his pocket. Wet the tip of a pencil with his tongue. "Okay, then. I need to know

178

everything I can about Mr Stevens and his associates. What they look like. Where they meet. Anything they may have let slip while you were cleaning the place around them. First and most important of all, though. I need to know your address."

Five

The old man spread the word amongst the family at church. Brought them back to the house: John's half-brother Hubert, his sister Audrey and her husband Emmett, plus their sons, Norman and Fred. Audrey arrived with a basket of fried chicken and three coconut cream pies.

"I used to make you these when you were a little boy," she said, standing the basket on the table. "They were always your favourite."

His big sis. Way she'd looked after him as a kid. Practically raised him after his old lady passed away. "I missed you, hon," he said, folding her in his arms. "You and your cooking."

She disentangled herself from his embrace. Flushed. "Thinking with his stomach. Just like a man." She smoothed down her dress. Looked him over. "You haven't changed," she said, her eyes damp. "Haven't changed a bit. You're still the little boy I used to lullaby when he couldn't sleep. Somehow I thought you'd be different after what they say about you in the news."

He dipped his finger in one of the pies. Licked off the cream. "Believe about half what you read in the newspapers, take the rest with a handful of salt and you'll just about have the truth of the thing."

Emmett hooked his thumbs behind his suspenders. "Some of the things they're saying about Crown Point. That the jailers were paid to let you out the place. That someone smuggled you a gun. Any truth in that, old man?"

"Lemme tell you something, big boy. If you don't know nothing, you can't tell nothing, can you?"

"No."

"Well, then. Let that be a lesson to you." He softened the remark with a smile. "Want to see something, Em?"

"Sure."

He plucked the blanket from the couch. "What do you think of this baby?" Unveiled a Tommy gun. "This is the one I bust outta jail with. Let me tell you something, Emmet, this thing could talk and it would tell a story. Believe you me."

His brother-in-law gingerly inspected the machinegun before handing it back to him. "And that's the piece got you out of Crown Point?"

"One of them, anyway." He conjured a second gun from his jacket. "And this' the one they say was smuggled in to me."

Emmett examined the firearm: the wooden pistol he'd bluffed his way past the guards with. "So it's true then. You really did it with a wooden gun."

"Sure as shooting I did." He supported the Tommy against his hip with one hand. Flourished the pistol in the other. "You still got that camera, Em?"

"Out in the car."

They went out to the yard. Johnny posed in front of the farmhouse with his arsenal for Emmett whilst Audrey set out a cloth and plates on the meadow behind the barn. They shot off a roll of film. Fooled like schoolboys. Joined the rest of the family for a picnic lunch on the grass.

It was peaceful there with the smell of the alfalfa and wild flowers in the air, swallows darting beneath the eaves of the barn.

182

For a while the world went away and they were a family again, eating and discussing births and deaths and marriages, just like regular folks gathered together of a weekend. It was almost possible to forget that the amiable brother joking and clowning at the centre of the gathering wasn't a wounded outlaw. The most wanted man in America.

And then a plane flew low overhead, throwing a shadow over the grass. It turned and began to head back towards the farm. Crossed over the meadow again.

"It's probably nothing," Emmett said, as it approached for the second time. "A crop-duster. Barnstormer from the county fair."

"You're probably right," Johnny said, getting to his feet. Discarding a chicken wing. "But that's not a chance I'm willing to take."

He dragged Billie into the house and began to pull their things together. Made sure the Thompson was loaded. Fastened his money belt. "The Hudson back of the barn. You want to run that into Mooresville for me, Hubert?"

"Sure, Johnny. Meet you down the gas station?"

"That where you working these days?" He nodded at the young man's affirmative. "And you sure it's safe?"

"Safe as anywhere. Don't worry, Johnny, no one's going to rat on you around here. Not on a local boy made good."

"You got a funny idea of making good, Hubie, boy." He looked to Emmett. "Can you run us down there when you leave, Em? I'll get down in the back. Stick a blanket over me in case the G are watching."

"Sure thing, Johnny. I'll get Fred to drive Hubie's car, if he's picking up the Hudson. Put Billie on the floor in back."

"That's swell, Em. Gets us out of here nicely." He went over to his old man. Stuck out his hand. "Well, dad. Looks like this it. I wish I could stay longer, but - you know how it is."

The old man's voice cracked as he held his son's hand. "I know you can't stay, son, but dear God, I wish you didn't have to go. Wish it with all my heart."

Johnny shied from the tears in his father's eyes. If he stopped to think, paused in flight, he'd never tear himself away. But his path was set. He had to go.

184

Knowing that he might never see them alive again. His old man. Audrey. The kids. That was torture. Worse than anything he'd undergone in the pen. But he stuck around any longer, waited for the law to sniff out where he was hiding, and he'd be back in the slammer. Either that or laid cold on a slab. "You ready, Billie?" he said, crooking the Thompson beneath his arm.

"Ready when you are, big guy."

"All right then. We got phone calls to make. A safe-house to arrange. Sooner we get back on the road the better."

Six

778 Rondo Avenue. Lucy Goodman's address. A faded white clapboard in the Black Bottom. Purvis took position in the kitchen with Goodman and Agent Notesteen, the latter toting a BAR, while Agent Gross manned the kitchen window with a Thompson. Rorer was noticeable by his absence.

"I thought you'd want to be in on this, Bill," Purvis had said, as the Inspector prepared to return to the Federal Building. "Think of the headlines if this comes off okay."

"And think of the headlines if it don't. I already got my tit in the wringer over that thing at the Lincoln Apartments. At least I could pin that one on the guys on the ground. Hoover thinks I bungled this one personally and he'll have my head on the block." He hesitated as he made to leave. "Be a real gold star for the man in charge if this goes right, though, Mel. Don't know if I'm doing the right thing leaving it to you after all."

"Don't worry, Bill. We take down Dillinger tonight and I'll mention you in my report to the boss."

His cockiness evaporated as the hours wore on, though. There were three guns in the house and Dillinger – or whoever it was – would be taken completely by surprise. It should be a walkover. Three college boys against a case-hardened killer, though. If he'd been a gambling man, he'd be looking to lay off some of his action right about now.

It was more than just the fact that 'Stevens' might get the drop on them before they could shoot, though. What if they got the wrong man? It was all down to Goodman's identification of the man as he approached her door. The light was fading and the street lamps were sparse in the Black Bottom. There was also the fact that they were relying on a Negress for identification. It was an established fact that they all looked alike to a nigger. What if the dumb coon pointed out the wrong man? Especially after the instructions Rorer had given Notesteen as he left for the Office.

"I don't want any messing around with this cocksucker. As soon as he shows his face, shoot him."

"Could you repeat that, sir?"

Rorer spoke slowly and emphatically. "If the nigger says its Stevens, shoot him. Shoot the son-of-a-bitch dead." He saw the

187

shocked expression on Purvis' face. "This isn't a courtroom, Mel, it's a battlefield. I'm not prepared to take any chances with these cop-killing bastards. Not after Kansas City." He slapped Notesteen on the shoulder as he left. "And don't worry about the paperwork. I'll take care of that. The asshole can't testify against us if he's pushing up daisies."

Shoot to kill. That was okay for Rorer. He'd been through the Argonne. Belleau Wood. The nearest Purvis had personally come to combat was skeet-shooting with his old man of a weekend after church.

Gross, at the window. "A car. It's stopping across the street."

Purvis joined him. A green Terraplane sedan. He pushed Notesteen towards the bedroom. "Cover him. If anything goes down, disable the vehicle." Braced Goodman as a figure strode up the path. "Is that the man?"

"Yes, suh. That's Mr Stevens."

"You sure now?"

"Yes, suh. That's the man from the apartment. Man who paid me to collect the cases." She started as the man hammered on the door. "Should I - ?"

"Give him the damn cases."

Goodman opened the door. Shoved the suitcases – freighted with wanted posters, rather than clothing – into the man's arms. Slammed the door in his face.

Gross cocked the Thompson. Looked at Purvis expectantly. He seized Goodman by the shoulders.

"That was him? That was definitely Stevens?"

"Swear to you, Mr Purvis. That was the man."

Gross looked at him again. "Sir? Mr Purvis?"

He didn't know who the man was. That was the thing. If he killed an innocent man, the newspapers would crucify him. Eat him alive. If he let the bastard get away though, walk from a prepared ambush, his career was over anyway. And anyone who had an arsenal like that in his apartment was guilty of something, Dillinger or not. Assuming that was 'Stevens' out there on the path.

Screw it. "Let him have it," he said.

189

Goodman shrieked as Gross unloaded from the window. Shattered the glass. An answering blast of gunfire came from the bedroom.

Purvis threw open the door. He covered the body lying across the path with his revolver. Turned him over with his foot.

It wasn't Dillinger. Van Meter, either. And the bastard had too many fingers to be Hamilton. He rooted in the downed man's coat. No gun. Turned up a wallet. Driving license. Clarence Leo Coulter. He wheeled on Goodman as she joined him on the path, crying hysterically. Restrained the urge to slap her. "You stupid nigger bitch. You made us kill the wrong man."

Seven

They hit Chicago late the following afternoon. He dropped Billie off in the Loop and drove out to the West Side. Parked in front of an apartment block in the Valley. This was the place, according to Piquet. Best let them get a look at him, though, before he sounded the bell. The mouthpiece had called ahead, warned them he was coming, but no harm being careful. It would be a pisser if he'd managed to walk from a police ambush in St Paul, only to be plugged by his best pals back in Chi.

He rested his hand on his piece as the door opened a crack. The whole thing could be a set up. It might not be Van and Red in the apartment. The guys behind the peeling green woodwork could easily be cops or, knowing Piquet, Syndicate guns.

The hand holding the snub-nose behind the chain, though. There weren't too many coppers with half their fingers missing. Syndicate guns, either. He let his hand fall away from his shoulder rig as the snub-nose vanished. The door swung wide as Hamilton's grin.

"Johnny."

"Red." He stepped quickly inside the railroad apartment. Snicked the door close behind him. "You boys made it out of there okay?"

"Homer managed to lose the bulls. Tipped us all off. We managed to get out of there before the feds moved in."

Van Meter emerged from the bathroom. Tucked in his shirt. "Christ, though. When I walked up the stairs and saw those dicks outside the door at your place, I was like to shit."

"How'd you get out of there, anyway, Van?"

"Said some crap like 'is your name, Johnson?' Walked away when one of them said no. His buddy asked me where I was going. I said I was a soap salesman. Said I'd get my samples from the car and ducked into the stairwell when the bastard tried to follow me. I pulled on him and chased him into the yard. The guy came back at me with his own piece, though."

"I saw that through the window. Real Keystone Cops stuff." He straddled a chair. "What happened then?"

"I managed to dodge him. Jumped a garbage wagon. Gave the driver $20 for his cap and coat. Drove past the roadblocks at twenty miles an hour and got hold of the rest of the guys. Beat it out to this place"

"Tommy and the kid get out, too?"

Hamilton nodded. "The kid daren't show his face in town since the Touhy mob went down, though. He knows the Syndicate is out for his hide. He's jungled-up with Tommy in a tourist court near East Chicago."

"Might not be such a bad idea for the rest of us, Red."

"That's what the kid said. We're going to meet him out in the sticks. Lay up somewhere peaceful while we plan our next job." He took a deck of Old Golds from his pocket. Shook out a cigarette. "One of us didn't make it, though."

"I read the newspapers."

Hamilton tapped a cigarette on the back of the deck. "They never gave him a chance to surrender. Shot him down like a dog."

"The way it's going to be for all of us, they ever get on our tails."

Van Meter twisted his lower lip. "They ain't shooting me down like a mutt in no alleyway. Not while I got a gun in my hand, anyways."

Johnny shifted position. Rested his aching leg. "Yeah, well. It doesn't have to come to that. Does it? The rest of us all got out of there in one piece. Us three, the kid, Tommy."

"And Billie. She make it out okay with you, John?"

Johnny bobbed his head at Hamilton. "I dropped her downtown. Supposed to be taking her over to some joint on the North Side tonight. She's seeing her old roommate's beau. He's setting up a safe-house for us. I'm running her over there when I finish with you guys."

"You coming back afterwards, though?"

Johnny nodded. "We can dope out what we gonna do next over supper. Play a few hands of poker. Things go like they should tonight, the guy comes through with the safe-house, and I shouldn't be more'n a couple hours. " He bummed a smoke and gimped towards the door. "I'll pick up some chow on the way back. The newspapers. See what's shaking with Eddie Hoover and his boys.

Stick a Schlitz in the icebox for me, break out a fresh deck of cards

and I'll see you both around nine, nine-thirty, okay, fellas?"

Eight

Ancker Hospital, St Paul

Tuesday, April 3

Purvis paced by the dying man's bed. Chain-smoked. His nerves still hadn't recovered from the shooting outside the nigger's place. The thought of what the consequences would have been if they'd killed a respectable citizen were too awful to contemplate.

The kill had been good, though. They'd wrenched a hysterical woman from the bullet-shattered wreck of the Terraplane. Once she'd recovered enough to talk, she'd admitted to the identity of the wounded man, her husband, Eddie Green, the Dillinger mob's jug maker. It was a major coup for the agents involved. Mr Hoover had sent his congratulations.

'The kill.' Not a redundant description of what had happened. Green was still breathing, but it wouldn't be long now. A slug had cut through his hat brim to enter the back of his skull. Came to rest above his right eye. Infection had set in. Meningitis. There was no way the wounded yeggman would come back from that one. It was only a matter of time.

The man was delirious. Rambling. There were tantalizing scraps of information in what he said. Places. Names. Fred. George. Lucy. The family, though, gathered around the bed. His mother reading from the prayer book she'd brought. Attempting to drown out her son. Exhorting him to say his prayers. And the brother, more straightforward. "Don't tell them nothing, Eddie. Don't say a thing."

He'd had them barred from the ward. Harsh when their boy was dying, but necessary. They were interfering in a federal investigation.

Now, though. Now that they were gone. He hovered over the bed as Green began to mumble again.

"I've got the keys. He wants them."

He opened his notebook. Stubbed his cigarette. "Whose keys are those?"

"John's."

"John who?"

"John Dillinger."

Son-of-a-bitch. He scribbled down the conversation. Leaned further over the bed. "You know where I can find John, Eddie?"

No response. Too direct. He tried a different angle. "Who was that at the Lincoln Apartments, Eddie? Who fired the shots at the cops?"

"You sure are a nosy fella, Doc." Something unintelligible. "Gimme a shot so I can sleep."

"I will if you tell me who was at the apartment, Eddie."

"You know as well as I do."

"No, I don't know."

"Gimme a shot, for Christ sake, Doc."

"Who was it, Eddie? Was it John?"

"Yes."

"John who?"

"You know without asking me."

""No, I don't know. Who was it, Eddie?"

"Dillinger. Will you give me that shot now, Doc?"

Rorer joined Purvis at Green's bedside. "Nice work, Mel." He grinned savagely. "You son-of-a-bitch."

Purvis reluctantly shifted his attention from Green. Managed an insouciant smile. "No guts, no glory, Bill. You should know that. Old soldier like you." He indicated the figure on the bed. "The leads he spilled earlier. The addresses. They pan out?"

"One of them didn't exist. The other did. We kicked-in the door on a fifty-year old steamfitter eating his dinner. His wife. Five year old daughter." He poked the bedstead with his shoe. "The bastard's screwy. The bullet scrambled his brains. We can't expect any sense out a guy been shot in the head. Best leave him to his relatives, the little time he's left."

Purvis disagreed. He was convinced the lead they were after was here somewhere. Hidden inside the dying man's ramblings. The mention of Dillinger just now. If only he could press the right button. "Eddie," he said. "It's me again. The Doc. I got you that shot. I need to know where Johnny is first, though, before you go under. Tell him where you're staying, okay?"

Green mumbled something in reply.

199

"Where is he, Eddie? Where can I find Johnny?"

Green muttered something indistinct.

"What's that, Eddie? Where's he staying?"

"Bohemia," the dying man said. "He's staying in Bohemia, Doc."

FOUR

LITTLE BOHEMIA

In the twenty-odd years of the existence of this division, no one ever has shot at any of our agents and got away with it. We run them to earth... We are going to run down the entire gang – J. Edgar Hoover

One

Manitowish, Wisconsin

Friday, April 20

I don't smoke much and I drink very little. I guess my only bad habit is robbing banks – John Dillinger.

The Hudson powered along the oil and gravel surface of Route 51, heading into the lake country of northern Wisconsin

"How's the leg?" Hamilton asked, hands at ten to two on the wheel. "Beginning to mend, John?"

"It'll put a cramp in my tango for a couple days, but otherwise it's jake. Not much more than a scratch."

Hamilton formed an air pocket in his cheek. "You were lucky. The cops had you cold there. Things had been different and you coulda ended up the same way as the rest of the boys. Back in the slammer. On the way to the chair." He watched the pine woods stream by outside the windows, the logging trails still heavy with snow. "St Paul ain't safe anymore. Them two brewers crossed the mob out there, Hamm and Bremer. Got themselves yaffled. No

202

wonder the G are all over the place. A big news story like that draws Eddie Hoover's boys like flies to shit."

Van Meter grunted. "You can't fix the bastards, either. They won't take a pay-off. Money we gave the Dutchman don't count for dick when it comes to the feds." His forehead creased as they slowed at a junction. He unfolded a road map with a single scribbled inscription in the margin. "*Little Bohemia.* Sounds kinda familiar to me from some place."

Hamilton made a left. "That Moran joint on the North Side. This guy Wanatka ran it for the Irishman a couple years back. He got outta town along with the rest of Moran's crew after that Valentine's thing in the garage."

"The Bohunk know who we are?"

"Jimmy says no, but he's a right guy. Done this kind of work before, you know what I'm saying?" Hamilton steered the Hudson down a corridor of pines. Passed beneath a whitewashed concrete arch bearing the resort's name and halted in front of the main lodge, a two-storey log construction with white wooden facing on the upper floor and an overflow cabin front right of the porch. "So," he said, killing the engine. "What do you think, John?"

203

The lodge stood around five hundred yards from the highway behind a concealing screen of pine trees. The single road into the resort meant there was only one way out of the joint, which was a disadvantage, but equally there was only one way in, the back of the lodge lying almost flush with a kidney-shaped lake. They had to hold off the G, local cops, the place was a fortress. And the surrounding pines meant they could scatter if forced. Lose themselves in the woods. "And the guy's expecting us, you say?"

"You think I'd drag you all the way up here if he wasn't?" Nelson's head protruded from the Ford as it drew up behind them. He crumpled his face. "Christ, I hate the boondocks. Try and get a decent cream soda or a first run movie in a dump like this. Jesus, I ask you."

Carroll stretched as he exited the Ford behind Nelson. "City boy. He can't smell the stockyards and he gets lonesome for home."

"Buncha frigging Hoosiers. You'll be walking around barefoot next. Sleeping with the pigs."

Van Meter elbowed Johnny. "Didn't know he was bringing his wife with him," he muttered.

Nelson stepped to him. "You got something to say to me, Homer, say it to my goddamn face."

Carroll moved between them. "This ain't the time. Time or the place." He worked his head towards the lodge house. "Mine host, ain't it, Jimmy?"

Nelson throttled back as a beaming fireplug in work boots and corduroys, a shawl-necked sweater buttoned over a plaid shirt, bustled down the steps. "Emil?" He moved apart from the gang. Shoved out his mitt. "We're the boys the Dutchman said would be stopping over a few days."

"Pleasure to meet you, Jimmy," Wanatka said, pumping the kid's hand. "You planning on staying long?"

"Couple days at the most. Just enough to relax some. Brush off a little of that city dirt." He tossed his head towards the lodge. "Got any other guests?" he asked casually, giving the joint the once over.

"Just you and your boys at the moment, I'm afraid." Wanatka sank his hands in his pockets. "We're having a dollar a plate dinner tomorrow, though. Should be quite a crowd in from the lumber camps. The CCC camp down the road."

"I thought we was going to have the joint to ourselves this weekend."

"The place empties out by ten. You'll have it to yourselves after that. Sorry for the inconvenience, but what the hell. It's the only thing keeps the place going these days." He shrugged apologetically. "The Depression. What can I say?"

Nelson scratched his ear. "Yeah, it's tough all over." He motioned to where the others were unloading their baggage from the cars. "You got someone can give us a hand with our trunks?"

"Sure, Jimmy. No problem. I'll send the guys from the bar." He whistled-up a couple of youths from inside the lodge. "Help these gentleman with their luggage, will you, boys?"

The two nodded. Strained as they hauled the trunks up the steps. "What you guys got in here? Lead or something?"

Johnny gave them a shit-eating grin as he followed them inside. "We travel in hardware." He crossed the lobby. The interior consisted of a barroom cum dining area with a small dance floor, plus toilets and kitchen to the rear. There were antlers and stuffed trout in glass cases on the wall and a log fire crackling in the hearth. The place smelled pleasantly of pine resin, wood smoke and frying steaks. "Nice and cosy," he said to Wanatka. "Just like home. Think I'm gonna enjoy my stay here, you know what I'm saying?"

"Thanks …?"

"Johnny. My friends call me Johnny, Emil." He signed himself into the guest book as John Edgar. Loosed his muffler. "Okay if we freshen up now?"

"Sure, Johnny. Only room for three upstairs, though. Two of you'll have to take the cottage."

"That's fine. I'll take the upstairs with Red and Homer, here." Glanced at Carroll. "If that's okay with you, Tommy?"

"Sure thing, Johnny."

"Jimmy?"

"Why can't you take the cottage, you fuck?"

Carroll put a hand on his shoulder. "No sweat, Jimmy. At least we get some privacy, yeah?"

Johnny flashed his bridgework. "Attaboy, Tom." Turned the smile on Wanatka. "You can rustle us up a couple them steaks I smell, Emil?"

"Sure thing, Johnny. You guys wash up. I'll give you a call when they're ready."

They helped the barmen lug the trunks up the staircase. Tipped the pair a sawbuck apiece. Locked the door behind them. Checked the place out.

It was a good set up. The front window overlooked the parking lot and gave a view of the road between the pines. The back window, meanwhile, opened on a still un-melted snow bank in the shadow of the building, a narrow strip of beach separating the lodge from the lake.

They'd be able to see anything coming before they were spotted. Be out the back window before the cops came in the front. And if things didn't go as smoothly as planned… "You better take a sprayer," Johnny said to Van Meter, breaking one of the Crown Point Thompsons from his luggage. Attaching the shoulder stock. "I think we're safe out here in the boonies, but best take precautions. Just in case."

"I got one of the mini guns the runt brought back from that gunsmith out West. Easier to carry under my jacket if we moving around the place, you know?"

Johnny laid the Thompson across the bed. "The kid has his uses," he said, fitting the pie-tin clip to the machinegun. "I can't say as I'm happy working with the guy, but I'll give him that."

Hamilton began to assemble the second Thompson. Drew a cleaning rag through the barrel. "The runt's screwy. Way he throws lead around on the job. He's going to get us all killed, way he draws heat."

"You don't think we're hot enough as it is, Red?"

"Not just the bulls I'm thinking of. The little guy's not so popular with the Syndicate at the moment, I hear."

Hamilton had a point there. Nelson's membership of the Touhy mob, the Syndicate's last remaining rival, had put him on a death-list, according to rumour. Besides, the new guy running things back in Chicago. The Barber. Whereas the Big Fella always had a soft spot for yeggmen, let them hide-out as long as they kept their noses clean, the Barber was a different proposition. With

Touhy locked-down in Joliet, the new guy was busy mopping-up the surviving opponents of Syndicate rule. Cleaning house.

Some of the poor saps who went down were obsolete Capone aides, Diamond Lou Cowen and Frankie Pope, Jack White, but enough outlaws were receiving a dose of buckshot in their soft and tenders to make any self-respecting yeggman look over his shoulder once he crossed the city limits.

Verne Miller had been the first to go, turning up naked with a clothesline around his neck after that thing at the railroad station. Barker yegg Gus Winkler had been next, whacked as he walked out a liquor distributor's on the North Side just before Christmas. A hundred and eleven slugs, according to the newspapers. Not as elegant as the way they'd taken out Touhy, but a blunt instrument was just as effective as a stiletto when it came to cleaning the streets.

Handsome Jack Klutas, meanwhile, leader of the College Kidnappers, had gone down at New Year, machinegunned to death in an ambush. It had been a cop holding the gun rather than a Syndicate shooter, but with Tubbo Gilbert barking the show, the dick that railroaded Touhy for the mob, it came to the same thing. It was no coincidence they'd started referring to the Big Fella's successor as the Enforcer, rather than the Barber, in the last few months. "You think Nelson's a liability, then?"

Hamilton clipped the Thompson together. Ran the rag over the breech. "Bulls or Syndicate, it don't really matter. The little guy's going to get us killed one way or the other. That's if he don't try and gun us his self." He wagged a remaining finger at Van Meter. "Way you ride him, Homer. Can't say as I blame you, but Jesus Christ. Good job you and him are bunking separate the next few days, is all I can say."

"Ah, fuck him. I ain't scared of the runt."

Johnny wrapped the Thompson in a towel. He laid it on the top of his trunk, within reach of his bed. Secured his money belt. "You oughta be. The squirt's always on the lookout to use his piece. He don't need a reason, neither. The little shit enjoys it." He unloaded his Colt. Dry-snapped it at the wall. Replaced the clip. "I think it's time we cut the punk loose. You. Me. Red here. Tommy, if he wants in with us."

"Him and Jimmy were together before we come on the scene. You think he'll play ball?"

211

"Tommy's a good guy. He'll do the right thing when the time comes."

"And if Jimmy don't want to run solo?"

Johnny tightened the buckle on his shoulder rig. Secured his piece in the holster. "The runt tries to push us and we'll push back. Push back hard."

Two

Purvis sat over the newspapers that morning, enjoying a rare day off. Not that going into the Office would have achieved much, anyway. The Dillinger manhunt had stalled. Leads were none existent. The bastard seemed to have evaporated into thin air. They were no nearer to running him to earth than they'd ever been.

They'd spent the last few weeks up in Michigan thanks to Youngblood, Dillinger's partner on the prison break. The spook had gotten drunk. Started throwing his weight around a Port Huron grocery store. When Sheriff Van Antwerp showed with a brace of deputies, Youngblood had got the drop on them. Plugged all three before they could pull.

Unfortunately for Youngblood, the grocer's son had helped himself to one of their holstered pistols as the escapee backed out the door. Put two in his brisket at close range.

Youngblood expired four hours later, but not before laying a false trail for his jailhouse partner by claiming Dillinger was in town with him. Purvis had spent two weeks up to his jock in snow, beating the bush along the Canadian border on the off chance the jig had been telling the truth. He'd come up with dick as regards Mr Dillinger.

At least he'd nailed the son-of-a-bitch's girlfriend. That was something, he supposed. The break had come from an informant, one Larry Strong, a boyfriend of Frechette's old roommate. Or rather ex-boyfriend, which was why he'd gotten on the phone shortly after Purvis returned from St Paul and informed the Chicago Office that he was due to meet Dillinger's moll in a few hour's time. Something about finding her and Dillinger a place to stay once they ducked back into the city.

Purvis had arranged to meet Strong at his place on the North Side, the Tumble Inn, shortly after eight. He recognized the informant standing behind the bar as he swung in from the street.

He took a stool. Ordered a beer. It wasn't the best lead he could hope for, but his only other option had expired when Green passed over earlier that day. The dying mobster had admitted to a half-dozen bank robberies, both with the Dillinger mob and Ma Barker's boys. His wife had provided even more information after he died, giving hard intelligence not only on the two robbery crews, but on Green's relationship with Harry Sawyer and the rest of the Minneapolis-St Paul underworld.

The Greens' info filled-out the Bureau's picture of the Twin Cities crime scene, something the feds had lacked up until then. It was all solid stuff. Unfortunately, it put them no closer to nailing Dillinger. Or rather, it put Purvis no nearer to that elusive goal.

He had Green's scalp hanging from his belt, enough to keep the Director off his back and draw praise from his colleagues. It wasn't enough, though. Hoover wanted Dillinger on a slab and he wanted him now. Every day the asshole stayed at large, the lustre of Purvis' achievements dimmed a little more. It was only a few months since he'd put Touhy in the slammer, but the newspapers, like the Director, had a short memory. It was Dillinger or nothing for him. The note Mr Hoover had sent him at the start of the manhunt was folded in his wallet. Cracking along the creases. "Well, son, keep a stiff upper lip and get Dillinger for me and the world is yours."

The alternative was too unpleasant to imagine.

He eavesdropped on Strong as mine host chatted to the customers. Sipped his beer. The informant was drunk. Didn't seem to recognize him. A few minutes later, the guy hailed a newcomer as 'Professor' and asked for a tune on the piano. The Professor pointed out that the joint didn't actually have a piano. The Tumble Inn was that kind of place.

He tensed. There she was. A petite figure in a pink checked dress. A bow at the front. A dark-haired, dark-eyed little slut. Dark skin. Enough makeup to grow a crop. Some kind of half-blood Indian, according to the reports.

No Dillinger, however. The bastard hadn't shown.

Goddamn it. The trap was a washout.

Still. Frechette. She was some kind of prize, anyway. He offered her a stool as she approached the bar. She declined. Stood between him and Strong. Showed him her back. He strained to hear their conversation as they talked. Drew a blank. Waited to see if the main target would show after all.

Five minutes passed. Ten. No sign of Dillinger.

Screw it. He finished his beer. Walked outside.

"Is the back of the place covered?" he asked the agent out front, Thompson visible beneath his mackintosh.

The agent nodded. "She still in there?"

He thumbed the safety on his revolver. "Where the hell else would she be?" Looked up and down the street. A Terraplane parked a few yards away from the agent, the driver sitting relaxed in front. A couple of kids pitching pennies on the corner. Everything quiet. He signalled the back up team from across the way. "Come on. We're wasting time here. Let's take the tramp while we can."

They hustled inside. Lined the clientele up against the bar. Checked their faces. No Dillinger. Carroll. Van Meter. A glance at their fingers. No Hamilton.

They waltzed Frechette out to their car. As they did so, the Terraplane on the opposite side of the street took off. A horrible thought struck Purvis. He buttonholed the agent with the Thompson.

"You check out the guy in the Terraplane?"

The agent shook his head. "You never told me to," he said.

"I tell you to put on your pants in a morning? Lift the seat when you take a leak?" He turned his attention to Frechette. "You. How'd you get here tonight? Come by car?"

"Someone drove me."

"You're not going to tell me who it was, I suppose?"

Frechette began to laugh as the car vanished into the distance, an indistinct figure behind the wheel. "You already know who drove me here tonight. Don't you, copper?"

Three

Johnny and the boys washed up and went down to dinner. Garlic steak and home fries. Chocolate ice cream for dessert. They ordered a pitcher of beer for afterwards and Johnny produced a deck of cards from his pocket.

"You play, Emil?"

"Pinochle."

"How about poker?"

They grouped around the table as Johnny dealt. Seven card stud. They played three or four hands. The pot stood at $34. The last two in were Wanatka and Johnny. The Bohunk reached for the dough as the bidding ended.

"Wait a minute," Johnny said. "Whaddya got?"

Wanatka showed his hand: kings and sixes.

"Too bad, Emil."

He turned up his cards: kings and eights. His coat swung open as he raked the pot, the Bohunk goldfishing at the sight of the

Colt beneath his arm. "You staying in, Emil?" he asked, as Wanatka scraped back his chair.

"I lost enough for one night. Think I'll leave you guys to it. Hit the hay."

Johnny closed his jacket as the Bohunk left the table. "You sure this guy is right, Jimmy?"

"You trust the Dutchman?"

"As much as I trust anybody." He boxed the deck. Followed Wanatka into the kitchen. Nosed over his shoulder at the newspaper in his hands. "Catching up on the headlines, Emil?"

Wanatka laid the *Chicago Tribune* by the sink. "It's a good likeness, Johnny. It wasn't for the moustache, I'd have made you before now."

Johnny's reflection looked back at him from the row of saucepans hanging above the stove. He smoothed his moustache. Billie told him it made him look like Ronald Coleman. He thought it was more Gable himself. William Powell. "The henna was a mistake, though. Different colour from my eyebrows. Think I'll go for black next time, same as Red." He laid his arm across

220

Wanatka's shoulders. Let him feel the iron beneath his jacket. "I heard you'd done this kind of thing before, Emil. Put guys on ice."

"I let racket guys have a couple days out the city to relax. Go fishing. Hunt. That kind of thing. It's the only way I can keep this place open, way things are with the economy. Guys like you, though, Johnny. Front-page news. Jesus Christ, man."

"Afraid of us, Emil?"

"Should I be?"

"Hell, no. We're just like those other guys you mentioned. All we want is to eat and rest for the weekend. We'll pay you well and get out after that. There won't be no trouble here. I promise you that." He let Wanatka leave the kitchen. Go to his bed. He wondered if he could trust him. The guy didn't want trouble, especially with his family on site. And he needed the money, he'd said that himself.

The reward that had been on his head since Crown Point, though. The smaller bounties for Nelson and the others. No fear of losing your business to the Depression with ten grand or more on your hip. It looked like he'd have to keep a weather eye on the Bohunk. Clear out of the lodge after the weekend.

Pity. It would have suited him to stay here longer. The city was looking an increasingly dangerous place for a yegg to lay his head. The article below the fold on the front page of the *Tribune*: Barker gunman Shotgun Ziegler executed gangland-style as he walked out a bar in Cicero. Another independent cut down by the mob.

Four

Frechette had given them nothing. They'd grilled her for two days straight under the lights in the Banker's Building, but the hard-faced slut had kept it buttoned. She did, however, reveal to the reporters that waylaid her and her escorts in the lobby that Dillinger had actually been in the bar at the time of her arrest. Which, falsehood though it might be, had gone down swell with the old man back in Washington.

"I am becoming quite concerned over some of these developments in the Chicago district. We have had too many instances where surveillances have not been properly conducted and where persons under surveillance have been able to avoid the same. I cannot continue to tolerate actions of investigators that permit leads to remain uncovered, or at least improperly covered. It is imperative that you exercise the proper supervision over the handling of this case."

No more 'Dear Mel' from the guy with the bulldog jaw. His career was hanging by the proverbial thread and he knew it.

He'd shipped the half-breed back to St Paul's for trial. Got her off his hands. There was always the hope that Dillinger might try to break her out of custody, but the way the yellow bastard had left his buddies to burn down in Lima, that seemed unlikely. The newspapers might like to portray these bank robbing sons of bitches as latter day knight errants, but he knew them for what they really were: anti-social parasites on the body of society, with no thought of anything but their own survival. The sooner the Barkers and Floyds and yes, the Dillingers of the day were tracked down and exterminated, the better.

He closed the newspaper as President emerged from the hallway. "Yes?"

"Telephone, Mr Purvis, suh. U.S. Marshall's office, Chicago."

Purvis took the call. Another Dillinger sighting, this one in Wisconsin.

He dialled the number he was given. Found himself talking to one Henry Voss.

"The man you're looking for is up here," Voss said.

"You mean Dillinger?"

"Could be."

He readied his notebook and pen. How many sightings did this make? Fifty? A hundred? What was it about a big case in the newspapers brought the kooks out the woodwork? "You want to give me the details, Mr Voss?"

"How'd you mean?"

"Well you could tell me where you saw Dillinger for a start."

"Oh, right. Well, he's holed-up at my sister-in-law's hunting lodge just outside Manitowish. Up on Star Lake."

"How do you spell Manitowish?" He 'uh – huh' 'd as Voss spelled out the name for him. "And this hunting lodge he's holed-up at. You got a name for the place, Mr Voss?"

The nib of his pen tore the paper as Voss answered.

"Sure I have. Little Bohemia."

Five

Saturday had been a lazy day for Johnny and the rest of the guys. They'd got up late. Dawdled over breakfast and the newspapers. Gone out in the woods back of the lodge to practice their marksmanship with a .22 rifle, potting at cans on a snow bank.

Johnny had asked Wanatka to join them, figuring to put a warning shot across the Bohunk's bows. Show them what they could do with a shooting iron. It might have worked if any of them could have actually hit the damn targets. Wanatka and Van Meter were the only ones who managed a bull's eye. Van was flushed enough with success that he trotted out one of the Thompsons and shot up the surrounding snow banks, knocking the needles out of the pine trees.

So much for playing it low-key.

Wanatka took a turn with the Thompson as well, then returned to the gravel parking area outside the lodge. Johnny and Nelson joined him in playing catch with his eight year old until the boy quit, complaining that Nelson threw too hard and stung his hands. Lunch followed, then Wanatka announced that he was taking the boy to his cousin's birthday party.

"Here," Johnny said, crooking a finger at the kid. "A quarter. Buy yourself an ice, okay, son?"

The boy looked at his father. Wanatka gave him the okay.

"You got a way with kids, Johnny."

"I'd like one myself someday. I ever manage to get out the life, that is." He rose from his chair at the dining table as Wanatka hunted up his car keys. "No need for that, Emil. Homer will be happy to run you into town. Won't you, Homer?"

Homer left off reading the funnies. He'd been briefed about Emil and the newspaper photograph along with the others. "Sure thing, Johnny. I'm sick of sitting around here as it is."

"It's okay, fellas. I don't want to put you to no trouble."

Johnny barred his passage. "No. I insist." He locked eyes with him. "Okay, Emil?"

Wanatka wilted. "Whatever you say, Johnny."

Johnny tousled the kid's hair. "Enjoy yourself, son."

The kid turned the quarter between his fingers. "Sure thing, Johnny." Preceded his father and Van Meter out the door.

Hamilton's brow creased as Johnny returned to his newspaper and searched the front page. "I don't like this, John. Too much coming and going for my liking. And that guy at the bar" - he indicated a weather-beaten figure enjoying a cigarette as he chatted with Mrs Wanatka – "he's got way too much to say to the Bohunk's old lady, far as I'm concerned."

Johnny turned to the sports pages. No headlines today. He couldn't say he wasn't disappointed. Chance to bone up on the Cubs. "I heard her say it was her brother-in-law. The local fishing guide. Guy gets on with his relatives, is all. You can't knock him for that." He finished with the newspaper. Handed it to Tommy. "We're getting out of here tomorrow, though. That's for sure. Wanatka's got that dollar a plate dinner tonight. That's way too many people for my liking. Place is more like Grand Central Station than a hidey-hole-in the woods."

Nelson lowered the copy of *Field and Stream* he was reading: an article on the new over and under shotgun from Browning. "Who the hell says we're leaving tomorrow? This is my gang, Dillinger, and don't you forget it."

Johnny unwrapped a stick of gum. Forked it into his mouth. "Well, I'm leaving tomorrow and I already talked it over with Van. And I presume Red's gonna throw in with me and Homer?"

Hamilton nodded. "You ain't got to ask, John." He turned to Carroll. "What about you, Tommy? You coming with us?"

Carroll glanced between Johnny and Nelson. "Getting pretty hot, Jimmy. The guys probably got a point, you know?"

Nelson stiffened. "So it's like that, is it?" He threw down his magazine. Stalked towards the door. "I'm gonna work on the cars. Make sure they're running okay. Somebody in this string's gotta do some work, rather than sit on their ass all day."

The others exchanged looks as the squirt left. So much for the problem of breaking with Nelson. Challenging the little guy's leadership of the gang. It looked like the mob had a new ramrod now. Johnny had toppled the punk without so much as raising his voice.

Six

Purvis fought the urge to vomit as he landed in Rhinelander, Wisconsin, after a three-hour flight. He considered grounds for arresting the pilot. The maniac had navigated from Chicago using a road map, then spun the plane on landing. How the asshole had managed to avoid piling them into the conifers hemming the airstrip, Christ alone knew. Taking on the Dillinger mob would be an anticlimax after that.

Still. He could handle airsickness. This was a chance to make up for missing Dillinger at the Tumble Inn. A chance for redemption. He'd already dialled Washington and relayed the good news to Mr Hoover. Got the okay to round up every stray agent and head for Wisconsin in reply.

The Director had ordered him to rendezvous at Rhinelander with Deputy Director Hugh Clegg, newly arrived to oversee the Twin Cities end of the case and the second operative Purvis had contacted after Hoover. Clegg had dispatched St Paul SAC Werner Hanni and a carload of agents overland, while arranging for Rorer, himself and three other agents to fly ahead. He'd suggested Purvis do the same. The Chicago SAC had immediately chartered a plane and set about collaring agents to fill it.

It had been chaos on the nineteenth floor as the word went out. Agents absent for the weekend had tumbled out of bed and hit the Banker's Building half-dressed in response to the summons, tyres smoking as they skidded to a halt outside. Purvis himself arrived knotting his tie, shirt unbuttoned as he ordered his men to break out every weapon available. The eleven man posse that drew up at the Municipal Airport a bare sixty minutes later were carrying the Chicago Office's entire complement of automatic weaponry. If they really had cornered the bastard, he'd have a hell of job slipping away this time.

Purvis left his men to unpack their armoury as he disembarked from the plane. He walked stiff-legged to the edge of the runway where Clegg and Rorer had gathered at the head of a trio of agents. Clegg, an officious pudge of a man, briar pipe gripped between his teeth, was bent over a notebook with some hayseed in a mackinaw and hunting cap. The latter was sketching a diagram with the Deputy Director's fountain pen.

"There's only one way in," the hayseed said. "Lake at the back of the place. Long as you stop them getting into the woods either side, you should have them boys trapped like flies in a bottle."

Clegg gave Purvis a ferocious grin as he joined them. "Hear that, Purvis? Dillinger and his whole mob bottled-up in the lodge house. I'd like to see the arrogant bastard thumb his nose to us this time, eh, Voss?"

"I wouldn't be too cocksure, Mr Clegg, sir. Them boys are packing some heat, according to Nan. They won't go easy, if what I seen in the newsreels is anything to go by."

"They've only been up against local police officers until now, Voss. Wait until they try their luck with federal agents. Right, Purvis?"

Purvis bobbled his head. The smell from Clegg's briar did nothing for his weakened stomach. What was the guy smoking? It smelled more like hot tar than tobacco, for Christ sake. "Are you sure it's them, Mr Clegg?"

Clegg tapped out his pipe on the heel of his shoe. Produced a buckskin pouch from his vest pocket. "Voss was only in there a few minutes, but he's positively identified Carroll from the mug shots I brought. And if Carroll's there, it's a racing certainty that the rest of the crew are the men identified from the Sioux Falls and Mason City jobs." He began to pack his pipe. "We've got to move fast, though. The gang are leaving tomorrow morning. The family is going to hide in the cellar before daybreak, according to Voss. We can take them then. While they're still in their beds."

"No chance of hitting the wrong people," Purvis said, remembering his first reaction to the Green killing.

Clegg struck a kitchen match. "Precisely." Held it over the bowl of his pipe. "First things first, though. We have to actually get to the lodge before we can initiate the arrests."

Voss pointed towards the township beyond the airport. "There's a Ford dealership in town. I'll run you over in the truck. Business being what it is these days, I'm sure the guy will hire you a couple cars."

The manager was unenthusiastic, however. "If you're out to bust moonshiners, you can forget it. Word gets out I'm working with the revenuers and half my business dries up."

Clegg bit down on his pipe stem. "I'm not about to divulge our business to a member of the public, but I can assure you that we're not after moonshiners." He puffed a noxious cloud into the clear country air. "Although I would like to remind you that it's your duty as a citizen to report any criminal activity you are aware of to the law."

"Yeah, right."

Clegg began to purple. "Are you going to rent me those cars or not?"

The dealer tweaked his earlobe. "How many you want?"

"How many have you got?"

The dealer swept his hand over the lot. "I can let you have those five there at the front. They come back damaged, though, and you're paying for the repairs, federal agents or not."

They dickered over the price a moment. Shook. Loaded up the cars. It was fifty miles from Rhinelander to Little Bohemia over unmade roads. Getting dark. The convoy would shed two vehicles along the way, victims of bad light and poor road conditions, the agents inside forced to complete the journey down Route 51 clinging to the running boards of the remaining Fords.

They made the trip successfully, however, rolling into Voss' place, Birchwood Lodge, a little after nine, the cars parking-up a bare mile from Little Bohemia. Time was running out, though. Wanatka's wife Nan, Voss' sister-in-law, had stolen out the lakeside lodge a half hour earlier with bad news for the FBI men. The mobsters were leaving early. From what they were saying, they wanted to be on the road as soon as possible. There was no time to plan or finesse the situation. The agents would have to go in immediately. Go in now and go in hard.

This wouldn't be like the arrest of Frechette. The Green killing. There were five of them this time, all armed. And the feds would have to actively bust into the place, rather than let the suspects come to them as they had before.

It was possible they might scoop the bastards as they made their departure in the morning, but that was unlikely. Odds on they were looking at a gunfight this time. And one thing the college boys weren't was experienced gunfighters. They'd never attempted a raid of this scale before. Never trained for a mass shootout. They all knew how things might end tonight if they bungled the operation and allowed the outlaws to return fire.

Kansas City. That was the event that was on all their minds as they charged their weapons. Fastened steel vests beneath overcoats and extinguished cigarettes.

The Massacre was the event that had kick-started the whole War on Crime, thrusting the Bureau to the forefront of the federal effort against interstate criminals. It had meant extra powers for the Bureau. New anti-crime measures passed through Congress. Three hundred fresh agents swelling the rolls.

If it hadn't been for Kansas City, they'd still be mere investigators, reliant on local cops for making the actual arrests. They'd still go into criminal situations armed with nothing but fountain pens and forms in triplicate. The Massacre had given them both the weaponry and the will power to go after the bad guys. As the Director stated, "no time and money will be spared towards bringing about the apprehension of the individuals responsible for this cowardly and despicable act… *They must be exterminated and must be exterminated by us, and to this end we are dedicating ourselves."*

The Kansas City Massacre had seen the birth of the Bureau as a national law enforcement agency. It had rescued it from the obscurity of the bureaucratic backwaters that had spawned it. The price, however, had been a terrible one: three agents and a trio of local cops cut down by machinegun fire in the parking lot of Kansas City railroad station on a warm summer's morning, barely a year before.

Two agents, Lackey and Smith, had accompanied local police chief Otto Reed in arresting escaped St Paul yegg Frank 'Jelly' Nash in the resort town of Hot Springs, Arkansas. They had cuffed him and loaded him onto an overnight train for Kansas City, from where he would be shipped back to Leavenworth to complete his thirty-year sentence for bank robbery. Two locally based agents, Caffrey and Vetterli, would be waiting on the platform for them, accompanied by a pair of city cops, Hermanson and Groom, with an armour-plated car to effect the transfer.

Something went wrong, though. A reporter nosed out the story in Hot Springs and flashed it across the wires. By the time the train steamed into Kansas City, the underworld knew they were coming. One member of the local criminal fraternity, Nash's best friend, Verne Miller, a Teutonic-looking former sheriff turned hitman and bank robber, had decided to act on the information and spring his pal from custody.

Things became hazy at that point. Miller had been positively identified as the leader of the rescue team, while a single fingerprint on a liquor bottle had linked Pretty Boy Floyd's sidekick, Adam Richetti, to the events that ensued. The exact composition of the underworld rescue squad was unknown, however, as was the reasoning behind their forthcoming actions. What wasn't in doubt, however, was what happened next.

As the Hot Springs officers made the handover of the prisoner and piled him into the armoured car, someone shouted.

"Up! Up! Get your hands up!"

The lawmen froze. A second voice called out.

"Let them have it."

Twenty seconds later, it was all over. Agent Caffrey was dead, as was Police Chief Reed and the two Kansas City cops.

Agents Vetterli and Lackey were wounded, the latter seriously. Only Smith escaped unscathed. Nash himself, the subject of the rescue attempt, lay dead in the front seat of the car, head blown apart by a shotgun blast, the balding yeggman's toupee hanging from the dashboard like a scalp.

Purvis had seen shots of the crime scene. The bullet holes puncturing the supposed armour plating of the car. Shattered windscreens. Blood pooled on the asphalt. Evidence of how easily four men could be transformed into cold meat in just a few seconds.

He fidgeted with his pistol. Practiced drawing it smoothly from the holster as they loaded back into the cars and took off for Little Bohemia. His nausea returned as they bumped along the unmade roads to the resort, passing the Koerner house, the last isolated cabin before the lodge. He wondered how much his upset stomach was down to the uneven highway and how much down to nerves as he prepared for the showdown to come.

Seven

There were seventy, seventy-five people at the dinner that night, blue-collar guys from the conservation camp and local lumberjacks. One of the latter had nailed Red at the bar and offered him a drink, threatening to pour it down his goddamn throat when Hamilton had refused. Hamilton had mugged at the others, "this guy is pretty tough. I better have a small beer," and the moment had passed, the rest of the night proceeding without incident.

The place emptied out as predicted by ten. Wanatka bid the last three customers good night, a couple of the conservation workers plus a mechanic from the village, leaving the boys to their nightly poker game. "Listen to those dogs," he said, as his two collies began to bark. "Wonder what's set them off now?"

Johnny never looked up from his hand. The dogs had put him on edge the first night there, but he'd quickly realized they'd bark at their own shadows when the mood took them. "Probably a jack rabbit. A skunk. You know how they are." He fanned his cards. "Anybody seen the runt?"

Carroll squirmed. "He's holed-up in the cabin with a gun magazine. That thing this afternoon." He folded his hand. "I better go see he's okay. If that's all right with you fellas."

Van Meter snorted. "Fuck him. We're better off without him."

"We was partners before you guys showed, me and him. I feel like I owe the guy something."

Johnny rocked back on his chair as he selected a card. "See what's griping those dogs while you're out there. They're going crazy tonight, for some reason."

And then a burst of machinegunfire came from outside the lodge. He slammed the four legs of the chair flat on the floor. "Jesus Christ." Scattered his hand on the table as he un-holstered his Colt. "Come on. Up the stairs. We need the Thompsons if we're gonna get out of here."

Eight

It was fully dark when the agents turned into the driveway to the lodge. There was no moon. The only light came from a single bulb hanging over the front porch of the lodge house. The cars parked in front of the place indicated the gangsters were still inside. It struck Purvis then that they might, just might, be able to carry out the raid successfully.

He ordered his driver to halt the car inside the cover of the trees. Helped himself to a Thompson from the arsenal in the trunk. Joined Clegg and Rorer as they powwowed by the Deputy Director's car.

"So how do you want to do this, gentlemen? Throw a cordon around the place, then straight in through the front?"

Rorer turned up his collar against the cold. Blew in his hands. "I say we go with Voss. Let the staff hide in the cellar and pick them off as they come out to the cars. Less chance of civilian casualties that way."

Purvis turned to the Deputy Director. "Mr Clegg?"

Clegg sucked on the cold stem of his pipe. He was an administrator rather than a field agent. A bureaucrat. The man had never made an arrest in his life. "I'd rather get this over with as soon as possible. Besides, they get outside the building and we may well lose them in the dark."

Rorer shrugged. "You may have a point, sir. Just - "

And then the dogs began to bark. A group of men spilled from the doorway of the lodge. Headed for a Chevrolet Coupe.

The agents reacted fast, fanning out into the woods to the left and right of the place to cut off any escape. Clegg and Purvis, accompanied by agent Baum, converged on the Chevrolet as the lights came on. Music leaked from the cab, Satchmo blowing *Potato Head Blues*.

They presented their weapons as the car reversed. U-turned. Made straight towards them.

"Police. Halt. Federal agents."

Two men appeared on the porch and began to shout and wave their arms. Their voices were drowned by the sound of the car engine, the music, the yelling of the agents.

"Stop the car. Stop the car or we shoot."

The Chevrolet surged onward. Purvis stood his ground. Opened fire.

The Thompson kicked against his shoulder. Jammed.

Son-of-a-bitch.

He tossed the machinegun and yanked at his pistol. It tangled in the lining of his coat. There was a loud rip as it tore loose. And then he was firing, the single cracks of the .38 melding with the hammer of the other Thompsons as Clegg and Baum pummelled the car.

Purvis ran forward as the Chevrolet ground to a halt. He skipped back as pistol shots kicked up gravel at his feet. Threw a round at the shadow exiting the cottage to the right as it vanished into the pines.

He refocused on the car in front of him as someone broke from the passenger seat and made headlong for the trees. Heard a 'halt' from the agents beyond the tree line. The crash of a shotgun.

Got the bastard.

More shots came from the opposite side of the lodge as Rorer sealed the rear. He tensed as the car door opened. Disgorged a wounded figure into the parking lot. "Identify yourself," he said, levelling on him with the .38.

"John," said the man on the ground, slumping onto the gravel. "My name's John."

Johnny and the boys sprinted up the staircase. Snatched at their cases. Carroll threw up the window. "Cover me." He hung a leg over the sill.

"Police. Stop."

Johnny loosed a burst over Carroll's shoulder. A shotgun boomed in return. Twice more.

Carroll pulled his pistol. Discharged the clip at the unseen copper. "Fuck it. I'm gone." He leapt into the snowdrift beneath the window.

Johnny gave another burst from the Thompson. "You next, Red?"

Hamilton nodded. Followed Carroll out the window. He beckoned to Johnny. Johnny emptied the Thompson and jumped. Van Meter landed beside him.

"What now, Johnny?"

"The beach."

They clattered down the wooden staircase leading to the lakeshore. Splashed through the shallows towards the woods. Halted inside the tree line. No coppers. There was gunfire from the lodge, though. Johnny headed them towards the road.

"We passed another lodge on the way up the road on Friday. It's sure to have a car. Get our hands on that and we can still make it out of here in one piece."

Shots continued to ring out in the darkness. Shouts. Purvis ordered an agent to bring a car up and use the headlights to illuminate the scene.

"I can't" the agent said. "McLawhon's got the keys."

"Well, get them off McLawhon, then."

"McLawhon's in the trees."

"So get in the trees and find him, asshole."

They finally managed to bring up the car. Lit the scene. What was immediately apparent was that the wounded man, elderly, heavyset, wasn't Dillinger. Purvis beckoned with his pistol.

"Federal agents. Come forward and identify yourself."

The man rose to his feet, then lurched backwards and pitched onto his rump. He extracted a flask from his pocket and drank deeply, then replaced the flask and, ignoring the commands to halt, tottered back into the lodge.

Rorer materialised from the trees. "They opened fire on us from the rear windows. We fired back. It was all quiet after that. Reckon they must still be inside." He took in the wreckage of the Chevrolet. The figure buckled across the steering wheel. "You got them, then?"

Clegg tucked his Thompson beneath his arm. Champed at his briar. "We got somebody, anyway." He aimed the pipe stem at Rorer. "Want to check him out, Bill?"

Rorer crawled cautiously towards the Chevrolet. He covered the man behind the wheel with his pistol as he opened the door. Held a hand to his neck. "Dead," he said, his expression flat.

They clustered around the car. Rorer switched off the engine. Retrieved the man's wallet and extracted his driving license. It was then that the three FBI agents learned that the man they'd just killed was a thirty-five year old conservation worker at the nearby CCC camp named Eugene Boisneau.

Nine

Johnny and the boys emerged at the edge of the highway. Kept to the shadows until they hit the neighbouring lodge. Hamilton sounded the bell.

"Any chance of a glass of water?" he asked the startled geriatric that answered the knock, before shouldering past him. Ripping the phone from the wall.

"You wouldn't be Dillinger, would you?" asked the householder.

Johnny led the others into the room. "You couldn't have guessed better." He noted the terrified expression on the old man's face. "Don't worry, pops. All we need is a car. Someone to guide us. I wouldn't harm a hair on your head."

The old man indicated an elderly woman lying on the couch. "I can't come with you. My wife's sick. Down with the flu."

Johnny draped a blanket over her. "There you go, mother." Placed a hand on the old man's shoulder. "The car."

"A Model-T. It's up on blocks."

Johnny checked it out with Van. It was just as the old guy said. There was a Model-A truck in the garage, though. Keys on the sun visor. "We'll try this." The engine growled. Refused to spark. He spotted a green coupe parked by one of the cabins as he re-entered to the house. "Whose is the coupe?"

"My carpenter. Bob Johnson."

"That his cabin?" He crossed the yard and rapped on the cabin door. Flourished his pistol as the occupant appeared in the doorway in his carpet slippers. "Sorry, Bob. This is an emergency. We need to borrow your ride."

Other than the wounded 'John', who could still be seen staggering inside the lodge, the place looked deserted. It couldn't be, though. The proprietor and his family, his staff, were still in there. Not to mention Dillinger, Carroll et al. The men they'd come for. The men that were going to pay for what had just happened outside the lodge house.

The agents waited. They'd shot an innocent man. Killed him in cold blood. The only way they could compensate for their error, balance the books, was by killing or capturing the mobsters trapped inside.

"I say we go in now," Rorer said. "Take them while they're still off balance. The longer we wait, the longer they have to organize themselves. Put together a defence. I say we take them now."

Purvis set his teeth. "And kill how many other innocent bystanders in the process? Not to mention losing any of our own guys." He held up his hand as Rorer made to speak. "This isn't the Argonne, Rorer. You're not going over the top now, you know. We're law officers not doughboys. I say we wait."

Clegg fussed with his pipe. The smell of hot tar filled the air as he coaxed it into life with a kitchen match. "I agree with Purvis," he said, releasing a toxic cloud into the trees. "The mob inside isn't going anyplace. Hanni and the men in the car should be carrying tear gas. Extra ammunition. We wait until they arrive and go in then. Smoke the suspects out in daylight when we can see them. Make sure we get the right guys this time when we open up on the bastards." He puffed on the briar as a new set of headlights swung into the driveway. "What the -?"

There was the sound of hammers locking as the vehicle approached them. An ambulance. The agents put up their guns.

"Where the hell did you come from?" Rorer asked, as a man with a doctor's bag debouched from the back of the ambulance.

"The CCC camp down the road. One of our workers rang from inside the lodge. Said he'd been shot."

'One of their workers.' Purvis cringed. "He give a name?" he asked.

"John. John Morris."

The guy from the car. This was getting worse by the minute.

The doctor stopped in front of the Chevrolet. "My God. What happened here?"

Clegg removed his pipe from his mouth. "We've a dangerous group of suspects trapped in the lodge." He looked into the middle-distance, avoiding the doctor's gaze. "The men in the car. They should have stopped when we challenged them."

"You mean you shot these guys? The cops?"

"We aren't cops. We're federal agents." He dropped his pipe as a figure appeared from the tree line. Snatched up his Thompson. "You there. Halt or I fire."

The man halted. Thrust his hands in the air. "Don't shoot me again. I'm already hit."

"Come forward and identify yourself."

The man limped into the headlights. He was bleeding from a shoulder wound. There were glass cuts to his face. "Hoffman. John Hoffman."

Another John. Purvis tried to place the name from his intelligence files. "He on our list of suspects?" he asked Rorer.

The doctor looked at him in disgust. "I doubt it. He runs a gas station in Manitowish." He nodded to Hoffman. "Come on, Hoffman. We better get Morris. Tell him it's okay to come out."

Clegg retrieved his pipe from the gravel. Brandished it at the doctor's back. "You'll do no such thing. This is a federal crime scene. I give the orders here."

The doctor ignored him. Joined Hoffman in calling the wounded man outside. They supported him down the steps as he

253

stumbled from the building. Behind him came three other men, their hands held high.

Purvis steadied his pistol. Dillinger and crew? Carroll? Van Meter?

He lowered his piece. Two of them wore aprons over their shirts and trousers. The other was dressed like a lumberjack. Looked about fifty years old. Whoever they were, they weren't gangsters. "Identify your selves," he said, as they approached the car.

The older guy dropped his hands. "I'm Emil Wanatka. I own the place. These are my barmen."

"Do you have any identification on you?"

"Do I look like Dillinger?"

"Christ sake," the doctor said. "I can vouch for him. It's Emil, all right?"

Wanatka balled his fists as he faced Purvis. "You bastards. Why did you kill our friends?"

"We shouted a warning. They should have stopped the car."

Hoffman supported himself against the bullet-torn Chevy. He pressed a handkerchief to his arm. "It was dark. We had the radio on. We didn't know you were there until the bullets started hitting us."

Wanatka opened and closed his hands. "We shouted when you opened fire. You ignored us, though. Kept firing."

"We never heard you. The gunfire. Never heard a thing."

The doctor intervened. "We can leave the post mortem until later. There are injured men here." He turned to Hoffman. "Can you walk, John?"

"Sure."

"Okay. Get in the ambulance." He motioned to two agents standing awkwardly to one side. "You two. Help Morris into the ambulance."

The two looked to Purvis. He nodded. Held a roll call of the men. Got them to call out their name and location. The last thing they needed was an agent missing. Down with gunshot wounds. "Where's Baum?" he asked, as the count came up short.

An agent directed him to one of the Fords parked in the trees. Baum sat in the rear of the car, cradling his head. He looked up as Purvis opened the door.

"He's dead. Isn't he?"

"The guy in the car? Yes, he's dead."

Baum grunted as if he'd been punched. "I killed him. I killed an innocent man."

"I was firing too. Mr Clegg. No one knows who fired the fatal bullet, Baum. It could have been any one of us."

"That doesn't help me. I know what I've done. " He pushed aside the Thompson lying across his knees. "It's over for me, Mr Purvis. All over. I can never shoot that gun again."

Purvis stood a moment. "Well." He eased the door close behind him. Left Baum to his grief and rejoined the others as the ambulance left. Tried to forget about the agent in the car. "What now?" he said to Clegg, as the latter tinkered with his pipe.

"Nothing changes. We wait. The gas should be arriving soon. It gets here by sunup and we go in then."

Rorer seconded him. "We ought to send someone down to Birchwood, though. Get them to leave a message for Hanni at Rhinelander. Tell him the situation. The best way to get here. And tell him to hurry."

Clegg agreed. He detailed an agent to take one of the cars and drive to the second lodge. "And take Baum with you," Purvis said, recognizing Agent Newman, a Mormon lay preacher. "Have a talk with him. See if you can straighten him out over the shooting here. A guy like you can do it if anyone can."

Another car showed in the driveway. This time they recognized the driver. Henry Voss. He picked up the shirt-sleeved Wanatka and his two barmen and drove them to the Koerner house to borrow coats. With the scene cleared of bystanders, the agents settled down and waited. It was just a matter of time.

The minutes ticked slowly by. The agents stamped their feet. Took turns in the cars to keep warm. It was only two hours since they'd first turned into the driveway leading to the lodge. Already it seemed like a lifetime.

Purvis started as someone burst from the tree line. Fumbled his pistol. "Hold it right there. Put your hands up."

The man attempted to raise his hands. Gasped for breath. "They're dead," he managed, eventually. "Down at Koerner's. All your men are dead."

The guy from the lodge. He swopped his pistol for notebook and pen. Time to bring some order to things. Follow procedure for once. "Your name, please."

"What?"

"Your name and address, please."

Wanatka stared at him. "Are you serious?"

"Name and address, please. I don't want to have to ask you again."

"Emil Wanatka. Little Bohemia Lodge, Manitowish, Wisconsin."

"Could you spell Manitowish for me, please?"

"M – a – t... no, M – a - n..."

"You can't spell the name of your own town?"

Wanatka exploded. "Who the hell are you after here? Me or Dillinger? Your men are dead and you act like you're giving me a traffic ticket. What the hell's wrong with you guys?"

Rorer stepped into the conversation. "Perhaps we better check this out, Purvis. The guy's obviously hysterical, but you never know."

Purvis grunted. Pocketed his notebook. He summoned the nearest two agents. "You two. Get this man to show you the way to the Koerner house. Check out his story." He tapped his fountain pen against his chin. The man was hysterical, of course. Rorer had been right there. Still. Something must have happened down the road. Shots exchanged, at any rate. Which meant that at least one of the outlaws had escaped from the house. "You're sure you drove them back when they tried to escape from the window, Rorer?"

"My men had the woods secured. They'd have run into us in the dark if they'd made it out the window. They've got to be inside."

Which left the figure that fled the cottage at the start of it all. They'd never apprehended the guy. And the fact he'd opened fire marked him as an actual suspect rather than another poor sap wandering into an ambush after an evening at the local bar.

He capped his fountain pen. The guy from the cottage. It had to be him.

It was only later, after Hanni arrived with the tear gas, that he realized just how right he'd been about the guy from the cottage. He couldn't have guessed at the carnage the fugitive had left in his wake, though. The damage done. It was just Baum and Newman's bad luck that they'd crossed his path as he headed for Chicago. Nelson had made it into the woods with a Colt machine-pistol in his hand and he wasn't stopping for anybody.

Ten

Johnny and the boys stuck to the cat roads as they sped south in the stolen coupe. They freed the carpenter at a country crossroads. Dodged the posses that were beating the bush for them. The roadblocks. Headed for St Paul.

There were three of them in the car, Johnny, Hamilton and Van Meter. Carroll had become separated from them somewhere in the woods. As for Nelson, there was no sign of him. It could only have been the runt that the bulls had opened up on at Little Bohemia. They were free of him, anyway. With any luck, the cops had punched him full of holes in front of the lodge house. Done them all a favour.

"I figure the Dutchman's our best bet. The guy can put us on ice for a couple days. Get us a clean car. After that, I figure we best head elsewhere. St Paul ain't safe anymore. Dutch can keep the local heat off our backs, but this federal shit is something else."

Hamilton watched the white line un-spool from the hood as they approached the Mississippi, the lights of the Twin Cities beckoning them onward. "And where you thinking of going, John?

Ain't no place safe from the federals. Those assholes can follow us anywhere."

"We hole-up back in Chicago. Hide in the crowd. Then we see about getting ourselves new faces. Getting back on our feet. One good score is all it takes and we can start making plans. Get ourselves a future."

"Wise up, Johnny. We ain't got no future. Not now they got the G involved. The bastards are everywhere. No hole to hide in with the government on our back. No place where the fix is in. We're one step ahead of them now, but there's a whole army of the fucks and they keep on coming. One day we're going to slip up and that's it, we're gone. There's too many of them. The cocksuckers are going to bury us all." He pressed his hand to his stomach. "They already got Eddie. The runt. Those guys down in Lima. We don't come up with something good and we going to be joining them soon, I swear to God."

Van Meter burned a Chesterfield. Flipped the match from the window. "We got to get out the country. That's the way I see it. Only way we going to avoid the feds is go where they can't touch us." He blew a smoke ring. Broke it with the cigarette. "Head down south. That's what I aim to do once we hit it big. The Caribbean. Brazil. A guy could live like a king down there, if he took off a good score. And plenty of those brown skin girls know how to treat an American with a suitcase full of dollars, eh, Johnny?"

"I already got me a girl, Homer. Sounds pretty good, though, way you put it." South America. Why not? It sounded the best bet all round. Sun, surf, sand. Somewhere to relax and enjoy life without the bulls breathing down your neck at every turn.

He pictured himself in a white suit and matching skimmer, Billie beside him in a sundress and sandals. Like Fred and Ginger in *Flying down to Rio*. If Piquet could put the fix in, spring her from the joint -

"Up ahead, Johnny. The bridge."

There. Barring the approach road. Minnesota State Troopers. He decelerated as they waved him down. Loosened his piece in his holster. "Don't shoot unless you have to. I think I can make it past them." He slowed the Ford to a crawl. Waited until the Troopers had almost reached the door.

Now.

The Troopers scattered as he floored it. Punched the coupe through the gap between the patrol car and the railing of the bridge. He flattened himself over the wheel as the bulls opened fire. Kept the pedal to the metal as Van Meter knocked out the back window, hosing down the roadway behind them with his machine-pistol as the police car gave chase.

"Move it, Johnny. They're gaining."

He hit a bend. Took it at ninety. A turning beckoned amongst the trees. "Hold on." He threw the Ford into a skid. Arrowed down the side road. "They following, Van?"

Van Meter ran his piece back into the car. "You lost them, Johnny. Best keep moving till we hit the city, though. See if we can get us another car." He reloaded the Colt. "At least this heap's still running. I thought we was gonna lose the tyres there. We take any hits?"

"A couple. Just bodywork, far as I can tell. Nothing going to slow us down none. See any damage, Red?"

"Johnny..."

"Red?" He stomped the brakes. "Ah, Jesus." Bent over the figure jack-knifed in the passenger seat. "Where does it hurt, buddy?"

"Behind."

There was a hole the size of a silver dollar in the small of Hamilton's back. The seat cushion was saturated with blood.

God almighty. A bad one.

He examined the wound. Plugged it with his handkerchief. There was little more he could do. They needed to get Hamilton to a doctor and fast.

First of all they needed a car, though, an unidentified vehicle to get them past the city limits. He flagged another Ford as it came towards them.

"My buddy's sick," he said, as the driver lowered his window. "We need to get him to a doctor."

"What's wrong with him?"

Van Meter uncoiled from the back seat. Shouldered a Thompson. "He's been shot. Now get out the car and keep your mouth shut and you might come out of this alive."

The driver let go the wheel. Put up his hands. "My wife and kid."

Van Meter peered into the back seat: a young woman nursing a child. "I'm sorry, lady, but we need your machine." He let fall the muzzle of the Thompson. "It's okay. Keep your hands down. We won't shoot."

Johnny assisted Hamilton from the coupe as the family vacated the hijacked car. Van Meter watched them, an unfathomable expression on his face. "What do you do?" he asked the husband, as he put an arm around his wife's shoulders.

"I work at the power company. I'm district manager."

"You're lucky to have a good job. A family. I hope you appreciate them."

Johnny patted the child on the head. "Don't worry. We like kids. You'll have a story to tell him when he's older."

He took the wheel. Sprayed gravel as they hit the road again.

St Paul was out the question after the shootout. The area would be swarming with bulls. Federal agents. There was only one place they might find shelter from the law. One place they still had

266

connections. The same place they might find themselves on a Syndicate death-list for the heat they brought with them.

Christ, though. They had no choice. He spun the car and made for Chicago.

Eleven

Hanni's men filled them in on what had happened a half mile down the road. The rest they pieced together later. Newman and Baum had driven to Birchwood as planned and left a message at Rhinelander for Hanni. As they finished relaying their message, the operator informed them that a Packard had supposedly been stolen in Manitowish. They'd motored into the village to substantiate the rumour, but came up blank.

A second message from the operator reached them, however, reporting a suspicious vehicle outside the Koerner house. Accompanied by a local lawman, Constable Christiansen, they'd gone to investigate.

This time, the rumour proved correct. Nelson had hijacked a car as he emerged from the woods, forcing the owner to take him south. The vehicle had stalled as it passed the Koerner house, however, and he'd bulled his way inside, corralling the driver and his wife with the Koerners as he ordered the latter to drive him towards town. And then a second car wheeled into the driveway.

"Who's that?" he asked.

It turned out to be Wanatka and the bar staff from Little Bohemia. Henry Voss. Nelson lined them up with the others as they entered the house.

"These people are my friends," Wanatka said, reaching for the Colt. "There's no need for this, Jimmy. No need at all."

Nelson swatted his hand aside. Wedged the gun beneath his chin. "Shut the fuck up." He glanced outside. "Anybody else in the car?"

"No."

"G-men?"

"I told you. The car's empty."

"All right, then." He bundled Wanatka towards the door. Grabbed Koerner. "I'm getting out of here and you two are coming with me."

He ordered Koerner into the back seat. Pushed Wanatka behind the wheel. Lodged a pistol beneath his ribs as he joined them. "Well? What are you waiting for?"

"The keys. I don't have any keys for the car."

Nelson bit his lip. "Jesus Christ." He slitted his eyes as a set of headlights washed the car. "Who the fuck is that?"

It was Baum and Newman, Christiansen in back. They saw the first car abandoned in the driveway, the second car full of people silhouetted against a white picket fence. Newman drew up beside the latter. Addressed the man behind the wheel.

"I'm looking for Mr Koerner." No answer. He fingered the pistol beneath his arm. "Who are you? Who's in the car?"

They never saw the small figure quit the passenger seat until it was too late. The first they knew was when a youth in a brown suede jacket thrust a gun through the driver's window of their Ford.

"Get out the car or I'll kill you. Do it. Now."

Newman reared back in his seat, hoping Baum would open fire with the Thompson sloped across his lap. He scrabbled for his pistol as Baum stared motionless at the pint-sized fury levelling at them through the window. Froze as the gunman poked the muzzle in his face.

"Pull that gun and you're a dead man. Now get out the car or I shoot."

Newman removed his hand from his pistol. He opened the car door. Gave the gunman a clear field of fire.

The first round creased his skull, dropping him stunned but alive to the floor. He felt Baum land on top of him as Nelson lit up the interior of the Ford. Saw his colleague scramble to his feet and try to run, the agent tumbling into the white picket fence bordering the driveway as a trio of slugs shattered his neck.

Christiansen was next. Two bullets snapped his hip as he careered into the car headlights, the impact spilling him into a ditch. Nelson put another three rounds into him as he lay in the dirt. Changed clips. Turned towards Koerner's car.

"You might as well have some too, you bastards."

The two hostages had a few seconds start over the lawmen in the rental, however. Wanatka leapt into a snow bank, bullets punching the ground behind him as he ran. Koerner was already in the house, the door locked behind him. No more targets for the squirt with the machinegun. Newman could swear there was a look of disappointment on the little man's face as he commandeered the shot-up Ford and tooled out the driveway. The agent managed to focus enough to get his pistol into play as the headlights dwindled, but too late. The kid Jimmy was heading southward, leaving havoc in his wake.

Twelve

Johnny and Van Meter made town late that afternoon. They toured every beer joint, gambling den and pool hall they knew. Hit up every ex-con, grifter and yeggman on the circuit.

It was no use. They were too hot. The pin-artists and sawbones that tended to underworld casualties refused to touch them. Federal heat had even the most venal of quacks slamming doors in their faces. One of them passed them a name, though. An address. They wheeled to a halt outside an apartment in Aurora.

"Volney? Volney Davis?"

The slim, dark-haired young man with the scar on his forehead kept one hand concealed behind the jamb as he answered the door. "Who wants to know?"

"The name's Dillinger. Johnny Dillinger. Maybe you heard of me?"

The slim man blinked. "Hold on a second." He closed the door on him. Reappeared a few seconds later clutching a newspaper. Double-checked the photograph on the front page.

"Jesus Christ Almighty. Come on in, John. Take the weight off your feet."

Davis was a machinegunner for the Barkers, an escapee from the Oklahoma state pen, who'd joined his fellow Okies on the spree of kidnappings and bank robberies they'd conducted across the Mid-West over the last two years. Although the two gangs had never worked together, they inhabited the same St Paul-based milieu and knew many of the same people. Tommy Carroll and Ray Karpis had dated the same set of siblings at one point – a third sister being married to the barman at Harry Sawyer's Green Lantern – and Karpis knew Nelson from Back of the Yards on Chicago's South Side. "Sure I'll help you," Davis said, after hearing about the wounded man in the car. "We got to stick together, way the heat's coming down with the feds."

"The Bremer kidnapping?"

"That and the Hamm thing. The payroll job at the St Paul post office. The one where we shot the two cops." He humped his shoulders. "Yeah, I know. Stupid. The Dutchman put us up to it, though. Same with the snatch jobs. The reform administration was pushing him, so he pushed back. Showed them what'd happen if they started to crack down on the yeggs paying protection. We never figured on the feds, though. J. Edgar Hoover's boys coming in from Washington."

"Kidnapping's big news since the Lindbergh baby."

"Fucking-A. We used to snatch bootleggers all the time during Prohibition and nobody batted an eye. They've all turned respectable businessmen since Repeal, though. We yaffle the same guys these days and it's all over the goddamn newspapers."

Van Meter cleared his throat. Jerked his head towards the street. "We better get Red in here before someone looks in the car. The backseat looks like a butcher shop, I swear to God."

Davis nodded. "Take the car round back. We can bring him up the fire escape. There's less attention that way." He lifted the phone receiver. "Dock's just down the road. I'll get him to scout the neighbourhood. Make sure everything's copacetic."

"There a drugstore round here?" Johnny asked.

"Sure. There's one on the corner."

"Too close. We don't want to lay a trail."

"There's another a couple blocks east of here. Out by the railroad tracks."

"I'll pick up bandages. Antiseptic powder. Do what we can for him till we get a doctor."

He backed the car down the alley and parked behind the apartment block, before helping Van Meter half-drag, half-carry Red into the building. They laid him on a Murphy bed set up by Davis. Skinned away his blood-soaked clothing. The stench struck them as they removed his undershirt. Van Meter blanched at the blue-green flesh around the bullet wound.

"You know what that means, Johnny."

Gangrene. Even with a doctor, Hamilton's chances were fading. "We better get moving, if we're gonna help the guy. Find that druggist Volney put us onto."

"He's not going to make it, Johnny."

Van was right. All they were doing was postponing the inevitable. Stretching out the agony. Still. "He's my buddy, Van. What am I gonna do? Stand there and watch him kick?" He creased a ten spot between his fingers. "I'll be back soon as I can. Try and make him comfortable till then, okay, boys?"

He made the run to the drugstore. Returned with the supplies. A bony, watery-eyed young woman in a floral print sundress was crouched over Hamilton, inspecting the wound. "How is he?" he asked, unloading the medical kit on the table.

"You know that as well as I do."

"He needs a doctor."

"There ain't no doctor, though. Even if there was, he couldn't help the poor guy, way he's going."

"So we just sit here and wait for him to die. That what you saying, sister?"

"I wouldn't let a dog die in the road without I tried to help him." She drew back her lips, revealing a gold-toothed smile. "The name's Edna, by the way. Volney's girl."

He remembered the handle the press had laid on her after she'd been nailed with her ex for highway robbery. The way she'd distracted guys during a heist. "The kissing bandit."

277

She coloured. "Volney calls me Rabbits after I dug my way out the state pen back in Missouri. Hooked up with him in KC." She sorted through the medical supplies. "Volney?"

"Sugar?"

"You lend me your razor? And that bottle of rubbing alcohol under the sink. I think I'm gonna need it."

Red was delirious by now, lapsing in and out of consciousness. A blessing with what was to come. Johnny wished he could have slept through it himself, instead of having to hold his buddy down while Rabbits went to work with the razor, carving open the bullet wound and extracting the slug with a pair of tweezers, gagging at the discharge staining her dress.

"You get my sewing box, Volney?"

"Beside you."

"Swell." She set a heavy darning needle and a spool of white thread to soak in the tumbler of alcohol containing her tools. Flushed the wound. "Sorry, sweetheart," she said, as Hamilton convulsed. "It'll soon be over for you one way or the other. Swear to God."

Van Meter licked his parched lips. "He's passed out," he said, releasing his friend's arm. "Better finish it quick. Before he comes round."

She threaded the needle. "No need to tell me twice, hon." She passed it swiftly and neatly through the wound, closing the ragged tear in Hamilton's back. "There." She broke off the thread. Discarded the needle in the glass of alcohol. "Finished. For what good it'll do the poor guy."

Johnny realized he was still gripping the unconscious man's arm. He released it. Swabbed his face with his sleeve. "Edna. Rabbits. If there's ever anything I can do for you. Anything at all -"

"I'd do the same for any guy in a fix. I told you that already." She tugged at her dress. Made a face. "That's one outfit ruined. Going straight in the ashcan."

Davis hugged her. "I'll buy you a new one next time we hit town. Buy you a dozen, you hear me?"

She shrugged him off. "Yeah, well. That's as may be. Ain't nobody going to hit town for a while, though. Not while we wait for this poor guy to pass."

Johnny put a hand on her arm. "Red's strong. He'll make it now. Way you dug the bullet outta him."

She kissed him on the cheek. "Guy's lucky to have a friend like you, you know?" She moved towards the bathroom. "Any of you guys need to use the can, you better do it now. I need a good long soak, I want to get this stink off me in a hurry."

Davis stirred himself. "We better get that car dumped some ways off. Anybody sees the state of the backseat, calls the cops, we're going to be in trouble." He looked to Johnny. "Want to do the honours, John?"

"I could do with a lift back, though, you want to tail me."

"Sure thing. Let Edna get her bath. Leave Homer to look after your buddy here."

They ran the car back to Chicago and abandoned it in a side street on the Southside. Got back to the apartment a few hours later.

"How is he?" Johnny asked, joining Van Meter by the Murphy bed.

"Not good. See for yourself."

Red was semi-conscious. Muttering beneath his breath. His face was the colour of old toothpaste. And the smell had hit him as he entered the room. "There's not much more we can do for him, is there?"

"All we can do is wait."

The speaker was a small man with the tragic eyes of a beagle. Moles on his face. Dock Barker, the youngest of the Barker boys. A bribed senator had arranged his pardon from a life sentence for murder back in Oklahoma, allowing him to join brother Fred and Karpis as part of the deadly trio at the heart of the Barker mob. He was an unthreatening figure at first glance, but Johnny knew the trail of shot-up lawmen and bank officials he'd left in his wake.

"Sorry to bring this to your door," Johnny said, shaking hands. "But we were desperate. Didn't know where else to turn."

Barker returned the handshake. "No problem. I hope someone does as much for me when the time comes." He indicated Johnny's leg. "Heard you stopped a bullet too, Johnny. Sorry we can't get you a sawbones. Perhaps later, when the heat's passed off."

"The leg's fine, Dock, thanks for asking. You know a quack does plastic and I'd appreciate it, though. Getting my map all over the newspapers the way I did, I could do with a new kisser. Especially with the government on my case."

"Federal heat," Davis said, shedding his coat. "We know all about that, don't we, Dock?"

"It's like we got leprosy since the Bremer job. We didn't have to launder the ransom money, I'd be south of the border now. Sunning myself in Cuba. Every time I hear a car pull up in the street, I think it's the feds."

Johnny grimaced. "We're all in the same boat since that asshole Hoover started to make a name for himself off our backs."

"At least he stepped on his prick with that Little Bohemia job." Barker handed Johnny a newspaper. "I picked up the *Tribune* on the way in."

Johnny skimmed the headlines. They all got out then. Tommy. The kid Jimmy. And the way the G had screwed up. The three guys shot as they walked out the lodge. The bulls dropped by Nelson. "This Purvis guy. He the best they can do?"

282

Van Meter grunted. "The rest of them are like that, we got nothing to worry about."

'The rest of them'. That was the problem. There was no end to the supply of men the government could throw into the game. They just kept coming. And no state lines to hide behind, either. "We best get some shut eye, Van. Take turns sitting up with Red. Until – you know."

"We did all we could, Johnny. At least it shouldn't be long."

Barker frowned down at the dying man. "At least he's gonna go with his friends around him. He ain't gonna die alone in a ditch someplace. Go out with his boots on."

Johnny made up a bed on the couch. "That's something anyway." Lighted a cigarette. "Perhaps the least a guy can hope for when he lives the way that we do. You know what I'm saying, boys?"

Thirteen

Hanni's men had been blinded by the lights of an oncoming car as they headed north along Highway 51. It was only when they were flagged by a wounded Newman they realized it was Nelson making his getaway.

They patched up Newman as best they could. Pulled into Koerner's driveway. Found Christiansen propped against the picket fence, wounded but alive. He would later make a full recovery. Baum was dead however. Nelson had unwittingly avenged the slaughtered conservation worker outside Little Bohemia. Blood for blood. This time the agent's Thompson had remained unfired.

Three innocent civilians shot down in cold blood. Three lawmen. Two people dead. One fugitive escaped. Things seemed to be getting worse by the minute. There was only one way of redeeming themselves now. Of alleviating the outrage that would fill the headline's of the nation's newspapers. They had to nail Dillinger as he left the lodge. Had to. Failure now was too much to contemplate.

At least they had the gas now. The extra agents. All they had to do was hold out until morning. Not such an easy task in a

Wisconsin winter, though. Spring might be on the way, but it was difficult to believe as they huddled in the lodge garage to keep warm as the night wore on.

Dawn was coming, however, and with it hope. Purvis roused as Hanni's men loaded the gas guns in the early morning light and sighted on the lodge house. Opened fire.

The gas cartridges thwacked against the wire mesh screening the porch. Vapour rose like early morning mist as the cartridges bounced back into the parking lot, leaving the interior of the lodge untouched.

Purvis and Clegg blinked at each other. Exchanged looks with Rorer.

"What the fuck do we do now?" the latter asked, biting off a hangnail.

Clegg began to charge his briar again. It was beginning to irritate Purvis. He stood out here much longer with the pompous son-of-a-bitch and he'd kick the goddamn pipe up his ass. "Someone will have to put one through the door by hand. It's as simple as that."

Rorer buried his fists in his overcoat. "You volunteering, Purvis?"

Purvis averted his eyes. "That's not what I meant," he said.

One of the other St Paul agents came forward. "I was a good friend of Carter Baum. If I can help flush out the bastards that killed him…"

Clegg pounded him on the back. "Good man, McLaughlin. I'll see your name goes down on my report. You can rely on that."

Purvis watched sourly as McLaughlin zigzagged towards the door of the lodge. Goddamn glory hunter. Still, the asshole had managed to put a cartridge through the door. The place was filling with fumes now. Vapour seeping from the doors and windows. Nobody could stand that concentration of gas for long.

He unlimbered his pistol. The bastards would be ready to run up the white flag by now. Either that or come out shooting.

Five minutes passed. Ten. Not a sound from the lodge. No sign of movement.

One of Hanni's men ran forward in a crouch. He cracked the front door. Peered inside.

He stood upright. Waved to the assembled agents "It's empty. The whole place is empty."

Purvis sank back on the running board of one of the Fords. Jesus Christ. He was finished now. That was obvious. Clegg was officially in charge of the raid, but he was the one that had initiated the whole thing. He was the public face of the Bureau in the War on Crime. The one the newspapers would home in on. That the buck would pass to. If he'd ducked the headlines in the past, he might be able to weather it, but he was too high profile. Too much the man of the moment. The papers would pillory him. Tear him apart.

He weighed the pistol in his hand. Imagined the feel of the barrel in his mouth. The taste of gun oil. No more 'Dear Mel' from the Director now. No more 'forget the Mr'. There was no room for an agent that brought bad publicity to the Bureau at this crucial stage in its growth. Killing innocent citizens didn't bring budgetary increases from a sympathetic Congress. Letting gangsters slip free didn't position the Bureau at the head of the federal reform movement. He was only a pawn in a higher game. Politics meant that he was heading for the scrap heap and he knew it.

Bureaucratic wheels ground slowly, however. If only he could have a second crack at the bastard before disciplinary moves were initiated. A chance to redeem himself for what had happened today. One more shot at nailing Dillinger could put his career back on course before the axe fell. Save him from the shellacking that was heading his way over today's fiasco.

That was all he needed. One more chance. He'd do whatever he had to do to survive the backlash over today's events. Pull out all the stops. And if that involved playing dirty, well. That was just tough shit on Mr Dillinger, wasn't it?

Fourteen

Hamilton never fully regained consciousness. He died two days later, in the early hours of the morning. Johnny had been drowsing beside the bed in a chair when he heard the death rattle. Saw the life drain out of his old buddy at last.

At least the pain was over for him. The running. The fear of capture. He'd died on the outside with his pal beside him. That was something, at least. Perhaps the most a yegg could hope for, as he'd said to Barker.

He shook Van Meter as the latter catnapped on the couch. "Homer. It's time."

Van Meter rubbed his face. "He's gone, then." He retrieved his pistol from beneath the cushion. Slotted it in the holster. "You know where we can take him, John?"

"I got a good idea." He wound the bloodied sheets around Hamilton as Van Meter ransacked the kitchen cupboards for lye. Knotted them around the dead man's head and body. Took a last look around the apartment at the soiled bedding. Empty medicine bottles. The bandages heaped in the sink.

"Going without saying goodbye, boys?" Edna closed a faded blue bathrobe at the waist as she eased the bedroom door shut behind her. Paused at the sight of the body. "At least it's over for him, Johnny. That's something, I suppose."

He finished tying off the sheets. "Yeah. That's something." He lowered his voice as Van came up with the lye. "We gonna let the guys sleep. Can't see no reason to get them involved in – you know."

She shivered. "Dock's got a hard bark on him, but Volney – he ain't got the stomach for this kind of thing. Never has done. Never will." She angled her head towards the alleyway. "You taking the car?"

"You got another?"

"Dock's ride's in the garage. We can always grab a fresh one we need it."

"Looks like this is it, then." He faltered. "You guys ever need anything, you know."

"Sure, Johnny."

"You're a swell kid, Rabbits. Volney don't know how lucky he is."

Van Meter clicked his tongue against his palate. "Be light in a couple hours, Johnny. We ought to get going on this."

He nodded. "We got a shovel, Van?"

"I checked the car. There's one in the trunk."

"Okay, then. Let's get it over with."

They carted the mummified figure down the fire escape to the alleyway in back. Folded it into the trunk of the car. Johnny drove while Van Meter rode shotgun. He kept a grip on his Colt as Johnny nosed the car beyond the city limits and routed south into Indiana.

They headed into farm country. Into the sticks. A sign pushed up beside a dirt track winding into the trees: *Danger: Keep out.* Johnny ignored the warning and followed the track to the bottom of a disused quarry. It was nearly light. "We better hurry," he said, extracting the shovel from the trunk. "Keep watch while I dig, okay, Homer?"

He attacked the loose, shaley soil. Excavated a waist-deep hole. Van Meter took a turn while he rested. He watched the sun begin to rise over the lip of the quarry as his cohort worked the shovel.

"That'll have to do, Van. We can't wait any longer." He cut the bindings loose from Hamilton's face and hands with his pocket knife. Opened the lye. "Red, old pal, I hate to do this, but I know you'd do the same for me."

He obliterated his friend's face and fingerprints as Van Meter looked on. Tossed the empty can. He blinked as Van Meter drew a butcher knife from his overcoat.

"Van?"

"I picked it up at Volney's. When I was looking for the lye. Figured they could spare it, you know?" He squatted beside Hamilton's body. Took a hold on the wrist. "Them missing fingers. As big a giveaway as his prints. We can dump it in a lake someplace on the way back."

Afterwards, they backfilled the grave. Stood a discarded role of barbed wire at its head. Some kind of marker. Not that the bastards would ever find the spot and identify him as Three-Fingered Jack Hamilton. Red had escaped the feds to that extent, at least. It was something they should be thankful for, Johnny supposed, as he accompanied Van Meter to the car and beat it back to Chicago.

FIVE

CHICAGO REDUX

Well, they had Dillinger surrounded and was all ready to shoot him when he came out. But another bunch of folks came out ahead, so they just shot them instead. Dillinger is going to accidentally get with some innocent bystanders sometime and then he will get shot – Will Rogers

One

When Dillinger was hidden in the woods of Wisconsin, they brought up a lot of young lawyers from the Department of Justice and turned them loose. They should have called on local authorities in Wisconsin... They fumbled it again - Senator Royal Copeland, New York

It was worse than Purvis could have imagined. They were already cursing his name as he caught the plane back to Chicago. A petition was circulating in Wisconsin demanding his resignation. URGE PURVIS OUSTER read the headline on that evening's *Chicago American* when he arrived back at the Banker's Building. DEMAND PURVIS QUIT IN DILLINGER FIASCO.

He ran the gauntlet of reporters on the nineteenth floor. Ducked into the bullpen. The agents still at their desks refused to meet his eyes as he made his way to his office. Failure was contagious. None of them wanted a share of their superior's misfortune if they could help it.

It was more than just careerism, though. Purvis could sense it. The college boys had come face-to-face with death for the first time and they didn't relish the sight. Suddenly it wasn't a game anymore. They'd known and liked Carter Baum. Realized it could have been themselves rather than their colleague lying dead in the woods.

Most of them had never planned to be lawmen. The Bureau was supposed to be a temporary measure after graduation. A way of tiding them over until the Depression eased and new jobs appeared. Being thrown into situations where they could be killed had never been on the agenda. Jerking sodas or pumping gas in their Mid-Western home towns seemed preferable to trading bullets with machinegun-toting hoodlums. The first resignations would land on Purvis' desk before the end of the day.

The resignations were the least of his worries, though. The bear-like figure in the ill-fitting suit emerging from behind his desk as he entered the office was of more concern to him at the moment: Sam Cowley, five feet nine and 170 pounds, the deceptively bland-looking son of a Mormon polygamist and a former missionary to Hawaii. The Bureau's current Director of Investigations. One of Hoover's most trusted aides. He held out his hand to Purvis as the latter tried to maintain his composure.

"Mr Cowley. This is an unexpected pleasure." He gave his superior's paw a brief squeeze. Released it quickly. "That thing in the woods. You'll have heard all about that, of course."

"Not at first hand, Purvis. Mel. I'll expect a report as soon as you've rested, though." He coughed into his fist. Looked ill at ease. "That's why I'm here, of course. That thing in the woods. The Director dispatched me here as soon as the news came through. Told me to find out what had actually happened. Take charge of things until they settled down again."

Purvis had been expecting it, of course. But not this quickly. Things usually went through channels. Took time. He couldn't believe the speed Mr Hoover had moved on this one. Damage limitation, of course. Cut out the rot quickly, before it spread. "I'm reassigned?" he said. "Demoted?"

"Officially this is just an inspection tour. You'll stay on as SAC for the time being. The Director wants us to show a united front to the press. Unofficially, I have carte blanche to reorganize the Chicago office. Direct the investigation as I choose. You'll be taking orders from me for now on, I'm afraid."

"I see."

"I'm sorry, Mel."

"You want my resignation?"

"Don't be absurd. We ought to be pulling together at a time like this. A combined effort's in both our best interest if we're going to catch Dillinger."

Purvis felt abashed, as if ticked off by a well-meaning schoolmaster. "You're right, of course. Just the strain I've been under. The events of the last twenty-four hours."

Cowley rested a fatherly hand on his shoulder. "Go on home, Mel. Get some rest. You look like you need it."

"Thank you, Mr Cowley."

"Make it Sam." He re-seated himself behind Purvis' desk and reached for the telephone. "I'm going to have an extra desk and chair sent in. Make a start on things tonight. Get a good night's sleep and join me in the morning. We've got a lot of work ahead of us if we're going to run down this Dillinger punk before he does any more damage to the Bureau's reputation."

Two

Dilinger and Van Meter dumped the car on the North Side, doors open, bloodstained dressings trailing onto the sidewalk. They caught a trolley to the end of the line. Phoned Piquet.

"We need a truck," Johnny said, as the lawyer picked up the phone. "A grocery truck. The kind with an enclosed back. Sliding doors. Throw in a couple mattresses and a camping stove and we can hide on the road until the heat dies down. The G are still buzzing after that thing in the sticks. We need to keep moving till we cool off with the feds."

"Things are never going to cool off for you and the boys, Johnny. Not now. Not ever. Haven't you realized that yet?"

Johnny spoke slowly but firmly, as if repeating instructions to a child. "We need a truck, Louis. A rig we can hide in till we find something permanent."

"You're asking a lot, John, say you still owe me money. Especially if you want me to defend Billie."

"I thought you were a fixer. Thought you could get my woman outta jail before it came to that."

300

"No fixing the feds, John. Thought you knew that by now."
He cleared his throat. "Now about the money."

"You'll get your money, counselor. And sooner than you
think. Now find us that goddamn truck. You'll have your money by
Friday."

He hung up the phone. Stole a car out to Indiana Harbor, East
Chicago's waterfront district. Toured the bars with Van Meter.

They found the guy they were looking for in the corner booth
of a hotel bar, a bobbed blonde in a green silk dress and roll
stockings beside him. Johnny wedged himself into the booth
between them.

"Sorry, sister. We got business with your boyfriend here.
Wanna go powder your nose while we talk?"

The blonde toyed with her pearls. "Zark?"

Zark pointed her to the bar. "Sorry, sweetheart. This'll only
take a minute." He waited for his date to make her exit. Set down
his martini glass. "Right, Johnny?"

"That depends. Depends if you're willing to do a favour for
an old friend or not."

"You're too hot, amigo. Local heat I can handle, but Washington gets involved and that's it. I don't want to know. Guy like me can get hung out to dry by the feds as easily as you can, you know what I'm saying?"

"A couple nights, Zark. That's all I'm asking. Couple nights till I get back on my feet, okay, buddy?"

"Forget it, John. You're a nice guy and all, but I'm not going down with you and your sidekick here." He killed his drink. Crunched the olive. "Now if you'll excuse me - "

Van Meter blocked his way. "You think you're dealing with a couple schmucks here? That it, asshole? Couple fucking greeners?"

Zark flashed his teeth. Slipped a hand inside his jacket. "You threatening me, punk? That what you doing, huh?"

Johnny noted the bulge beneath Zark's armpit. Eased the two apart. "Nobody's threatening anybody here, okay? Just we need a favour and you're the guy that can do it for us." He let a smile slide across his face. "After all, it's as much in your interest as ours that we stay outta the hands of the G."

"And how do you figure that, wise guy?"

Van Meter snickered. "Hoover's boys are like to hang you out the window on the nineteenth floor if they find you been helping a couple yeggs like us, copper or no copper."

Johnny plucked a wad of notes from his suit. "Not that they'd ever find out if we stay on the street, Zark. Know what I'm saying?" He tucked the greenbacks into the bagman's pocket. "There'll be more where that came from, once we find Tommy Carroll. Help put us together with Tommy and we can get back to work soon as possible."

Zark removed his hand from his jacket. "I hear where Carroll is, I'll put him in touch with you." He smoothed his pocket. "A couple days is all I can keep you on ice, though. After that, you're on your own."

"Couple days is all we need, if things go to plan. You can run interference for us with the local law after that, though, and we'll keep the long green coming your way. Help you keep the little lady in the manner she's accustomed to." He hooked his thumb at the blonde as they backed out the booth towards the door. "Nice ass, by the way. You know how to pick 'em, Zark. Gimme her phone

number and I'll throw in a couple extra grand as a bonus, okay?"

Three

Purvis perched in the spectator's gallery of the St Paul courtroom. Cowley had asked him to stakeout the place in case Dillinger attempted to break his moll out of custody. Purvis suspected the Director of Investigations was sidelining him while he reorganized the Chicago Office in his absence, especially after the rocket he'd received for attempting the same tactic with Makley and Pierpont.

Nevertheless, he wasn't totally unhappy to be present in court as Frechette went to trial. The place had good associations for him. It was the same courtroom he'd seen Roger Touhy go down for a ninety-nine year stretch in a few months previously.

The memory gave him a warm glow as he watched Agent Reinecke go under the hammer with Piquet. Reinecke had been one of the officers that had questioned Frechette and Piquet wanted the world, or at least the jury, to know how the feds treated a helpless girl when she fell into their clutches.

Q. Isn't it a fact, Mr Reinecke, that you yourself slapped this girl in the face?

A. I did not slap this girl in the face at any time.

Q. Isn't it a fact that you continually went like that to her under the chin? (indicating with right hand).

A. I think I can explain what you are alluding to, if you will permit me.

Q. All right, go ahead.

A. Miss Frechette had a manner of not looking me in the eye when I was talking to her. When her head would be down, I would take the tips of my fingers, on one or two occasions, and raise up her chin, and I said, "Please, Evelyn, look at me when you are talking to me, and answering my questions."

Which wasn't the way Frechette had it when Piquet got her to open up on the stand.

Q. By the way, did you hear Agent Reinecke say that he on several occasions lifted up your chin with his finger, and asked you "Please, Evelyn, look me in the eye."

A. Yes, I heard him say that.

Q. Did that occur?

A. Well, he didn't lift up my chin, and he didn't say "Please."

Q. But he did have his hand under your chin?

A. Yes. I would say he hit it up, instead of lifting it up.

Q. And you were, or were you not, faced with a lot of lights in that room?

A. Well, when I first got into that building Monday night I was. I remember one fellow coming over there and saying, "Well, maybe Evelyn wouldn't like these lights," and he shone them right in my face.

The jury weren't buying it, though. Piquet had the tramp tricked out in virginal white, long sleeves, buttoned neck, but anyone could see what type of woman she was. Reinecke, by comparison, a blonde, blue-eyed law graduate, looked like any mother's son, and was more than capable of holding his own with an ambulance chaser like Piquet.

Truth be told, they had been rough with the girl when they'd picked her up. With no other lead to Dillinger and the Director breathing down their necks, they hadn't much choice. He had to admit to a grudging respect for the way she'd stood up for two days under the lights without food or drink before they'd eased up on her. Or before Doris had made them ease up on her, anyway.

"This' inhuman," the secretary said, as Purvis broke from questioning her. Passed her onto Reinecke. "You can't treat a woman like this, Mr Purvis. It's just not right."

Purvis swabbed his face with a handkerchief. Those lights were hot, all right. He compared the wilted look of the bedraggled half-breed to the crisp, laundered look of the fresh young blonde in front of him. "What the heck are we supposed to do, Doris?" he said, embarrassed that he felt the need to explain himself to a secretary. "We need answers and we need them now."

"That's no excuse, Mr Purvis. You're college boys. Government men. Not local flatfoots. Chicago cops. Don't you realize how you lower yourself when you act like them?"

Well. She'd caught him on the raw there, he had to admit. Men like himself, the other agents, were better than the brass buttons they reluctantly rubbed shoulders with in the courtrooms. She was right, they ought to act with the dignity their office called for.

Circumstances, though. If the round-heeled slut could give them Dillinger, he was prepared to lean on her and deal with his professional pride later. "So what do you suggest we do then, Doris? Call her a cab and cut her loose?"

"At least let me bring her a sandwich. Let her have a few hours sleep."

"Are you suggesting we put her in a hotel or something?"

"There's a couch in the lady's room. Let her have an hour there." She looked at him beseechingly. "Please, Mr Purvis. If you're the man I think you are, let the girl have a break."

He considered. It could actually work in his favour. Good cop-bad cop. Doris as the figure in white. "All right then. For you, Doris, if for nobody else."

She'd beamed at him then. Squeezed his arm. "For you, Mr Purvis. For your conscience. For the kind of guy you really are underneath that professional exterior."

Purvis had shrugged modestly. "Go on, Doris. Take care of the little tramp before I change my mind." He'd become uncomfortably aware of her fragrance perfuming the air around him. "And keep an ear open for anything she tells you. I want a full report once she's asleep, you hear me?"

He wondered if he'd stuck to the interrogation, failed to give her that break, she'd have spilled as to Dillinger's whereabouts. As it was, he had to be content with sending her up the river in the yeggman's place. Assuming the twelve good men and true below him weren't swayed by Piquet's eloquence as he launched into his closing speech, that is:

"Evelyn Frechette loved Johnny Dillinger and although she knew he was a desperado, she was willing to take a chance with him. We all know where Dillinger belongs, but are we going to punish other people who become entangled in his net? Miss Frechette was willing to go to the end with this Public Enemy Number One because she loved him. She did not harbour him under the statute she is being tried under. Give her back her freedom."

The jury seemed to take more notice of the Judge's remark that she knew he was an escaped convict and had taken a car across a state line. The bitch got two years for harbouring.

Four

Johnny grinned at the flat-nosed figure at the back corner table of the tavern. "Tommy."

Carroll squinted at him over his stein. "Johnny boy. Van." He waved them into a seat. "You guys made it then."

"Red, though."

"He…"

Van Meter lit up a smoke. "We hit a roadblock in Minnesota." Left the deck on the table. "You know how the guy drew lead. Don't know how he lasted long as he did, the poor schmuck."

Johnny helped himself to a cigarette. "Kinda thought we'd lost you too, Tommy." Struck a match. "Till we talked to Zarkovich, anyway."

Carroll drained his glass. "Well, it got pretty hairy out there, I gotta say. Especially after I split with you guys. I managed to reach the next village okay, sneezed a car, but I ran up a logging road. Got stuck in the mud. I hadda walk through the woods after that. Ride the rods into town with a buncha hobos. I woulda got rousted for vagrancy, I hadn't run faster than the railroad bulls in the stockyards there." He signalled the barkeep. "Either that or busted a cap onna bastards, you know?"

Johnny averted his face as the barkeep delivered the beers. Waited for him to withdraw before continuing. "Speaking of which, I heard the runt made it outta there too."

"Yeah. He jungled-up with some Indians on the reservation. Stole a car out the woods once the heat died down. Hit town just the other night."

The runt had walked in on a couple of Chippewa Indians tapping maple syrup, according to the newspapers. Paid them to put him up for a couple of nights. The redskins had a good idea he wasn't the guy on a fishing holiday he claimed to be, but the .45 beneath his pillow was the stick to the carrot of the two hundred dollars he offered them for room and board. Even after he spilled the syrup they were boiling when the smoke from the fire became noticeable. Shot their dog for barking. After all, two hundred dollars was two hundred dollars. Not something a couple of dirt-poor Chippewa could afford to turn down at the height of the

Depression. And a .45 was a .45, whatever the state of the economy.

Besides, they didn't have to put up with the kid for long. When their provisions dwindled to the point where all they could offer their guest was lard, he decided he'd had enough. Got the elder of the family, one Ollie Catfish, to walk him to the highway.

Catfish protested he was sick. Nelson doctored him with a prod from his Colt and they started down an abandoned railroad line towards civilization. Six miles in, they spotted a campfire. They joined the three men around it and warmed their hands.

A Chevrolet Sedan appeared. Parked fifty yards away.

Nelson got to his feet. "Who the hell's that?" Approached the car as a second vehicle, a Plymouth, drew up by the Chevy. He hailed the driver of the Plymouth, another Chippewa, as he emerged from behind the wheel. "This your car?"

The driver helped the two occupants of the sedan unload fishing tackle from the boot. "What the hell is it to you? What authority you got to be on our land, anyway?"

Nelson showed his pistol. "This authority enough for you, Geronimo?" He jerked his piece towards the fire. "Now get over there with your buddies and shut your mouth."

The Indian deadpanned. Joined the others by the campfire as Nelson yanked the distributor from the Chevy. Marched Catfish towards the Plymouth.

"Me sick," the Chippewa said, massaging his stomach.

"You'll be a hell of a lot sicker if you keep trying to fuck with me, old man."

He pushed Catfish into the car. Got the Indian to guide him towards Highway 71, before dropping him by the roadside and motoring towards Chicago, losing himself in the tourist country north of the city.

It made Johnny uneasy to think the runt was out there and he didn't know where. Especially after the bad blood brewing between them at the lodge. "You and him bunking together, Tom?"

"We're hiding-out in a motor court. The kid's idea." He humped his shoulders. Looked embarrassed. "Me and Jimmy. We go back a ways, you know?"

"No sweat, Tommy. I figure we should all hang together while the heat's on, though."

"Try telling the kid that, Johnny. He's still pretty sore about the way you took over the string in the woods."

Van Meter pulled at his beer. "You figure it's safe for us to show our faces at the court, Tommy?"

"I wouldn't, Van. Not yet awhiles, anyhow."

"Work on him, Tom. I don't like to think a triggerman like the runt's got a hard-on for me. Especially as me and Van are planning to go back to work as soon as possible. If you're up for it, Tommy, that is."

Five

The anteroom to Piquet's office was aggressively modern in its design, all chrome and glass and stripped white pine. The secretary was pretty up to date too, a frosty blonde in a tailored business suit and an expression on her face suggesting Purvis was something she'd picked up on the sole of her shoe. "You have an appointment?" she asked, the distaste in her voice almost palpable.

He flipped open his badge. "I don't need an appointment, sweetheart." Louis Piquet. Since Dillinger had failed to show at his paramour's trial, the Syndicate lawyer was the only lead he had. The fact that a high-priced mouthpiece like Piquet had defended Frechette suggested that someone other than the seemingly-penniless hatcheck girl was paying the bills for the attorney's services. The lip's previous appearance at Pierpont and Makley's trial seemed to confirm the Chicago SAC's suspicions. If the slippery bastard wasn't still in touch with the Indiana prison system's answer to Houdini, Purvis would eat his hat. "Melvin Purvis, FBI. Pleased to make your acquaintance, miss."

"I know who you are. One moment, please." She vanished into the inner office. Reappeared. "Mr Piquet will see you now," she said, reinstalling herself at her desk. Pecking at her typewriter as if he was no longer there.

He stood there flat-footed, badge out. Licked his bottom lip. "I'll just go through, then." Failed to get a response from the secretary. "Okay, then." He pocketed his badge as he entered the office.

Piquet lifted his eyes from an artfully-arranged spread of paperwork on a heavy oak desk. He remained in his seat. "Purvis."

"You know me, then?"

The lawyer seemed to be restraining a smile. "The man who nailed Touhy for the Factor job."

"Something about that seems to amuse you, Mr Piquet."

Piquet let the smile show for a second, before folding it neatly away. "A fine piece of detective work, Mr Purvis. Almost up with the one you pulled out the hat at Little Bohemia."

"If it wasn't for certain members of the legal profession helping shield armed robbers and murderers, Little Bohemia would never have happened. Dillinger would be in custody by now and we wouldn't have had to go haring off into the woods in the first place."

317

Piquet rested his elbows on his desk. "So much for subtlety. Cut to the chase, eh, Purvis?" He steepled his fingers beneath his chin. "That why you're here then, Melvin? Trying to get a lead on Johnny?"

Purvis helped himself to a chair. "Why the hell else would I be here, Piquet? There's a million things I'd rather be doing than talking to you, given the choice."

"I say you could have a seat?" He grinned when Purvis failed to respond. "Chicago's rubbing off on you, Mel. Quite the little tough guy, aren't we?"

"Listen, Piquet - "

"What are you going to do, Purvis? Hang me by the heels from the nineteenth floor until I squeal?" He nodded at the expression on Purvis' face. "What's a matter, kid? Think I don't know what goes on over there?"

"Rumours…"

" 'Vigorous but appropriate' methods, you guys call 'em. Breaking phone books over suspects' heads. Feeding them the goldfish." Piquet curled a thumb at his chest. "My town, buddy. Not much goes down here without me picking up on it, capisce?"

" 'Capisce?' "

"Type of clientele I got, you tend to pick up the lingo."

"The Syndicate, you mean."

"Whatever the funnies are calling it this year." He lounged back in his chair. Plaited his fingers over his pot belly. "The type of clientele that don't appreciate me talking to coppers, federal or otherwise. I told you what you wanted to know and pretty soon I wouldn't have a business left. That's if I was lucky."

"You mean - "

Piquet mimed shooting a pistol. "Chicago ain't no cissy town, Mel."

"We'd protect you, Piquet. If you helped us, that is."

"Sure you would. Until five minutes after I'd testified."

"You want to go to jail, counsel?"

"Lawyer-client privilege. No law against that, Purvis."

"There is against harbouring a federal fugitive." He thrust out his chin. "If you know where he's hiding, Piquet, why don't you help us? Dillinger's no Syndicate gun. Why should the Barber be a threat to you?"

"Johnny won't be around much longer. Oh sure, he's making a sap of you and Hoover for now, but he's only one guy against an army. He'll slip up soon – probably over a broad, knowing John – and when he does – well, it's life on the Rock, if he's lucky.

Me, though, I got to survive in this town after he's gone. Make a living. Guys know I sang once, they'll know I could do it again. Don't matter if the guy I sent up the river's Syndicate or not, they'll think I'm a bad risk. Type of risk the Barber's likely to eliminate just to be on the safe side." He examined his manicure. "Careful guy, Mr Nitti. Not that I know him, you understand."

"Sure you don't."

Piquet squared the papers on his desk. "If there's anything else, Purvis… "

"Mr Hoover won't like this, Piquet."

"Screw Mr Hoover. Though from what I hear, he might rather enjoy the experience."

"You could be looking at jail time if we make the connection between you and Dillinger, counsel."

"I'll take my chances."

"You can't fix the federal government, Piquet. No matter how good your local connections."

The lawyer studied Purvis for a moment. "Well." He tapped his thumbnail against his teeth. "I will give you this. There's a guy out of East Chicago looking to peddle a deal to the law about Johnny. The local cops gave him the elbow, though. Didn't want to dirty their reputation."

"Sure they didn't."

"We're talking about Stege here. Head of the Dillinger Squad. The captain might beat you to death in a stationhouse basement, but he'd take a bullet before he took a bribe." He looked uncomfortable at the thought. Centred his tie. "Anyways, I'll pass on your name to the guy in question, assuming you're interested. Give him your number. Tell him the federals aren't as choosy about where they get their information as the cops."

"That still may not be enough if we can prove collusion between you and Dillinger, counsel."

"You got me shaking in my boots, Melvin. Swear to God." He smirked at Purvis as the agent made to leave the office. "I caught the act with Dolores out there when you came in, by the way. If it's any consolation to you, she rooms with a bull-dyke

tennis professional up in Tower Town. Waste of a good woman if

you ask me, but what the hell do I know, eh?"

Six

Carroll had been up for the bank job, just as they'd hoped. The target was Fostoria, a rail hub forty miles south of Toledo. The lines crisscrossing the downtown area gave the bank the reputation of being bandit-proof, a reputation the three of them were about to disprove as they drew up opposite the First National shortly before closing time.

Johnny and Van Meter strolled into the lobby, overcoats slung over their arms. It was a bad set up: a mezzanine overhead and a side entrance leading into the neighbouring jewellers. No time for second thoughts now, though, as Johnny threw aside his overcoat, revealing the Thompson in his hands. "Stick them up. This is a raid."

He left Van Meter to handle the staff while he cleared the cash from the counters. A uniformed figure broke from the jewellers as he filled a laundry bag. Van Meter triggered a burst. The cop back-pedalled. Collapsed into the store.

Fuck him.

Johnny cleared the remaining cash and backed towards the door. Seized a couple of tellers. "This way. Through the jewellery store."

Outside, Carroll was policing the street, breaking up the crowd with machinegun fire. One guy was down, clutching his foot. Another hobbled away, leaving a blood spoor from his leg.

The getaway route was clear, though. They stood the bank staff on the running board and made it out of town. Dumped the hostages. $17,000. No muss, no fuss.

That night they paid the proceeds of the job to Piquet at a tourist camp at Crown Point, the last place anyone would think of looking for them. Picked up the truck. There'd been enough of the long green to square the bill for the rig and pay the bulk of the fee for Billie's defence. Enough for a down payment on plastic surgery. Not enough for that fresh start they'd been talking about, though. For a new life outside the U.S.A. Somehow, it seemed, no matter how many jugs they cracked, how much dough they heisted, there was never enough for that.

<u>Seven</u>

Purvis sat at his desk after returning from the meeting with Piquet. He perused the paperwork in front of him. It multiplied daily as the leads came in, the results of underworld tip-offs, mail-covers and sightings. Suspects questioned, 'vigorously' or otherwise. Reports submitted by agents in the field. A growing paper trail marking the Bureau's pursuit of the nation's most wanted outlaw.

And what did it add up to? Nothing. That was what. A big fat zero. He'd applied all the techniques of scientific detection taught by the Bureau in Washington. Collected fingerprints. Analysed ballistics. Recorded the evidence. Filed it. Sent copies to headquarters. And all it added up to was dick. He might as well have stayed home and watched the daisies grow for all the good it did him. Or sat in the bathroom and jerked-off. He was no nearer nabbing Dillinger than he'd been in February, when the manhunt began.

He considered the underworld deal Piquet had mentioned. Wondered if the lawyer had passed on his number. That kind of deal-making and compromise had always been anathema to Purvis.

He'd liked to think he and his fellow agents were above such manoeuvres. They were scientific investigators, after all. Analysts. Not the kind of cigar-smoking, blackjack-wielding meatheads that manned the local detective squads. The kind of thugs that used bribes and threats to do their work for them, playing divide and rule within the underworld in order to get results.

Nevertheless, he'd spent long enough in the murky waters of big city crime by now to know that that was the way things went down on the streets outside the Banker's Building. If they ever did catch up to the Hoosier outlaw, it was because somebody had traded him for a break with the law or set him up for the reward money, rather than because they'd tracked him down via the resources of the Bureau.

The door opened a crack. Doris. She looked good. Smelled better. He'd not really talked to her since he'd returned from the Frechette trial in St Paul. The whole episode where she'd intervened for the half-breed had affected him. For good or ill, he couldn't say. He wondered how he felt about her. How she felt about him. Working at close quarters each day the way they did.

They were human after all. Not made of stone. "Yes, sweetheart? What can I do for you?"

"Just to say I was finishing for the day, Mr Purvis. Unless there's anything else you want me for?"

He restrained the obvious answer. Kept it professional. "No thanks, Doris. That'll be all for the day." He twitched his nose as she made to leave. "What's that you're wearing, honey? Something expensive?"

Doris touched the hair at her temple. "Gosh, Mr Purvis." She fluttered her hands. "It's nothing special. A girl like me can't afford more than vanilla essence on what the government pays, you know?"

"Still. It suits you, Doris. A clean, natural smell. Not the kind of thing some of these gangland floozies drench themselves in, believe you me."

"If I had some guy to spend money on me the way the rackets boys do, Mr Purvis - "

"Don't say that, Doris. Don't ever say that. Not a nice girl like you."

"Every girl likes a man to spend money on her, Mr Purvis. These gangland molls don't have a monopoly on that, you know."

He looked at her severely. Jutted his jaw. A move he'd practiced in the shaving mirror the last few mornings. "Government men don't get paid the same as these racketeers and bank robbers do, but at least we can hold our heads up in public. Sleep easy at nights. That's something you might want to consider next time you compare yourself to one of these underworld tramps, Doris."

"At least the yeggs and rackets boys know how to show a girl a good time, Mr Purvis. They don't spend every waking hour sat behind a desk."

"Unlike myself, you mean, Doris?"

"You're putting words in my mouth, Mr Purvis."

"Please, Doris. Call me Mel."

"I don't think that would be right, Mr Purvis. Not in front of the other staff. People would talk, you know?"

"Office gossip? I suppose you're right." He mused on what the secretary had said. What his life consisted of. The office. Paperwork. Stakeouts. Interrogations. The bachelor apartment awaiting him at the end of the day. It was all so different from the fraternity parties and romantic trysts of his college days. Petting in lover's lane. Another lifetime now…

"Mr Purvis?"

"Doris? "

"Can I go now, Mr Purvis?"

"Sorry, honey. Sure you can. I'll see you tomorrow, okay, sweetheart?" His eyes focused on the papers on his desk as she left the office, trying to extract some kind of sense from them as the words ran together. He concentrated on his work as the only thing in his life that had some kind of purpose, some kind of meaning, for him.

"Melvin?"

Purvis raised his head. "Sam?" He looked around the room as if searching for an escape route. "How long have you been there?"

"I just came in. Passed your secretary as she walked out the door."

"Sweet kid," Purvis said, his voice wobbling. "A real sweet kid." He ran a finger inside his collar.

"Are you okay, Mel?"

"I'm fine, Sam. Never felt better."

"Well, you don't look fine, I have to say." He sat opposite his subordinate. Gave him a concerned look. "I think you might be working too hard, Mel. Letting the case get to you. I think you might be ready for a rest."

'A rest.' He knew what that meant. All the Mormon bastard needed was an excuse and he'd be shunted aside. Dumped from the case. "Heck, no, Sam. I'm full of pep here. A good night's sleep, I'll be right as rain. Never felt better, you know?"

"Well. If you're sure." He patted Purvis on the arm. "What you need, son, is a good woman. It doesn't do a man any good to pull in single harness too long, you know. The playboy lifestyle might seem attractive to a gadabout like yourself, Mel, but a man wants to make a career in government service, he's best to find someone to stand by him when the times are tough. Find himself a wife."

Like Hoover, Mel thought, biting his tongue. At that moment in time, though, it seemed like the Director might have the best

330

idea. You wanted to see your life turned on it's head, see yourself transformed into some kind of patsy, put your heart in the power of some Jezebel and let her get to work on you.

Same with this punk Dillinger, from what Piquet had said. He almost felt sorry for the guy. The outlaw might not have showed at Frechette's trial as he'd hoped, but he had a gut feeling that it was a woman that would finally bring the yeggman down in the end, just as the lawyer had stated. *Cherchez la femme.* That was the key. Find the woman and they'd find Dillinger himself. It was only a matter of time.

Eight

East Chicago, Indiana

Thursday, May 24

The back of the truck stank. Old food. Socks. Stale cigarettes. And the fumes from the stove gave Johnny a headache. Same as the company, unfortunately. Confinement was getting to his old buddy Van Meter. Making him ornery. The constant flow of complaints as he sat cross-legged on the mattress, cleaning one of the Thompsons. Slapping at a flea.

"I didn't become no yeggman to live like this. This' worse than the can. How much longer we gotta hide in this stinking rust bucket?"

Johnny changed gears as they approached a gas station. "Piquet should have arranged something more permanent for us by now. A place to rest up. Plan another job. Get those new faces we talked about." He decelerated as they rolled onto the forecourt. "Anyway, this ain't so bad. You can use the bathroom while I fill her up. Grab yourself a wash and shave. What the hell. It's better than Indiana State, ain't it?"

Van Meter reassembled the Tommy gun. "It ain't just the accommodation that's bothering me. It's paying off Zarkovich." He slapped a magazine into place. "I don't trust the fuck. The guy didn't wanna help us in the first place. And after we braced him in the hotel bar – well, I'll be happier when we leave East Chicago behind us, get back to the city, you know what I'm saying?"

Johnny nodded. Getting wrong side of a powerful figure like Zark was a dangerous move. Still. As long as he kept topping-up the sergeant's bank account, he should be safe from a double-cross. As long as the bastard didn't decide to go for the reward, that is.

"Shit."

"What?"

Two figures in hats and overcoats stepped from behind a parked Ford. Waved them down as they slowed before the pumps. Bulls? If they were lucky. The fact Nelson was still alive meant the Syndicate was as big a threat to them as the law. Why they daren't show their faces in Chicago until Piquet had arranged a safe-house for them.

Carroll was still bunking in a tourist camp north of the city, keeping an eye on the runt. Stopping him leading the Mob to their door. Not that the Mob needed Nelson as a marker when it came to tracking their targets. He lowered his window as the truck came to a halt. "Anything I can do for you guys?"

"You can take the keys out the ignition and step out of the cab."

"And why the hell would I want to do that?" He saw the second guy begin to slide open the rear door of the truck. "Leave it."

The second guy rotated his head. "Say what?"

Too late. The blast from the Thompson lit-up the interior of the rig. Knocked the poor sap off his feet.

The first guy started towards his partner. Made to clear leather. Took a burst full in the face.

There was a ringing silence, broken only by the chime of ejected cartridges striking the asphalt. Van Meter hopped down onto the roadway, smoke curling in a question mark from the snout of the machinegun. "Jesus Christ. What have I done?" He

334

approached the first figure. Prodded him with the gun barrel. "They're both…?"

Johnny joined him. Hunkered down. "Dead as Kelsey's nuts." He wormed a hand inside the second one's jacket. Came up with a shield. Bulls, then. That was a relief. If the two had been Syndicate guns, they were already dead.

Still, though. Two dead cops. You couldn't get hotter than that. East Chicago, too. They lingered any longer on the outskirts of the town and the law would be on them like white on rice.

He skimmed the shield into the undergrowth. Zark. It had to be. The two dicks were probably honest. On the sergeant's shit-list. He sent them up against Johnny and either they or the yeggs in the truck would go down. One less problem however it fell out, the son-of-a-bitch.

He put the truck into gear. Goddamn Zark. Soon as the bastard heard him and Van were still kicking, he'd be aware of the danger. Out to neutralise them before they came looking for him. Or were captured and spilled to the law.

It was time to get off the highway. To find themselves a more permanent hideaway. Somewhere in the city. Hidden in the crowd. He cast a last look at the bodies lying at the roadside amidst a scatter of brass, broken dolls, puppets with their strings cut, then spat and turned the truck around and headed for Chicago.

SIX

PROBASCO'S PLACE

I'd like to have enough money to enjoy life; be clear of everything – not worry; take care of my old man, and see a ball game every day – John Dillinger

One

Johnnie's just an ordinary fellow. Of course he goes out and holds up banks and things, but he's just like any other fellow, aside from that – Mary Kinder, gang moll.

Dillinger and Van Meter spent the next night suspended between floors in Clary Lieder's garage on Division and Oakley. Lieder specialized in trading hot auto parts and customizing underworld cars with smokescreen generators and bullet-proof glass. He was one of the Chicago contacts they'd picked up from Nelson. A right guy. He could keep his mouth shut about the yeggs cooping in the truck on his service elevator. It was no long-term hideout, though. They needed somewhere secure. Somewhere a surgeon could work on them.

Piquet went about making the arrangements. In the meantime, he stashed them at Jimmy Murray's Rainbo Barbecue up on West North Avenue. The chalet-style diner came complete with a secret room tucked beneath the eaves of the roof, its walls equipped with gun ports and a 360-degree field of fire, a high-rent hideaway accessible only by a concealed staircase at the rear of the building.

Murray himself was a plump, moustachioed ward-heeler, a fixer who'd used his connections with the Thompson machine to weasel out of a twenty-year stretch for his part in the two million dollar Rondout train robbery. "I had the contacts to fence the bonds, the hot money. Keep the local bulls off our backs. Doc Newton hadn't accidentally shot his self, gone to a doctor, we woulda got clean away." He wagged a finger at Johnny as they sat over a bottle of Schlitz. "That was ten years ago. There ain't no reason it wouldn't work again, though, given the right guys. I'm fixed better than ever with the pols. The law. Got a guy in the Federal Bank can tell me when the Reserve's coming in. Kinda thing could set up a fella for life, if it came off okay. Get him out the country before the feds could bust him, you know what I'm saying?"

Van Meter pinched the bulb of his nose. "Train robbing. Thought that went out with the Wild Bunch. Frank and Jesse James."

Johnny necked his beer. "A Pullman's gotta be easier to crack than a bank vault. Hit it out in the boondocks and there's no cops to bust you, same as there is in town. You can vanish into the sticks. All you gotta do is stop the thing. Find a guy as can handle the soup for us and we're in." He clinked bottles with Murray. "Any rush on this, Jimmy?"

"We can hit it soon as I can get the finance together. Might take time, though. Even a guy like me has problems, way the economy's gone to shit."

"You looking for seed money, we got a load of bonds hid upstate. We was going to put them out in St Paul, till the feds hit town. Figure you might be able to move them through your connections, if anyone can."

"I can get you thirty-five, forty cents on the dollar for railroad or security bonds. Eighty-five to ninety for Liberty Bonds. Might take time, though. Depends how quick you want to get going on this."

"No immediate rush, Jim. We gonna be in town a good while yet. Me and Homer here, we'll make a trip out, drop them off with you and after that – well, we got an appointment at the doctor's, you know what I'm saying?"

Two

The peeling, once-white frame cottage stood behind a Shell service station on North Crawford Avenue. There was a dense green hedge at the front of the place and a high board fence at the rear. Two German shepherds in the back yard threw themselves at the boards at their approach, before a stream of rapid fire Italian brought them to heel.

The place Piquet had found them looked good. Secluded. And the guard dogs. After Little Bohemia, Johnny appreciated having a couple of on-their-nerve mutts looking out for him.

The guy himself, though. Jimmy Probasco. Some kind of horse doctor with a sideline as a fence. The reputation he had for dodging convictions might mean he was protected, a good thing for himself and Van. Or then again, it might mean he was way too friendly with the bulls. The thought of lying there helpless on the chopping board while the guinea dropped a dime on him was the kind of thing could give a guy nightmares if he let it.

And there was another thing. The smell as the wop opened the door to them. One hundred percent proof. The guy stank like a distillery. He seemed to be holding it together though, as he led

341

them inside. Offered them a drink. "Or I can make coffee, you prefer it," he said, after they shook their heads, seating themselves around the kitchen table.

Johnny turned down the offer. "Keep me awake this time of night."

Probasco drained a water glass of Canadian Club. "You probably got a point there." Poured himself a refill.

Jesus Christ. "You know who we are?"

"Sure I do. You'll be okay here, though. Tucked out the way. And King and Queen there"- he indicated the back yard – "make sure we won't get any unexpected visitors sticking their noses where they're not wanted."

"The price, though. How much we paying?"

Piquet cut into the conversation. "Jimmy says fifty dollars a day." Teased his pompadour. " Isn't that right, Jimmy?"

"What we agreed on, yeah."

Johnny frowned. "Don't you think that's high?"

Probasco recharged his glass. "You're pretty hot, but I want you to be satisfied. What do you think is fair?"

"How about thirty-five a day?"

"That's all right with me. Thirty-five a day, then, for room and board."

Johnny turned to Piquet. "The sawbones. When can he work on me?"

"Make with the scratch and he can be here tomorrow night."

"He good?"

"He worked on Ma Barker's boys. Fred. Dock. Old Creepy. I didn't hear no complaints from them." He held out his hand. "He won't work without a down payment, though. I told you that already."

Johnny counted out three thousand in twenties. "You'll get the rest after the operation."

Piquet added the cash to his roll. Opened his hand again. "And there's the balance for defending Billie. Two thousand dollars, yeah?" He curled his fingers as Johnny stared at him. Hid his hand in his pocket. "I did the best I could for the gal. Two years

343

is nothing compared to what they coulda thrown at her. I'm not Clarence Darrow, for God sake. I mean, Jesus Christ, John."

"They want to make an example of her," Van Meter said. "Use her to get at you. There was no way she was going to walk out that courtroom a free woman, Johnny. No way in the world."

Yeah, well. Perhaps Van was right. He didn't like it, but what the fuck. Sometimes you just had to eat it. Show some class. "You'll get your money, counsellor. Don't worry about that. Johnny Dillinger ain't no welsher. I pay my debts." Billie. It broke him up to think of her rotting in the pen, but there was nothing he could do about it. Same with the guys in Ohio. Local law was one thing, easy to fix. The fucking federals, though. As the last few months had taught him, they were something else again.

Three

Piquet brought the two doctors to the house the following evening: Doc Loeser, a fifty-eight year old parole violator, who'd been living in Mexico after skipping-out on a three-year bid for dealing dope out his drug cupboard, and Harry Cassidy, twenty years the Doc's junior, an alcoholic pin-artist with an ex-wife eating him alive with alimony demands. The older guy looked like a gone-to-seed Erich Von Stroheim, while the younger one sported a puss full of broken veins. Used the same brand of cologne as Probasco.

Not a pair to inspire confidence in a fella looking to go under the knife. Anything but.

"You sure these boys are up to it?" Johnny asked Piquet, as the lawyer introduced the two medics.

"They did good work on the other guys wanted to change their faces. Besides, no one else will touch you, John."

"Yeah, I know. People keep telling me. I'm too damn hot." He eyeballed the elder of the pair. "You the one who's cutting me?"

The kraut bent slightly from the waist. "Harold will act as my assistant and provide aftercare. The charge is one hundred dollars per day."

"On top of what you get for the surgery."

"That is correct." He examined Johnny's face like an artist contemplating a subject. "What do you want me to do?"

"The moles" – he pointed to his face – "and the dimple" – flicked his chin with his index finger. "The scar on the lip. And a facelift. Smooth out the lines. Straighten my nose while you're at it. Think you can handle that, Doc?"

"The moles are easy. As for the facelift, we cut you behind the ears where the scars don't show. Pull back the skin. Tighten it with kangaroo tendons" – a quick smile – "put a spring in your step. We can use the excess from the incisions to fill the dimple. You want a general or a local anaesthetic?"

"A general. That would put me right under, wouldn't it?"

Loeser nodded.

"You going to be here, Homer?"

Van Meter turned a little green. "If you want me to stay, John."

Lying unconscious with a reward on his head in front of these two gravediggers was the last thing he needed. "That's what I want, Homer." He held out his hands. Spread his fingers. "You can erase my prints for me?"

Loeser mimicked Johnny's actions. Displayed fingertips blurred by scar tissue. "I lifted my own down in Mexico. You like what you see, I can do the same for you." He motioned towards the staircase. "Another time, though. The operation on your face is enough for one day. When you're ready, that is."

They trooped up to the front bedroom. The Doc scrubbed his hands in the bathroom.

"Have you eaten today?"

"Why? Will it make any difference?"

"It will if you vomit while under the ether. You could choke to death on the table."

He'd had steak and eggs an hour or so earlier. Fuck it, though. He'd take the risk. He'd wanted it safe and easy, he'd have stayed on his dad's farm in Moorseville. "I had coffee and grapefruit for breakfast. Toast." He stripped his shirt. Lay back on the cot. "Okay, Doc. I'm ready."

The two medics assembled their equipment on a card table placed beside the cot. Cassidy began to drip ether onto a towel.

"You still there, Homer?"

"Don't worry, Johnny. I'll be here till you come back round."

The towel descended over his face. The smell of the ether was nauseating. He began to go under. Panicked. Struggled to stay awake.

"He's fighting it, Doc."

"Use the whole tin."

The smell increased in a rush. Darkness met over him. Like slipping below the surface of a river. That time he fell in the local stream as a kid. Fall Creek. He'd hauled himself out by a tree branch. Went back later and mastered his fear. Learned to swim. Dive. Mastered it as he mastered any physical activity. Any chance to parade his skill and daring.

The summers at the swimming hole thereafter, cooling of with the other kids from the neighbouring farms. Trying to impress the girls. It was another diversion to add to the sandlot baseball games and the long, lonely rambles through the woods with his dog and his .22 as he struggled against the monotony of farm work, attempting to flee the cold, motherless house. The distant father.

The way she'd left him. The memories of her body laid on the table as he mounted a chair, trying to wake the figure inside the coffin as the pallbearers entered the kitchen. The beatings his father handed out the way other men handed out candy. Affection. As if the boy reminded the old man of the woman who bore him. The woman he himself had lost.

The way he hitchhiked into Indianapolis as the sandlot and the swimming hole palled. The older bunch he hung with in the speakeasies and pool halls, tough guys with prison haircuts and homemade tattoos. Their stories of easy money and the women it could buy. The whorehouses he'd already begun to visit when he had the money. The drink to steady his nerve.

The goddamn drink. Rotgut cooked in basement distilleries by the dagoes. Moonshine from surrounding farms. He'd been sitting on a stoop slugging the latter from a Mason Jar when Ed Singleton had suggested rolling Mr Morgan on his way to the bank.

Mr Morgan. The only guy he'd ever regretted robbing. Someone who'd treated him to candy when he'd visited his store as a kid. He'd cried when the grocer confronted him later. It had been the drink, though. He couldn't even remember the job. Just waking up the next day with a throbbing head and a couple hundred dollars in his pocket. A bloodied length of pipe by the bed.

Throwing himself on the mercy of the court seemed the best way to go after what he'd done. He couldn't ask his old man to pay for a lawyer. Not after letting him down that way. Besides, it was a first offence. Surely they wouldn't give him hard time for what he'd done? Especially after Singleton drew a two-year bit.

So he'd pled guilty. Let the bench decide his fate.

He'd expected to be punished for what he'd done. Accepted it. Seeing the old man's head laid open that way. Like striking his own father. When the judge hit him with a ten to twenty year sentence, though, he thought the world had come to an end for him. Instead it was just the beginning...

"He's not breathing."

Something hard pounding against his chest.

"Oh my God. He's dead."

"You killed him, you mick quack, and you're dead too."

The pounding continued. He coughed. Turned his head.
Vomit spattered the floor beside the cot.

"Easy, gentleman. Our patient has come back to us." Loeser
arched over him as he opened his eyes. "Welcome back, Mr
Dillinger. We thought we'd lost you."

"Might as well have been now as some other time." He
managed a small laugh. "The operation?"

"Things went well." Loeser proffered a small hand mirror.
Revealed a bloodstained mummy. "I'll return in three day's time to
remove the bandages. Harold will stay with you until then. After
that, we start on the fingerprints. Unless you'd prefer we started on
your face first, Mr Van Meter?"

Van Meter paled. "I'm in no rush to let you carve on me, you
damn butcher."

"Very well, then. Fingerprints first." He opened the windows to vent the ether. Stowed his tools into his doctor's bag. "Three day's time, then." Headed for the door.

Four

The Doc returned with Piquet on the Thursday morning. Cut away the bandages. "Well. What do you think?"

The moles were gone. The dimple. Jesus Christ, though. The way Loeser had carved on his face. "God Almighty. I look like I been in a dogfight."

"The incisions still have to heal. Wait until I take the sutures out. See what you think then."

Piquet threw an arm around his shoulders. "Christ, John. Try and see it without the knife work. You look like a new man."

"You think so?" He returned the gaze of the stranger regarding him from the glass. That was the thing. The stranger. Handsome-looking bastard, too, you ignored the scars. He grew his moustache back in, got himself some window glass spectacles, dyed his hair again, his own father wouldn't know him. "Okay. I can see it. Way he's going to look in a few weeks time."

Loeser admired his handiwork. "Happy?" he said.

"Good enough, Doc. Good enough." He displayed his mug to Van Meter. "What do you think, Van? Ready to give it a go?"

"I wouldn't trust that bastard to cut the tail feathers from a pigeon."

The Doc opened his medical bag. Removed a number of small coloured bottles. A scalpel. "The fingerprints, though. You still wish me to work on them?"

"Johnny goes first, though. He's got a damn sight more faith in you than I have."

Johnny unfastened his cufflinks. Rolled his sleeves. "Suits me. I'd rather get it over with as soon as possible." He set his face as Loeser swabbed his fingers with antiseptic. Injected each one with cocaine. "Are you ready, John?"

"I'm ready."

"Very well, then. We begin." He unsheathed the scalpel and began to peel Johnny's fingertips with the blade. Once the right hand was finished, he dipped the now raw digits in a solution of hydrochloric acid and left them to soak a moment, before transferring them to a solution of caustic soda. He switched to the left with his blade as the chemicals worked on the right, before whittling away any ridges that remained once the chemicals had done their work.

He paused as he finished with the scalpel. Laid it aside. "Could you use a drink, John?"

"Yeah, I'd take a drink. I'd take about anything I could get right now."

The Doc snapped his fingers at Probasco, who'd joined Van Meter and Piquet as they watched in horrified fascination.

The Italian poured a jigger of scotch. Handed it to Johnny. He watched him hold the glass awkwardly between his palms as he killed the shot. "Anybody else?" he asked, hovering the bottle over a couple more glasses.

Johnny set his teeth as Piquet and Van Meter grabbed for the tumblers. "What's a matter, boys? Not got the stomach for this?"

Van Meter downed his drink. Beckoned Probasco to give him a refill. "I'm game, Johnny. You know that. Just…"

"Yeah, Van. I know." He parked his empty glass. "Okay, Doc. Let's finish it."

Loeser applied the caustic solution to his left hand. Touched up the blade work. Bandaged his fingers and gave him a shot of morphine. "You won't know much of what's going on for a few hours, but at least you'll feel no pain." He leered at Van Meter. "And while you're out I'll work on your colleague here. Fingers and face, Mr Van Meter?"

"You don't knock me out if Johnny's hopped up, though."

"Just a local anaesthetic? The pain will be considerable, you know."

"If you think I trust you shitheels enough to see us both on dope you got another thing coming." He unbuttoned his shirt. Stretched out on the cot. "All right, sawbones, let's get it over with. Better now than never. Cut away you bastard and be damned."

Five

Loeser transformed a vertical scar on Van Meter's hairline to a horizontal one and trimmed down his lip. He reset his broken nose, then burned a tattooed anchor bearing the motto 'Good Hope' from his forearm with acid. As far as Van Meter was concerned, though, when the bandages were removed a few days later, the tattoo's erasure was the only part that had worked.

"Look at my goddamn face," he said, hurling the dressings on the floor. "I pay out five thousand dollars and this is what I get."

Johnny studied the lumpy mess dispassionately: now that his own wounds were beginning to heal, he was starting to fall in love with his new mug. "Quit griping. You got to give yourself a few weeks to heal before you start spouting off about the way you look after the op."

"That's easy for you to say. You got a good job. I got a lousy one. And look at these fingers." He splayed his hands. "That's going to leave nothing but a buncha scars."

Loeser tutted. "My own fingers, though, Mr Van Meter." He displayed his own digits once again. "See? Completely smooth. Once your own have healed - "

357

"You goddamn butcher. I ought to take my money back. Take it out of your hide."

"A few more days, Mr Van Meter. If you are not completely satisfied, then perhaps we can renegotiate as to my fee. As it is, I am prepared, for no extra charge, to furnish you with new identities to go with your new faces."

"You can do that?"

"Give me a few moments." He beckoned a bleary-eyed Probasco, who was watching the confrontation from behind his customary glass of rotgut. "You have writing paper? A pen?

"Sure. Hold on." He groped in a drawer. "There you go, Doc. Knock yourself out."

Loeser installed himself at the kitchen table. Scratched away at the foolscap. "There." He presented Van Meter with the paper: *Received $30.00 from Henry J. Adams four miles west of Amorita, Oklahoma in full for confinement of Henry J. Adams, Jr., born January 2, 1899, to Henry J. Adams and Mollie Johnson Adams (maiden name of mother Mollie Johnson).* "If the details are acceptable to you, I am able to transfer them to a blank document and forge the signature of a long dead physician."

Van Meter blinked. "You can do that?" he repeated.

"I developed considerable expertise in such things when selling out of the drugs cabinet in my former practice. It was the carelessness of one of my former clients that landed me in Leavenworth, rather than my own penmanship. And as for the marks of your surgery" – he recharged the fountain pen: *Received from Henry J. Adams of Chicago, Illinois, $37.00 in full for care of injuries to distal phalanges palmar aspects of both hands, to ventral surface of right forearm, to forehead of left side near median line.* "The result of an automobile accident, shall we say?"

"Well, I look like I been in a goddamn car crash," Van Meter grumbled. "Still." He handed the document back to Loeser.

"You can do the same for me?" Johnny asked.

"Of course." He set to work again: *Received $25.00 from James C. Lawrence of six miles south of Byron, Oklahoma in full for confinement of Joseph C. Lawrence, Jr., born January 11, 1904, to James C. Lawrence and Mary Lawrence Harris (maiden name of mother Mary Lawrence).*

"And as to your scars."

Received from Joseph C. Lawrence of Chicago, Illinois,
$44.00 in full for care of injuries to chin, to nose, to distal
phalanges of both hands palmar aspect, to upper lip on left side
near median line, to both cheeks below the ear, to chest.

"I will write these up tonight, if they are to your satisfaction. Have Mr Piquet deliver them on his next visit. I trust you will find my paperwork acceptable. On which note," he added, capping his fountain pen, "we reach the conclusion of our business together. Congratulations, gentlemen. With your new faces, new identities, you are, in criminal terms, once again virgins. Your past has been erased along with your fingerprints."

Johnny studied his new I.D. "You're a wizard, Doc. What can I say?"

"I would not not grow too complacent, Johnny. The federal manhunt draws closer every day. Even with your new faces, new documentation, your lives are still in danger if you remain in the United States." He closed his doctor's bag and shrugged into his overcoat. "With the money from your operations, I intend to return to Mexico and life as a respectable citizen. I advise you to do the same. With your names in the headlines and a price on your heads, it will only be a matter of time until someone betrays you. This may be the last opportunity you have to escape with your lives. If I were you, gentlemen, I'd follow my example and head for the border. Get out of the country while you still have the chance."

Six

Johnny and Van Meter spent the next few weeks laying up at Probasco's while their wounds healed. They talked over moneymaking schemes with Piquet, ideas to cash in on their notoriety that didn't involve dodging bullets. An interview with the *American* was proposed, a reporter being driven blindfold into the sticks to meet with Johnny. Piquet would handle the $50,000 fee. When the magazine's editor grew leery and dropped the deal, Piquet suggested making a movie instead.

"We can rent the equipment," he said, splitting a bottle with Probasco. "I know a guy in the newsreel business. He can handle the cameras and lighting equipment for us. You can give your life story. Run down a couple of jobs to people. Tell them crime does not pay."

Van Meter bobbled his head. "I can give out a message to the youth of America," he said.

Johnny raised an eyebrow. "Steady, Van. We just want to tell them that crime doesn't pay."

Van Meter considered. "Okay. *I'll* give out a message to the youth of America and *you* tell them crime don't pay. How 'bout that, huh?"

Mostly, though, they lounged around the house, Van Meter tinkering with the radio, monitoring the news reports and police broadcasts, while Johnny read the newspapers. The item announcing that Johnny now rated a $15000 reward to Nelson's $7500 was one that went into the clippings file. "Watch the little prick burn when he finds the G put a higher price tag on my head than his. And you, Van. You don't rate at all." He smirked as Van Meter gave him the finger.

They were getting antsy, though, especially Johnny. Sick of their host. Probasco was an argumentative drunk. He was too leery of his guests to give them any trouble, but a booze-fuelled argument with an equally lushed Piquet spilled out onto the sidewalk one night, threatening to attract heat. And when he tried to enlist them in gunning a business partner, some guy he was buying a tavern with, it was all Johnny could do to stay in the room with the prick.

Besides, now his face was mending, he was eager to try out his new face on the streets. His first jaunt was a Cubs game at

Wrigley Field, where he goosed an unsuspecting Piquet in the ribs. He enjoyed watching the lawyer jump until Piquet pointed out Captain Stege, head of the Dillinger Squad, standing two feet away from them, resulting in a quick fade from the freshly-minted James C. Lawrence Jr.

Other outings were more successful, however. He took in the movies. The World's Fair. And he began to frequent Anna Sage's place on the North Side. The whorehouse he'd patronized when he first raised from the pen.

Billie. He missed her. Two years without was a long time. He'd be waiting when she came out. Send for her if he was abroad. The train job came off and he'd have enough to keep them on easy street for the rest of their lives.

Two years, though. That was a hell of a long time. Too long for a man to go without. He'd already lost nine years to the state prison system. Be damned if he was going to lose another two to the feds.

A man had his urges. His needs. And a whore. There was no connection there. No love. It was just a means to an end. A way of getting himself straight when the mood was on him. In his heart, he was faithful. He'd be there when Billie walked out that gate. Waiting for her. Ready to start that life they'd promised themselves in the sun. A life where the law couldn't touch them.

That was what he promised himself. That it was just a physical thing. That he'd stay faithful in his heart.

The heart has it's own agenda, though. He was bleeding inside and he needed something to staunch the wound. Or rather someone.

Polly.

Polly Hamilton.

She was a waitress in a North Side restaurant. Divorced. A redhead who turned tricks on the side to eke out her wages. She lacked that flint-faced, calculating quality he associated with the hardcore hooker, though. There was still the air of an ordinary girl about her. The enthusiastic amateur. He tried hard enough, he could almost fool himself they were a regular couple. That he wasn't an impostor. That she truly cared for him. A little make belief and he could almost believe they were in love.

She looked like a farm girl, with a clear complexion and blue eyes. A Swede or mick. And she had a way about her when she laughed, sweet and innocent. Difficult to believe she made the rent on her back in a North Side call house, but what the hell. She thought he was Jimmy Lawrence, clerk at the Board of Trade coming off an automobile accident. It wasn't perfect. But, then again, what was?

And they enjoyed themselves. Christ, yes. Every day was a holiday. With his new face and the safe-house at Probasco's, they could have fun openly. Like that regular couple they pretended to be.

Riverview Park was one of their regular haunts. They'd ride the roller-coaster, screaming on the downward slopes, kissing on the curves. He'd win her a kewpie doll at the shooting gallery, the other customers queuing to watch as he set the targets flying. They'd stroll by the water. Eat cotton-candy. Have themselves a ball.

They'd take in a movie afterwards, Beery in *Pancho Villa*, Fields in *You're Telling Me*, a gangster flick if one was playing, then move on to a restaurant or club, the Grand Terrace or French

Casino. He'd ask the orchestra leader to play his favourites, *All I Do is Dream of You* and *For All We Know*, then croon in her ear as they played. Lead her onto the dance floor for the carioca. The way he had with Billie.

He called her 'Countess' or 'Contessa'. Bought her an amethyst ring. She gave him a gold ring with an inscription inside – *With All My Love, Polly* – and a watch with her picture inside. Just like a regular couple.

But like a regular couple, it wasn't all fun and games. Money was running low. The guy had to earn a crust. And there was a job on offer. It was time to get the gang back together. Time to go back to work.

SEVEN

GOLDIGGERS OF 1934

He had his weaknesses – women, for one thing and a flair for the spectacular – J. Edgar Hoover

One

We can't all be saints – John Dillinger

The job had come through Jimmy Murray at the barbecue stand. It turned out Nelson was back in town. The runt wanted a meeting. Had a jug lined up. A good one. And they were part of the string, if they wanted in.

"What do you think?" he'd asked Van Meter that morning, as they lingered over breakfast at Probasco's. "Reckon the little guy's setting us up?"

"He wouldn't try nothing in Murray's place. The guy's too well connected. The offer's gotta be jake." He slurped his coffee. Drew on a Chesterfield. "Taking him up on it, though. That's something else again, you know?"

Yeah, Johnny knew, all right. But funds were running low. They needed a cash injection. The squirt must be in the same straits as themselves, if he'd decided to forget about the flare-up at Little Bohemia. Invited them along on the heist.

He was still mulling things over when he left Probasco's. His survival-sense switched off. The first indication that he'd walked into a trap was a revolver punched into his spine as he emerged from behind the Shell station. Made to cross the avenue.

"Inna car, punk. Somebody wants a word with you."

He found himself sandwiched in the back seat of a Hupmobile, the two legbreakers sitting each side of him like bookends. The silk shirts and hand-painted ties told him they weren't coppers, anyway. The garlic on the speaker's breath, breaking through the expensive cologne as he leaned across and relieved him of the Colt in his shoulder rig, gave him a good indication of who they actually represented. "Can I ask where I'm going?" he said, as the car merged with the downtown traffic.

"You can shut the fuck up, is what you can do," the first one said.

"Don't sweat it," the second one, added. "We got orders to drop you back at your apartment afterward. The guy just wants to talk to you, is all. This' one ride you'll be coming back from."

Their destination was an office block in the Loop. They took an elevator to the third floor. The black lettering on the marbled glass door read *Motion Picture Operators' Union.* A portly, moustachioed Italian in a grey flannel business suit and horn-rimmed spectacles manned the cheap pine desk inside. Behind him sat a thick-set, middle-aged mick with a hostile expression and, over in the corner, a younger, dark-haired guy with the high colour and collapsed cheeks of a lunger: West Side boss Klondike O'Donnell and St Valentine's Day lookout and sometime Barker sidekick, Byron Bolton respectively.

The Italian, who appeared to be chairing the meeting, was Phil D'Andrea, former head of Syndicate trucking operations i.e. beer running, and, despite his almost professorial aura – rumour had it that he'd put in two years at Hamilton Law school before throwing in with the family cartage business at the outset of Prohibition – a skilled marksman and trusted bodyguard to the Big Fella before the taxman sent him up the river. "Have a seat," he said, as the bruisers withdrew, taking up position outside the office. "The boys weren't too rough with you, were they, Johnny?"

Johnny eased into the hard-backed chair as if it was made of glass. Or rather, ice. The thin variety, which is what he appeared to be skating on at the moment. "Uh-uh. Never laid a finger on me. Didn't harm a hair on my head."

"That's good. Very good. Some of the fellas we got on board these days can get carried away with the heat of the moment. We was looking to hurt you, you wouldn't be here now." He pressed his hands together in front of his breastbone, as if praying. "All we want to do is talk, get me? Just have a little conversation with you, is all."

"You have to stick a gun in my ribs for that?"

O'Donnell grunted. "You'd a come in otherwise?"

Johnny wound it in a notch. "No. I guess not." Gave his attention back to D'Andrea. "So. This talk we gonna to have. You want to fill me in, D'Andrea?"

"You know who I am, then?"

"We might not be in the same profession, but we drink from the same well, so to speak."

O'Donnell popped his knuckles. "Drinking from the well's one thing. Pissing in it's another."

"Come again?"

Bolton coughed into a handkerchief. "The kid Jimmy. We got a problem with him."

D'Andrea flattened his hands on the desk. "The prick's in tight with the Touhys. We see the bastard back in Chi and he's dead before he can draw breath, you get me?"

"What the hell's that got to do with me?"

O'Donnell gave him the fish eye. "You run with the squirt, don't you?"

"We worked together in the past. The runt brings too much heat, though. We cut him loose a while back."

The tension in the room lessened. Bolton looked at O'Donnell. "Didn't I tell you this guy was jake?"

"Just cause you run with Karpis and them Okie bastards don't make you an authority on yeggmen, Bolton." He creased his eyes at Johnny. "You ever work with Touhy, kid?"

"I never even met the guy."

D'Andrea allowed a quarter-inch of smile to show beneath his moustache. "We know there's no connection between you and the Irishman. We had to ask, though." He hooked off his spectacles. His eyes contracted as he polished the lenses with a square of yellow cloth. "You're really finished with, Nelson?"

"I don't owe him a thing."

374

"You know where he is, though."

"Why the hell should I know where he is if I cut the prick loose?"

"Why indeed?" D'Andrea replaced his spectacles. The lenses flashed in the light as he stared intently at Johnny. "If you were to run into the squirt again, though."

"Drop a dime on the kid, you mean?"

O'Donnell cut in. "If you know what's good for you, asshole."

D'Andrea raised a hand. "Easy, Klondike. No need for unpleasantness." He practiced his smile on Johnny again. "Let's just say that if you did decide to inform us where the little guy was jungled-up, someone near the head of the organization might be, eh, inclined to look on you with favour, shall we say?"

"Nitti, you mean?"

Bolton examined the back of his hand. "We don't use names," he said.

Johnny shrugged. "Whatever." Crossed his legs. "What do you mean by 'grateful', anyway, D'Andrea?"

"He means we let you live, is what he means, you punk."

375

D'Andrea gave O'Donnell a disapproving look. "The Big Fella always had a soft spot for you guys, Christ knows why. Let you have the run of the place, long as you anted up a percentage, same as everybody else wanted to operate here.

The new guy, though. He's a different kettle of fish. A businessman. He don't see no percentage in letting you kids run loose playing Jesse James. Don't like the heat you bring. You don't stay outta this burg and you're likely to end up in the county morgue with a tag wired to your toe. Unless, of course" – he went for a benign expression – "you could prove useful to the organization. You help us out and we help you out. Providing you don't try and pull no bank jobs within the city limits, that is."

"You're asking me to rat on the kid. Turn into a goddamn squealer."

"You don't owe him nothing. You said that yourself."

Bolton set light to a Sano. "Wise up, Johnny. Do yourself a favour here."

"This ain't the law talking," added O'Donnell. "You can't run from us. We found you today, we'll find you again if we want to. No problem there, kid."

No problem? Easy for them to say. One thing he'd never do was turn stool-pigeon. Even on an asshole like Nelson.

The alternative, though. There'd be no place to hide if he crossed the Syndicate. They owned Chicago. Put a hair across the Barber's ass and he'd be signing his own death warrant.

Tell them what they wanted to hear and they'd be off his neck for the meantime, though. He couldn't turn in Nelson, anyway. The squirt had vanished since Little Bohemia. He couldn't have ratted on him even if he wanted to. "So all you want me to do is keep my eyes open for the runt. Get in touch if I find him."

"Give us what we want and we guarantee we lay off you and your buddies whenever you're holed-up from the law."

"There's no guarantee I can deliver, though. Like I say, me and the kid are finished."

"You run in the same circles. Mix with the same people. You'll get a lead on him eventually and when you do, we want to hear from you."

Johnny blew out his breath in a long sigh. "Okay, then. Whatever you say. I run into the half-pint again and I'll give you a call."

D'Andrea beamed. "I'm glad you seen sense, Johnny. You got your racket like we got ours. There's no need for us to bang heads if you're willing to see sense." He clapped him on the back as he escorted him out the office. "You're all right for a farm boy, Johnny. Shame you got to thieving instead of coming in with us."

Johnny resisted the urge to swat the guinea's hand away. He wasn't a hood and he didn't associate with hoods. He was a thief. A man who went out and worked for a living. Put his neck on the line. Not some guy who sheltered behind a big organization. A punk who put the arm on tavern owners and union guys. Working stiffs. Guys that couldn't hit back. "Can I get a ride back uptown?" he asked, twitching his chin at the two heavies standing guard outside the office.

"Sure you can. The boys'll drop you wherever you ask." D'Andrea withdrew behind the desk. "And you find Nelson, ring the office here. It's a legitimate front. No names over the telephone, but we can arrange a meeting. The number's in the book."

He got the two hoods to drop him outside Probasco's. Took a cab uptown from there. He was still half expecting a tail as he dropped off at the barbecue stand. Some silk-suited greaseball

378

eyeballing him from beneath a streetlamp as he walked in the door. The Syndicate was a hell of a lot more efficient than the feds when it came to keeping tabs on a guy. Hell of a lot quicker to take a guy off the street when they wanted, too, judging by the number of yeggs they'd sent to the county morgue in the last six months.

"What do you think, Jimmy?" he asked Murray, as they settled in the hidden room. "You're connected in this town. How do you think we stand?"

The ward-heeler knuckle-stroked his moustache. "They didn't just hit you in the head means they think they can use you. Soon as you fink on the kid, though, you're history."

Van Meter nipped at a beer. "I say play them along. Long as they think you can hand up the runt, they'll lay off us. Give us time to fence the bonds. Pull that train job." He drained his bottle. Pushed aside the empty. "Speaking of which, this bank heist the kid's pushing. You still up for that, Johnny?"

"I don't see as we've any option. Cash's running low. We need something to stake us until we pull the big one, you know?"

Murray flamed a cigar. "Word's gonna get out that you're working with the kid again, though. And once it does…"

"You managed to move the bonds yet, Jimmy?"

The ward-heeler belched smoke. "Christ sake, John. These things take time, okay?"

"That's what I thought."

Murray made to retort. Paused at a knock on the door. "Yeah?"

The counterman stuck his head round the jamb. "Some kid to see you, Jimmy."

"Sour-faced little fuck? Newsie's cap?"

"That's the one. Want I should send him up?"

Murray looked at the others. Johnny nodded.

"Looks like we're working with Nelson again, after all." Johnny concealed his pistol in his lap, hoping he wouldn't have to use it. He wondered which was more a danger to him: Nelson himself or the guys trying to put a hole-in the little prick's head.

Two

Purvis furtively unbuttoned his collar as he worked his way through the IN tray that Friday afternoon. The city was in the grip of a heat wave, the temperature rising towards the nineties as the day wore on. The streets were full of women in sundresses and shirtwaists, a consolation prize for the guys in undershirts on stoops and street corners, smoking and spitting as they whiled the days away waiting for jobs to materialize, a winter of snow clearing and cardboard shacks waiting a bare three months in their future.

For now, though, it was summer, the streets a passing carnival for any guy lucky enough to have a job and enjoying his weekend off. Purvis wished he could join them, shed his jacket and tie for shirtsleeves and slacks, treat himself to a snow cone or soda, but there was work to do. The flood of paperwork on Dillinger never seemed to abate. The bastard got around more than a stray dog, if you believed half the sightings that turned up on his desk.

Following them up was a pain in the ass, but it had to be done. There was always the possibility that one of them might prove true. Ignore a report that he'd been spotted out in the boondocks and you could bet your roll that was the tip that would have led to his capture. Dillinger was only one man, for Christ sake, and they were an army. He was bound to slip up eventually. Surface again somewhere soon. Wasn't he?

The phone rang. Captain Tim O'Neil, East Chicago police department. "We know you guys don't get on too good with the bulls in the city there, but what the hell. We got the skinny on this Dillinger fuck and we thought you ought to know about it."

He'd had the real bunk on Dillinger handed him too many times in the last few months to raise his hopes here. The Indiana State Police had already phoned in a sighting in Culver City that day. Dillinger and Van Meter casing a bank.

Still. There might be something useful here. Piquet's reference to "a guy out of East Chicago" looking to cut a deal over Dillinger. You never knew. "Okay, Captain O'Neil. Any information you can give us on Dillinger would be greatly appreciated."

"This ain't just some bullshit tip, Purvis. We got the goods on the cocksucker this time. Can we meet someplace? Sort out the details?"

"You can't just tell me over the phone?"

"You want this prick on a morgue slab?"

"Well…"

"All right, then. We'll pick you up outside the Banker's Building at six. Make a meet. Piquet says you're interested, but you're not outside when we pull up, you can forget about it. We let you spend the next six months out in the boondocks running down leads that go no place. Getting laughed at by the newspapers. The local cops." The captain clicked a cigarette lighter at the other end of the line. "Think it over, Purvis. You got nothing else to hang your hat on. Way things are going with this Dillinger asshole, way he's making a fool of you and the rest of them college boys, we're the only hope you got."

Three

Johnny knocked at the second floor apartment. A dark, soulful eye appeared around the corner of the door. A prow of a nose. The voice, when it came, was low and melodious. Accented like Dietrich. "Johnny?"

"Who else, baby?"

He hugged the woman as he entered the room. She was an attractive, heavy-bosomed Latin type in her early forties. The blue silk kimono she wore parted to reveal muscular , but well shaped, calves as she led him inside. Like many madames, she'd gotten out of the game early enough to keep her looks. For one bizarre moment, she reminded him of his last hostess, Sheriff Holley up in Crown Point. Anna Sage had followed a very different profession from her Lake County compatriot, however.

Better known as 'Katie from the Kostur', she was the former manageress of East Chicago's most infamous cathouse, the Kostur Hotel, a bucket of blood catering to longshoremen and sailors and notorious for the donnybrooks that periodically left the fixtures shattered and the walls pock-marked with bullet holes. A series of busts had led her to relocate from the lakeside port's notorious

Indiana Harbour section to Chicago's North Side, where she operated from a string of call houses while fighting deportation to her native Romania. She was Polly Hamilton's roommate and employer and, for the foreseeable future, Johnny's new landlady while he doped out the railroad job with Van Meter.

The Syndicate meeting had spooked him. He didn't know if Probasco had got lushed and opened his mouth about his location or if one of the quacks had spilled, but he knew it was time to find a new hideout if he was going to work with Nelson again. Moving in with Polly seemed the ideal solution. Nobody knew where he was except her and Van Meter and that was the way it was going to stay until they hit the Reserve train and got out of the city for good. "My room ready?" he said to Anna, resting his suitcase on the carpet beside him.

"I gave you the double with Polly. Moved Steve into her old room."

Steve Choliak, her unemployed son. "The kid okay with that?"

"He thinks you're a right guy, Johnny. Besides, he don't know who you are. Thinks you're just some two-bit hustler from back East hiding-out on a gambling charge." She loosened the belt of her kimono. "I'm the only one as knows who you are, Johnny. You're secret's safe with me."

"You're trying to tell me Polly don't know who I am?"

"Sure, Johnny. As far as the girl knows you're just Jimmy Lawrence from the Board of Trade."

"Yeah, sure." He cased the apartment. Overstuffed furniture. Striped wallpaper. A canary in a cage. "Polly not in right now?"

"She's at the restaurant. As you well know."

"No need for her to stick with that while she's with me. I'll have a word with her. Get her to quit." He looked at Anna. The way the kimono clung to her curves. Parted at the cleavage. "And Steve. He's downtown checking out the jobs, I suppose."

"Checking out the pool halls more like. You know Steve."

"Just the two of us then."

She angled her head towards the bedroom. "You want to check out the arrangements, Johnny? Check out the new bed?"

He cupped a hand to her rump as he followed her into the bedroom. Polly Hamilton. What the hell. How could it be cheating when the girl was a whore?

Four

A blue Packard kerbed outside the Banker's Building as Purvis departed the lobby. A dyspeptic-looking individual in heavy black spectacles wound down the window. Loosed a cigarette bass at the Chicago SAC. "Purvis?"

Purvis tried not to appear too eager. The mention of Piquet had persuaded him there might be something to the police captain's offer after all. This could be the break he'd been looking for since the start of the case, the tip off that finally put the Hoosier bandit in his gun sights. If it panned out, this could get him off the hook for Little Bohemia. Put him back on the Director's Xmas list. Back on the front page where he belonged. "Captain O'Neil?"

O'Neil thumbed him into the back. "Cowley. Your boss. He in on this?"

"I phoned him straight after you left. He's staying at the Great Northern Hotel while he's in Chicago. He's expecting us." He scrambled into the car. "You need directions?"

The driver twisted his head and smiled over the back of the seat at him, a handsome, dark-haired sheikh with bedroom eyes. A

388

black cigarette holder set between his teeth. "It's okay, Purvis, I know the way. Stayed there a couple of times myself when I've been in Chicago on business."

They rode the few blocks to the Great Northern. Took the elevator to Cowley's room. 712.

"You want coffee?" Cowley asked, as he answered the door to them. "I can have some sent up before we begin, if you like."

O'Neil grunted. Perched on the edge of the bed. "You got anything stronger?"

"Against my faith, I'm afraid." He dragged up a couple of hard-backed chairs. Positioned himself and Purvis opposite the captain. "I'll take that as a no, then?"

"Take it any goddamn way you like." O'Neil evaluated the bedroom's Hollywood Modern décor. The crisp white bed linen. The Degas reproduction over the marble fireplace. "Pretty nice. You federal boys do yourself good living off the government tit. Nice to know what my frigging tax money goes on, anyway."

The dark haired man sat on an embroidered damascene chair at the centre of their impromptu circle. He fitted an Abdullah to the cigarette holder. Set it afire with a slim gold lighter. "You want to get down to business, Tim?" he said, streaming smoke at the ceiling rose. Propping an ankle on an impeccably-tailored knee.

"The hell with it. We all know why we here. Dillinger. You want him. We can deliver him. Guarantee us that fifteen grand on his head and he's yours."

Cowley sat forward. He brushed his hair back as it fell over his eyes. "Details," he said. "How. Why. Where. Persuade me you're not just blowing smoke and we'll start talking money, Captain."

The dark haired man entered the conversation. "I've an informant I've worked with for years. A good one. Her flatmate's dating Dillinger."

"You're sure it's him?"

"It's him all right. My informant's known him professionally for years."

"Professionally?"

"She's a whore, Mr Cowley. Or rather a madame. Dillinger's been a regular customer of hers in the past."

Cowley let the distaste show on his face. "A whore." He exchanged grimaces with Purvis. "Are you sure you can trust her, Mr - ?"

"You can trust her all right. The bitch is fighting deportation. She can't afford to lie. Guarantee she can stay in the country and she'll deliver the bastard on a plate." He grinned disarmingly. Proffered a manicured hand. "I ought to have introduced myself earlier. The captain's not one for the social graces, I'm afraid. I'm Zarkovich. Martin Zarkovich, Sergeant East Chicago Police Department. Pleased to make your acquaintance, Mr Cowley."

Five

South Bend, Indiana

Saturday, June 30

The Hudson arrived at the intersection of Wayne and Michigan in downtown South Bend at 11.30 a.m., directly opposite the Merchants National Bank. There were four of them that day. Three of them had worked together before. Johnny and Van Meter and Nelson.

Johnny and Van Meter had considered taking the job away from the punk after the warning from D'Andrea, cutting him out the string, but the jug was a fat one and the meeting at Murray's had been an unexpected success.

"Past is past," Nelson had said, looking him in the eye. "Besides, this' a one-off deal. We don't have to become running buddies. Once this' over, we never have to set eyes on each other again. Strictly business, okay, Dillinger?"

Johnny had nodded. "Okay, Jimmy." Shaken hands on the deal. "Whatever you say."

Besides, there was a bonus in the shape of the fourth man they'd added to the string. The only guy that matched Johnny when it came to newspaper headlines. Pretty Boy Floyd himself.

"Forget that 'Pretty Boy' shit," Floyd had said when they met him the night before, an amiable-looking, dark-eyed fullback, Indian blood showing in his broad, flat features and black, centre-parted hair. "That's something the newspapers made up. Most people know me as Choc."

"Choctaw?" Van Meter asked.

Floyd displayed the bottle in his hand. Choctaw Beer. He patted the overlap at his belt. "I got a taste for the stuff when I was working the harvest crews as a kid. Better that than the moko this bastard swills all day," he went on, indicating the dazed-looking figure cradling a Mason jar at his side. "He hadn't been drunk at the station that morning in Kansas City, lost his head with the chopper, and the feds wouldn't be hunting us the way they are now."

The guy with the Mason jar belched. Took a hefty swig of corn liquor. Smacked his lips. A jug-eared wop, unshaven, a bouquet of gin blossoms adorning nose and cheeks: Adam Richetti, Floyd's sidekick and a former inmate of Indiana State, which is how the two crews had connected. The bastard would be too hungover to make the forthcoming job, something for which Johnny would be silently grateful.

"The fed in the backseat hadn't panicked, loosed off his scattergun, and the guys in the front seat would still be alive now," Richetti said, knocking a cork into the neck of the jar. Rubbing the heel of his hand against his eye.

Floyd went to speak. Gave a dismissive wave with his fingers instead. Like he'd had it out with the wop before. Was sick of the subject. "Federal heat. There's nothing worse."

"Except for the Syndicate." Johnny watched Nelson busy himself beneath the open hood of the car, monkeying with the spark plugs. "What happened to your buddy. Miller. Guess you're on the same list back in Kansas City."

"Which is why we headed up North. Last place the feds are gonna expect an Okie like me. Same with the Syndicate boys in KC." He tilted the beer bottle to his lips. Emptied it in a rush. "You got a good one for us, Jimmy?" he said, giving a backhanded swipe to his mouth. Pitching the empty into the bushes.

Nelson surfaced from beneath the hood. Cleaned his hands on a rag. "Think I don't know my game, Choc? Things go okay on this one and we'll have enough on our hips to hole-in for the next six months."

Enough to hole-in for the next six months? Johnny hoped so. The money went out as fast as it came in, though. Protection. Lawyers. Doctors. Always bills to pay. A line of mooches with their hands out. There was no difference between him and the working stiffs that read about him in the newspapers. The only difference between him and John Q. Public was that your solid citizen was likely to die in his bed, while he… well. He didn't want to think about that now. Not as they were preparing to crack a jug. "We set?" he asked, draping a handkerchief over his hand.

The others nodded.

"Okay, then. Let's do it." He led them out the car, leaving Nelson to guard the Hudson. Noted the cop directing traffic at the crossroads. A high school kid checking them out as Van Meter took position on the sidewalk. "What the hell are you looking at?"

"Nothing."

He drew back the handkerchief, revealing his pistol. "You better scram." Shouldered through the weekend shoppers into the bank.

They were old hands at this by now. Van Meter barred the entrance, while Johnny went for the scratch, kicking open the waist-high swinging door and scooping cash from the counters. Floyd took the floor, corralling the customers against the wall with his Thompson, Johnny flinching as the big man loosed a volley into the ceiling, showering plaster onto the hostages' heads.

"What the hell was that for?"

"Keeps the suckers in line." He goofed at Johnny through the descending dust cloud. "Hey, it gives me a thrill. I gotta have some fun, ain't I?"

Yeah, well. Having fun was one thing. Drawing heat was another. He gestured to Van Meter. "The cop from the crossroads."

Van Meter raised his Winchester at the sound of the police-whistle. "I got him, Johnny." He chambered a round as the cop dropped his whistle, reached for his revolver. "Leave it, you prick."

"Screw you, you son-of-a-bitch."

Van pressured the trigger. "You dumb fuck." He ejected the spent cartridge as the copper hit the asphalt. Called to Nelson, crouched by the Hudson with a machine-pistol. "Watch it, Jimmy. The jeweller's across the street."

Nelson turned as the jeweller opened fire from the shop doorway. Hit him in the chest, the slug caroming off the half-pint's steel vest, knocking him off-balance. The jeweller snapped off a second round, pounding the brickwork by the runt's head, then dodged back inside as Nelson returned fire, striking a man inside a stationary car and a passer-by. Sending the Saturday morning shoppers screaming for cover.

Nelson paused to reload. That was when the high school kid made his play. He leaped onto the yeggman's back, clinging to him like a monkey as they reeled across the sidewalk.

Van cocked his piece. "Snot-nose punk."

Nelson shrugged his assailant. "I got him." Pitched the kid through a plate glass window. He tugged a revolver from his waistband and sent a bullet through his opponent's hand. Finished reloading as the kid passed out. Focused his attention back on the street.

More cops. Van Meter strung a half-dozen hostages across the front of the bank. Opened fire. Sent the lawmen ducking amongst the cars parked along the kerb. "It's getting hot out here," he hollered into the bank. "You guys nearly through?"

Johnny scooted a full sack to Floyd. Slung a second over his shoulder. "We're coming." He thrust his Thompson at the bank president and one of the cashiers. "Okay, you two. You're walking us out of here."

The cops let rip as they hit the street. Dropped the hostages, shot in the legs. Johnny snagged the president as he nursed a smashed ankle.

"Come on you. Keep going."

Nelson covered them as they dragged the hostages towards the Hudson, shooting out shop windows and perforating the marquee of the nearby movie house: *Stolen Sweets* with Sally Blane and Charles Starrett. Substituting his revolver as the machine-pistol jammed. "Hurry it up, for Christ sake. I can't hold them much longer."

They dumped the moneybags in the Hudson. Made to follow. Van Meter stumbled. Sprawled across the running board, his head laid open.

"I'm hit."

Johnny barged the hostages aside. "I got you." Boosted him into the roadster. "Move it, Jimmy."

"Sure thing."

They raced the bullet-holed Hudson towards the town limits. Ran the git. Johnny inspected Van Meter's skull as they hit the highway. A surface wound. "I always knew you had a hard head," he said, applying salve. Bandages. "I thought they took you off at the goddamn neck."

"Fuck you, Johnny." Van Meter ground his teeth together. "I'm dying here."

"We'll get Cassidy to check you back in Chi. You'll live." He gave his attention to Floyd, as the Okie rifled the sacks. "We hit a good one, Charley?"

"She'll do. Enough for me and the wop to hole-in for a few months, anyway. Head back home." He glanced at Nelson. "What about you, kid? Back to Chicago with these two guys?"

"Frisco for me, Choc. I got contacts out there. Friends that can hide me." He glared at Dillinger and Van Meter. "Like I said at Murray's, this' a one-off deal for me. I ain't forgotten about that thing in the woods, even if you have. I ever see you two assholes again and I'll kill you, understand me?"

They switched cars behind an abandoned school house. Floyd and Richetti headed south, bound for Oklahoma's Cookson Hills, Nelson for the West Coast, while Johnny nursed Van Meter back to Chicago. Failed to raise Cassidy. It was left to Probasco, the former horse doctor, to tend to the wounded Van Meter. He cleaned the wound with alcohol. Something his place wasn't short of, anyway. "I called Cassidy a dozen times, but the fuck never showed," he raved the next day, as Piquet showed with the faked I.D. from Loeser. "We had to rely on that harp son-of-a-bitch and Van Meter would be dead by now. Good job I know my stuff from the gee-gees. Hey, Van. Show Louis your head."

"Christ, Probasco."

"I saved your life, didn't I? Why, I was up all night picking hairs out the wound."

Later, after the guinea passed out over a bottle, Johnny filled the lawyer in on the bank job. Floyd had been over-optimistic about the take. Six grand a piece. Enough to keep them holed-in for a few weeks longer, but chickenfeed compared to the big score they were looking for. Van Meter was more concerned about the jeweller, however, one Harry Berg according to the *Tribune*, the storekeeper who'd opened up on Nelson as the runt guarded the car.

"We'll have to go back to South Bend in the next couple days and take care of that little Jew," he said, fingering his bandaged head. "We can't let the prick get away with this kind of thing, you hear me, John?"

Johnny snipped the article from the newspaper. "Sure, Homer." Fattened the bundle in his wallet. "Whatever you say. He's on the death-list, right?"

"Hey, I'm serious here. I was looking right at the son-of-a-bitch when he came running out that store. The asshole was trying to kill us. I swear to God."

Johnny laughed outright at the expression on Van Meter's face. The knock on the head must have turned him screwy. "Okay, Van. You might have a point there. We can't afford to let a guy go on living that can shoot that straight. Reward we got on our heads these days, the bastard might shut up shop and come looking for us. And he couldn't make a worse job of catching us than Eddie Hoover and his boys, could he now?"

Six

The lawmen rendezvoused with Sage on the North Side, parking across from the Children's Memorial Hospital at 707 West Fullerton. They walked down to the lakeshore. The beaches were crowded with bathers escaping the heat wave that gripped the city, but this particular spot was deserted.

"You sure she'll show?" Purvis asked, wiping the back of his neck with a handkerchief.

Zarkovich selected an Abdullah from a gold cigarette case. Offered it around. "She'll show all right. She can't afford not too."

O'Neil fed one of his subordinate's cigarettes into his mouth. Accepted a light. "This the cunt now?" he asked, as a second car appeared outside the hospital.

Zarkovich curled his lips as a plump, obviously female figure stepped from the car. "That's her, all right. Anna, baby. How you been?"

"Marty." She smiled on one side of her face. Dipped her head to the others. "You're the federal men?"

Cowley took charge. "Mrs Sage? I'm Cowley, Director of Investigations, FBI. This is my associate, Mr Purvis. I understand you may have information on the whereabouts of John Dillinger?"

"He's probably on the town right now. Him and my, ah, associate, Polly. Polly Hamilton."

Purvis flared his nostrils. A fat, dago-looking whore smelling of face powder. Dime store perfume. "Your *associate*," he said, loading the phrase with as much contempt as he could muster.

"Anna's roommate," Zarkovich added. "Right, Anna?"

Sage looked at him gratefully. "That's right, Marty. My room-mate. The girl who's been dating Dillinger."

Cowley bulged his tongue behind his lip. "You're sure it's him?"

"I knew right from the start. He denied it, but I confronted him with a newspaper photograph and he admitted who he was. It's Dillinger, all right." She glanced at Zarkovich. "Could you let me have a cigarette, Marty? This' kind of hard for me, you know."

"Sure, sweetheart." He sparked her up. "You want to let them have the good news, Anna?"

She inhaled a mouthful of smoke. Let it plume from her nostrils. "He's staying at my place. Staying with Polly. We're supposed to be going to the movies tomorrow night. The Marbro. Get the immigration people off my back and I'll walk him right into your hands. He'll be yours for the taking, I guarantee it."

Seven

The Syndicate caught up with Johnny a few days after the Sioux Falls job. Byron Bolton was the messenger boy, dapper in a sport shirt and seersucker suit. Florsheimer shoes. The gunman pushed himself away from the side of the parked Chrysler Imperial he'd been lounging against as Johnny walked out a movie house. Fell into step beside him as he walked down Lincoln. "Guy wants to see you, Johnny. Says it's important."

"Same guy as before?"

"Not this time."

"Who then?"

"The guy himself. Guy at the top."

Johnny halted. "Nitti?"

"Christ, John."

"What the hell does Nitti want with me?"

"You tell me. Must be serious. Two-bit yeggmen don't get to see the Barber less it's something important."

No sign of a Syndicate torpedo, which didn't mean shit. The greaseballs would have him covered if they wanted to take him.

You never saw the bastard that got you. That was a given. "I got a choice in the matter?"

"Sure you got a choice. Come in for a talk with the boss or don't. You don't come in when you're asked, though, and you risk pissing the Barber off some. And believe me, my friend, one thing you don't want is the Barber and his, uh, associates on your ass." He spread his hands. "We're doing this friendly here. No guinea muscle pushing you into a Hupmobile. No threats. No heaters. Just yours truly making a friendly request from the guy on top, okay?"

Standing on a crowded street, a cinema queue beside him, and he might as well have been on a desert island, the help he could expect if things went down. Despite what Bolton had said, he knew what choice he had in the matter if he wanted to keep his head on his shoulders. Which was no choice at all. "This your ride?" he said, indicating the Chrysler.

"She's a lulu, ain't she? Hop in the front and I'll drive you down to the Capri."

The Capri turned out to be a modest-looking Italian restaurant on North Clark Street, all striped awnings and plate glass windows, just around the corner from the garage where the Moran

407

mob had been wiped-out a few years previously. The place was deserted except for the barman and an elderly Negro porter sweeping around the tables, the dark leather booths empty of the crooks and politicians that gathered there to hash out pay-offs over meatballs and spaghetti. Waited to see the guy that held court from the private room in back.

Bolton slipped the Negro a ten spot. "Beat it, Uncle. That's enough for today." Turned to Johnny. "Want a drink?" he asked, as the Negro docked his broom and left.

"Just a beer." He stood with his back to the bar as Bolton vanished behind a beaded curtain, keeping an eye on the place as he sipped his brew. It wasn't likely the Barber would pull a stroke in his own restaurant, but you could never be certain. The guy had him hit in the head in the privacy of the back room, shlepped him out the alleyway, and nobody would ever know he'd been in the place except for the bartender. And looking at the forearms on the guy, the scar tissue on his knuckles, he wouldn't be the type to holler law anytime soon.

He burned a Lucky Strike: the six-minute cigarette. Halfway through the butt, Bolton reappeared and beckoned him towards the curtain. He killed his smoke and, grinding it beneath his shoe, followed the gunman into the rear of the restaurant.

The back room was panelled in the same dark oak as the dining area. A long banqueting table draped in a stiff white linen cloth dominated the centre of the room. At one end of the table sat a dapper little guy with Chaplin eyes and a busted nose, a half-eaten chicken dinner turning cold at his elbow, a glass of Chianti at his hand. There was a scar on the side of his neck where he'd been shot by a cop the year before. His hair was dark and parted to the left. Immaculate: Francesco Nitto a.k.a. Frank Nitti a.k.a. the Barber. Or, as he was becoming more commonly known on the streets these days, the Enforcer. He closed the leather-bound ledger he was reading as they entered the room. "You don't take your hat off when you walk into a guy's house, huh? His place of work?"

Johnny doffed his straw skimmer. "You bring me here to lecture me on my manners?"

"In a manner of speaking, yeah." He gestured him into a chair. "You and me, Dillinger. We need to talk. That agreement you had with us. How did it go? You told us where Nelson was and we'd stay the fuck off your ass. That was the deal, wasn't it?"

Johnny settled in his chair. Sat his hat on his lap. "I said I'd tell you if I knew where Nelson was hiding-out." He shot his cuffs. "I don't know where Nelson's hiding-out. Simple as that. I couldn't help you if I wanted to. Know what I'm saying?"

"Trying to get smart with me, kid? You were identified as pulling that Sioux Falls job with the half-pint just a couple weeks ago. The one where you shot the cop. Or you going to deny that? Lie to me to my face. Disrespect me in front of Bolton here?"

Bolton squirmed. "You want me to wait outside, Mr Nitti?"

"I want you to shut the fuck up, is what I want you to do. Sit there and shut up and do your frigging job like I pay you to do." He turned back to Johnny. "So? You going to deny it, punk?"

"I'm not going to deny a goddamn thing. Yeah, sure, we pulled that job with Nelson. And no, I don't know where he's hiding-out at the moment. I didn't know at the time. He was north of the city in the Chain o' Lakes country till Tommy Carroll put him back together with us. Moving between motels, tourist lodges far as I know. Nowhere near Chicago, which is where I assumed you were looking for him. Nowhere I could track him for you even if I wanted to."

"And now you pulled the job. Where is he now, smart guy?"

"The West Coast, far as I know. The kid used his split to stake himself out in Frisco. The runt used to run beer out there before he came back East. Figure he's got friends out there he can cool off with till the heat passes in Chi."

"The heat ain't gonna pass this time. Not with the burr you put under J. Edgar Hoover's saddle. The heat ain't gonna pass till you guys are in the slammer. In the slammer or under the ground."

"You threatening me, Nitti?"

"Tough guy. All I got to do is snap my fingers and you'd be dead before you reached the end of the block. Only thing stopping me is the heat that kinda thing brings." He took a sip from the wine glass beside his plate. The light winked from the star-shaped diamond on his finger as he replaced it on the table. He rotated the ring beneath his thumb as he continued. "Hit the small fry and nobody bats an eyelid. It makes the inside cover of the *Tribune* at most. Joe Public gives you ten seconds over his toast and coffee, then moves on to *Moon Mullins. Gasoline Alley.*

Front page stuff, though. That's something else. The Big Fella found that out when he whacked those guys in the garage there on Valentine's Day. Al wouldn't be doing no ten years on the Rock he hadn't stirred the law up gunning those North Side boys the way he did. Got the feds on his ass for tax evasion."

"You giving me a pass?"

"I ever hear anything more about you and Nelson and this time you go down with the punk, whatever excuse you got."

"Otherwise?"

"Otherwise you get out of town. Get out and stay out. You had your day, Dillinger. You and them Okies of Ray's. You had a good thing going with those small town banks for a while. Small town cops. That racket's over, though. Finished. It was done with soon as the feds got involved and started tracking you interstate. All you doing now is screwing things up for the rest of us. Guys trying to operate a business here. Provide a service." He surveyed Johnny's face. "Looks like you might be thinking on the same lines yourself, though, state of your puss. Guy done a good job on you. You should be okay for a new start somewheres once the scars heal over. Another reason I'm giving you a pass 'stead of dumping you in the drainage canal with a couple cement blocks wired to your feet."

"Soon as I got a bankroll together, I'm gone, Mr Nitti. One big payday's all I need and then I'm outta here. Leaving the goddamn country."

A shadow flitted across Nitti's features. "You got a job planned? Something major? In my neck of the woods?"

"You know I'm not gonna tell you nothing about any job I got planned, Mr Nitti. With respect, all right?"

Nitti stiffened a finger at him. "I'm warning you, punk. I hear you're hanging round this burg with any of your old crew, Hamilton or Van Meter or that prick Nelson and heat or no heat, you're gonna go. I already lost three guys to that bastard Stege when he thought they was you and your sidekicks. The feds might be on me like flies on shit, but nothing the way they would be you knock over a bank or a payroll in the Loop. I get just a whiff you been seen on the streets or you planning a job and that's it, brother. You're on your way to the big jail yard in the sky and no time off for good behaviour, capisce?" He withdrew his hand. Reopened the discarded ledger. "I see you again and new face or no new face you're gonna end up on a morgue slab. Now get out of my sight before I change my mind. Let the wrecking crew loose on your ass,

you hear me?"

Eight

The four lawmen huddled beside their cars as Sage departed. Cowley looked at the others.

"Well, what do you think?"

Purvis crimped his mouth. "I think it's a load of hooey. If she knew it was Dillinger all along, why did she wait until now to contact us?"

Zarkovich unscrewed a spent cigarette from the holder. Ground it underfoot. "She didn't have to." He emphasized his words with the cigarette holder, like a conductor with a baton. "These aren't regular tax-paying citizens we're dealing with, Mel. People like Anna only cut deals with the law when they have their backs to the wall. She didn't get that letter from immigration two days ago and Dillinger could have stayed there until the bicentennial as far as she was concerned."

O'Neil spat. "The bastard's been paying her good money to hole-in there until now. You can bet your ass on that."

"What about the girl?" Cowley asked. "This Polly Hamilton?"

Zarkovich shrugged. "One of Anna's whores. She knows the score. Anna tells her to hand him up when the time comes and she'll do what she's told." He inserted the cigarette holder in his inside breast pocket. "You can help her out with immigration, Sam?"

"I can write them a letter. Tell them she's been of great help in our investigations etc. Nothing I can do for her officially, though. She doesn't do something that benefits immigration directly and they won't want to know." Cowley worked his shoulders. "Government. You know how it is."

"Kind of tough on the broad," O'Neil said.

Zarkovich gazed out over the lake. "Perhaps it would be the best thing all round if Anna left the country once this was over. This kind of deal-making looks pretty bad in the headlines. Perhaps it would be best if there were as few witnesses to what happened to Dillinger as possible." He dipped an eyelid at his superior. "Right, captain?"

O'Neil stirred himself. "The reward for Dillinger. The fifteen grand. That pays out dead or alive, right?"

416

Cowley formed an air pocket in his cheek. "I think I see where this' going," he said.

"That's right, Cowley. You want the cooze to play ball with Zark here and that's our condition. Dillinger goes down when we make the pinch or the deals' off."

Nine

Johnny settled into his new life at Anna's, relaxing with Polly after the excitement of the bank job. He'd help her clean up around the apartment, something he'd got used to in his cell at the pen, washing the dishes, a towel wrapped around his waist for an apron. They'd play pinochle or rummy. Double date with Steve and his girl. Eat sundaes at the corner ice cream parlour and meals at the Seminary restaurant.

He'd have his shirts starched and his hats blocked at neighbourhood cleaners or go out to buy new socks and underwear - it impressed a broad the way he changed them every morning, same with the way he took a bath twice a day. It kind of threw Polly that he wore the same grey suit all the time, but what the hell. He liked to wear a jacket and trousers then throw them away, buying a new set when he became bored with the old. At least it saved on laundry bills.

He grew bolder. Polly had hung up her old job at the S and S Sandwich Shop, but decided to apply for another when he hinted he might have to travel out of town soon, a job that needed medical certification. Driving her downtown, he found that the medical examiner's office was in the same building as the detective bureau. Four times he waited outside the examiner's office on the thirteenth floor, while Stege directed the search for him two storeys below. Risky, but it was a kick, and he savoured the danger, the had to admit.

It was good to be able to move around the city undetected. With his new face, he felt like the Invisible Man. He knew it couldn't last, though. Not with the bounty on his head. In a time and place where the threat of repossession and bankruptcy hung over everyone, $15000 could mean the difference between security for a man's family or a Hooverville by the railroad tracks.

Or deportation to Europe, for that matter. He liked Polly and Anna, trusted them as far as he could, but a whore was a whore at the end of the day and it would be foolish of him to think otherwise. In the dark watches of the night, Polly breathing softly beside him as she slept, he knew they'd eventually betray him. They might not want to turn pigeon, might wrack their consciences after the fact, but they'd be unable to help themselves. Turning the trick. Trading love for money. That was the definition of a whore. He was dumb to expect anything more of them. It was the way they were made.

The train job, though. They'd obtained the timetable and stops. Planned a git via maps from the county surveyor's office. Murray's plant had obtained the layout of the express car and the type of safe they'd be dealing with. They'd tracked down a source for the soup. Murray could handle the take. As soon as they had the finance from the bonds, they'd be ready to roll.

It was just going to be him and Van Meter this time, with Murray to launder the dough. A few more hands would have been useful, though. Floyd would have been the obvious choice, but he'd holed-up back East and couldn't be contacted. Nelson was back from the coast, hustling for funds, and they'd considered cutting him in after the last job, despite the bad blood between them. That was before the events of July 16th, however, when a couple of state troopers had approached a group of men parked up a dirt road north of the city at two in the morning.

"What's the trouble?" one of the troopers had asked, climbing out of the patrol car.

"No trouble here," answered a voice, followed by a burst of machinegun fire.

Both troopers had gone down, one with six bullets in him. The law had blamed post-Repeal bootleggers after uncovering a still in a nearby barn, but the job had Nelson written all over it.

They weren't the only ones who would have recognized the runt's signature, either. The guineas knew the kid Jimmy was back in town and they'd want his head. And if Nelson had his name on a Syndicate bullet, the rest of the magazine was earmarked for himself and Van Meter. There was nothing as certain as that.

Ten

Purvis started at the sight of the white-haired man ensconced behind his desk as he returned from the meeting with Sage. Captain Stege, head of the Dillinger Squad.

"You take the offer?" Stege said, failing to rise as Purvis entered the office.

"Excuse me?"

"Zarkovich. O'Neil. Zarkovich's squeeze."

"Zarkovich and Sage are... ?"

"She was cited in his divorce. A tramp like that pays off in more than U.S. dollars when she's dealing with a cooze hound like Zarkovich." He sniffed at Purvis' bewilderment. "You don't know who you're dealing with, do you? Zarkovich is a bagman. He handles the fix for the law in Lake County. That's why I threw him and that fuck O'Neil out the stationhouse when they came to me with the Dillinger thing."

"Do you have any proof to back up your allegations, Captain?"

"Zarkovich was indicted for corruption three times before they finally nailed him for bootlegging five years ago. The only reason he survived was because half the city government was beside him in the dock." He gave Purvis the wrong end of a glare. "The offer, though. Dillinger in return for the reward. You took it, didn't you?"

"I don't think that's any concern of yours, Captain, do you?"

Stege exhaled slowly. "You dumb son-of-a-bitch. You know it's a set-up, don't you?"

"What do you mean?"

"The fact they want Dillinger dead. It's a set-up. They're covering their tracks. Where do you think Johnny boy's been hiding since Little Bohemia?" He stood. Pushed back his chair with his calves. "It wouldn't surprise me if Nitti's backing Zarkovich's play, either. This thing's got the guinea's fingerprints all over it. He's already used you to take Touhy off the board. Why shouldn't he do the same with Dillinger? Get you to pull the trigger on the prick, the same way that crazy wop did for him with Mayor Cermak down in Florida."

Purvis swallowed the Touhy dig. The bullshit about Nitti. He figured the old fuck was trying to get to him. The Factor case was good, even if nobody else seemed to believe so. "You think he'll double-cross us?"

Stege came around the desk. Torched a stogie. "Oh, you'll get Dillinger, all right. Zarkovich will make sure of that." He shook the flame off the match. "You'll be helping cover the tracks of corrupt police officers, though. Dirty politicians. You really want to be a part of that, Purvis?"

"You work in the gutter, you sometimes have to dirty your hands. You're a Chicago cop, Stege. You should know that better than anyone."

Stege's complexion paled to match his hair. "Government agent or not, you better watch your mouth, boy."

Purvis swallowed. Stege might be short and pushing sixty, but he was still powerfully built. He could well believe the rumour the Captain had once beaten a drunk to death with a fence picket for insulting his mother. "I have my orders, Captain. Getting Dillinger takes priority over everything else."

"Even if it means murdering the poor bastard in cold blood?" He clapped his derby on his head. Wrapped his hand around the doorknob. "Still, you guys proved you ain't too fussy how you get your results up in St Paul. Personally, I'd give any man a fair chance to surrender and take his medicine in court. Even a cop-killing son-of-a-bitch like Dillinger."

Eleven

Johnny met up with Van Meter at the barbecue stand. He ordered a couple of red-hots as they waited for Murray. Word was the fixer had managed to fence the first of the bonds for them. There should be enough to provide them with walking around money. Enough to start putting together the job on the Reserve train.

There was something else on their minds, though. Tommy Carroll. Nelson had shown unexpectedly the previous evening, his eyes raw. Voice cracking.

"The bastards got Tommy down in Iowa."

Carroll had become careless. Steered his tan Ford into a small town service station, his latest pick-up beside him as he vacationed away from the Chicago heat, and asked the mechanic to check the tyres while he grabbed a bite at the diner across the street.

The mechanic had spotted a bundle of false plates beneath the lap rug, though. Called the cops. There had been two of them waiting when Carroll returned from lunch.

"Hey," one of the dicks called, emerging from the unmarked police car. "Just a minute. Who are you?"

Carroll went for his piece. "More to the point, who are you?"

The dick closed with him. "Police officers." He threw a right as Carroll drew. Dumped him on his ass.

The ex-pug came up quickly, though. Sprinted down the sidewalk. Turned to fire.

The dick fired first. Hit Carroll beneath the arm. Knocked the pistol from his hand.

Carroll staggered, then regained his balance. Lurched in back of the diner.

Dead end.

The second dick set his feet and fired. Three shots. The last two found their mark. Carroll went headlong amongst the ash cans and empty bottles.

The cop stood over him. Shut out the sky. "Who are you?" he repeated, cocking his revolver.

"Carroll. Tommy Carroll." He touched his chest, indicating his wallet, as he expired. "I got seven hundred dollars here. Be sure the little lady gets it. She's got nothing to do with this. Don't know what it's all about, you hear me?"

The news had sobered the survivors, bringing them temporarily together, just when Johnny needed an extra pair of hands on the Reserve job. He was leery of working with Nelson again, scared of what the kid might do, but Nelson was chastened by the news of his buddy's death. Acting like a professional, for once in his life.

"We oughta forget the bullshit between us," he'd said, shaking hands before departing. "There ain't that many of us left that we can afford to fight. You got anything brewing and need someone as can handle a car or a gun and I'm your man, okay, Dillinger?"

Which sounded good to Johnny. The cops Nelson shot outside of town, though. That was the thing. The Barber would be onto the little guy if the bulls weren't. Blaming the killings on bootleggers was going to turn up the heat under the Syndicate. Even if they did get out of booze after Repeal.

And then there was Van Meter.

"Screw the little bastard. I never did care a hell of a lot for the guy, anyway."

Johnny grinned, in spite of himself. "He was always bitching about you too."

Van Meter uncapped the mustard. "We had it pretty heavy a couple times, didn't we? I thought we was going to draw on each other that night at the Dutchman's." He seasoned his red-hot. "The kid was okay at Sioux Falls, though, I'll give him that. Held it together. If nothing else, he's a hell of a wheelman."

"One way of keeping a gun out his hand, anyway. And trying to take the train with just two men ain't gonna work. We're gonna need a half-dozen guys at least if we're gonna stand a chance."

Van bit into his roll. "That thing with the cops the other night. Sounds like the kid's putting together a new string. We could use the extra hands. I say we tell Murray to get back in touch with him. Cut him and his crew in when we're ready to go." He looked up as a dapper-looking figure breezed in from the street. "Speaking of which -"

Johnny indicated the briefcase in the fixer's hand. "That what I think it is, Jimmy?"

Murray nodded. "I got you a good deal on the bonds." He stepped behind the counter. Opened the door to his office. "Enough to get things rolling with the Reserve train, anyway."

Van Meter licked mustard from his thumb. "Screw the Reserve train. This calls for a celebration. We deserve a night on the town." He dumped his red-hot in the trash. Blotted his mouth with a napkin. "I got a hot date tonight with chorus girl from the Green Mill. I figure she can find a friend for my buddy if I ask her nice. The kinda gal as knows how to show her, ah, appreciation, to a guy with a roll on his hip. If that's something you'd be interested in, Johnny?"

Johnny thumb-stroked his moustache. "Sounds pretty good, Van, but I gotta say no. I told my gal I was taking her to the movies tonight. There's a new gangster flick at the Biograph, *Manhattan Melodrama*. Dick Powell and Clark Gable. Myrna Loy as the love interest. And from what they say in the *Tribune*, it's gonna be a doozy."

Twelve

Cowley and Purvis talked things over in the office that night.

"The whole thing stinks," Purvis said. "Shooting Dillinger down like a dog rather than giving him a chance to surrender. That's not why I joined the Bureau, Cowley. I'm a federal agent not a hired gun. I say we leave it to the cops and to hell with it, Sam."

"You can't pussyfoot around with these guys, Mel. Stand on procedure and you end up like Carter Baum. Those guys in Kansas City." He sucked his teeth. "It never bothered you when you took down Green. Or when you opened fire at Little Bohemia, for that matter."

"That's a pretty cheap shot, Cowley."

"That's the problem, though, isn't it, Mel? That thing in the woods?"

Little Bohemia had been a disaster. And that had been in the middle of nowhere. Some log cabin out in the sticks. He launched a full-scale police ambush in a crowded city street, killed a half-dozen innocent bystanders and forget the headlines, they'd lynch him from the nearest lamppost.

431

It wasn't just that, though. "This deal with the Sage woman. Pretending we're going to help her with her immigration problem. Deceiving her that way. It's just not right. She might be a whore, but she's still a woman, Sam, no matter how she's disgraced herself."

"That Southern Gentleman routine won't wash, Purvis. Your career's hanging by a thread here. Mine too, if I screw this up." His voice softened. "We can't afford to play by the rules anymore, buddy. Not if we want to bring this bastard down. He's made a fool of the Bureau for far too long, Mel. Made a fool of you and me into the bargain. Dillinger goes down tomorrow night, whatever it takes. Or we go down in his place."

"And if it takes the government double-crossing this Sage woman. Dillinger being killed in cold blood?"

"You won't have to get your lily-white hands dirty, Melvin. The East Chicago boys will do the actual shooting. I'll see to that."

"And the Bureau comes out smelling of roses. No matter what went on behind the scenes."

432

"The winners write the headlines, Mel. Nobody has to know what happened behind the scenes, do they?"

Purvis lapsed into silence. He gazed out the office window at the shining bed of lights spread below him. The deal with Sage. The East Chicago boys. He knew it was necessary in order to finally nail Dillinger. To save his career.

They were supposed to be the good guys, though. Federal law. And here they were cutting deals with dirty cops. Whores. Planning to murder a man in the equivalent of a gangland killing. If he'd ever thought it would come to this on the day he'd applied to join the Bureau, he'd have torn up his application form. Took his chances with the Depression.

It had been a long time since he'd been able to afford those kind of scruples, though. He was a cop now. Same as Zarkovich. Same as O'Neil. Down in the gutter, with the rest of them. "Okay, Sam. Whatever you say. We take down the larcenous son-of-a-bitch now we've finally got the chance. But no police execution this time. The guy gets a chance to surrender or I'm blowing the whole thing off."

EIGHT

THE LADY IN RED

Never trust a woman or an automatic pistol - John Dillinger.

One

We had a lot of fun. It's surprising how much fun we had –
Polly Hamilton

Cowley and Purvis spent the next day by the phones on the nineteenth floor. They'd informed all available agents to stay in touch in case something might break. Zarkovich and O'Neil joined them shortly before lunch, accompanied by two of their own men, Stretch and Sopsic.

"How many guys you got to stake out the picture house?" O'Neil asked Cowley, sparking a Camel.

"Fifteen. That should be sufficient, I think."

O'Neil snorted. Flicked the curled match on the office floor. "You ought to bring in Stege and his guys. Make sure the asshole's got no chance of slipping the net."

"No local cops. You can't trust them. The bastards are all on the take to the Syndicate."

"Stege's as straight as a die, the prick. He's got a weakness for talking to reporters, though. Hogging the headlines."

Zarkovich joined the conversation, immaculate in tan linen and a blinding white Panama. "Not that that would constitute a reason for cutting him out of the show. Right, Cowley?"

"No local cops," Cowley repeated. "We handle this ourselves or the deal's off."

O'Neil hunched forward. Blew smoke at the linoleum. "If this goes wrong because there's not enough men on the ground, I'm damned if the East Chicago Police Department's going to take the blame."

Purvis bristled at the burned match on the office floor. "You'll be quick enough to take any credit if this goes right," he said, nudging it aside with his shoe.

O'Neil exposed a set of suspiciously white, even teeth. "That's right, junior. That and the fifteen grand reward."

Purvis made to retort. The phone cut him off.

Sage.

"He'll be at my place tonight. I'm making dinner. We're going to the movie after that."

"What time?"

"Around eight. I'll ring again later when I know something definite."

Purvis hung up. He filled in the others on the details. "We better get ready. Call the men in. We'll plan a briefing for tonight."

They began to work the phones. The agents began to arrive mid-afternoon, jackets removed, ties loosened in defiance of regulations. They sipped soda pop. Smoked. Fanned themselves with newspapers in the stifling heat. No orders were given or speeches made. There was an air of expectancy in the bullpen, though. This time, the tip might be for real.

Johnny sat left foot propped on right knee at Anna's dining table. He wore lightweight grey slacks over white Hanes briefs, size 34, with black socks and red Paris garters over white buckskin Nunn Bush shoes. His white Kenilworth broadcloth shirt was unbuttoned over his undershirt and money belt, his red print tie hanging un-noosed at his neck. He smoked a La Corona-Belvedere cigar as the two women busied themselves preparing fried chicken, the way Billie used to in their few months together.

438

It gave him a pang to see Polly's body outlined beneath the thin material of her white blouse and blue summer skirt. He'd grown to feel something special for her over the last few weeks. It wasn't love, but he couldn't deny he was more than fond of the broad. It was a shame this might be one of their last nights together, what with the train job ready to go, a shipment due next week according to Murray. He knew she was a whore, but still. It'd be a shame to let her go.

"Hey, Countess," he said. "You still wanna catch that movie tonight once we've eaten?"

She dimpled at him over her shoulder as she peeled the vegetables. "The Temple movie? The one at the Marbro?"

"I thought we were gonna see the Gable movie tonight? The one at the Biograph?"

She made a moue. Gave her attention to the potatoes. The carrots. Sliced beets. "I'm sick and tired of gangster flicks. Can't a girl catch a Shirley Temple movie once in a while?"

He'd rather have Loeser carve on him again than sit through a Temple flick. *Little Miss Marker*, for Christ sake. But what the hell. He was feeling good today, the train job on track, the belt at his waist fat with bond money. And he was going to cut the tramp loose soon. He didn't want to upset her. Call him sentimental, but…

"You really wanna see the Temple movie, Contessa?"

"If you don't want to, Johnny…"

"Hell, if you wanna see it, I wanna see it." He arched an eyebrow at Anna, curiously quiet as she prepared the chicken. "What do you say, Anna? Gable or Temple? The casting vote, sugar. It's up to you."

She gave Polly a sharp look. "If you'd rather watch some little kid than a good-looking hunk like Gable."

Polly pouted. "I wanna see the Temple movie," she said.

"You're sure of that?" Anna asked.

Polly dug her heels in. "Johnny says I could and what Johnny says goes."

Johnny laughed. Clapped his hands together. "You heard the little lady, Anna. Looks like we see Gable another night, don't it?" He crushed out his cigar in the ashtray as Anna dried her hands. Removed her apron. "Going somewhere, baby?"

"I just realized. I ran out of butter." She ankled towards the door. "Give me five minutes. I'll just run down the store and get some."

Six o'clock. Seven. Still no word from Sage. It looked like another failure. Another bust.

The men in the bullpen. The eager expressions on their faces. Like hounds scenting possum. Purvis didn't know how he'd face them if this turned out to be another false alarm. Another waste of his and everybody else's time.

Five after seven. The phone rang. "Sage?"

"He's here. We'll be leaving soon. I don't know where we're going, though. The Biograph or the Marbro." She rang off.

The Biograph? Nobody had mentioned the Biograph. He trailed a finger down the diagram of the Marbro pinned to the office wall. Cowley had spent the previous evening surveying the place. Charting entrances and exits. Now this. "Why the last minute switch?" he said, after informing the others. "You think she's getting windy? Trying to wriggle out of things now the arrest" –

Cowley twitching at his choice of words – " is about to go down?"

Zarkovich tipped back his Panama with his forefinger.

"Could be that. Or it could be nothing at all. The Marbro's on the

other side of town from Anna's apartment, though. The Biograph's

just around the corner."

"How do you know that?" Cowley asked.

"It's my business to know." He snapped his fingers at one of

the agents wafting himself with a *Tribune*. "Hey, kid. Gimme that

newspaper a minute, will you?"

The agent looked to Cowley. Handed over the newspaper at

his nod.

Zarkovich flipped to the entertainment section. "Here we go.

Headlining at the Marbro tonight. *Little Miss Marker*, with Shirley

Temple. And at the Biograph. Clark Gable in *Manhattan*

Melodrama. A gangster movie with Dick Powell and Myrna Loy."

He passed the newspaper back to the agent. "I'd keep a couple guys

on lookout at the Marbro just in case, but if I was a betting man, I'd

put my money on the Biograph as the place that Johnny Boy's

going to show his face tonight. Or gambling against your faith as well, Sam?"

"It is when the game's rigged."

The two sets of lawmen faced each other: Zarkovich had been just a little too smooth on the comeback when it came to the change of venue. The last minute switch had thrown off Purvis and Cowley's plans for setting up the arrest. Left them wrong-footed.

Zarkovich had presumably scouted out the Biograph beforehand, however. Or visited it with Sage, if the information Stege had passed to Purvis had been correct. The East Chicago cops would have the upper hand when it came to taking Dillinger tonight. They could rig the thing to go their way if the feds decided to go back on their promise to kill the son-of-a-bitch. The bastards had to be sure the yeggman went down, eliminating any incriminating secrets he might be carrying on local law officers and their underworld ties.

Zarkovich picked lint from his trousers. "What exactly are you trying to say here, Sam?"

"You swear you don't know anything about this last minute change, Zarkovich?"

"We're all tense here. Edgy. That's understandable given the circumstances. That doesn't excuse sniping at each other this way, though. We're all on the same side here. All cops. As long as we remember that, things should go okay tonight outside the Biograph. You agree with me on that, Sam?" He tilted his head towards the bullpen before Cowley could answer. Uncoiled from his seat. "Enough bullshitting for one night, anyway. We've got an arrest to plan. Get your men together, Purvis. It's time we gave them a briefing."

Johnny eased aside his plate. He whittled a morsel of meat from his teeth with a pick. "Well, girls, I got to say. You fry a mean chicken between you. Best I ate since I came off the farm."

Polly blushed. That she could still do that, the profession she was in, kind of lifted his heart.

"Ah, Johnny. Things you say."

The way she'd slipped into calling him 'Johnny' these last few weeks. He wasn't sure whether she'd known from the start, or if Anna had pulled her coat when he'd moved into the apartment, but it didn't really matter now that things were coming to an end for them. "I mean it, Contessa. You'll make some man a good wife some day. You can take that to the bank." He scanned the carriage clock on the mantel. "Almost seven. Time we were making a move, if we're gonna catch that Temple picture."

A look flickered between the two women. Polly stared down at her shoes.

"Well, I was thinking, Johnny. I can always catch that Temple flick with Anna when you're away. If you'd rather watch the Gable movie…"

Anna pressed his foot beneath the table. He dropped her a wink.

"You sure, Countess?"

A grin broke at the corner of her mouth. "Well, that Gable. He is kinda cute."

"I wouldn't go that far, but he's some kinda guy." He took a second cigar from his pocket. Considered. Decided to save it for later. "You ladies gonna dress, then?"

Anna rose. "I just got my dress back from the cleaners. The one you bought me the other week, Johnny."

"The black and white thing?"

"No," she said. "The red one. Tonight I'm going to be the lady in red."

Seven fifteen. The agents jammed into the office, pistols showing over their shirts. The air was thick with tobacco smoke, the electric fans attempting to cool the overheated atmosphere causing the fumes to swirl like a London fog. Cowley introduced Zarkovich and O'Neil. The latter remained in the background. Let Zarkovich do the talking.

"You've probably already guessed why you're here." He nodded at the murmurs of 'Dillinger' from the assembled agents. "That's right. He'll be showing at one of two separate movie theatres tonight: the Marbro or, as is more likely, the Biograph, up

446

on the North Side. He'll be accompanied by two women. A younger, good-looking girl and an older woman. The older woman will be hard to miss. She'll be wearing a red dress. A bright red dress.

You may not be sure of Dillinger's identity when you first see him. He's sporting a moustache now. Dyed his hair black. And he's undergone plastic surgery. Lost the moles on his face. The cleft chin. You see a woman in a bright red dress though, accompanied by a pretty girl and a guy in a straw boater with a Gable moustache and you'll know you've got your man." He made to step aside. "That's all from me for now. Mel?"

Purvis took centre stage. Cleared the debris from his throat. "It is the desire of the Director that John Dillinger be taken alive, if possible, and without injury to any agent of the Bureau. Yet, gentlemen, if he appears at either of the two picture shows and we locate him and he effects his escape, it will be a disgrace to our Bureau. This is the opportunity we have all been awaiting, and he must be taken, no matter what the consequences. Do not unnecessarily endanger your own lives in the process, however. If Dillinger offers any resistance, it will be up to each of you to do

447

whatever you think necessary to protect yourself in making the arrest."

O'Neil muttered beneath his breath. "What a crock of shit."

The speech seemed to have gone over with the men, though. And Zarkovich slapped him on the back as they filed out of the office. "Attaboy, Mel. A tonic for the troops, huh?"

Purvis coloured. "Whatever." He joined Cowley in the bullpen. "How do you want to play this, Sam?"

"You take the bulk of the men and stake out the Biograph. I'll put a couple of men on the Marbro just in case. Both groups stay in contact through me at the office. You see Dillinger enter the theatre and I'll rush the rest of the men over there from the other location and we take him as he comes out at the end of the show. Any questions?"

"Who takes the Marbro?"

"Agent Winstead and one of the East Chicago cops. Zarkovich?"

Zarkovich stirred. "Trying to keep me away from the glory, Sam?" Disarmed the remark with a smile.

He was probably right, though. Zarkovich was the brains behind the East Chicago contingent. Keeping him away from the Biograph as long as possible was probably the best way of ensuring the stakeout remained under the control of the Bureau, rather than the East Chicago cops. "He shows at the Biograph and you should be able to make it before the show turns out," Purvis said. He gave his attention to Cowley. "What guns should we take? The Thompsons?"

"Only your pistols. Things go to plan and we shouldn't need the backup. Besides, we can't risk the Thompsons in a built-up area." He caught Purvis' eye as his subordinate made towards the basement garage. "Not after that thing in Wisconsin, anyway. Another public-relations disaster like that would finish us. You hear me, Melvin? We don't turn the streets into a shooting gallery. One thing the Bureau can't afford is another Little Bohemia."

Two

Strolling down the alley from Anna's with an attractive woman on each arm, dark glasses, hat sloped rakishly over one eye, Johnny had the world by the tail. Polly was the looker of the two, but Anna was no Tugboat Annie and the blazing red dress she wore drew the eye like the neon sign lighting the movie marquee ahead of them as they turned onto Lincoln:

Essaness

BIOGRAPH

Iced fresh air

Cooled by refrigeration

The latter was as much an attraction as the movie itself on a night like this. Boy, it was hot. Drinkers had spilled out of the Goetz Country Club Tavern next door to the theatre and street vendors were doing a brisk trade in orange juice and snow cones. He treated himself and Polly to one of the latter, an orange juice for Anna, and walked them into the movie, the weight of the .38 automatic dragging at his pants. Wearing a jacket hadn't been an option on a night like this, but it robbed him of the opportunity of wearing his usual shoulder holster.

He hoped it wasn't too obvious he was carrying. Like the Mae West line: 'That a gun in your pocket or you just pleased to see me?'

"What are you smirking at?" Polly asked, as he paid for the tickets.

"Nothing for you to bother your pretty little head about," he said, steering her and Anna towards the front of the house. He positioned himself between them, an arm along the back of each seat, and stole a kiss from her as the lights went down, then removed his sunglasses and skimmer and settled into position to watch the show.

Purvis took the Pierce Arrow alongside Agent Brown. Stretch and Sopsic, the East Chicago cops, sat mute in the backseat, Cro-Magnon faces over Sulka neckties and hundred dollar suits, pistols swelling their jackets, as the big, old-fashioned jalopy led the federal convoy towards the Biograph. Anybody spotted the vehicle as it headed through town and they were liable to mistake the passengers for a Syndicate crew on the way to a hit. Which, if things went as Zarkovich and, Purvis suspected, Cowley, wanted, they wouldn't be far wrong.

They arrived outside the theatre at seven thirty-five. Took position on the sidewalk. Purvis loitered by the box-office. If Dillinger showed, he was to light a cigar, a signal for the others to make their move. Brown, meanwhile, stayed in line of vision. Every five minutes, he jogged to the phone booth at the corner and kept Cowley up to date at the office. And from the office itself, Cowley kept in regular touch with the Director, sitting in his library at home by the telephone as he waited to relay to the newspapers the news that Dillinger was finally under arrest. Under arrest or dead.

Eight fifteen. The theatre began to fill with people. Still no sign of the outlaw, though. The picture began at eight thirty. Something was wrong. The bastard wasn't going to show. It was another washout. Another bust.

And then he was there, in front of him, a dapper figure in a straw skimmer and moustache, a woman on each arm. A younger, attractive girl in cloche hat and open toed sandals and Anna Sage in a blinding red dress. He disengaged their arms as he paid at the box-office. Pecked the girl on the cheek as he led them inside.

Purvis couldn't believe it. After all these months. There he was, acting like he owned the goddamn place. John Herbert Dillinger. Son-of-a-bitch. It was him at last.

Brown had seen him too. He signed to Purvis and sprinted for the phone box, while Purvis bought himself a ticket. He pushed his way inside the crowded theatre. Found himself drawing curious glances from the audience as he searched the darkened seats for the outlaw trio. Came up blank.

He reversed into the lobby before he tipped his mitt, the hot summer night wrapping back around him like a blanket after the air-conditioned cool of the cinema. There was no chance of taking Dillinger while the picture was playing. They'd have to wait for the show to turn out. Grab him when he hit the street.

He went over the running times with the girl at the box-office. The movie lasted ninety-four minutes. With newsreels and shorts, the whole program topped out at just over two hours. Two hours and four minutes to be precise. If he stayed for the entire show, Dillinger should exit the Biograph at ten thirty-five.

Cowley arrived shortly after nine, followed a few minutes later by Zarkovitch and Winstead from the Marbro. O'Neil showed around the same time, shadowing Zarkovitch as he took up position between the theatre and the alleyway leading to Sage's apartment. The rest of the team fanned out along the street and the alleyway, blocking the side and rear exits and cutting the escape routes up and down Lincoln.

Purvis and Cowley, meanwhile, covered the front of the place along with a handful of their best shots. They were taking no chances. There was no way Dillinger would be able to break through the cordon surrounding the theatre.

The same way he'd supposedly be unable to break out of the escape-proof prison at Crown Point. The trap at Little Bohemia.

At least the son-of-a-bitch was alone this time. No Van Meter or Hamilton to cover his back. And no jacket, either. No place to conceal a Thompson. The most he could be packing was a pistol and a pretty small calibre one at that. Purvis kept that in his thoughts and he might just get through what was to come without having to rush home for a change of underwear.

He took up his post by the box-office again. Scoped the street. The other members of the team were the only members of the crowd not in shirtsleeves. Their dark suit jackets stood out like niggers in a snow bank. John Q. Public might not notice anything out of the ordinary, but a man like Dillinger, a man attuned to the ever-present danger of arrest, would spot them the instant he left the theatre.

He chewed on the end of a cigar. Wished to Christ he was anywhere other than here. Consulted his watch again. Ten twenty. Jesus. Almost time. Why on earth had he agreed to go along with Zarkovitch and -

A sedan halted in front of the theatre. Two cops in blue pants and blouses, their uniform jackets doffed due to the heat, emerged. One of them packed a twelve gauge. He rocked back the hammers as he approached Purvis at the box-office. "Step back from the ticket counter. Do it now."

Purvis inched backward as if walking on thin ice. "I'm a federal agent. This is a stakeout. You're interfering in an important operation here. I'd advise you to get back in - "

The cop's finger tightened on the trigger. "You sassing me, punk?"

His colleague placed his hand on the gun barrel. He gently lowered the muzzle towards the floor. "Easy, Lou. This pansy ain't no yeggman. He might just be telling the truth." He chin-nodded to Purvis. "Better show some identification, buddy. And make it slow, okay? Lou don't take the heat too well. Move too fast and he might just blow you in two."

Purvis tweaked his shield from inside his jacket between thumb and forefinger. Presented it to the cop.

The cop examined it. Turned it over in his hands. Did everything but sniff the damn thing, before reluctantly handing it back to him.

"Put up the scattergun, Lou. This guy's jake." He removed his cap. Mopped his forehead. "The manager rang in. Couple suspicious guys hanging round the front of the theatre. Thought you was like to heist the place. Take off with the box-office money."

"That why you here?" Lou asked, seating the hammers on the shotgun. "Somebody going to knock the place over?"

Purvis returned his shield to his jacket. "Sorry, fellas, that's confidential. Federal business, I'm afraid." Not that he'd be inclined to share confidences with this asshole anyway, after having a shotgun stuck under his nose.

Lou spat. "Federal law. Goddamn college boys. Why n't you stick to your law books and leave busting the bad guys to the real cops?"

"On your way, hotshot. Go peddle your papers."

The second cop studied him. "I'll remember you, buddy. One day you'll run into me when you're not wearing that badge and we'll see what a tough guy you are then, asshole."

Ten thirty. He didn't have time for this bullshit. Not now. Not with the show about to turn out. "You want me to call your superiors? That what you want, huh?"

The cop held his gaze a fraction longer. Nodded to himself as if memorizing something. "Come on, Lou. We'll leave this fag to it. Any luck and he'll shoot his prick off when he draws. Same way him and his buddies did at Little Bohemia."

Cowley hurried up to him. "What the hell was all that about?"

Purvis was still smarting from the Little Bohemia remark. "Local law. A misunderstanding. They thought we were here to rob the place, that's all." He closed his eyes momentarily. Opened them again. "Christ. More of the assholes."

They stepped into the middle of a face off between the East Chicago cops and two city detectives. Flashed their shields. "Sorry, men," Cowley said. "This' a federal stakeout. I'm going to have to ask you to leave."

One of the detectives hiked his thumb at the two East Chicago cops. "You're trying to tell me these two are federal agents?"

"East Chicago police. They're here with us. A joint investigation."

"They're out of their jurisdiction, is what they are." He prodded one of the two in the chest. "You got no right to be here, punk. I oughta arrest your ass right now. Throw you in the can."

Stretch – or was it Sopsic? – drew back his lapel, revealing an Army Colt in a shoulder rig. "Wanna try it, you fuck?"

Cowley interposed himself between them. "Please, gentleman. This isn't the time or the place. This' too important to get into a jurisdictional dispute over."

The city detective's partner glared at Cowley. "If it's that important, why didn't you inform the station house you'd be running a stakeout on our turf? Federal law too high and mighty to talk to the flatfoots on the ground?"

The flow of pedestrians increased around them, separating Purvis from Cowley and the cops. Ten thirty-five. The show was over. People were coming out of the theatre.

There. In the crowd. A white straw boater. A flash of red. He plugged a cigar into his mouth. Fumbled for his matches. Nearly spilled the damn things as the guy passed within arm's reach of him, Cowley and the two city cops oblivious as they argued the jurisdictional toss.

He came close to swallowing the cigar as Dillinger's eyes met his. The bastard had rumbled him. It was all over.

And then the outlaw's gaze swept past him. He stepped left around Purvis, guiding the women by the arm as they proceeded towards the alleyway.

It had been a pretty good show. There'd been a Walt Disney and a March of Time newsreel. A Charley Chase as support. And the main flick, *Manhattan Melodrama*. Gable as a gangster and Dick Powell as his boyhood pal, now the local D.A. Myrna Loy as the broad that came between them.

Powell was nothing much, a jumped-up hoofer, but Loy was hot and Gable was something else. The way he died at the end to protect his buddy, though. Letting himself go to the chair. Kind of made him squirm, to tell the truth of it. He was glad when the lights went up. Left him sitting between the two best-looking broads in the house.

"Gable," he said, as they sauntered out the theatre, arm in arm. Mixed with the crowds. "He remind you of anybody in particular? Way he brushed his hair back? Wore that moustache?"

Polly punched him playfully on the bicep. "Check out the swell head on buster here, why don't you, Anna?"

Anna gave a strained smile. "Who else would they base a mobster on, Polly? He's the best-known gangster in the country. Front page news." She fell behind them. Loosed his arm. "Ain't that right, Johnny?"

Purvis waved a match over the end of the cigar like a signal beacon. Cowley and the cops were too involved to notice, though. Ditto the agents on the street. Zarkovitch was moving, however. O'Neil. They closed with Dillinger, one each side of him. Sage lagged behind as the East Chicago detectives homed in on their target, pulling the girl free of Dillinger's arm as she did so.

"Anna?" He half-turned as the older woman tugged Polly away from him. Saw a guy mount the sidewalk from the gutter.

Looked right. A guy in a linen suit stepping out a doorway, a panama tipped over his eyes.

He knew it then. Began to run for the alleyway. A hot wire seared his back as a pistol snapped. Another in his side. Then somebody punched him in the back of the neck, sending him lurching into the woman in front of him. He staggered the last few steps. Collapsed face first into the alley.

Someone rolled him onto his back. Tore the pistol from his pocket. Stripped his money belt.

"Zark?"

"Shut your damn mouth."

He watched the money belt vanish beneath Zarkovich's jacket as the cop crouched over him, pressing the Colt into his hand as he rose. It was like looking upward from the bottom of a well, the sides closing in as the bulls gathered around him. Shutting out the light.

He saw Billie. His mother. The long dark coffin laid out on the kitchen table. A pistol bloom in the detective's hand.

There was a single flash of light. A thunderbolt. And then there was nothing. Nothing but the darkness.

Dillinger sprawled on his face in the mouth of the alley as the two cops pressed in on him, bending over the body. There was another shot, muffled this time. The two of them straightened as Purvis pounded down the sidewalk, buttons flying from his blazer as he wrenched loose his pistol, skidding to a halt over the body of the dying outlaw.

"Don't move," he said, knocking the automatic from Dillinger's hand.

Zarkovich holstered his piece. "You're a little late, Mel. The guy won't be moving again this side of Judgment Day."

"You shot him down in cold blood. Executed the poor bastard. You didn't even try to arrest him, did you?"

O'Neil stepped over the body, smoke wisping from the barrel of his Smith and Wesson. "We gave the prick what he asked for. What your boss agreed to at the start of all this." He poked the dead outlaw with his toe. "Don't look much for $15000, does he?"

Zarkovich glanced disinterestedly at the corpse. The broken spectacles angled over the nose. The bullet hole above the eye. "He was just a punk who got lucky. Nothing special. Not the hero the papers made him out to be, anyway. Anything but." He looked at Purvis standing impotently by, cigar drooping, as the onlookers began to gather, the murmur 'they got Dillinger' running through the crowd. "Same with the guy who nailed him. They'll write him up as some kind of plaster saint, an all-American hero, rather than a dumb-ass college boy who got lucky. Let a couple local cops do his dirty work for him."

O'Neil shrugged. "Like I give a fuck." He holstered his pistol. "Let's get moving before the reporters show. We got a claim to put in. Let the G get the glory while we think how we gonna spend that reward money."

Cowley appeared at Purvis' elbow as the East Chicago cops sloped offstage. "Is he dead?"

"If he's not now, he never will be." He saw the anger flare on Cowley's face. "Those two bastards. Zarkovich and O'Neil. They played us like fools. Called the shots all along. I know this' what we were after, but I feel like we failed somehow. That they took us for suckers."

"He's dead, Mel. That's all that counts. Whatever secrets he had on the East Chicago boys died with him and perhaps that's for the best."

"You think this was part of a cover up, Sam?"

"I think that I better call Mr Hoover in Washington, is what I think." He wheeled on the spectators edging in on the body, dipping handkerchiefs, strips of newspaper, even the hems of their dresses in the dead man's blood. "Get away from here. Get away from here, damn you, or I'll have you arrested."

The mob scattered. They reassembled at a distance as the two detectives who had argued with Cowley reappeared on the scene.

"Is what they're saying true?" one of them said. "You got Dillinger?"

Purvis nodded. "That's right. He tried to pull on us, so we opened fire. It was a legitimate killing, officer."

The detective grunted. "There's a first time for everything." He looked down on the corpse. "You call a meat wagon?"

"Uh – no. Should I have?"

"Jesus Christ." The detective fished a dime from his pocket. Headed towards the booth where Cowley was phoning Washington. "You keep these grave robbers off the stiff while I phone a hospital. The Alexian's just round the corner. Shouldn't take them more than five minutes to make the pick up."

"Not that this guy's in any hurry to see a medic," his partner said, lighting a Chesterfield. "The only place he's headed is the morgue."

The line outside the city morgue stretched down the block. There were men in shirtsleeves or undershirts, women in summer frocks. A few in beach wear. An estimated fifteen thousand spectators queued to view the body of John Dillinger laid out on a zinc-coated wooden slab in the building's basement, a sheet covering his body, a five inch yellow tag wired to his toe. One blonde, carefully reapplying lipstick after her first visit to the formaldehyde-reeking room, expressed disappointment at the experience.

"He looks like any other dead guy," she said. "But what the hell. Guess I'll go through again."

Commercial ventures also showed an interest in the spectacle. A street vendor made a good profit selling fruit juice to the parched crowd on the sidewalk. Another hawked strips of stained brown material guaranteed soaked in the blood of the dead man inside.

Others were less fortunate in their attempts to make money off the corpse. A team from an embalming college had the death mask they lifted from the corpse confiscated by police, while a $10,000 offer from a carnival for the dead man's body was turned down by the Dillinger family. The dead mobster's brain was later ascertained to have gone missing, however, although an investigation revealed this was carelessness on the part of the coroner's staff rather than the result of ghoulish souvenir hunters. A rumour that the dead man's penis was donated to the Smithsonian was later revealed by the Institute to be just that, a rumour.

The body was claimed by Dillinger's father a few days later and buried in his hometown of Mooresville. Scrap iron and concrete were poured over the coffin to deter ghouls. A four-foot high obelisk was erected over the grave bearing the single word

Dillinger. His true epitaph appeared on the wall of the alleyway

flanking the Biograph a few hours after his murder:

Stranger, stop and wish me well

Just say a prayer for my soul in Hell,

I was a good fellow, most people said,

Betrayed by a woman all dressed in red.

Epilogue

For the Record

Billie Frechette and Polly Hamilton later married and faded into obscurity. Anna Sage was deported, despite her role in the Dillinger shooting, and died of liver disease in her native Romania in 1947.

***

Louis Piquet was tried for aiding and abetting Dillinger during his post-Crown Point crime spree. He served two years in Leavenworth and, having been struck from the legal register, returned to mixing drinks for a living. He succeeded in obtaining a pardon from President Truman, however, and was on the point of being reappointed to the bar when he succumbed to a heart attack in 1951.

***

Zarkovich became chief of detectives in East Chicago, succeeding O'Neil as police chief when the latter retired. He never bragged about his role in the Dillinger shooting, merely relating, "I just did my job."

***

Jimmy Murray abandoned the idea of robbing the Reserve train after his fellow conspirators' deaths. He did, however, continue to operate as a fence and fixer from his Rainbo barbecue, undisturbed by either the Syndicate or the law. Later FBI reports described the former ward-heeler's political connections as strong enough that local police simply refused to serve warrants sworn against him.

***

John Dillinger Sr. joined a carnival sideshow, lecturing on the theme 'Crime Does Not Pay', and appeared at the Dillinger Museum set up by Emil Wanatka at Little Bohemia between 1935 and 1936. Dillinger replied to criticism of what he was doing with the simple truth that his farm was failing and he needed the money. His dignity and evident distaste for what he was forced to go through in order to secure his livelihood moved all who met him. He passed away in the late 1940s.

***

Frank Nitti was indicted for extortion of the movie industry and committed suicide in 1943.

***

Dock Barker was arrested in Chicago in January 1935 and received a life sentence for his part in the Bremer kidnapping, as did gang member Volney Davis and Harry Sawyer, the underworld fixer behind the crime. Byron Bolton received four concurrent three-year sentences in exchange for testifying against his fellow gang members.

Dock was killed while attempting to escape from Alcatraz in January 1939.

Fred Barker was killed a week after his brother's arrest in a gun battle with federal agents in Ocala, Florida. His mother, Kate Barker, was also killed in the exchange of gunfire. On finding that his men had shot to death a senior citizen with a clean criminal record, Hoover's publicity machine transformed the dead woman into Ma Barker, leader and mastermind of the killer brood.

Alvin 'Ray' Karpis, the true brains behind the gang, was personally arrested by Hoover in New Orleans in March 1935, the last casualty of the War on Crime. He spent thirty-three years in Alcatraz, becoming the longest serving prisoner on the Rock, and emigrated to Spain on his release, a move supposedly funded by the proceeds of the Hamm and Bremer kidnappings. He authored two volumes of autobiography and died in the late seventies, having outlived Hoover by several years.

***

Jimmy Probasco died after falling from the nineteenth floor of the Banker's Building while undergoing FBI interrogation. Rumours that he was being held out of the window by the ankles in order to extract a confession were ignored by the official enquiry, which brought in a verdict of suicide.

Probasco and the Barkers weren't the only ones to meet a violent end before they finally closed the casebook on Dillinger, however.

St Paul, Thursday, August 23, 1934

Homer Van Meter left the car dealership on the corner of University and Marion. He wore a blue suit with matching tie and white oxfords and carried a brown leather holdall in his right hand.

The holdall contained $6000. There was another $2000 in his money belt. It was enough to see him out the country, with any luck. Enough to fund an exit from the Twin Cities, at any rate.

St Paul wasn't safe anymore. Not since the feds had swarmed into the place after the Barker kidnappings and arrested the Dutchman. Besides, he was too hot. The local gang powers that hadn't been lifted by the G made that plain enough to him. Leave under his own steam or via a wooden box.

It was going to be the former if his ride arrived, though. The ride that was going to be the start of his journey over the border. The start of a new life beyond the U.S.A.

The figures waiting on the sidewalk, though. Three guys in baggy suits. Dented fedoras. Pistols in their hands. And a big guy in banker's pinstripes and a freshly-blocked hat. A riot gun lodged against his hip.

"Hi, Homer. How you doing?"

His scalp contracted, as if he'd been doused in ice water. The bastards had set him up.

He took off running, throwing a couple of shots over his shoulder as he hared down University Avenue, dodging through the traffic as he turned onto Marion. Swerved into an alleyway.

No exit.

He wheeled as the cops blocked the way to the street. Lifted his pistol as Big Tom triggered the riot gun. Blew him against the wall of the building. He tried to stand, but all four opened fire. Sent him sprawling amongst the spent rubbers and broken glass.

Big Tom skinned the money belt from his body. Snapped up the holdall. It was every man for himself since the feds hit town. Still, a nest-egg like this should compensate him and the boys for the breakdown of the O'Connor system. And nobody could accuse him of harbouring criminals after wasting the piece of shit at his feet. He displayed the holdall as he turned to his cronies. Flashed them a grin. "Xmas' come early this year, fellas. The drinks are on me, okay?"

East Liverpool, Ohio, Monday, October 23, 1934

The call had come while Purvis was on an inspection tour of the Cincinnati office, one of the humiliatingly mundane tasks the Director had saddled with since the Dillinger shooting. Pretty Boy Floyd had surfaced at last, flushed by local cops when his car ran off the road somewhere in southern Ohio on Friday night. Richetti was already in custody, but Floyd himself was running loose in the wilds south of Youngstown. If Purvis could get there fast enough, he could trump the local cops before they caught the Okie bank robber in their net. It was a chance to grab the credit for the Bureau and shore up his deteriorating relationship with Mr Hoover.

The Dillinger shooting should have made him at the FBI, wiping out the stain on his record stemming from Little Bohemia. Instead, the missives from Washington had become increasingly terse, the tasks delegated to him increasingly trivial. He had the feeling he was being sidelined. Jealousy, he guessed. The way the newspapers had focused on him rather than on Hoover and his precious Bureau.

Cowley had the right idea. The way he'd sunk into the background after the Biograph shoot-out. Let naïve Little Mel stick

475

his head above the parapet. Get it cut off by the Chief down in Washington.

Perhaps he should have followed Cowley's lead and avoided the cameras. He had a feeling it wouldn't have made much difference, though. Little Bohemia had already soured the Director on him. It made you wonder if the rumours about Hoover and his aide, Tolson, were true. He certainly acted like a woman scorned.

Purvis tried to forget his feelings as the car pulled into the farmyard, one of half a dozen they were to check that morning. The team consisted of himself and three other agents in one car and the East Liverpool chief of police and three of his men in another.

Working with the Ohio cops went against everything the Bureau believed in, but they had the local knowledge his agents lacked. Teaming with them as they beat the brush was the best chance his own men had of being in at the kill rather than leaving the credit entirely to the yokel cops. Even if the kill – the arrest, he had to think of it as the arrest – went to one of the hicks, he had the experience and the sophistication they lacked when dealing with the press. Play his hand correctly and he could seize another front page for himself - or rather the Bureau. That should be enough to clear him with Hoover, surely to God?

And if it wasn't, fuck him. He'd enjoy the attention. The time in the sun. He'd already fielded book offers. Sponsorship deals. The guy down in Washington tried to keep him in line, he'd get a shock. The Golden Boy would walk. Make his own way in the world. See how the fruit behind the Director's desk liked them apples, hey?

He was jolted loose from his reverie as the car bounced to a halt on the potholed farm track. The East Liverpool cops were already spilling from the other car. "It's him," one of them shouted towards the federal vehicle, as he pointed towards the figure weaving amongst the farm buildings. "It's Charley Floyd."

Purvis made to draw his pistol. Remembered to unbutton his coat. "Federal agents. You're under arrest." He swept the jumble of outhouses and chicken coops. The pigsties. Nothing.

He offered up a silent prayer that the bastard wouldn't slip through their fingers this time. Where the hell was he?

One of the agents stiffened like a hunting dog. "Behind the corn crib. Look."

There. In the gap beneath the elevated floor of the crib. Mud-caked shoes. Suit trousers. The way he scurried from side to side. Unsure what to do. Where to run.

"Come on out, Floyd. Come out with your hands raised or we shoot."

One of the East Liverpool cops raised his twelve bore. "Look out. He's going to run."

He emptied the scattergun as Floyd made his break, gouts of earth erupting at the outlaw's heels as he swerved behind the farmer's garage, putting the outbuilding between himself and the law as he zigzagged across a field, sprinting for the trees.

Purvis brought his pistol into play. "Let him have it." He braced himself as the other agents opened up beside him with pistols and a lone Thompson, the local cops joining in with riot guns and revolvers.

Floyd almost made it. The burst from the Thompson had gone high, chewing up the farmer's apple tree, but missing Floyd. The pistols and shotguns were good for street cleaning, but hopeless at long range. Another twenty, thirty feet and the big Okie would have made it into the tree line and lost himself in the woods.

Someone got lucky, though. Floyd seemed to slip. Went down heavily in the mud. Purvis half-expected him to get back to his feet and keep running. Not that he was going to give him that chance.

"Come on," he said, slapping another clip into his Colt, his hands stinging from the recoil. "Don't let the bastard get away."

The East Liverpool cops were ahead of him as he scrambled across the freshly-ploughed field. One of them grabbed Floyd's gun hand as he swung a .45 auto in their direction, twisting it from his grip. A second officer snatched a .22 from the fallen man's waistband. Stepped back and jacked the rounds from the chamber as Purvis skidded to a halt.

"What's your name?" the cop asked the man on the ground, as Purvis fought for breath.

"Murphy."

"Bullshit. What's your name?"

"My name's Murphy."

Purvis thrust his face into the pinioned outlaw's. "Your name's Floyd," he said. "Isn't that correct?"

Floyd deadpanned.

"Is your name not Charles 'Prettyboy' Floyd?"

Floyd's mouth twisted. Another time and place, it might have been a smile. "Stow that 'Prettyboy' shit. You know who I am."

The East Liverpool police chief joined them. He rested his hands on his knees as he examined the outlaw. "How bad you hurt, son?"

Floyd bleared down at himself. There were two merging bloodstains, one high on the right side of his chest, one below the heart. "You done for me. Hit me twice." He let his head fall back. "Jesus. I'm all shot to pieces."

Purvis inserted himself between the wounded man and the police chief. "Tell us about Kansas City, Floyd. The shooting at the train station. Were you involved?"

"To hell with Kansas City."

The police chief looked uneasy. "We best get him a doctor," he said to Purvis.

"A doctor can't help him now. He's dying."

Floyd looked at him resentfully. "I know I'm through."

"Then do the decent thing and tell me what you know about the massacre at Kansas City station."

Nothing.

"Is it not true that you, Adam Richetti and Verne Miller did the shooting at the train station?"

Floyd coughed blood. "I ain't telling you nothing, you son-of-a-bitch." He tried to rise. Found himself pinned by the cops. "Fuck you."

Purvis moved back as the yeggman began to choke.

"I'm going," Floyd said, and died.

***

Adam Richetti was later tried and convicted for his part in the Kansas City Massacre. Despite perjured evidence given by the FBI, it is likely that Floyd's partner was one of the gunmen responsible for machinegunning Nash and his escort at the railroad station. He died in the gas chamber at Jefferson City, Missouri, on October 7,

1938.

Ohio State Penitentiary, Sunday, September 22, 1934

The guard heard the steel outer door to Death Row close behind him. Just him and eight men with nothing between them and eternity but the slim hope of a reprieve. All right, so they were sealed in their individual cells each side the corridor, but he still wished to Christ they'd let him carry his piece with him onto the landing. Thank God he was working a different shift the coming week.

He knew the argument against going armed onto the cellblock. That if one of the assholes in there got hold of a gun, they had nothing to lose by using it. Shit, it was the way most of them had ended up queuing for Old Sparky in the first place. Which didn't make him a whole lot easier about having to face the bastards armed with nothing but a nightstick on his hip.

That cocksucker Pierpont, especially. The way the guy never spoke to him gave him the creeps. It was the way he looked at a fella. Reminded him of the wolves he'd seen at the zoo in Cincinnati when he was a kid. No fuss or hollering, but you knew they'd tear you to pieces you ever ended up in the cage with them. You could take that to the bank.

483

He wheeled the breakfast cart up to the convict's cell. Slopped the oatmeal into the bowl. "You know the routine, Pierpont. Stand back from the door if you want to be fed."

He waited for the prisoner to back up. Slid the bowl through the slot in the door.

"Hey, guard."

He started. "What - ?" Goggled at the pistol in Pierpont's hand. "Oh my God."

"He can't help you now. Do as I say, though, and you won't have to meet him yet." He levelled the muzzle at the guard's head with one hand and reached through the bars with the other. Unhooked the keys from his belt and unlocked the door. "Inside."

He exchanged places with the guard. "Up against the wall, motherfucker. You know the routine." He rifled the latter's pockets. Kicked his legs out from under him before exiting the cell and locking it behind him. "You try and holler, shout for help, and I'll plug you, so help me. I'm already due to burn for one copper. Figure that means I get the next one for free. Bastards can't fry me twice, you know?"

"Harry? That you, buddy? You got the keys?"

He stepped quickly along the corridor. Loosed Makley from his cage. "What about the others?"

"We got a better chance if there's a bunch of us. Gimme the keys." He worked down the row of cells. Freed the other condemned men from their cages. "Now for that goddamn door."

He tried the various keys on the ring. Shit. The bastard wouldn't open. He stalked back down the corridor to his cell. "Hey, you. The outer door. How do we open it?"

"You don't." The guard twitched as Pierpont raised the gun. "It opens and shuts from the outside only. They know you guys are desperate. Got nothing to lose. Same way they don't let me carry a piece when I bring in the food."

"You're lying to me."

"I swear to you, Pierpont. Harry. There's no way you can unlock the thing from this side."

"I'm going to count to three. You don't give me the answer I'm looking for and I'm going to spread your brains all over that goddamn wall. One."

"Please, Harry. I'm telling the truth here."

"Two."

"Christ, Harry. I swear to you. Swear on my children."

"Three." He hesitated. Something seemed to be holding him back. "Your last chance, buddy. What's it gonna be?"

"Harry. The door."

Pierpont swung around at the sound of Makley's voice. Readied his pistol as a couple of armed guards doubled towards the cellblock. "I'm warning you, coppers. One more step - "

The first blast of gunfire knocked him off his feet, the pistol skittering from his hand. Makley made a lunge for the piece and took a shotgun charge to the head. The rest of the prisoners folded, hands raised as the posse entered the cellblock and backed them into the cells. One of them prodded Makley with his gun barrel.

"Looks like your buddy got lucky. Took the easy way out. You still got a date with the chair, though, Pierpont."

One of his colleagues plucked the pistol from the floor of the corridor. He began to laugh. "I'll be a son-of-a-bitch." The handgun disintegrated as he squeezed it in his fist. Soap. He couldn't believe it. The crazy bastards had tried to bluff their way off Death Row with a pistol carved from soap.

***

Pierpont was executed on October 17, being carried into the death cell on a stretcher. He had been nursed back from potentially fatal wounds by the prison medical staff in order to keep his date with the electric chair.

Lake Geneva, Wisconsin, Tuesday, November 27, 1934

Nelson kept his eye fixed to the mirror as he motored down Highway Twelve. He'd been paranoid since he'd returned from hiding-out on the West Coast with John Paul Chase, a buddy from his bootlegging days in Frisco, but the two guys he'd disturbed at the tourist lodge just now sure had the look of the G about them.

Perhaps he'd made a mistake returning. If it hadn't been for the robbery Murray had been touting after Dillinger and Van Meter got theirs, he'd have gone back to California. As it was, he'd spent the last couple of weeks holed-up in the lakes, putting out feelers to the few contacts remaining to him in Chi. He was looking to find a bolthole. Protection. Somewhere to lay low until he hit the Reserve train.

He thought the Lakeside Inn had been the place, but obviously not. Somehow the feds had gotten on to him. Someone had finked. Thank Christ he still had his armoury with him. He ever found out who the squealer was and he'd make sure it was the last time they'd ever talk to John Q. Law. Talk to anybody, period.

The two agents Nelson had disturbed had been following-up a lead from a girlfriend of Chase's the Bureau had picked up in San

Francisco. She'd travelled with the two outlaws before falling out with Nelson and returning home. The threat of prosecution coupled with a tour of the lake country north of Chicago had jogged her memory and pointed towards the Lakeside Inn as a possible Nelson haunt. The possibility turned out to be correct. All they had to do now was get back on the little bastard's trail after he'd caught them with their pants down. First of all, though, they phoned the office on the nineteenth floor.

Cowley fielded the call. He was short-handed. Most of the agents were on assignment. He'd have to improvise. "Ryan and McDade are in the area. I'll call them. You two stay put in case he returns."

"Are you sure two men are enough, sir?"

"I'll take Hollis. Check out the situation myself. Keep the office informed if there any further developments." He put through the call to Ryan and McDade, then collected his hat and coat. Stuck his head in Purvis' office as he headed for the elevator. "Babyface Nelson just left Lake Geneva. Move fast and this time we might catch the little prick."

Purvis surged up from behind his desk. "What are we waiting for? Let's get going."

"That won't be necessary. Hollis and I are just going to cruise around and see if we can spot the car on the highway. When we get set, I'll phone you."

Purvis dwindled into his seat. So that was the way it was going to be, was it? Keep Little Mel away from the limelight. Tie him down behind a desk. "You want me to phone Washington?" he said.

"The information's pretty vague. Just stay here and cover things until I get back. You can manage that, can't you?"

Ryan and McDade were already on the road, the license number of Nelson's car clipped to the sun visor of their Ford coupe: 639578. They monitored the oncoming traffic as they passed through Fox River Grove and cruised towards Wisconsin.

And then a black Ford punched past in the opposite lane, heading south for Chicago. Their eyes met. 639578.

"Turn around," Ryan said. "Let's take a closer look at this sucker."

McDade pulled a U-turn and closed with the black Ford. He frowned as it slowed, curving into the meridian, before pulling into the northbound traffic on the tail of the FBI agents. It hovered behind them for a few moments and then powered forward.

McDade eased his foot down on the accelerator. "I don't like the look of this. Let's keep ahead of them."

Ryan worked his .38 from the holster. "Let them keep coming. The bastards try anything and they're in for a shock."

The black car drew level with them. The driver wound down the window. Sounded the horn. "Pull over."

A scowling kid in a cap and sunglasses. Nelson. It had to be. And a dark-haired guy in the back seat. Jesus Christ. A BAR in his hand. Ryan raised his pistol.

"Floor it, Dade. Get us out of here." He opened fire.

Nelson yanked his own piece. He steered one-handed as he emptied his Browning at the G. Screamed at Chase as the windscreen exploded. "Don't just sit there, you dumb prick. Let them have it."

Chase knocked out the side window and let fly with the heater. The FBI car was drawing ahead, though. The volley went wide.

McDade kept the pedal to the metal. "We losing them?" he said, as the outlaw Ford fell back.

Ryan nodded as he reloaded. "We must have hit the motor. They're out of sight." He gestured towards the side of the road. "Pull off here. We can make a stand if they catch us."

They ran the coupe into the long grass at the side of the road. Readied their weapons and waited.

The fight had already passed them by, however. It was Cowley and Hollis, driving north past the gun battle in a Hudson sedan, who took up the challenge, crossing the meridian and intercepting the black Ford as the engine failed.

"We're gaining," Hollis said, pumping the accelerator. "Another twenty feet and I can run them off the road."

Cowley rammed a magazine into his Thompson as the distance shrank between the two cars. He was a deskman. A bureaucrat. He'd never fired a gun in action before. Never even bothered to qualify on the pistol range. That didn't matter, though. At this range, he couldn't miss. "Hold her steady," he said, sighting the Thompson. "I'm going to take a shot at her."

He leaned out the window of the Hudson and drew a bead on the figure in the backseat of the Ford. Opened fire.

Missed.

"Hold her steady, damn it."

Cowley refocused his aim. Nelson wasn't prepared to sit and take fire without hitting back, however. He spun the steering wheel hard right as they approached the outskirts of Barrington and skidded the Ford into a side road, jumping onto the running board and readying a BAR as the federal car barrelled past. It slewed to a halt 150 feet away, diagonal across the blacktop from Nelson and Chase, the latter two opening up over the hood of the Ford as the federal men killed the engine.

Hollis and Cowley broke from the sedan as automatic fire tore-up the bodywork. Cowley dropped to one knee. He brought his Thompson into play. Put a six-round burst into Nelson.

The squirt refused to go down, though. Adrenalin kept him on his feet. He returned fire, bowling Cowley into a roadside ditch, two bullets through his stomach and chest, before slamming back into the Ford as Hollis gave him both barrels of a sawn-off shotgun.

Nelson pushed himself off from the car as the automatic rifle jammed and rearmed with a Thompson from the back seat. He lurched towards Hollis like something from a Karloff movie as the terrified agent hurled away his empty weapon. A .45 slug struck the G-man in the forehead as he dodged behind a telegraph pole, exiting behind his left ear, dropping him amongst the crab grass and daisies at the edge of the highway. Killing him instantly.

Nelson swayed like a drunk in the middle of the road, then crawled into the driver's seat of the Hudson. He managed to get it into gear. Reversed it towards the Ford.

"Get their guns and we'll get moving." He gagged. Spat a mouthful of arterial blood onto the dashboard. "You'll have to drive. I'm hurt."

Chase obeyed instructions and gathered the dead men's firearms. He took the wheel as Nelson passed-out in the passenger seat. At seven thirty the following morning, the runt's body was recovered from a roadside drainage ditch in suburban Niles Center. There were seventeen separate gunshot wounds in his body: two in the chest, five in the stomach, five in each leg.

There was no way he should have been able to stay on his feet after being hit by Cowley and Hollis. No way he should have been able to return fire and knock over the two lawmen like plaster ducks in a shooting gallery. Nelson was already dead when he slaughtered the two agents. Cowley and Hollis had, to all intents and purposes, been taken out by a corpse.

Chase was picked up a few weeks later and received a life sentence, eventually serving over thirty years on the Rock. Cowley, meanwhile, became a martyr to the cause. A dead man was no threat to Hoover's position as the public face of law enforcement. The Director of Investigations was installed as the Bureau's pre-eminent hero in the War on Crime. He remains the highest-ranking agent ever to be killed in the line of duty.

South Carolina, February 29, 1960

Purvis sat in his study and brooded over his clippings. He had been the hero of the hour. While Cowley faded into the shadows, he was interviewed by reporters and photographed with the Attorney General. He knew the damage the publicity was doing to his relationship with the Director but he couldn't help himself. It was like a drug to him. He couldn't resist the attention.

The killing of Floyd kept him in the headlines. Even Cowley's death at the hands of Nelson gave him an opportunity to vent, swearing blood vengeance for his fallen comrade in arms. There was only room for one publicity-hungry egomaniac in the Bureau, though, and that man occupied the Director's seat in Washington. Purvis left the Bureau in 1935, never to work in law enforcement again. His subsequent book, *American Agent*, made no mention of Hoover in its depiction of the War on Crime.

His life after the Bureau was an unsuccessful one. His attempts to practice law or find another police position were frustrated by Hoover. The movie offer was blocked. The closest he came to show business success was hosting the Pop Toasties Junior G-Man club. Business ventures failed. And now this:

"There were sinister motives by Captain Gilbert and the politico-criminal syndicate for wanting to remove Touhy permanently from the scene. With Purvis as their unwitting tool, they worked to see Touhy convicted of something. That Touhy was convicted at all in the Factor case is something for which the Department of Justice should answer."

He crumpled the report into the wastebasket and removed the chrome-plated Colt automatic from his desk drawer. The pistol had been a leaving present from his colleagues in the Bureau: *To Little Mel. All the best from the boys on the nineteenth floor.*

He jacked the slide. Placed the barrel in his mouth. The bullet-shattered visage in the alleyway gazed into his. Welcome to Hell, Melvin. He squeezed the trigger.

***

Twenty-three days after his eventual release, Roger Touhy was shotgunned to death on his sister's doorstep by Syndicate gunmen. "The bastards," he said, as he expired. "They never forget."

Afterword

No other criminal in American history ever so captured the imagination of the public. His insouciance, his cynical attitude, his put on good humor when bullets did not serve the immediate purpose he had in mind, were as much a part of the legend of this super criminal as his uncanny ability to shoot his way out of traps or his unfaltering courage in battle - Chicago Tribune, July 23, 1934

In 1936, a young actor named Humphrey Bogart would find acclaim playing opposite Bette Davis and Leslie Howard in Archie Mayo's *The Petrified Forest*. Bogart's character, one Duke Mantee, was clearly modeled on John Dillinger. The outlaw bore a remarkable facial similarity to the future movie star and, in the early 1930s, enjoyed a celebrity that would have been the envy of many a Hollywood A-lister.

Eighty years on, Dillinger's front-page charisma still shines out of the grainy black and white newspaper photographs. The eyes look up from under the brows with a knowing humor. He sports a sardonic grin. It's easy to see how the wisecracking figure beneath the headlines could turn an arraignment into an impromptu press conference or place ahead of Roosevelt and Lindbergh in newsreel popularity polls. It was a fascination with the face in the photographs that led me to begin researching Depression-era crime and, eventually, to produce the book you now hold in your hands.

Although I have tried as far as possible to stick to recorded fact in the writing of the novel, the demands of narrative forced me to alter the actual characters and events on several occasions. My sins are largely ones of compression or elision rather than outright invention, however. I have, for instance, combined the character of Captain Stege of the Dillinger squad with his equally ferocious sidekick, Sergeant Frank 'Killer' Reynolds. Similarly, several major figures in the outlaw's life fail to make an appearance, most notably his stuttering Croat nemesis, Captain Matt Leach of the Indiana State Police.

My main departure from fact is in having FBI agent Melvin Purvis hop-scotch around the Mid-West from his base in Chicago as he observes or initiates trials and arrests in St Paul and Lima. This was a convenient way of covering a plethora of events from the law enforcement angle without introducing numerous fictional viewpoints. For the sake of familiarity, the Bureau itself is referred to as the Federal Bureau of Investigation rather than the Justice Department's Bureau of Investigation, the title the organization bore until 1935.

The classic study of Dillinger's career is John Toland's *Dillinger Days*, although Robert Cromie and Joseph's Pinkston's *Dillinger: A Short and Violent Life* is also worthy of note. The Dead Sea Scrolls of Dillinger studies, however, is Russell Girardin and William Helmer's *Dillinger: The Untold Story*. Compiled from interviews with participants in Dillinger's career shortly after his death, it was shelved due to legal complications and sat on a shelf in Girardin's garage for almost sixty years until tracked down by Helmer and published at his instigation in 1994.

Paul Macabee's *John Dillinger Slept Here: a Crook's tour of Crime and Corruption in St. Paul, 1920 – 1936,* meanwhile, provides invaluable background on the Mid-West underworld of the Prohibition and War on Crime eras. Highly recommended.

The book which made me believe I could actually turn the Dillinger story into a novel, though, was Bryan Burrough's *Public Enemies,* an express-train of a narrative which unfolds the careers of Dillinger and the other Depression outlaws in fascinating detail and sets them in the context of New Deal politics and the Justice Department's War on Crime. Don't let the lacklustre movie adaptation put you off: this is a must read for anyone interested in the Public Enemy era and can't be recommended enough.

Appendix One

Nitti, Touhy and the assassination of Mayor Cermak

On February 15, 1933, a deranged lone assassin named Joseph Zangara opened fire on President-elect Franklin D. Roosevelt as he addressed a Democratic rally in Miami, Florida. The assassin fired wide, however, the shots striking Mayor Anton Cermak of Chicago, who died of complications resulting from his wounds the following week. Zangara was subsequently found guilty of murder and executed in the electric chair on March 20 1933.

That's how events are recorded in the history books. An alternative theory is that the bullets were intended for the mayor all along, part of an ongoing struggle for underworld domination between Cermak on the one hand and the Nitti Syndicate on the other. Zangara, a former Italian army marksman, was either the assassin himself or a Lee Harvey Oswald-style patsy, providing a diversion for the Syndicate gunmen acting as backup. Whichever version is correct, Cermak ended up dead and the greatest threat to Syndicate control of Chicago was over.

'Pushcart Tony' Cermak was elected to the Mayor's office on a reform ticket in 1931. The price of reform as far as the new mayor was concerned was elimination of Syndicate control of the rackets and replacement by his surrogates, chief of whom was Des Plaines bootlegger and Teamster boss Roger Touhy, the last holdout against Syndicate control in the greater Chicago area since the destruction of George 'Bugs' Moran's North Side crew on St Valentine's Day, 1928.

The mayor's motives may have been corrupt, a bid for personal control of the Chicago rackets. It's more likely, however, that Cermak recognised vice as an intrinsic part of the urban environment, a blight that should be controlled where it couldn't be eliminated. Rather than leave bootlegging, gambling and prostitution in the hands of an all-powerful Syndicate, he attempted to replace it with a weaker, more malleable organisation directed by City Hall, rather than vice versa.

Whatever Cermak's motivation, the practical results of the mayor's decision were a series of raids on Syndicate operations by the Chicago police department, coupled with municipal support of Touhy, police officers riding shotgun on the suburban bootlegger's beer trucks in order to dissuade Syndicate hijackers.

These raids were followed by the attempted 'arrest' of Syndicate head, Frank Nitti, by two police sergeants, Harry Lang and Harry Miller, the latter brother of West Side gambler and bootlegger Herschie Miller. The two men entered Nitti's office at 221 North LaSalle Street bearing a search warrant and shot him at point blank range, Miller inflicting a flesh wound on himself in order to claim self-defence. Both men survived their wounds – and their subsequent trials for attempting to murder the other – and Cermak hastened south to attend the Democratic convention, where he met his fate at the hands of Zangara and, possibly, persons unknown a short time later.

With Cermak out of the way, the Syndicate moved on Touhy. Their tool in the District Attorney's office, Captain Dan 'Tubbo' Gilbert, widely regarded as Chicago's most corrupt cop, approached Chicago SAC Melvin Purvis with information linking the Touhy mob to the kidnapping of brewer William Hamm, one of the high-profile abductions that followed in the wake of the Lindbergh baby case in the early thirties. Touhy was arrested and put on trial, but acquitted, the kidnapping of the St Paul brewer eventually being laid at the door of the Barker gang, acting in concert with Twin City fixer Harry Sawyer.

Touhy was immediately rearrested, however, and tried for the Factor kidnapping instead. With Factor himself as the chief prosecution witness, Touhy received a ninety-nine year prison sentence. His partner, Matt Kolb, was gunned down in a roadhouse shortly afterwards and Nitti's men swarmed into Des Plaines, effectively ending the last serious challenge to Syndicate rule in the greater Chicago area.

Appendix Two

The Box Score

Bank robberies

July 17, 1933 – Commercial Bank, Daleville, Indiana, $3500.

August 4, 1933 – Montpelier National Bank, Montpelier, Indiana, $6700.

August 14, 1933 – Bluffton Bank, Bluffton, Ohio, $6000

September 6, 1933 – Massachusetts avenue State Bank, Indianapolis, Indiana, $21,000

October 23, 1933 – Central National Bank and Trust Company, Greencastle, Indiana, $76,000

November 20, 1933 – American Bank and Trust Company, Racine, Wisconsin, $28000.

December 13, 1933 – Unity Trust and Savings bank, Chicago, Illinois, $8700

January 15, 1934 – First National Bank, East Chicago, Indiana, $20,000

March 6, 1934 – Securities National Bank and Trust Company, Sioux Falls, South Dakota, $49,000

March 13, 1934 – First National Bank, Mason City, Iowa, $52,000

June 30, 1934 – Merchants national Bank, South Bend, Indiana, $29,890

Killed: the good guys

October 12, 1933 – Sheriff Jess Sarber, killed Lima, Ohio, by Harry Pierpont

December 14, 1933 – Sergeant William T. Shanley, Chicago police, killed by John Hamilton

January 15, 1934 – Officer William P. O'Malley, East Chicago police, killed by John Dillinger

March 16, 1934 – Under sheriff Charles Cavanaugh, killed Port Huron, Michigan, by Herbert Youngblood

April 22, 1934 – Eugene Boisneau, CCC worker, killed Little Bohemia Lodge, Rhinelander, Michigan by FBI agents.

April 22, 1934 – Carter Baum, federal agent, killed Little Bohemia Lodge, Rhinelander, Michigan by Babyface Nelson.

May 24, 1934 – Detectives Martin O'Brien and Lloyd Mulvihill, East Chicago police, killed by Homer Van Meter

June 30, 1934 – Officer Howard Wagner, Indiana State Police, killed South Bend Indiana, by Homer Van Meter

November 27, 1934 – Director of Investigations Samuel P. Cowley and federal agent Herman E. Hollis, killed Barrington, Illinois, by Babyface Nelson.

February 29, 1960 – Melvin Purvis, former SAC Chicago, death by gunshot wounds (open verdict), South Carolina.

Wounded

September 26, 1933 – Finley Clarkson, clerk, wounded in thigh and abdomen, Michigan State Penitentiary, during prison break.

September 30, 1933 – H.J. Graham, cashier of the American Bank and Trust Company, Racine, Wisconsin and Sergeant Wilbur Hansen, Racine police, wounded during bank robbery.

November 20, 1933 – Hale Keith, police officer, wounded Sioux Falls, South Dakota, during bank robbery.

March 13, 1934 – R.H. James, secretary of school board, wounded during bank robbery, Mason City, Iowa

March 16, 1934 – Sherrif William Van Antwerp, Deputy Howard Law and Fields 'a negro', wounded while attempting to apprehend Herbert Youngblood, Port Huron, Michigan

April 22, 1934 – John Morris and John Hoffman, citizens of Mercer, Wisconsin, wounded at Little Bohemia Lodge by FBI agents

April 22, 1934 – Federal Agent J.C. Newman and Constable Carl Christiansen, wounded at Little Bohemia Lodge by Babyface Nelson

June 30, 1934 – Perry G. Stahley and Delos M. Coen, bank officials, and Jacob Solomon and Samuel Toth, citizens of South Bend, Indiana, wounded in bank robbery

July 22, 1934 – Miss Theresa Paulus and Mrs Etta Natalsky, Chicago citizens, wounded by stray bullets during the shooting of John Dillinger

Killed: the bad guys

March 16, 1934 –Herbert Youngblood, killed resisting arrest, Port Huron, Michigan

April 3, 1934 – Eddie Green, killed by federal agents, St Paul, Minnesota

April 23, 1934 – John Hamilton, fatally wounded by police whilst escaping Little Bohemia. Died approx. April 27.

June 7, 1934 – Tommy Carroll, killed by police, Waterloo, Iowa

July 22, 1934 - John Dillinger, killed by federal agents and East Chicago police, Biograph Theatre, Chicago

July 26, 1934 – James Probasco, defenestrated, FBI office, Chicago

August 23, 1934 – Homer Van Meter, killed by police, St Paul, Minnesota.

September 22, 1934 – Charles Makley, killed during prison break, Ohio state Penitentiary, Columbus, Ohio

October 17, 1934 – Harry Pierpont, died in the electric chair, Ohio state Penitentiary, Columbus, Ohio

October 23, 1934 – Charles Arthur 'Prettyboy' Floyd, killed by federal agents and local police, East Liverpool, Ohio

November 27, 1934 – Lester Gillis (a.k.a George Nelson a.k.a Babyface a.k.a. the kid Jimmy) fatally wounded by federal agents, Barrington, Illinois

January 15, 1935 - Fred Barker and Kate 'Ma' Barker, killed by federal agents, Ocala, Florida

October 7, 1938 – Adam Richetti, died in the gas chamber, Jefferson City, Missouri

5 January, 1939 - Dock Barker, killed while attempting to escape, Alcatraz Federal Penitentiary, California

19 March, 1943 - Frank Nitti, committed suicide, Riverside, Chicago

Glossary

AEF – American Expeditionary Force. The American armed forces dispatched to France in World War One.

BAR – Browning Automatic Rifle.

Cat road – back road, minor road.

CCC – Civilian Conservation Corps. A Depression-busting work creation scheme involving the unemployed in reforestation, erosion control etcetera.

To be fed the goldfish – to receive a beating with a length of rubber hose

Git – escape route.

Guinea stinker – cheap cigar.

Hooverville – shantytown inhabited by the unemployed. Named after Herbert Hoover, president at the time of the Wall Street Crash.

Jack – money

Jackroller - mugger

Jug – bank.

Moko/moko-loko – moonshine, illegal liquor. Also known as panther piss, radiator juice etc.

NRA – National Recovery Administration. Federal body involved in emergency reorganization of national business and government in the face of the Depression. Included reform of the banking system.

Pin-artist - abortionist

Pulled his coat – wised him up.

Raised – made parole.

The Rock – Alcatraz Federal Penitentiary

Roundheels – a slut i.e. a woman who could be easily laid on her back due to the aforementioned anatomical peculiarity.

SAC – Special Agent in Charge. The FBI agent in charge of a local office.

Scratch – money

Sheikh – playboy, Lothario. After Rudolph Valentino's turn in the motion picture of the same name.

Sneeze – steal

Soup – explosives, specifically nitro-glycerine

Tiger – the gunman responsible for controlling the street outside the bank during a robbery.

Turned out – initiated e.g. as an armed robber.

Yaffle – kidnap

Yegg/yeggman – armed robber

Lightning Source UK Ltd.
Milton Keynes UK
UKOW05f0809270714

235832UK00002B/61/P